HUNTER

HUNTER

WILLIAM COFFEY

BLACK & WHITE PUBLISHING

First published 2003
by Black & White Publishing Ltd
99 Giles Street, Edinburgh
Scotland, EH6 6BZ

ISBN 1 902927 74 5

A CIP catalogue for this book
is available from the British Library.

Cover design and photograph: www.hen.uk.com
Printed and bound by Creative Print and Design

HUNTER

1

There was something about the fella that Hunter couldn't go.

It wasn't just the expensive suit, the poofy shoes with tassels and the noisy tie. Was it noisy or loud? He wasn't sure but he didn't like it anyway. Yellow silk, with diagonals of wee brown animals that looked like arse-holes. Just like the guy who was wearing them. Hunter had called him Dr Calder, just to get up his nose.

The psychiatrist's nostrils had flared, just for a sec. Mr Carmichael, he had corrected, smoothing the wee arseholes and urging the cop just to call him Calder.

The priest from the archdiocese and the rich bitch, the ones who would decide exactly how much public cash went to the shrink's drug clinic, had been giving it Calder this and Calder that. Hunter shouldn't have been there – literally – he was just standing in for the Chief Constable who, surprisingly enough, had found an urgent appointment elsewhere in Glasgow.

Carmichael was talking and that was what the cop really didn't like. Not what he was saying, not even the tight, constipated vowels that sounded as if he had a wee jaggy animal up his arse. It was the volume or lack of it. For he spoke so softly – it was calculated, Hunter was sure of it – that you found yourself bowing towards him to listen. Superior bastard.

'He can't write, this chap, not even his name, and he can't count to ten. He's well dressed – suit, white shirt and blue tie, shiny shoes – but he's got real problems. So I ask him, something safe – something about his folks to put him at ease.'

Carmichael rose from his desk and went to pour the coffees. He knew that he had them in the palm of his hand, the priest and the woman, and the Detective Inspector did not have a vote. The money was as good as in the bank. So he took his time, taking them into his inner sanctum but careful not to betray any professional confidences. That would give the wrong impression entirely. He spoke over his shoulder and it was even more difficult to hear him.

The woman leaned forward, chin on the palms of her hands, elbows on invitingly open knees.

'And the bloke mumbles something about his mummy – mummy, mark you, and this chap's in his fifties – so I move on quickly.

'Milk, everyone?'

Hunter declined.

'"Hobbies?" I ask him, "Do you have any hobbies?" But he doesn't even know what a hobby is. I suggest football but he shakes his head. "The telly?" But he doesn't watch TV either.

'Sugar?'

Only Hunter took sugar – two spoons, no, three, seeing it was a mug.

The psychiatrist continued, 'Now, I admit it, I'm struggling here but I ask, "What do you do with your time?" And he says, "Painting."'

Carmichael brought the coffees over on a tray, with a plate of ginger nuts, and picked up the thread of his anecdote again. '"Painting," says I, trying not to sound surprised. Now, I've heard about chaps like this but I've never actually met one. You know – severely mentally impaired but endowed with one supreme gift. Like a blind man who can hear a mouse fart at fifty paces. Oh, sorry, Nigella.'

The rich bitch tried to force an upper middle-class blush but failed miserably. Hunter wondered if the shrink was making a move on her. She was certainly gagging for it.

Carmichael carried on again, '"Painting," says I, "now that's interesting. And what do you do – watercolours or oils?"' He lifted a ginger nut and cracked it in half, just for the dramatic effect. 'And the chap says, "Aw, naw, sur, bathrooms and sculleries."'

The priest and the rich bitch laughed. Even Hunter cracked a smile but he was trying to remember where he had heard the story before. Connolly? No, it would be too well known. It was before the Big Yin anyway. Chic Murray or maybe Hamish Imlach.

Carmichael, quieter than ever, was getting to the sting now. 'Over the course of the weeks,' he said, 'the chap consistently told me that he was "happy enough". Always used those very words. And which of us, if we're honest,' he paused, looking each of them in the eye to make sure his point was not lost, 'wouldn't settle for being "happy enough"?' He dunked one half of the ginger nut in his coffee and Hunter could just tell that Carmichael was thinking that tagging that last bit on had been quite a nice touch – a common touch, suggesting that he had nothing to hide.

The rich bitch agreed that 'happy enough' was, indeed, a rarity, saying, 'Quite, quite.' And, just as the priest was starting to pontificate on the subject, there were two sharp, efficient raps on the door. Carmichael's wife entered. She nodded politely towards the three guests, then said, 'It's Matthew, Darling.'

Carmichael said, loudly, 'Yes?'

She looked uncomfortable, didn't want to say it in front of them, but he made her go on.

'Attempted suicide, I'm afraid.'

Carmichael paled. His wife walked to him and put a hand on his shoulder. She said, 'Don't worry, he's all right. Absolutely fine. No lasting effects.'

Carmichael fished an inhaler from his jacket pocket and took a deep puff.

'Heart,' he said to Hunter. 'Dodgy ticker.'

And then, to his wife, 'He's okay? Honestly?'

She squeezed his shoulder. 'Yes, honestly, he's fine, physically fine. But . . . it was so strange. It would have to be, I suppose, with Matthew, but, well, he was smiling – not manic – but he seemed . . .'

Carmichael took another sook at the inhaler, then he finished her sentence, 'He seemed to enjoy it.'

He rose, then said, 'You must excuse me. This is Zara, my wife. Take care of our guests, Darling.'

She tried to stop him. Said that Matthew was in his room, sedated, a nurse at his side. She wanted her husband to take a minute, just a minute, to relax a little.

But he wouldn't have any of it. He excused himself, promising to be back soon, and left the room.

The rich bitch sympathised with Zara. How awful it must have been for her.

She started on about it and almost forgot to finish. 'He seemed . . .' she searched for the word, was unable to find it and settled for '. . . happy. Swallowed a roll of toilet paper, most of it anyway. Nobody's fault – you can't watch them all the time, you know. One of the other residents who found him. In the loo, in a cubicle. I heard the alarm go off. When I got there, they were pulling the paper out of his mouth. Two of the nurses were. It was a bit like the Andrex puppy advert.'

She let out a nervous little giggle. 'At first it came out easily, like a big orange ribbon, I guess his mouth was dry and it just pulled out, then it would break and they'd get hold of it again and yank out some more, smaller and smaller bits. And his face was turning blue because he wasn't getting any air and it must have been, well, uncomfortable, sore, I mean,

3

one was sitting on his chest and the other with his fingers down his throat and Matthew's . . . smiling. He's enjoying it. Not the pain, the discomfort, but . . .'

She stopped, then said, 'I'm sorry, I'm rambling. Calder's upset because, you see, Matthew's his favourite.'

She gave them an embarrassed little smile. 'It might be unprofessional to say that, but it's true. We took Matthew in . . . when? More than a year, anyway. He's a poor soul. Not ill enough to be sectioned – committed – though, if a suicide attempt isn't reason enough, then what on earth is? But that's the National Health Service for you. He did attend a hospital day clinic, then he stopped going altogether. And they, well, they just washed their hands of him. When we heard about him he was living in a dingy bedsit – rent paid by the DSS straight to the landlord – and the boy was just a rickle of bones. He had no one, no parents, relations or friends. So we took him in.'

She was good, Hunter thought, too good. It was just too slick. The timing was spot on, rehearsed. If he had her in an interview room she'd be in soapy bubble. The Hunter's antennae were twitching.

'He's damaged, of course,' Zara was saying. 'Calder will tell you the correct medical terminology, but Matthew will never be . . .'

'Well,' the rich bitch filled in.

'Quite, quite,' Zara said. These two clearly spoke the same language. 'He's Calder's first call every morning. He calls him the boy who can remember his dreams. He can, you know, Matthew. He's quite animated when he tells you what he dreamt about. Calder says that it's the closest the boy gets to reality.'

2

Sandy Hunter cursed, slammed on the anchors and his Vauxhall Vectra stood on its nose. The young roe deer cleared the road in three graceful bounds but got a fright at the height of the hawthorn hedge – a splattery brown fright – and landed that wee bit lighter on the other side and high-tailed it into the Scots pine forest. Bloody countryside, nothing but shitey animals, pissing rain and more wind than the Forfar Farting Federation. And Bella wanted him to live in it. What was it with his darling wife anyway? He'd said as much to her on the way to her sister's in Luss.

'What is it with you, anyway? You been reading *Animal Farm* again? Two legs bad, four legs good.'

But she'd had the edge on him, she'd prepared for it for God knows how long, decided, if he did this, she'd do that and, if he said that, then she'd say this and, when he had pressed the usual buttons, she had failed to respond as per but just given him her long-suffering smile.

'Now Sandy,' she had said, nice as ninepence. 'I believe you're a reasonable man. Fair-minded and open to suggestions. I believe those very words came out of your own mouth this morning when you decided for us that a dishwasher was really not needed since there's only the two of us in the house now. And I can see your argument – I hadn't considered the plumbing or the upheaval and the expense of new worktops and all that. You were – no, you are, quite right. So all I'm asking is for you to have a look. That's all, just a look and that can't hurt, can it?'

She had stroked the two house schedules on her knee and sighed. It was the sigh she'd used thirty years ago, when he'd tried to get the leg over and she'd said, 'Oh, no, not till there's a ring on my finger, and then, Darling, then.' She'd re-enlisted Darling, brought it right up to the present.

'I'm not saying we're buying, Darling. It's not as if our own house is even advertised – not in Slater Hogg and Howison's window, is it? Now don't look at me like that – but it would surprise you just how easy it is nowadays and it's not as if you'd be involved in any of the work or anything like that now, is it? The only packing you did was your pipes and you didn't know where you put them and you . . . but that's all water under the bridge, eh? And it would be so much easier this time – this last time, Darling – because it's not as if I'd have two young children under my feet now, is it? Unless, of course, the country air made you a bit . . . frisky. Snuggle in at night. It's been a while, you know.'

Whisky makes you frisky, tequila helps you feel 'er, Bella had been on the whine and Hunter wanted lager to slag 'er. But he was on guard. He had noted the surfeit of 'is its?' and didn't know how to bliddywell answer them, did he?

'And it would surprise you just how much we'd get for the house. It's really sought-after. Netta got £95K . . .'

Jesus H, this was getting serious. Into estateagentspeak.

'. . . for hers and it doesn't even have a brick-built garage.'

He'd thought of pressing the nuclear button, mentioning the menopause, guaranteed to get her to blow a gasket, then get all guilty, then sulk. She used it herself and, even when she was wrong, she had the perfect excuse. Made him feel like a shit when she said, 'I should know better than to expect sympathy from you. You've no idea what it's like.'

If you said you did, you didn't and, if you said you didn't, then you should. Where were the equal rights campaigners when it came to the menopause? Shaving their eyebrows and plucking their legs, probably. Where were they during the night when the duvet was up and down like a hoor's knickers? And, anyway, surely it should be the personopause. It was enough to drive a man to personslaughter. Hunter stifled a chuckle. Fucking menopause. More like the no-fucking menopause. Easier to get your leg over a roe deer than his old dear. Now maybe that was the attraction of the country . . .

He switched on the car lights, just in case Bambi's brother had been on the same kamikaze course. He put the car into gear, accelerated, then cursed through clenched teeth as it stalled. It was crying out for a service and the brakes badly needed attention. Just as well he had a contact – a guy with a good garage and a bad drouth. Hunter had killed The Drouth's drunk-driving charge. One good turn deserves several others. That was how the city worked. It was big enough to hide a small misdemeanour. But try explaining that to Bella, his Darling wife.

Hunter gave the car plenty of wellie and it took off with a belch of smoke. Bella even now was rambling through her big sister's log mansion in Luss. It hadn't taken a detective to figure out how her mind was working. There had been two schedules for houses on the kitchen table. Both in Luss which – in estateagentspeak – was not a handful of streets of old hovels behind the back of beyond but a sleepy village of homes full of character on the bonnie, bonnie banks of Loch Lomond. Big Sis must have been winding her up again. Big Sis and her snobby, retired bank manager husband. Happy as pigs in shit in the land that time forgot. What did it have? Two pubs, both charging tourist prices, a kirk and the graveyard the busiest place. And Bella thought she could persuade him to move there? Well, Big Sis might wear the trousers in her house, she might be happy with the kirk socials and garden and crosswords, but it wasn't for him. He'd win in the end – he always did – but not without a few cross words. But everything had its price.

Bella kept mumping on about seeing her sister. She couldn't recall the last time they'd visited. Must have been really memorable, Hunter thought, but resisted the temptation of saying it out loud. Anyway, Bella had gone on, said when they were there they could take a look at the two houses – not go in, not a real appointment, just a wee look and, tonight when he was home early, well early for him, why not kill two birds with the one stone?

Three, actually, Hunter reckoned, as he let her have her way. Carmichael had extended an invitation for cocktails on his yacht 'If it is convenient, Sandy, we'd be delighted, delighted. Catch you later, ha-ha.'

It had turned out to be very convenient, thank you very much. So he'd burled the Vectra round past the two hovels. The big one, up the hill, might have had Psycho's mummy in an upstairs room and the other, the 'bungalow in need of some modernisation', had a wee tree – honest to God, it was a bliddy tree – growing in the guttering.

He'd said, 'D'you think it's a willow. I think it is a willow. They like it dark and dank. That's where the weeping comes from.'

And it nearly did. Bella hadn't even asked him to get out of the car. And she'd restricted her wrath to a scornful snort when he'd told her, as he dropped her off at Big Sis's, that he had to go on to an interview and would pick her up later.

In a way, he hadn't lied. Okay, so it wasn't an interview, as such, and there would be a bevvy going, but he wanted to have another look at the Carmichaels. All was not quite what it seemed with them. He'd got a young WPC, a dark-haired girl with big bazookas, to trawl the internet. Calder Carmichael had some honourable mentions in the press, the broadsheets mainly, and all of them glowing. The practitioner-patient relationship, whatever the hell that was, came in for a lot of praise. But it was just the usual guff from reporters who didn't have an effin clue but were perfectly capable of taking dictation and regurgitating it.

Zara was the star. She was the managing director of the Carmichael Fertility Clinic, with the same registered address as her husband's junkie shop outside Busby, on the outskirts of the city. Zara was into more high-class stuff. It cost two hundred and fifty quid, plus VAT, for a first consultation. Now what would that entail – heavy petting? Might get a tequila thrown in. But the dosh would be nothing to her clientele. Hunter could picture them, middle-class; rapidly approaching middle age; and barren. Willing to pay the price for a wee bundle of immortality. They would change its nappies now and it would change their incontinence pants in a couple of decades' time. Happy nappy pappy. Hunter had no such long-term plans. He was a man who looked forward to getting pished tonight.

The Carmichaels had no children of their own. Now that was interesting. Was that a lifestyle decision? Dinkies – dual income no kids. Somehow, Hunter doubted it. Just as he was confident that it was Calder who couldn't do the biz. And Zara wasn't bad. Not bad at all, actually. Bit on the skinny side – he liked a bit of meat on them – but she wasn't what he'd call jaggy. He wasn't into that. She'd have to shut up, too. He couldn't go thet poash axnt. It made her just too . . . clinical. Yes, that was the word he'd use to describe Zara Carmichael, MBE. Awarded in the New Year's Honours list two years ago for her services to charities. Her passport must read like a timeline of disasters in the western world. Romania; Albania; Kosovo; Afghanistan, to name but a few. Jesus, you should start to worry if she turned up on your doorstep. She dragged disaster around in her petticoats, then bathed and fed the waifs and orphans. What was in it for her, besides an MBE? Or was it just a redistribution of wealth – taking from the well-heeled west to give to the needy in the east of the continent? Strange hobby, but it takes all kinds . . . Still, he made a mental note to have a root around in the running costs of her charities. Zara had expensive tastes. There had been his'n'her Mercs – little change out of a hundred thou – outside their Busby empire. And then there was the yacht. Maybe that was why they put themselves out so much for the drug dosh – what was it? – twenty grand. How far would that go? Hardly enough to keep him in ties.

Hunter eased back on the throttle. There was a funny smell in the car, burning, stronger even than his thick black tobacco. But he could see the masts rising like erect dicks in the marina, saying 'Look at me, I've got a big one. I can't use it now, but I bet you wish you had one.'

Oh dearie me, what a fucking shame.

He parked the Vectra at the marina – alongside a Bentley, chauffeur and all – and followed the burning smell all the way to the front wheel. He put his hand down and felt the heat from a foot away. This was a job for a professional, a man with a drouth.

It wasn't hard to locate the Lady Zara. Big bugger with Hooray Henrys and Henriettas on deck giving it laldy with the guffaws. Carmichael saw him coming and greeted him at the bottom of the gangplank. Mine host was smart but casual – open-necked denim shirt, white chinos, yacht shoes, with the leather laces, and no socks. If he was surprised to see Hunter, he disguised it well.

'Sandy! So happy he could make it – come aboard.'

Hunter said, 'Wow, what a beauty. Is she yours?'

Carmichael preened himself, 'What, this little thing?'

Then he let his new friend into a secret. 'Most of her belongs to the Bank of Scotland, floating mortgage, you know, but what the hell – you're only middle-aged once, what? Now, a refreshment? Whisky, I'll bet.'

No, you don't, Hunter thought. You've not got the balls to gamble.

Carmichael said, 'Malt, of course. Anything in it? More whisky ha-ha-ha.'

An imperceptible hand movement beckoned a flunkey, then Carmichael excused himself for a minute which stretched till the end of the night.

The fragrant Zara was gliding about on deck, a smile painted on her face. Hunter watched her, intrigued. She flitted from group to group, a touch on an arm here, a brief, whispered secret there, never lingering too long, always on the move, working hard, the conductor of an orchestra bringing the units together to play her tune. Quite a different person to the one this afternoon who seemed so vulnerable, so fragile. Or maybe the same person just playing a different role.

A generous whisky was put into his hand and Hunter instantly felt at ease. He was at home here. Not one of them, Lord forbid! Not a member of any group, just the way he liked it. An outsider, eariewigging, hanging on the edge of a conversation, contributing nothing, free to move on to another group when he got bored. He sauntered around the deck in a clockwise direction (was there a nautical term for that?) and found himself up at the sharp end when he realised that he had made a fundamental navigational error. The flunkies – there were three of them – took on cargo at the stern. He relieved one of the waiters of another glass of malt – well, it was October, after all, and a man was in need of some central heating – and set off for the business end of the boat.

He had to belly dance a passage through a heavy team of pearls and blue rinses. An evening out from the Bearsden Conservative and Unionist Association, perhaps? All bums and boobs, cheating gravity by a feat of engineering to rival the Forth Road Bridge. Jesus H, one more of them at this side and they'd have the Lady Zara over sideways. And any old trout who went in face down was a goner. Take the Finnieston crane to right her. Maybe just decide to leave her there, as a memorial.

For those in pearls on the sea.

One dame was quite excited about the maestro, who was in town, apparently, to maest at the concert hall where the acoustics, exually, were superb. She made it sound like soup herb. Hunter squeezed past and one of the old dears farted on him, a wet one, which escaped out of the leg of her drawers like the air from a balloon with its neck held tight. He made it upwind just in time.

A snippet of conversation caught his attention. A hotelier in soapy bubble, allegedly, the rumour-monger stressed, and running out of creative accountancy options. But the alligator snapped it shut when he realised The Hunter, a stranger, was hovering. He moved on, enjoying for a minute or two a group of new mothers – Zara's clientele, no doubt – discussing their nippy nipples and how long it had taken for their haemorrhoids to migrate due north. Plums in their bums and bools in their mooths.

He followed a flunkey into the galley which served as a makeshift, but well-stocked, bar. Hunter lifted a bottle of Glenmorangie, cracked the seal and poured himself a generous glass. Not the best of malts, but it had one wonderful quality. It was so pale that you could drink it neat and everyone thought that you were a man of moderation sipping a little whisky with a lotta water.

Hunter's attention was drawn to a chink in the curtains of the cabin. Through it, he could see Carmichael, clearly in doctor mode, the head nodding in sympathy. His 'patient' was vaguely familiar. He was an old man, or maybe a very ill man, who was writing, slowly. He tore off a cheque and handed it to Carmichael. The figure on it brought the flicker of a smile to the psychiatrist's face, then he began talking again, leaning forward.

The man with the pen that could write big figures did not have to bow to Carmichael.

Hunter drained his glass, refilled it and wandered back out to the deck and stood looking out at the other craft in the marina. They really made quite a racket, splish-sploshing about, wire ropes rattling and clanking. Rich man's toys, not working vessels. Mine's bigger than yours. And Carmichael has one of the biggest. What was it worth? If you have to ask, you can't afford it.

A strong smell of perfume wafted downwind. It appeared to be coming from a suicide blonde, dyed by her own hand. She had her back to Hunter, a suntanned back with glittery make-up glistening in the fading sun. A bit broad in the beam but, hey, who wasn't nowadays? She half-turned and a puff of October wind sneaked inside her deep-green, silk dress, fluffing it out then moulding it to the generous contours. Not Marilyn Monroe over the air vent in the movie but not bad, all the same. She turned all the way around and Hunter noticed that she was smuggling rugby studs in her bra. She was on her tod, odd one out in a group of seven, and on the pull. No spring chicken and displaying all her goods in the shop window. Built for comfort rather than speed, she wasn't this year's model and she'd be dear to run, but well worth a test drive.

The Glenmorangie was hitting the spot, it was maybe just as well that the Vectra had given up the ghost. He could always bell the local bobbies for a lift home. One of the benefits of rank. The plods were always happy to Panda to you.

Oh, Christ, Bella. He'd better phone her, too. She liked the place so much she could bliddywell spend the night there. He fished his moby out of his jacket pocket and then realised that he didn't know Big Sis's number. Oh well, he'd tried. Tough titty.

Speaking of which, Blondie's nips were out now like organ-stops. Or maybe organ starts. She caught him staring at her good points and lowered her eyes to dwell on his groin. Captured and just as the one-eyed trouser snake was coming up for a peek, too. Then she looked him straight in the eye, picked the olive out of her martini and licked at it with a small, sharp tongue. Subtle as fuck, eh? A liquid droplet fell from the olive and disappeared into her ample cleavage.

He walked his sexy walk over to join her.

She said, 'It's nice out, isn't it?'

He said, 'Yes, but put it away. I'm a policeman.'

She said, 'Is that your truncheon in your pocket or are you just pleased to meet me?'

It wasn't original but it had been once.

3

Hunter sat at his usual table at the window of Joe's Cafe, a greasy spoon off Glasgow's once splendid Victoria Road. It was his favourite hidey-hole, a place where he could gather his thoughts and get some free grub. He called for a second mug of sweet, milky tea and had decided to risk a roll on lorne sausage. Who or what was lorne anyway? Short for forlorn, most likely, a staple of down-and-outs and cops nursing hangovers. Joe's rolls were well recognised booze soaker-uppers and a warning to a stomach feeling sorry for itself that life could get worse. But not much.

Blondie had been plenty keen. They'd been dropped off by some yahs in a four-wheel drive at her tidy bungalow in Milngavie and she hadn't wasted any time. Practically carried him over the threshold. Stepped out of the silk dress and led him by the hand to the bedroom. Just like the movies. Unfortunately the truncheon had suffered a bit from wet rot. Not at its best, what with the Glenmorangie and all. They'd had a go at making the beast with two backs but, well, it happens to the best of us. Credit to her, though. She worked hard at it. Kissed and sooked, but the pink parrot would not come up to play. And Blondie gave it plenty. Got up on top, grinding and sweating, golden globes bouncing and the raspberry ripples burling like Catherine wheels on shaky pins at bonfire night.

She seemed grateful enough in the morning, too, wanted to do the whole breakfast bit, but he declined. Still, fair play to her, she gave him a lift into town. Nice wheels, a Saab. Cheap to run, too, when you didn't pay the bills. The ex-Mr Blondie picked up the tab. Price he had to pay for being caught with his trousers down, she told Hunter with a wicked little chuckle. Oh well, you know what they say, he who laughs last didn't see the joke. Hunter took pride in his sense of humour.

Blondie had dropped him off at Queens Park. She'd sussed that he was married and was smart enough not to question why he was making an exit in the middle of nowhere. But she'd slipped him her phone number and held on to his hand for a second.

He'd caught a fast black home, intending to nip in for a shit, a shave and a clean pair of Ys. But Bella was there and she had other plans. She was not a happy badger. She gave it the usual – treated like dirt; how dare he?; who did he think he was?

Jesus H, he'd said sorry, umpteen times, but she was on her high horse.

It was the shame of it, the disgrace. There with her sister and her brother-in-law, holding on, not knowing when he'd be back, and then realising that he wouldn't and not even the decency of a phone call.

He said he'd been on a job, drugs smuggling – in Loch Lomond – and got away with it. Sandy Hunter, scourge of the poppy fields of Rowardenan. She was so angry she didn't see how ridiculous it was. He suppressed a smile behind his shaving foam.

She ranted on. When she came up for air, he explained that he didn't have the number. But that had just made it worse. One sister she had, one, and he didn't know her phone number. Didn't consider it worth his while to make a note of it.

Christ on a bike. He'd got rat-arsed, stayed out all night shagging (well, the intention was there) a blonde bint with big boobs and he was getting grief for not knowing her sister's phone number. Bella's nagging bouncing back off the tiles. And he already had a bit of a head, but he decided not to make a thing of it. He said sorry again, sorry that he'd missed her sister. Did she drop Bella off and just turn round again?

He was drying his face on one of the tartan towels when she returned with a receipt in her hand. A taxi receipt, from last night, thirty-five quid, and she wanted the money back and she wanted it back now.

He didn't say a word but it didn't make any difference. She had rehearsed the row, honed it to a razor sharpness, and she wouldn't be denied it by anything as submissive as silence. The denouement appeared to hinge on lots of nots, what he/she would not do; and if he thought he/she would, he was not on.

He had dressed quickly and tried to leave. But she barred his way at the door, the taxi receipt in her left hand, her right open waiting for the money. So he shook her hand, took the receipt, wiped his arse with it and left her to nurse her wrath.

Effin women – you couldn't live with them and you couldn't kill them.

He enjoyed the memory of the classy departure. It would cost him, he knew that, and there would be hell to pay when he got to the station too, if he went empty handed. They wouldn't be quite so impressed with the poppy fields of Rowardenan or the Balmaha triangle.

It was, what, 10.40 a.m. Oh, Jesus, the Vectra. It was still in the car park at the marina, cowering in the corner with a broken leg. He phoned The

Drouth, the garage owner, and arranged for one of his guys to collect the keys. Then he phoned the station, got one of the young Detective Constables and told him to take a couple of days to check out the hotelier who was using a creative system of accountancy.

'Just take a look-see,' he said, 'I've had a wee whisper.'

Nothing would come of it. But it covered him for last night and, come to think of it, for this morning too.

Joe brought the roll and a fresh mug of tea. He turned a chair around and sat astride it, resting his arms on the back. He'd been watching old gangster movies again – Edward G, Bogie – the good old days when things were black and white.

Joe said, 'Thinkin bout givin the place a makeover.'

'Oh, aye.'

'Thinkin bout a big open-plan area an wan wee booth at the back.'

'Interesting.'

It wasn't going exactly the way Joe had anticipated but he persevered. 'Booth's fur you.'

'I'm touched.'

'Big bit's fur customers – y'know, folk who pay.'

He paused, so his point would not be missed. 'The kind that aren't here cos you are.'

'Are you trying to tell me something, Joe?'

'Polis're bad fur business,' he said, throwing his arms open to display that his establishment was full of emptiness. Unfortunately, the impact of the grand gesture was overtaken by the impact of the sauce bottle (glass, HP, brown) smashing on the tiled floor (dirty green, rapidly turning brown.)

Hunter got up, reached into his pocket and took out a tissue. He wiped a spot of sauce off his shoe, folded the tissue, then placed it neatly on the table. He lifted the roll and headed for the door. He turned and said, 'Maybe I'll give environmental health a wee ring. This place looks like a shithouse.'

Hunter's office was so clean you could eat your dinner off the floor. But that would change. His desk was busy, but tidy. The four murder files were neatly arranged. Three at one side, one at the other. His computer was running, two personal documents on the desktop, DRUGDEATHS and BIZDEATH.

He had worked his way through the drug murder files, the honest-to-god paper entries, and come up with nothing new. Unusual. He would expect to find something, a thread or two to pull at to see what unravelled. The troops were getting sloppy and the reason was the bliddy computers. The youngsters hooked up to them like life-support systems and the sickos and the pervs used them for their jollies. The computers had their place in the polis – fine and dandy for storage, instant retrieval of data from various locations – but they were . . . inhuman. No errors. The troops just followed the format, keyed words into the boxes, ran the spellcheck and it all ended up looking right. The paper files had been phased out completely for less serious crimes, but Hunter had insisted on their retention for the biggies. The guys were getting sloppy. Nevertheless, he made a mental note to call in the plods to check their notebooks. There was nothing to beat verbatim recordings, misspellings, bad grammar and all.

But, in his heart of hearts, he felt that it would make no difference. Everyone knew who was responsible for the drug deaths. The score, to date, was two-one to Jimmy Stone, aka The Stoneman. The next move, the eye for an eye, was up to Danny Boyd. Neither, he was sure, had thrust the knife or pulled the trigger or pushed Larry The Laundryman out of the back of a Ford Transit doing 100 mph on the M8. But they had given the orders. They were responsible.

Hunter turned to the murder of Andrew Knox, aged fifty-seven, an architect, respectable and respected, well connected and comfortably well off. His killing was the kind that touches the chattering classes, that makes the opinion column and letters page of *The Herald*. The kind that makes murder real, not just the thing you read about. Not just a junkie or a ned. But your own dad or son. Or your husband.

It was dangerous territory for a copper. You had to deal with intelligent people, people who knew their rights, people who could afford lawyers, people who were lawyers. The kind of thing that could end your career. Hunter opened the Knox file. He didn't need to look. He knew the facts and, more importantly, the unanswered questions.

He let his mind drift back, almost three weeks, 4.30 a.m., nice morning, too, if your name wasn't Andrew Knox.

Digger Burns, his Sergeant, already at the murder scene. The dead guy, in the driver's seat of his big Audi, head back on the headrest, mouth open, looking as if he was just sleeping.

Hunter had said, 'Jesus Holy Christ, it's Des O'Connor.'

Hunter did that, put a famous name to them, so he could recall the faces easily.

'So, we're looking for a music lover.'

Digger knew that he wasn't meant to comment.

Andrew Knox, grey hair, balding on top; weak chin, average height, average weight. Mr Regular in a regular suit. The kind of bloke you see in town every day but don't really because you never give him a second glance. Mr Insignificant. Mr Invisible. Nothing out of the norm. Until he was murdered. It was the way with so many folk – didn't make their mark in life until they were dead.

Half a dozen uniform coppers and three other detectives hanging about like spare pricks at a wedding.

Burns gave him the details, in the order he liked them.

'Andrew Knox, fifty-seven years old, married for thirty-three years; three grown-up children; lived in Fintry. Killed . . .'

He waggled his hand, to show it was a guesstimate.

'. . . between 1 a.m. and 3 a.m. The body was found by his wife, Mary, at around 4 a.m. He was killed by a stab wound to the neck. You can see if you open the back door.'

Hunter did so. Burns opened the driver's door and gently eased the head forwards.

Hunter said, 'Where is she, the wife?'

Burns had been dreading this bit. He said, 'We took her home.'

Hunter exploded. 'You off your fuckin head? She finds her old man dead or says she finds him and you . . .'

'Not me, Sir.'

Burns never interrupted his boss but it was the time to make an exception.

'Chief Constable's orders, Sir.'

'Aw for fuck sake, Digger. You let The Toby Jug contaminate a murder scene? I'd be better working with that bliddy boy over there.'

He lowered his voice a little but the other cops could still hear him, even though they were all facing away.

'How the hell did The Jug get here? Was he lost or something?'

Burns said, 'He had been at a function, in Edinburgh, and heard it on the radio. Told the driver to come here.'

He paused, expecting another rant, but Hunter was examining the corpse.

Burns went on, 'Single blow, through the vertebrae. The doc reckons it must've severed the spinal column and gone up into the base of the brain. Said it looked like one wound.'

Hunter stopped him and called over one of the coppers.

Hunter said, 'What was it with The Jug anyway? Just taken in by the widow's tears, decided to show her the compassionate face of policing, eh?'

Burns whispered, 'Seems they have mutual friends – you know, mix in the same circles.'

Hunter said, 'What, the bliddy Magic Circle? Does he reckon, now she's the Widow Knox, he'll get her to play with his wand?'

The young cop stood, embarrassed, a couple of yards away.

Hunter said, 'C'mere, kid, not going to bite you. Just shine your magic wand on the wound.'

The young man trained his torch beam through the glass.

Hunter saw the lad was afraid. He said, 'In you go.'

The cop got into the car, realised he would be in Hunter's way and scrambled on to the back seat. He perched there, on his knees, and shone the torch beam on Knox's head. Hunter leant in, but his trousers brushed against the young cop's shoes.

Hunter rubbed at his legs and snapped, 'Get your arse out of my face. What are you, bliddy rugby poofter or what?'

The young cop swivelled around on the leather seat. His hand was trembling.

Hunter had a close look, then said, 'Okay, son, put your torch out. Your first murder?'

'Yes, Sir.'

'Then remember this. He's feeling no pain and you shouldn't be either. Know what I mean?'

The young man hesitated, then said, 'I'm not sure, Sir.'

Hunter's voice was gentle. 'It's just a dead man. Couple of hours ago he was breathing, mibbe heavy breathing, too, eh? Know what I mean now?'

The young man understood. He tried to smile.

Hunter went on, 'Well, he's not breathing now so he's dead, and a dead guy can't hurt you and he won't haunt you either cos you're one of the good guys. You're going to catch the one that did it. Right?'

The young cop nodded his head.

Hunter said, 'Good. Now bugger off.'

The young man went back to his colleagues, not sure if he had been favoured or rebuked.

Hunter walked to the back of the car and Burns followed.

Hunter asked, 'What else did the quack say?'

Burns said, 'He said the blow was delivered with precision and the wound was caused by a strong, slender, bladed weapon . . .'

17

Like a hatpin, Hunter thought. The kind of thing a woman would have. A woman of a certain age. A woman like a wife . . .

Hunter stuck his pipe in his mouth and sparked a match – was all set to kindle up – when he remembered the ban on smoking. He phoned security – security, in an effin copshop, that would quieten the fear and alarm of the lieges. Good, he recognised the voice, an old-timer, who knew a thing or three.

He said, 'Sandy, here. Seems to be a problem with the fire escape door at my office. Just going to check, so ignore the flashing light on your consol, eh?'

The security guard knew the score. The Hunter was going out on to the metal fire escape stairway for a smoke. The old guy said something about the fire brigade and received a mouthful.

Hunter took a fire extinguisher and wedged the fire escape door open. Jesus H, it was like being back at school, lying and skulking outside for a smoke. He put a match to his pipe, sucked in flame and exhaled plumes of smoke. He'd been battling the no-smoking brigade for years, fighting a rearguard action, yielding territory all the time. First it was the general office, then three-quarters of the canteen and, last year, smoking was only allowed in half a dozen self-enclosed hen hutches. He had nabbed one of them, smucking fartly, but it was a short-lived victory. The bean counters had done a deal with the insurance company, which had expressed concern about the rising numbers of claims of passive smoking-related illnesses, and agreed a 25 per cent reduction in policy price for a no-smoking building. Hunter had ignored the ruling or, as he put it later, he had failed to remember. He'd lit up in his office – and triggered the fire alarm. It could have been overridden, of course, but the Chief Constable had set down standing orders. The first offence had to be handled as if it were a real fire. To set an example, he said. So the firefighters had driven their big red fire engines, mee-maws blaring, to the copshop, had a chuckle, then driven their big red fire engines back to their station. And the cops' bean counters had earned their fat salaries by pressing some buttons and a bundle of taxpayers' money moved by magic through the ether to the fire brigade's bean counters who, by a strange coincidence, also received fat salaries from taxpayers' money.

The Toby Jug had given The Hunter an official arse-kicking. Should have known better; no exceptions made; had to set an example; etc, etc. Hunter had come in on the Monday with a big chocolate cigar and took delight 'smoking' it all round the office. Another item of confectionary had mysteriously appeared in the canteen, accompanied by a list requesting

18

suggestions on the most suitable custodian. The Chief Constable won the chocolate teapot by a distance.

Hunter tapped his pipe on the stairway, watching the last embers of tobacco flicker away like fireflies lost in the daylight. He went back inside, retrieving and replacing the fire extinguisher on the way, and returned to his office.

His phone was ringing. It was the switchboard. Was the Chief Constable with him? No. In that case, would he take a call from a Mr Carmichael?

'Sandy! Calder Carmichael here. Sorry to disturb you.'

Hunter said, 'Oh no you're not – disturbed folk are your business, eh?'

Carmichael said, 'Now that's a good one, very good. I'll use that one. Tell you why I'm calling. I was looking for Tobias, actually. You see we've got four tickets going a-begging for the Royal Concert Hall tonight. Now I know it's short notice, but it's was not every day you got the chance to hear Josef Paborsky, is it? So would you be interested, Sandy?'

Interested? In something for nothing? Does the Pope wear a funny hat?

Hunter thanked his new found friend, made arrangements for a plod to collect the tickets and said goodbye. There was something he had to do.

Find out who the hell Josef Paborsky was when he was at home.

Lisa poured a glass of expensive white wine and took a sip. She let it dwell on her palate, savouring the moment. Cool, mature, full-bodied, with just a trace of bitterness. So was the wine. She glanced again at her Cartier watch. Dinner was almost ready and, judging from the aroma escaping from the oven, it was going to be worth the wait. For the past week she had been on Corsica. She liked French food and the chef in the hotel had been pretty damn good, but there was nothing quite like home cooking.

She tore a roll open and buttered both sides. Then she removed the box of McCain's chips from the oven. Carefully, taking account of texture and size, she laid the chips on the roll. Longways, so she could bite through them. She added salt, vinegar and a snake of tomato sauce. She plonked the top down, giving it a squeeze with just the right amount of pressure that only experience brings. She paused just long enough for the butter to begin to melt, then took a bite.

Bliss.

Lisa lifted a dish towel and tucked it into the top of her Chanel T-shirt. Then she took the roll and the wine through to the sofa in front of the telly. She did a bit of channel hopping and stopped at an Aussie soap. Slobbing out, just the biz.

Ten minutes later, she lifted the phone, then put it back in its cradle.

19

Where was the mobile? Oh, yes, in the kitchen. She punched out Mum's number, then topped up the wine glass. She's going to tell a lie.

'Hiya, Mum, it's me. No, I'm in London.'

Just a white lie.

'I'm fine. Yes, honestly, a bit tired, but fine, really. Yes, the film shoot went well. Oh, the usual, clothes, you know, blouses, skirts.'

A black lie.

'I'll be home tomorrow. Yeah, Saturday. I'll phone. Of course, I'll see you. Have you taped *Corrie* and *Eastenders* for me? Great, I'll get them tomorrow.'

They chatted easily for five minutes, then Lisa said, 'Love you too, Mum. See you tomorrow. Bye then. Bye.'

She felt a bit guilty and thought about Louise, her younger sister, just a five-minute taxi ride away in the new Gorbals. What was Louise eating now? Last week it was mince and Sugar Puffs. Together. The week before, it had been banana fritters – breakfast, lunch and dinner. She was pleading temporary insanity on account of her pregnancy. Lisa ran a bath and took the mobile with her. If the guilt returned, she would ring Wee Sis. But she didn't want to take any chances. Did not want anyone arriving at the flat unexpectedly. If the mood came on her tonight, she did not want any distractions.

She replenished the wine glass, then stripped off. She caught sight of herself in the bathroom mirror and smiled. It wasn't hard to figure out what men saw in her. It didn't matter what she ate, she never put on an ounce. What was it Mum said? You can't fatten a thoroughbred. Same weight now as when she had left school, what, ten years ago. Five foot nine, eight stone six pounds. Boobs firm, stomach flat and, at last, a little shape on hips she always thought too boyish. She cupped her breasts. No silicone there. No, sir, what you see is what you get. And without any effort, either. Some of the girls had to work hard at staying in shape. Demanding routines in the gym, pounding the streets in their Nikes. Living on lettuce and LSD. Not for Lisa. She was just as God had intended her to be.

She put a generous amount of Molton Brown bath oil into the water, then added some ylang-ylang oil for relaxation. She put a shower cap on her head because she didn't want to have to wash her hair. She slipped into the water and lay back for a while, trying to unwind. Really trying. But it wasn't working. She thought about killing the bottle of wine, maybe popping a sleeping pill too and zonking out. But she'd tried that before. Tried it three weeks ago and it hadn't worked.

She got out of the bath and put on a soft towelling robe. She went into the living room, to the big window with the view over the Merchant City. A clock chimed ten. She was born here, just round the corner, in a tenement that the City Fathers had later demolished in what they endearingly called a slum clearance. The slum dwellers had been cast to the winds in the peripheral housing schemes. Oh, dear God, how she had hated Easterhouse. Thirteen years old, neither girl nor woman, uprooted and deposited with no say in the matter. She banished the thoughts from her mind. They were too painful to remember.

She looked out over the city, her city. But it isn't anymore. She doesn't belong here. At least she had that in common with the neighbours she rarely saw. None of them came from here and none wanted to remain for any length of time. It was a stepping stone for the young couples who bought their furniture from Ikea and looked forward to the time when it could be unbolted and moved to a place they wanted to call home. The businessmen saw the place as an investment and city base to see out the last few years to retirement. There were no prams in the close, no children playing in the back courts. The new blocks of flats could have been in any city in the civilised world. They had been thrown up in less than a year. Roots sunk as the crocuses faded and people in just before the first frosts. Yellowish bricks clicked together like a Lego set, characterless and anonymous compared to the solid, imposing sandstone tenements they had usurped.

Lisa went to the bedroom and slid open the mirror doors to reveal a vast array of clothing. She would not be sad tonight. The city was just coming to life and she would go out, have a good time. She chose a little black dress, figure-hugging but not too revealing, and laid it on the bed. A black bra, just to curtail the nipples, didn't want to appear provocative. She took a black thong and two lace-topped black hold-up stockings from a drawer and then picked out a pair of black Kurt Geiger shoes. Sexy, yes, but stylish. Then she surveyed the wigs, perched on the polystyrene heads on the top shelf. The blonde might look brassy and a bit of a challenge. A redhead? – too fiery for tonight. Brunette then? Nah, too nothing. So it would be black, same colour as her own hair but shorter. Just in case. If the mood overpowered her tonight, the police would be looking for a woman with short black hair. Yes, the short, black wig. As an insurance policy. Just in case.

Lisa dressed quickly, appraised herself in the mirror and liked what she saw. Confident and classy. Pretty Woman.

Just one choice left – the big one. Which coat? She reached for the black suede one. It wasn't going to rain tonight. It would be safe. But at the last minute she grabbed the leather coat. The brooch was there. A large silver cross, fastened over the left breast, its shaft disappearing into the raised piping. She put the coat on and took one last look at herself. Yes, girl, you'll do. What was it her mother used to say? Oh, yes.

Dressed to kill.

Josef Paborsky entranced almost the entire gathering at Glasgow's Royal Concert Hall and cemented his reputation as one of the most fastidious technical violinists in the world. He had started with an impeccable performance of some twiddly Handel, elbow up and down like a copper at a free bar.

But, just as the audience was looking forward to more of the same, he had indulged himself in a lugubrious, mournful interpretation of the slow movement from 'Winter' in Vivaldi's *Four Seasons*, then gone on to Massenet's 'Meditation' from *Thaïs*, a languorous and weepy piece.

Hunter knew the Vivaldi – could have whistled along to it – from Classic FM on the car radio. It was, Bella's sister said at the interval, music to die for. Hunter restrained himself from correcting her grammar – music for which to die. He had sacrificed his night and wasn't going to blot his copybook for one smartarse remark. The tickets were £40 each and Bella thought that he had paid for them himself. Little did she know that they had cost a body-swerve of The Jug and a wee wave earlier in the evening to Calder Carmichael who, thankfully, was too busy lording it to waste time on them. It was Carmichael's concert – his wife's really – to raise funds for poor piccaninnies in Kosovo or Afghanistan or some other godforsaken place. Bella had slipped him the dosh earlier and, if the truth were told, he'd been sorely tempted. But The Hunter was a reasonable man. He'd given her £40 back, saying 'I want to pay for your ticket myself.'

She'd given him a big kiss (a wet one) and a cuddle (quite a sore one) and said, 'Sometimes, Sandy Hunter, oh sometimes . . .'

Whatever the hell that meant.

Hunter had read in the programme that the truculent Czech fiddler was reluctant to reveal his age, which was put at anything between fifty-six and sixty-four, but, the witty writer added, 'even the latter might be somewhat of an underestimate!!' Two exclamation marks to be sure that you got it. Well, fuck me, fuck me. Hunter reckoned that no matter his age, Mr Paborsky was not a well man. The picture on the front of the glossy pamphlet showed the guy amid swirling smoke, a fag in his hand. His agent, Patrik, looked on adoringly. Patrik was also described as his long-term companion. Heard the one about the fiddler with two fags in his hand? Paborsky listed his hobby as smoking and his pet hate as 'small-minded people who infringe my civil liberties by trying to prevent me from doing so.'

Wasn't all bad, then.

Hunter's mind wandered ten minutes or so into the second half. He found himself wondering what would happen if he kindled up his pipe in the concert hall, explaining that he was only exercising his civil liberties. No doubt the smoke police would pounce to arrest him. He would be restrained, with sufficient physical force as deemed necessary, and ejected. He might be taken away for remedial treatment. What would that be? Pipe smokers would have the tips of their thumbs amputated. Couldn't light a match or spark a lighter without them. Fag smokers, just to be on the safe side, would have the first and middle fingers amputated, so they couldn't hold their smokes. He'd heard a good story about the archers at Agincourt. The smart guys with the longbows, out of harm's way themselves, who rained down arrows on the enemy. So, when the baddies captured them, they didn't kill them but simply cut off the two fingers on their right hand – the ones that held the arrow on the bowstring – and sent them back to put the fear of God into their buddies. It had been the beginning of the good old V-sign. The archers at Agincourt gave the enemy the fingers to let them know what was coming. Get it right up you (or should that be into you?), Pierre.

Perhaps the smoke police would not be allowed such latitude nowadays. A more humane remedy might be considered appropriate – something like ECT. Slap some petroleum jelly on the napper, plonk on the jump-start leads, plug it in and zap the nicotine receptors. Carmichael could do it at his clinic. Bit of the Frankenstein about him anyway. There really was something iffy about that place. The junkie money he got would hardly keep the Mercs in petrol for a week. So where the fuck does the real dosh come from? Oh, pardon me, I meant to say, from where the fuck does the real dosh come?

Bella caught him smiling and misinterpreted it. She took his hand and gave it a loving squeeze.

Well, gently fuck me.

There was one funny bit, when Paborsky, or the maestro as he preferred to call himself, nearly fell. He had stumbled, staggered back and collided with the cellist – a big dame who could crack coconuts between her thighs. She'd stopped the Czech bouncing by cradling him with one big arm, but the maestro nearly fell flat on his arse. He had shrugged it off with a flamboyant flapping of his bow and, according to the aficionados, it did

23

nothing to impair his performance. But, when (thank the Lord) it was all over, the guy looked near to exhaustion. He was led back on to the stage but performed only one encore – the slow section from Alban Berg's Violin Concerto, which was funereal and resigned. Much to the disappointment of the adoring audience, he took only one bow.

The night had served its purpose. Bella was beaming. All dolled up with the costume jewellery twinkling, she had fitted in perfectly with the crowd. Better than her dowdy sister anyway. Hunter had been pleased she had persuaded him to put on his suit. It enabled him to sit anonymously, which was more than Big Sis's man had done. Blue velvet jacket and cream trousers, the writers of rhyming slang were really spot on. What a merchant banker. And the bugger had deep pockets and short arms. Last time he bought a drink, he got change out of a ten-shilling note

They wandered down Buchanan Street towards Central Station. Time for the old fogeys to go home; time for the bright young things to come out to play. One of the trendy clubs had been taken over for the evening for a private function – the Press Fund Ball. Hunter knew he could bum his way in, slap a few backs, crack a few jokes, down a few drams. But it would cost him all of his hard-earned Brownie points. So it was back to the house for a wee sherry and, who knows, might even be time for a game of Trivial Pursuit. Haud me back.

Lisa had no such commitments. She just strolled into the ball.

The bouncer approached her with enthusiasm.

'Ticket, madam?'

Lisa loosened her coat buttons slowly, glancing at him. She put a finger to her lips, looked up at him like a child and he was not having paternal thoughts.

She said, 'Now where did I put it? Maybe you could give me a hand.'

She opened the coat invitingly and moved in close, letting him smell the perfume. He took his hands and put them around her waist. He stopped there, unsure for a couple of seconds, then he let his hands drift on, around, then south, to her hips.

She wriggled provocatively, and said, 'Find anything?'

She brought her palms slowly up his thighs, brushed her fingertips over his groin.

Then she stood on tiptoe, gave him a peck on the cheek and whispered, 'You keep cool, I'll keep it warm.'

She turned away and went to the cloakroom to deposit the leather coat.

Philip Macintosh had watched her skilful performance. He had been on the point of rising from his table, to ensure that she was not turned away, and was disappointed that his intervention had not been required.

Lisa flitted easily between tables, sipping wine, always leaving a little in the glass – in case she had to return to a safe haven – then moving on. She was aware of Macintosh's interest. She recognised him but was not able to put a name to the face. She had worked for him, what? Five, six years ago. The PR guru, the man with the Midas touch. She had been part of the window dressing in a couple of his publicity stunts, just a piece of ass in the background of a promo – one was for a new car showroom but she couldn't remember the other. It had been okay work when she was trying to make it as a model. An hour's work, just a flash of flesh, a twinkle of the pearly-whites for the cameras. Fifty pounds please, in cash, that'll do nicely. He'd tried it on, of course, but no more than any the others. Dirty Mac, that was what the girls called him.

Macintosh was watching her all right. And he liked what he saw. Not just the body, although that was an appealing prospect. He liked, most of all, his chances. She was on her own and thus, in his eyes, available. It had been a hard night. His two business partners had talents but they did not include the art of entertaining. The burden of mixing and matching the guests had fallen entirely on his shoulders. It was essential to keep them happy and always leave them laughing. A perceived slight could fester and come back to hurt him. In the pocket. The evening had gone well, apart from the wee fisticuffs session between the lawyer and the aspiring rock star, but that had been more handbags at dawn. Still, he'd had to go through the pretence of separating them. They parted eagerly, like marshmallows, but Macintosh did a bit of puffing, as if it was an effort, just to preserve their dignity. They had shaken hands, preened themselves a bit and sat down thinking that, for a second or two, they had lived on the edge.

Their timing was terrible, for Macintosh was all but fixed up with one of the birds who had flown in from a hen night. She had been no oil painting but then he was no artist. And he only wanted a bit of the other, not to spend the rest of his life with her. Unfortunately, by the time he had calmed his guests she had done a runner.

But the blackbird had seen him, he was sure of that, because she had perched at all the other roosts and assiduously avoided his table, which this year – as well as the feather-duster-weight boxers – included three million-aires, a newspaper editor, footballers from Rangers and Celtic and Miss Scotland. She was a looker, all right, but thick as mince and a voice that was an oral contraceptive. He'd tried it on with her earlier and the current holder of the tartan sash had told him through a thin smile that, if he tried to feel her up one more time, she would 'knee him in the balls'.

He had taken that as a no. At another time he might have put it down to frigidity but that was clearly not the case according to her response to the less subtle approaches of the Rangers player. She had asked if he wanted to tickle her bellybutton from the inside. The attraction must have had something to do with the sash his father wore. Whatever, he was going to get his flute played tonight.

Macintosh had the rest of the night off. His twenty-five-year-old wife, eighteen years his junior, was at home looking after their two children. Freelance opportunities were rare nowadays and thus more valuable. So he was not going to miss the chance. Besides, he was really in the mood. And the blackbird was becoming more and more attractive.

Lisa, standing at the bar, sensed he was behind her. She didn't turn round, didn't even look in the long mirror above the impressive display of whiskies. She didn't know when, exactly, he had arrived but she could sense the presence. And she knew it was him. She thought of leaving. Just collecting her coat and walking out. No words, no scene, no damage done. But the urge was there. In the pit of her stomach, growing in intensity, but still under control. She let it run. There was no small talk. In fact, he didn't talk at all. He just leant over and lifted some nuts from the plate on the counter. The pressure pushed her body against the bar and he held it there to ensure that she could feel his erection in her buttocks. Exercising his power. She could smell him. Aftershave and after it. Okay, then, mister, you're asking for it. You'll get it.

He ordered, 'Your place.' Then walked away.

She waited about thirty seconds, then followed obediently. She collected her coat. Her fingers darted to the brooch, the silver cross, its long shaft disappearing into a razor-sharp point concealed in the piping.

Zara Carmichael drove her Merc right up to the door of the Royal Concert Hall. The multistorey car park across the road had long since emptied, the streets were deserted, but even so she had insisted that all the lights in the building be extinguished. The evening had been a superb success but at what price? Paborsky was terribly weak but he had been absolutely brilliant. God bless his big bloated ego.

Calder had not wanted him to perform – even ten minutes before curtain up – said that the concert was important to her refugees' charity but, if the old fellow were to falter, if his body was to give in to the ravages of time and his life of excesses, then everything they had worked for could be jeopardised. Zara had handled it well, cosied up to the old chap, whispered that she knew how much the performance mattered to him, but said that his health and strength were of paramount importance. The audience would be disappointed – of course they would be, they had come to hear the maestro, after all – but they would understand if he called off. First fiddle could step up to save the day. That had done the trick. Hit him right where it hurt – his vanity. Paborsky had thrown a tantrum and insisted that he would go on stage if it was the last thing he did. It nearly was and he knew it. Zara recognised the significance of his encore, the Berg, which built on a chorale by Bach entitled 'Es Ist Genug' – it is enough – Christ's last words on the cross

Zara got out of her car and opened the rear doors. The figures emerged from the shadows. Paborsky, stooped and feeble, leaning heavily on Patrik, his lover and agent, and Hubner, his personal physician. They helped the old musician into the car. Hubner lifted his legs in, as you would a child close to sleep, and locked the door. Then he entered the rear of the car by the other door, closely followed by Patrik, who was crying.

4

'What way's Mecca?' Hunter said.

A young Constable giggled nervously. The other three cops smiled, a compromise of obedience to their superior and respect for the body in the bin shelter. It did look like a Muslim at prayer, on his knees, face down, arms stretched out. His jacket had been pulled up over his head. Holy shit, what a way to go. In his prime, worth a bob or two, judging by the suit, hand-stitched soft leather shoes, and lying dead at 6.53 a.m. in the midden.

Hunter had just arrived. He took in the scene quickly. No blood. Strange, you would expect blood.

He said, 'Pound to a pinch of shit I can tell you what happened.'

He had known immediately it was the second businessman murdered and he felt instinctively it wouldn't be the last. There was a contemptuous challenge about this scene and the brown stuff would really hit the air extractor when it leaked out, so he wanted the boys with him. And The Hunter knew how to do that.

He held up a £1 coin and said, 'Any takers?'

Detective Sergeant Digger Burns had seen similar performances but the others, Murdo, his Detective Constable, the tall, gangly lad who had just come over from Islay, and the beat bobby were astonished.

Burns played along. 'Can't put my hands on a pinch of shit at the moment, Gaffer,' he said, taking a coin from his pocket, 'but I'll match your pound.'

Hunter spotted an old dear watching them from her bedroom window. She would be the one who phoned in about 'the drunk in the back court.'

Hunter edged into the bin shelter, out of her sight, and beckoned the others to follow him.

Then he said, 'Just stop me if I go wrong, right? So, you were thinking, poor guy, out for a swally – that's a refreshment in Glasgow, by the way, Murdo,' he said to the Islay lad, 'in case you're not fully conversant with the vernacular. So he has a good swally and he's on his way home but he gets caught a bit short so he nicks in here for a single fish.'

Murdo was puzzled. Hunter wiggled his finger as if he were urinating.

'A pish, Murdo, c'mon, keep up, Son. So, the guy's busy with the syphon of the python and wallop, God turns his lights out – thrombo, brain haemor-rhage, something like that, eh? What d'you reckon, Digger? That what you're thinking?'

Burns knew the role he had to play so he nodded in agreement.

Hunter took the £1 coin out of his Sergeant's hand and said, 'Then you're wrong. This guy died because of his Nat King.'

Burns played the straight man. 'His what?'

Hunter tutted like a disappointed headmaster. 'He was after his Nat King Cole – his hole – y'know, Murdo, copulation, fornication, multi-plication.'

The photographer arrived and Hunter ushered them out into the open so the man could take pictures of the corpse in situ from every conceivable angle.

Hunter lowered his voice and spoke conspiratorially. The young coppers responded. Of course, they had heard about The Hunter, some good, some bad. But they would make up their own minds. What a guy! Not like some of the other top tecs who treated them like shit. They were now fully paid-up members of The Hunter's gang.

Burns, for years now, had been trying to get out of it.

Hunter was laying it on thick. 'And you say you've not touched anything lads, eh? Nothing at all? That's good. You've done the right thing. Good.'

He chatted easily, his gaze fixed on the body, turning away unerringly seconds before the photographer's flashlight exploded.

'Just as well it's you that found him. You wouldn't believe what some of your gaffers do. I'm thinking of one guy – no names, no pack drill – but let's just say he's English and for argument's sake we'll call him The Toby Jug.'

The beat bobby laughed. They all knew who he was talking about.

'Well, if The Jug had been here – oh, dearie me, did I say that out loud? Anyway, he'd have combed the guy's hair, so he looked his best for the photographer.'

Even Digger smiled.

Hunter said, quietly, 'Now, lads, I want to ask a favour. You don't need to and I'll understand if you don't want to cos, well, I know how it is and the pressure that's put on you. But it's just that, well, it'd be a big help to me if there was wee delay in writing this one up. Know what I mean?'

He could have asked them to eat a pinch of shit. The cops, taking their cue from Digger, were nodding like wee dogs on the parcel shelf of a car.

Hunter said, 'You will? Oh, good lads. That eases the pressure, I can tell you. Now don't change anything, nothing underhand. Just hold off a bit and give me a call before you file, eh?'

It was, at least, a bit of breathing space. Hunter had one overriding priority – to keep a lid on this, to win some time. He would need it because, if his gut was right, there was a serial killer on the loose.

And he didn't have a clue what to do about that.

Now he was sending the cops on their way, reminding Murdo to keep a civil tongue in his trousers.

'You'll get a decent cuppa at the cafe across from the train station,' he said. 'But, of course, I don't have to tell you that, do I? Give it about an hour, lads, then start knocking on doors. You know the drill. And bring the overtime sheets to me. Fuck the bean counters, eh?'

He let Burns start off with them, then beckoned him back.

'Thanks for the call, Digger – even if I did only have a couple of hours kip. And you were wise not calling in the cavalry. Who else knows?'

Burns said, 'No one that matters. No link with Knox, if that's what you mean.'

'That's what I mean,' Hunter said curtly. No one to impress now. No need for an act.

The photographer had finished taking his pix of the body in situ. Burns knew what was next. He took a pair of latex gloves from his pocket and put them on. Then he bent down and, gently, as if he were turning a new-born baby in his cot, he eased the body over on to its side. It was an it, now. Not a son/husband/father. That was how Burns handled it. Professional, dissociated and dispassionate. He knew that, all too soon, he would have to break the news to a mother/wife/child. That would be the time for compassion, for understanding and sympathy. But now it was an it.

The photographer snapped away, even as Burns turned it on to its back. That's when they saw the blood, not a lot of it, but it had come from one single, fatal wound in his temple. Much bigger than the one that had killed Knox. Big enough to have a tampon stuffed into it.

Zara switched on the powerful battery of lights above the operating table and a myriad of diamonds sparkled on the surgical instruments on the stainless steel trays. She had checked them off one by one but still she consulted the printed sheet on the clipboard and methodically went over the list again. It was her role in the operating theatre, her part in the crime that was being committed. Josef Paborsky would soon receive a new heart. The donor was a perfect match. Not only in blood and tissue, but also in Calder's most critical test. He was NM$_2$ – Neither Missed Nor Mourned.

Zara was dressed head to toe in surgical greens, with a mask over her nose and mouth. Her eyes fell on the razor-sharp edges of the scissors and two scalpels – even for a procedure as intricate as this, Clive would use only two blades. The theatre was cold – an essential environment for the impending operation – to keep the temperature of the patient low, slowing the heartbeat and reducing the flow of blood. She was surveying the array of scalpels when Clive tapped her gently on the shoulder and a shiver ran up her spine.

He said, 'Time for a break. A coffee, some caffeine, a st . . . st . . . stimulant.'

It was his way of breaking the tension. They had worked steadily for over two hours and she had been fighting to maintain her concentration. Hardly surprising since she'd only had four hours' sleep after the concert.

She said, 'That's a good idea. Will instant do?'

Clive smiled. He had the saddest smile, forced and false, like those she had seen on the faces of the starving throughout the world. The features differed, the skin colour changed, but it was the same display of teeth and cold eyes of those trading dignity for the meagre rations of charity to keep body and soul together.

He said, 'I'll do it.'

She said, 'Sure? Are you finished here?'

They were in what masqueraded as the Carmichaels' intensive care suite. It was the most sacred part of their Busby empire, built from scratch in what had been the stables of the old house and existing, ostensibly, to respond to any life or death emergency which might arise when an elderly mother was giving birth. Most of the equipment has been mustered on this pretext, although the cardiopulmonary device, commonly known as a heart-lung machine, had been acquired for cash dollars in Eastern Europe, where no questions were asked, and brought into the country, literally, on the back of a lorry. The IT suite was, in fact, a fully-equipped operating theatre. All that was missing was the expertise and that would arrive as soon as they had polished off their bacon and eggs.

Clive walked back to the deathly still body on the trolley at the far side of the room. It was a young man, a big boy really, handsome apart from the strawberry birthmark which stained most of the left side of his face. He was Romanian, a refugee, alone in this country and, very possibly, this world. His sternum had been split and rib cage wedged open with large clamps. Ironically, he was attached to tubes and machines which ensured that his healthy heart continued to beat. That was the prize – the heart – and it would be removed soon and the original owner would cease to be.

Clive, out of habit, checked the readings on the machines.

He said, 'Look at the size of his heart.'

Zara stepped forward, a little reluctantly, and looked into the young man's body. Was his soul here or had it gone already to hover at the portals of purgatory?

The heart was huge. She balled a fist and thought that the organ was almost three times its size.

Clive said, 'That's one decision made. It will have to be orthotopic.'

Zara nodded her head. She knew that the preferred option was a heterotopic transplant – a kind of piggyback procedure where the native heart is left in place and the donor organ attached in such a fashion that it acts as a booster pump to the circulation. Paborsky had not undergone any chest operations and there was still a reasonable amount of residual function in his old heart, so the heterotopic process should have been possible. But not with this big heart. There simply was not enough room to accommodate it. So it was to be an orthotopic transplant – Paborsky's heart would have to be removed and the new one sewn into its place.

The maestro lay on the operating table in the centre of the room. He, too, was in the twilight world twixt life and death. Michael Sørensen, the anaesthetist, an unpleasant, thoroughly obnoxious man, had practised his black art then gone blithely to have breakfast. He had said, as he left, that both patients would 'remain unconscious at least for two hours and probably for ever'.

Paborsky had been given immunosuppressive medications to ensure that the defence mechanisms in his body would not attack his new heart as an alien invader. Sørensen had inserted two intravenous lines – one into the internal jugular vein in the neck and a peripheral one into the back of his hand. The anaesthetist would use these to monitor the blood pressure during surgery and to draw blood where necessary. Intravenous catheters had also been inserted.

Zara herself had shaved Paborsky from chest to knees. Opinion varied on whether this reduced the likelihood of infection setting in post-operatively but shaving was common practice before birth and she wanted to think of this as the beginning of the old fellow's new life.

Clive said, 'We're all done, for now. A coffee, then. I'll make it if you could tell the others the operations will begin at . . .' he looked at the clock on the wall '. . . 8.30. That'll give them the best part of an hour.'

They left the theatre and helped each other to disrobe. Clive held the kettle under the cold water tap and Zara noticed that his hands were trembling. He needed some medicine. She took a bottle of Smirnoff vodka from a cupboard and poured a generous measure into a mug. Clive saw it happening, though he never lifted his head.

She said, 'Just to steady the nerves.' Then she left and made her way up to the big house.

Poor Clive. The drink was a physical need. Had he been a patient, Calder would have been understanding, sympathetic. But he was not a dependent, he was an asset, booty plundered from his own terrible misfortune. Calder had been angry with him last night. Caught him drinking in a quiet corner of the bar at the concert and scolded him as if he were a child. Zara had intervened, warned off her husband, through her fixed smile, and sat with Clive. She had bought him another whisky – a large one, too, waited until he finished it, then took his arm back into the hall to listen to the maestro. Clive was an alcoholic, seventy per cent proof. Couldn't work because of the drink and couldn't do anything without it. But get the dosage right and there was none finer.

The final members of the transplant team were finishing off breakfast as she entered the house through the conservatory. They called themselves the Ramblers, a kind of acronym fashioned from their names – Ramsey, Black and Erskine. Calder knew two of them – Ramsey and Black – from his days at university, and Sørensen had recruited the other. They all shared certain characteristics, a lust for money and a callous disregard for human life.

Black waved a piece of toast at her and mocked, 'Zara, love of my life, do we have time for a quickie?'

Zara said, 'In your case, Darling, I'm afraid that never would be too quick.'

Black said, 'Should I take that for a no?'

Zara said, 'No, the operative word was never. And since we are on the operative subject, your presence is required elsewhere in twenty minutes.'

Sørensen rose from the table. He said to Erskine, 'Let's be having you then, although I do not believe our presence will be required for long. I say, again, this is lunacy. To my knowledge, only one man of old Pabo's age has survived a heart transplant and it was carried out in the Methodist Health Care System in Houston, Texas. If this one is successful, it will be the second miracle in a stable in the past two thousand years.'

Hunter was in his magic mode, a craft that few knew existed and none performed better. He had switched to it subconsciously, instinctively, an animal reaction to avoid risk and injury. It was a gift that he had been born

33

with, and he had made the most of it, developed it to what was now close to an art form. Always on the move, clearly visible, available to all who didn't want him and able to disappear before the very eyes of those who did. Now you see me, now you don't. And that's magic.

A cup of coffee would have gone down well – a caffeine jag – but it was too risky. He would be a sitting target in the canteen. He had stopped, twice, at the coffee machine and twice thought better of it. The daft plastic cup would only be a hindrance. So he kept on the move, like a shark quartering its territory, patrolling the corridors in busy, deliberate style, never retracing his route lest he be cut off, but always within spitting distance of Conference Room One. He would be inside it soon enough, with Tobias Fastnett, the Chief Constable, James Smith, Assistant Chief Constable (Crime), along with the force's experienced Press Officer.

The hacks had already begun to descend on the Pitt Street headquarters of Strathclyde Police. Details of the news conference had been put out over the Presswire and the crime corrs had been e-mailed. Fat lot of good that would do since it was a Saturday and the guys on the dailies – the hairy-arsed reporters who really knew the score – would be in bed with a hangover or on the way to the pub for a pint of antidote to try to stave one off. The information given out was scant: murder; male; Glasgow city centre; news briefing 11 a.m. The journos knew that they were unlikely to be given a name. Families have to be informed, etc. But the press statement had concluded 'it would be in your interest to attend'. Shorthand for there's a story in this one. Maybe a particularly gruesome death – good copy, gruesome deaths – or a personality. The victim might be a weel-kent face.

The TV crews had been first to arrive. The lighting guys were rigging up their gear in CR1, at the moment, and the cameramen were taking shots of the outside of the building, just for padding in case the producer wanted to tease out the item. The telly journos – a cracking-looking bird from the Beeb and from STV a boy who didn't look old enough to shave – would set the pace, under orders from their newsrooms to deliver for the lunchtime bulletins. The guy from the Press Association might be troublesome. He used to work at the *Record* but had been sacked for taking a swing at a news editor, so he was now working twice as hard for half the poppy. The troops were calling him Bruno to his face and arsehole behind his back. He'd be out to make a name for himself.

Hunter knew that the media was a necessary evil. A newspaper printing a picture of the victim, or the telly showing the locus of the crime, could be what it took to bring witnesses to the copshop. In the company of journalists, he was a great advocate of the fourth estate, freedom of the press, freedom of information and all that crap. It didn't cost anything to butter them up and it didn't do to cross them. But, once you started to feed the media, it became voracious, demanding to eat every day, sometimes three times a day. You had to be careful not to create a monster, so you had to eke out what you had, feed them scraps, little and often. But, today, a Saturday, should be a skoosh case. A stern face for the telly, a sombre voice for the radio and a smile for the wee lassies from the Sunday papers.

Fastnett was in a flap and that was why Hunter was in magic mode. He had been in the old dear's house, the one who spotted Toshie's body, when his mobile had rung. Eight o'clock on an effin Saturday morning and The Jug was on the job. Doing his best to look industrious, impressive. Probably switched on his computer the instant he got in hoping that it was logged somewhere by some IT nerds who had been asked to take an electric look at his devotion to duty. But today Fastnett was not a happy badger. He left absofuckinlutely no doubt about that.

He had asked if the phone line was secure.

Hunter wanted to say no, get Moneypenny to phone back and put it on the scrambler. He actually said not really. The Jug had ordered him to report to him ASAP, actually used those four letters, just to fool anyone under the age of forty who had tapped into the moby.

He complied, of course, and reported as soon as he had concluded the interview. Oh, yes, and devoured the bacon roll the old dear insisted on making him. And, well, just one more cuppa.

The Jug had only one theme, a middle-class murder, another middle-class murder. And he wanted to know if there was linkage

Jesus H, he'd been at the American books again.

Hunter had played it straight down the line. It wasn't so much what he said but what he didn't say. There was, he said, no proof. The word he didn't say was – yet.

The snapper had been diligent, produced the glossies quickly, and The Jug had looked in amazement at the pictures of Toshie's body.

Strange, he said. Freaky, he said. He stabbed the tampon with his pen, as if he didn't want to touch it even in a photograph.

He had said – what a brilliant piece of observation – that the tampon was a signature.

Hunter had agreed. It was good to agree with The Jug. But he did not say that the handwriting was bad. Bloody awful, in fact.

SOCO, the Scene of Crime Officers, had not yet come up with anything useful. They had collected the usual detritus in the usual poly bags, but nothing that looked remotely interesting. The pathologist had yet to report back but he had ventured the early opinion – not to be taken as gospel, of course – that there were no evident indications of a struggle. But a blind man could see the cause of death. With a tampon sticking out of it. The time of death he put at between 2 a.m. and 3 a.m. Same time as Andrew Knox had been killed.

The plods had got nothing from knocking on doors and the old dear had been no joy either. She'd seen nothing, heard nothing. End of story. She was a nosey old shite, too. Could tell you the life story of all her neighbours.

The back court was surrounded by a five-foot brick wall. The gates – the ones the dustbin men used – were secured with a chain and padlock, and there was no indication that they had been forced open. The front entrance had a security system, one of the push button codes, but the old dear said that it hadn't been working for weeks. It didn't take Einstein to work it out.

The guys had rapped on the other doors and drawn a blank. One young couple had come home around four. They had noticed nothing unusual but that meant nothing. They had been on the bevvy.

Fastnett had asked about developments on the Knox case. Hunter had had the merry widow in the frame for it but Toshie had changed that.

Hunter had tried to waffle but The Jug clearly wasn't buying it, so he changed tack, asked the Chief Constable how he wanted to play the press conference. Did he think they should volunteer that they were linking the two murders?

It worked. You never got a straight answer from The Jug. He didn't do straight answers. He did meetings.

Hunter's mobile phone had gone off. One of the lads from the Masons had said the ring was dull. It needed to be customised, he said. That's why it played 'The Billy Boys'. Hunter had choked it smartly and gone to the window to pretend to get better reception. Fastnett got on the internal phone and told his secretary to get James Smith and the Press Officer, ASAP.

When Hunter's phone call ended, Fastnett, a trained observer with a musical ear, had asked if that was 'a party tune'.

'What, eh? Oh, no, sir,' Hunter had said, 'only the wife, worried about me.'

The Press Officer, a shrewd operator, had handled Fastnett well. Said yessir, yessir, three bags full sir. And then, almost as if he had been talking to The Hunter in the lavvy fifteen minutes before, almost as if The Hunter had warned him to cover his own back, he said that, perhaps, there might be a potential problem. Did they want to link this killing with that of Knox?

The Jug had been remarkably concise. Just spread out his hands, palms up, one aimed at Hunter, the other at Smith.

Hunter had found his shoes fascinating. Smith, accepting the responsibility of rank, cautioned against any mention of Knox. Treat it as a straightforward murder.

And if, the Press Officer ventured, the question were asked from the floor?

Comfy brogues . . . maybe due for a visit to the cobbler, though.

Smith said that such a question, were it to arise, could be answered honestly. There was no evidence to link the two incidents. It would be a straightforward press conference, death by a bladed instrument and an appeal to members of the public who might have seen anything, no matter how apparently insignificant, to get in touch with their local police station.

The Jug was happy with that. The purpose of his meeting had been achieved. It had been what Hunter considered to be Arse Out The Window Time, a quaint little Glasgow expression, derivation unknown, meaning implicit. It was up to Smith now to avoid the double-glazing and they could go on to discuss both cases freely.

The tampon was the strange thing. Macabre, the Press Officer had said. There had been none in the Knox killing. It was, compared to Toshie, a straightforward stabbing. But it had a sinister element, too. One wound, executed with precision. No one mentioned a serial killer, though each of them thought about it.

Hunter had answered questions but been careful not to proffer an opinion. He had a bad feeling about this. It was going to bring no medals and a lot of arse-kicking. He asked whether he should relinquish control of one or both cases. Did they think that having one man in charge of both would suggest linkage?

The Jug was on to him in a flash. Nice try but no cigar. But he did win one concession. Smith would take the press conference. That was a result. It would allow The Hunter to hover, to keep an eye on Bruno.

The Jug, never one to miss a bonding opportunity, concluded their meeting with the brilliant observations of how an early arrest was essential. How the entire force would be under scrutiny and, as leaders, they must not freeze in the heat of the spotlight.

More moron than oxy.

Lisa woke slowly, like a cat, unfurling one limb at a time until she occupied all four corners of her double bed. Sleep, God's own medicine, left her refreshed in body, mind and soul. Sunlight streamed through the bedroom window. A nice day, a day to be enjoyed, savoured. Not hot like the Mediterranean, where the burning rays had to be avoided, or humid, like the West Indies, with its steamy air catching in your throat. Sunny Glasgow, God's own country.

She got up, put a dressing gown over her naked body and slipped her feet into a pair of huge slippers, two giant, grey mice, a Christmas present from her sister Louise's oldest. What age was she? – not yet five – and Louise already with her third child well on the way. Twenty-three she was, going on forty. Trapped with a husband who neither worked nor wanted to and, Lisa was certain, was a bit too free with his hands – though Louise denied it. She was just accident-prone. Bumped into things; fell a lot.

Lisa banished the thought from her mind. She went to the loo and splashed cold water on to her face. Mum always said that cold water gave you a good complexion. She had a pee and changed her tampon. God damn the curse.

But it was a beautiful morning, what was left of it, and Lisa was determined to enjoy it. She took a couple of crumpets from the freezer, popped them in the microwave, then covered them with golden syrup while they were still hot. From the kitchen window she could see three girls – she was no good at ages but was sure they were still primary school pupils – in the back court. They were just hanging about. They didn't look unhappy or anything like that but they didn't seem . . . happy. They would have their Walkmans and mobile phones and money in their pockets to have lunch at McDonalds. Kids nowadays were smarter, more sophisticated, but they had forgotten how to play. Lisa couldn't remember the last time she heard laughter in the streets. She had played in those streets with Louise – daft games, harmless fun, but it wasn't just the buildings that had been changed. The era had gone too. It was the end of innocence.

Lisa ate her breakfast with a fork, twisting the slippery strands of syrup around the tines and sucking at them like spaghetti. Despite her years of practice, she could not avoid some sticky threads dripping on to her chin. Her mother used to tease her about that – keeping some for after, are you? Bet you wish it was after. And she did then and felt guilty about it. Even as a child, Lisa knew what guilt meant. It was shame. It was feeling bad about how you felt. But that was baggage that she had long since deposited in the left luggage locker of her past. Everything had a price. You paid it and didn't look back. Je ne regrette rien.

She sponged her face, patted it dry with a fluffy towel, then went to the living room. She had been away from her flat for just over a fortnight and a mountain of mail had built up. She sorted it into two bundles. The larger

38

pile of what was clearly junk mail she binned without opening it. She gave the remainder her undivided attention. There were no personal letters – she didn't get personal letters here. Her family didn't write them and no one else knew where she lived. There was a phone bill and a gas account. Neither of any significance since both were paid monthly, by direct debit. There were statements of both of her current accounts – one with the Royal Bank of Scotland, the other one Lloyds TSB. She must do something about them. Too much money building up there doing nothing.

Lisa kept till last the letter from her independent financial adviser – not the one in Grand Cayman but the nice woman in Glasgow who handled some of her investment trusts. They were healthy – but, when the sums are approaching six figures, your financial affairs are never exactly poorly. Still, the nice woman wrote, the Jupiter and Fidelity investments had been disappointing and she was recommending transferring into Newton Higher Income and Gartmore European Selected Opportunities. The figures on the paper brought Lisa pleasure. You've made it girl, you've arrived. And now they're desperate to keep you. Changed days. It wasn't so long ago that they couldn't get rid of you quickly enough.

Decisions, decisions. Deliciously delightful. Lisa kissed the letter. The wealth and what it could buy were wonderful. She would never have to worry, as her mother had, about paying the rent. And nice things were nice. But the bonus, the dividend, was the liberty that financial security provided. It wasn't that she could afford anything she wanted. Not even being able to make sure that Mum lived in comfort. Money meant freedom; it offered options. She could choose whether to work or not. And she could make other decisions, too . . .

She went to the CD, lifted a Robbie Williams but chose instead a disc she had picked up last month in Hungary. *Baroque Favourites*, all strings and organs and harpsichord. It started with Tomaso Albinoni Remo Giazotto, 'Adagio in G Minor'. Funeral music. Crème de la crem.

She smiled and went and sprawled on the white leather settee. She pulled the money paper to her open lips. She could taste freedom and it was all she had ever wanted. No man had considered that. She had heard thousands of weasel words, listened to all the hollow promises, but none of them had thought of offering that. Not even when they were playing a part, mouthing someone else's words, sweating for the camera. And, now that she had it, no man could get close to her. They could paw and lick and thrust. And she would simper and writhe in supposed orgasmic ecstasy. But they would not touch her. Not now. Not ever.

She was in control. She had absolute power and it was so sweet. Sweeter than syrup. A surge of adrenaline coursed through her body, tingling her nerve ends, and started those butterfly wings fluttering inside her tummy. She stood up, shrugged off her robe and lay down gloriously naked. She closed her eyes, waiting for the Handel. 'Concerto in B Flat, Op. 4, No. 6', the box said.

And what did you do this morning?

Oh, I listened to a little Handel, 'Concerto in B Flat, Op. 4, No. 6', actually. No, I wouldn't say I enjoyed it. It's not so great, actually. A bit too pompous, too full of its own importance, if you ask me. But then again, if you ask me again, Handel was full of shit, actually.

She laughed aloud at the very thought. She could do it now. She could say exactly what she wanted when ever she wanted. And all because of the numbers on this piece of paper. Gently, she pulled the paper up flat, over her stomach. The letterhead was embossed and she could feel its slow drag on her skin. She traced the mounds of her breasts, concentric circles, smaller and smaller, ever so slowly nearing the pink pert nipples. When she did so, she used only a corner of the paper, lightly, gently, angel kisses, until she began to moan with pleasure. Down now, between her legs, the paper held in both hands like a scroll.

Starting so softly, rhythmic and light, backwards and forwards, parting the lips, gently but firmly, finding the clit, tummy is tingling, pressure increasing, pleasure is mounting, fluid is surging, nearing crescendo, can't hold it back, saying the love words, shouting the name, and it's Lisa. Lisa Lisa.

Hunter was in the canteen in the copshop, drinking coffee and eariewigging. Toshie's murder was all the goss and, he was pleased to note, none of the troops mentioned a name or the tampon. The young cops from the crime scene must have kept a lid on it. Good guys. Murdo and the other bloke, thingmi. Never forget him.

The press conference had gone well and well it should. They had asked the obvious questions, taken no for the obvious answers, then raced off to catch their deadlines.

Hunter had winkled out Bruno beforehand, said he'd see him in the usual pub after the weans had left. It had been enough to keep the hack's tongue between his teeth. So they'd had a quick pint – Hunter had paid for them, too – and said that the story was a biggie. Said Bruno should give him a bell later and he'd give him the victim's name. He suggested around 9.30 p.m. and Bruno agreed with glee. He knew The Hunter was doing him a turn, giving him the story to himself. He could put it out on the Press Association wire right away – might even catch the national TV news bulletins – and it would definitely make all the city editions of the papers. That should ensure that the smug staffers got their fat, superannuated arses kicked when they turned up on Tuesday. Bruno was on the way back – and punching his weight.

Hunter was relieved that the journos hadn't a clue who the victim was. But he had known. As soon as the young cops turned Toshie face up, he had known. It had given him a bit of a fright. He wasn't scared – he'd seen enough stiffs not to be affected like that anymore. No ghosts with muddy faces invaded his dreams now. Anyway, Toshie was one of the better-looking deaders. A touch of class, right to the end. But seeing a mate lying there had given Hunter a surprise, no a shock, and it was many a long year since that had happened. Barely a mark on Toshie, not a scratch or a trace of blood. Yet The Hunter had turned his back, instinctively, and moved away. Digger Burns, the eternal Sergeant, had noticed it but had the sense not to say anything. Hunter had gone for a wee walk round the back court. Kindled up his pipe and had a puff.

He'd been away for the weekend with Toshie what, three weeks ago? No, it was four, before Knox was killed. Great time, too. Weekend fishing up the west coast, a distillery, one of Toshie's clients, picking up the tab and providing generous liquid refreshment. A dozen of the boys – press mainly, another cop, from Inverness, and a couple of high-flying businessmen. Friday and Saturday under canvas. Landed a couple of good brown trout, too. One of the guys had got his dick caught in his zip while he was having a piddle. What was his name? The sheep-shagger from the *Press and Journal*. Thingmi. Screamed like a stuck pig. The middle of the night, pitch black, and there they were like schoolboys, shining a torch on it and offering obscene advice. Carry On Zipping. All of them pished. No option, of course, but to yank (no rhyming slang intended) the zip down. Poor bugger, his pride and joy had come out like a burst salami. But he lived to shag another day. They'd spent the Sunday in a posh hotel, good nosebag, decent kip and helicopter back to Glasgow early Monday in time for work.

Good guy, Toshie. A man's man. A mate, really. A shame. What a fucking waste. He'd gone out in style, though. Would be remembered for a while. The tampon murder. And all because of he couldn't keep a civil tongue in his trousers.

It was sex. Hunter had no doubts about that. But why? Toshie didn't seem to have a problem pulling the birds, so it wasn't as if he was desperate. So why not a hotel? There were plenty around, lots of places not to be seen. Bottle of wine, decent bed for indecent acts, what's the prob?

The Jug had hinted, not come right out and said it but alluded, that was the word, he had alluded to it.

Poovery.

He had asked Hunter to consider the possibility that Toshie was . . .

A shirtlifter?

. . . not all that he seemed. The circumstances were unusual. There was nothing to suggest that the victim had not gone into the back court willingly and, with the choice of such clandestine surroundings, it would be negligent not to consider the possibility of homosexual practices.

He made it sound really dirty.

Two men just seizing the moment.

Aye, and one of them having his period.

Or a trap, The Jug had said. Lured into the darkness by a young woman where a man . . . or men . . . or women were waiting.

It was the why that was puzzling Hunter. He was ruling out a domestic. Like he's going to leave his nice sandstone house in Newlands to give his wife one among the dustbins in the Merchant City and she's going to do away with him there and then and hail a cab and go home to her two bairns. Robbery was a non-starter, too. Sure, his readies had gone and Toshie always kept a good wedge in his wallet. But the credit cards were still there and his watch, which must have been worth a bob or two, was still on his wrist. So what was the motive?

Find the motive and you'll find the killers, The Jug had said helpfully. Then he buggered off and that was the most helpful thing he had done.

Knox's wallet had been dipped, too. Only the dosh. His plastic and watch were not touched and the keys were dangling in the ignition of his Audi. Same killer? Jesus H, Hunter hoped so. Two loonies on the loose at the one time didn't bear thinking about.

He couldn't see Toshie as a horse's hoof. Not even for a wee change, something different. Christ, he'd been in a tent with the guy last month. He'd have known. Charged Toshie for loitering within tent. No, poovery was a non-starter. But it was nookie, Hunter could feel it in his water.

He began to compose his mental Photofit. Some guys could go for an old slapper but not Toshie. Wasn't his style. No, he'd be on to a young bint, youngish, and a looker. Confident. Cocky, that was better, easier to remember. She was cocky, up for it. Game for a bit of danger. It wasn't Toshie's idea to have it away in the midden. It was hers. A shag out in the open, a bit of rough. For a change. What was it they said? The tramp wants to be treated like a lady and the lady like a tramp . . . So she had a few bob, too. And she had the chat. Dirty talk. You can't lick it. She'd got Toshie down on his knees and then she'd stabbed him. Either that or she was eight feet tall. One wound, same as Knox. One lethal wound. So a bit of knowledge of anatomy. More than a bit. A lot. And she's got a crossed wire, a blown fuse. Sex is the lure, love the promise and killing the outcome. She's a doctor or a nurse. Where death isn't a stranger.

Dr Strangelove.

Zara sat in one of the old leather armchairs in her fertility clinic on the outskirts of Busby. She had kicked off her shoes, tucked her legs underneath her and lit a cigarette. She dragged the smoke deep into her lungs, held it there for several seconds, then exhaled parallel plumes of smoke through her nostrils. She repeated the exercise and this time felt the nicotine hit her head like champagne bubbles. It was invigorating, decadent, wicked. She smoked so rarely now that each cigarette was like the first, the taste bitter, unpleasant; the habit foolish, dangerous; and the heady swirl worth it all and then some. A cigarette meant a triumph, a reward for achievement, and it had to be savoured, alone and uninterrupted. Calder disapproved but that only made it doubly delicious.

Zara yawned. The past week had been hectic, juggling all the usual balls and also having to keep a tight rein on the arrangements for the concert. The media interviews had been particularly difficult, and she had fended off requests for personal interviews – 'The charity is the cause and the maestro the star' – but she had been at every conference, vigilant, alert, conducting the orchestra without a baton and directing Josef Paborsky. He had almost blown it once, introducing Hubner as his personal physician, and some fresh-faced photographer had snapped them together. Zara had told the lad about the maestro's wicked sense of humour, said that Hubner wasn't his real name and he was merely a minder. The photographer had believed her – even said thanks for keeping him right – and the picture had not appeared in any of the papers. And the Lord be thanked for that. The last thing in the world that Zara needed just now was some fool of a journalist wondering why Paborsky had felt it necessary to travel with a heart transplant surgeon.

Zara finished the cigarette and lifted her glass of whisky – a large one, because she deserved it. She drank greedily and felt the raw spirit burn its way to her stomach to heat the cockles of her heart. The transplant operation had been – as far as they could tell – a success. The Rambers had returned to the big house just after 2 p.m. She had listened to them – noisy, boasting, as if after a victory on the rugby field – and known it had gone well. They had got stuck into the booze right away and she had gone to scold them, told them to keep the noise down. Did they want to attract

43

attention? They had told her to chill, to relax, enjoy herself, and she had left quickly, ignoring Black's suggestion that she should sit on his face.

They really were odious but, for the immediate future, a necessity. Each was a specialist in his own field, with a conceit that exceeded the common bounds of morality.

There had been a crisis, about an hour into the operation. Zara had gone to the theatre, to peep in and to pay particular attention to Clive. The donor organ had been harvested, without complication, and Clive was about to cut away Paborsky's heart. It had been bypassed and his blood diverted to the heart-lung machine. This would keep him alive, after a fashion, taking the blood which normally coursed through the heart and lungs, cleansing it of carbon dioxide, replacing it with oxygen and pumping it out to the body tissues. Clive had to remove the heart, leaving part of the right atrium so the donor organ could be stitched on to it. But he had stopped, doubting himself, as he was about to sever the nerves. Hubner, the most knowledgeable, had spotted it first, then Sørensen, who said, 'Come on, you old sot, just bloodywell get on with it.'

Clive's hand had trembled, then started to shake.

Calder had coaxed, cajoled, then ordered Clive to 'do his duty'.

But it was Zara who helped him. She caught Calder's attention and, using frantic signs, told him to bring Clive to her. Outside the theatre, in the pre-op room, Clive broke down and wept.

'I can't . . . do it. It's not fair. I'm not fit. Hubner must finish. I'm just, I'm just a drunk.'

Zara wanted to hug him, comfort him, let him take some of her strength. He was the best of the lot of them and at least he recognised his weakness. She hushed him with soft, gentle words.

'Slowly, Clive. Easy, relax a little. That's it. That's good. Good. No hurry, no rush. Just breathe, breathe deeply – that's it, big breaths. Not too much, don't want you hyperventilating, do we?'

He tried his sad smile but there was fear and panic in his eyes.

He said, 'I can't do it, can't help him, can't . . .'

Zara put a hand on his arm and squeezed gently. She said, 'I can help you, Clive. Relax. Calm. Calm. Trust me. Will you do that for me? Eh, Clive? Will you do that for me, please?'

She led him away from the window, out of view of the men in the theatre. Then she got the vodka. Clive groaned, a self-deprecating condemnation.

Zara said, 'I know, Clive, I know. I know how you hate it. But it's not for you now. It's for Paborsky. For your patient.'

She took a mug and half-filled it with vodka.

'Will you drink it, Clive? Please, drink it for me. Then you can help your patient.'

He took his medicine and she spoke in a soothing monotone.

'You can do this, Clive. You know that. You do, Clive. Focus. It's what you're trained to do, what you were born to do.'

Clive drank again.

'You can save the life of a genius. You're the only one who can. Save the life of a man whose music enriches the lives of millions. He's dead just now, Clive. As good as dead. Hubner can't save him. But you can.'

Clive said, 'But the boy . . .'

Zara said, 'He's dead, Clive. He is dead. We know that. Nothing will change that. And we did it. But will I tell you how I handle it?'

Clive nodded his head. Good, he was listening – he was taking it in.

She went on, 'I rationalise it this way, if the technology had been available in the days of Galileo, da Vinci, Einstein, would they have been kept alive? Of course they would. It's the law of the jungle. The strong devouring the weak – red in tooth and claw.'

Clive raised the mug again and she saw that his hand was not shaking.

Zara said, 'Just do your best, Clive. No one can ask for more. Even the Russians refused Paborsky because the risk was so great. The old man knew that. The worst that can happen is that he dies. That's the surgeon's cross and his salvation – you told me that, Clive.'

He smiled and his eyes were calm. Zara helped him to scrub up and he returned to theatre. She went in after him and lined up the surgical team behind Paborsky's still body and raised a Polaroid camera. Hubner protested, turned his back. But Calder spoke to him. It was, he said, an insurance policy. A musketeers' policy – all for one and one for all. Zara took seven photographs. One picture, she said, for each of the magnificent seven. Calder, Clive, Hubner, Sørensen, Ramsay, Black and Erskine. She asked Hubner to take the camera and she took his place in the line-up. The camera flashed again.

Then Clive took up his blade and severed the nerves in the heart. These nerves help to regulate the rate of heartbeat. In a younger man they might grow back, but this was unlikely in a man of Paborsky's age, so small pacemaker wires were attached to the new heart and brought out through the skin near the base of the incision. The wires would be attached to a temporary pacemaker box to help regulate the heart rate. In a couple of days, they would attach a permanent pacemaker under the skin.

The remainder of the five-hour operation went well, except for the first time they allowed the blood to flow through the new heart and it had produced a massive haemorrhage. They had reverted to the cardiopulmonary machine but not before their blood supply had almost been exhausted. But Clive had remained calm, took control and they had weathered the storm.

Hubner assisted with growing admiration. Clive's hands were steady, the scalpel strokes confident, quick and clean. And, thanks be to God or Baal or Beelzebub, the transplant had been successful.

Poor Clive. A brilliant career ruined by drink and all he was left with was a conscience. He had ignored two warnings from his hospital management. The third time, when a patient had almost died, had resulted in an appearance before the General Medical Council and a suspension of two years. And that, in turn, had led to a divorce. His wife cited mental cruelty and he lost his house and his kids. And then the wheels had really come off the wagon. He had found little comfort in the bottom of a bottle although that didn't stop him from looking.

The transplant team – even the boorish Sørensen – had recognised Clive's skills in the operation. Patrik, Paborsky's agent/partner/lover, had expressed it all. He had not actually said words but had sobbed his gratitude and clutched Clive's hand. At one point, Zara thought that he was actually going to kiss it. Calder had disappeared to make a phone call, one consignment, to be collected this evening.

Clive, embarrassed, had returned to the operating theatre, to the lifeless body of the young Romanian donor, with eight black bin bags. He began by severing the legs above the knees. Then he cut the thighs from the torso, removed the arms and finally the head. Zara had waited, until the powerful saw was silent, then she had returned to the theatre. Clive had the vodka bottle to his lips. He ordered her out. He would clean up. It was his responsibility.

Zara rose from the big leather armchair and opened a window wide. The blast of air would cleanse the clinic of smoke but Calder would still smell it on her. But, hey, a girl had to do what a girl had to do.

Almost on cue, her husband came into the clinic. His nose twitched but he did not comment. He was carrying a number of drawings.

'Look at these,' he said. 'Fascinating, utterly fascinating. What do you see.'

They were pencil drawings of insects, little bodies and long legs, the kind David Attenborough whispers about as you see them magnified a thousand times.

Calder was too excited to wait for Zara's comments on the work of Matthew Whittle, his favourite patient.

'It's extraordinary,' he said. 'These are the fruits of Matthew's suicide attempt. It was, he said, simply the best thing he had done in his whole life. It had taken him on to another plane. And he wanted the staff who saved his life to know that he didn't hold it against them. Can you believe that? He was offering forgiveness, said they were only doing their job, said that he understood that. And he could always try it again. Maybe get farther. Maybe go the whole way.'

Calder stopped and shook his head in astonishment. 'Now isn't that extraordinary?'

He examined one of the drawings. 'And all the time Matthew was drawing these.'

He tapped the paper.

'I said they looked like pond-skaters, you know, those insects that walk on water. But they're not. I asked Matthew what they were and do you know what he said?'

Zara knew what she was meant to do. She obliged and shook her head.

Calder went on, 'Matthew said, "They're me.".'

Calder paused and Zara did her best to look engrossed.

Her husband continued, 'He said he had seen them, seen himself, after he had lost consciousness, and they had gone when the staff revived him.

'They live,' he had said, 'in my mononucleic acid.'

'Can you believe it? A boy from Barlanark, no education to speak of, and he is telling me about mononucleic acid. And he knew all about it, MNA. How much do you know about it?'

Zara almost told him. She would have used her quiet, clinical voice, pointed out that, in eighteen years in nursing and even longer with an arrogant psychiatrist, she had more than a passing acquaintance with the receptor of signals to the brain, the motorways that carry them to the right locations, that enable them to be deciphered and acted upon. But she let it pass.

Calder was talking again, his voice quivering with excitement, 'I spent six years learning about MNA. Freud said that the unconscious mind contains essentially only instinctive drives and conflictive complexes. Jung believed that there is an enormous reservoir of shared unconscious wisdom and ancestral experience transmitted throughout the generations to the whole of humanity. He called it the collective unconscious experiences. And Matthew, the boy who can remember his dreams, drew pond-skaters and called them his intelligence.'

Calder took a few drawing pins from Zara's little desk-tidy tray and said, 'I'll stick a couple of them up on the wall, okay? Who knows, I might get some of his intelligence some day.'

47

He pinned up three of the crude drawings, then stood back to admire them.

'His intelligence, eh? And who's to say he's wrong? He's up there with the best of them, Zara. A freethinker, a genius.'

And, she thought, completely off his trolley.

In truth, the afternoon had dragged a little for Lisa. She had looked forward to this break at home and, when she first realised that she was becoming enveloped in ennui, she had fought it. She decided to go to see a movie but realised she didn't have the energy for it when she couldn't be arsed getting dressed. So she tied her dressing gown tight, put on the rubber gloves and set about the bathroom with the scouring pads and potions. Her mum said that she could only relax, really relax, when she'd earned it, after she'd done a decent job. Unfortunately, it didn't work for Lisa. The loo gleamed – when the cleaner came in tomorrow she would think that she'd died and gone to Cif heaven – but there was no reward. So Lisa accepted that there were some things you could control; others you simply had to suffer with good grace. Lisa yielded to it, put on the baroque CD again and lay back to let it happen.

There had been only one incident of interest; a breaker in the tedium. She had written to her financial adviser, just a brief note accepting the advice and authorising the sale of two batches of investment trusts and the purchase into two new ones. It had happened as she licked the flap of the envelope. Somehow, probably a bit spaced out because of her period, the paper's edge caught her top lip. That was not exactly how it happened, for the paper did not move, it remained still as the dead. It was Lisa who moved, her head that moved, right to left, tongue out, licking, and her top lip ran along the flap's edge which cut deep like a razor. For an instant, there was nothing then, even before the blood, came the pain. A sharp, delicious pain that brought tears to her eyes. And at that instant she was alert, acutely aware, really alive again.

She hurried to the bathroom, to the mirror. Corelli was playing. Music stripped to the bare minimum.

Her kind of guy, old Arcangelo. No romance for him, no foreplay. Just pleasure and pain. He understood the thin divide between agony and ecstasy. And the time when the lines crossed.

In the mirror, tears on her cheeks and the blood appearing on her lip. On her labium. Good grief, she still remembered that from college. And that it was an erogenous zone, because of the large number of nerve ends and blood vessels there. Sexy stuff, blood. Then it started to flow, over both lips, into her mouth, warm and slightly salty, but not unpleasant. How could it be? She was only tasting herself. Too quickly, the agony receded to a throbbing ache. She pressed on the wound and the blood flowed stronger but she could not revive the sharp edge of the pain. She slid open the mirror door of the cupboard, revealing the extensive first aid kit.

Once a nurse always a nurse. She located the 'Newskin', unscrewed the top and smelled the sharp edge of the liquid, withdrew the spatula and applied it to the cut. Despite herself, she cried out, balled her fists and stamped her feet. Then the anaesthetic kicked in. But she had the moment. Like a moth on a light bulb. Halve the longevity but double the brightness.

Shit. She raced to kill the CD but it was too late. Pachelbel's 'Canon' started. The opening notes on the harpsichord, a hammer on the ribcage of a corpse.

He'd told her, Simon, her first real boyfriend, that it was music for the soul.

And she'd believed him.

'Just lie back,' he'd said, easing her on to his bed, 'close your eyes and open your mind.'

She trusted him.

'You're an artist and your mind is the canvas. Just let the composer paint it. He's laying on the wash, golden yellow, smooth, broad strokes.'

And his hands stroked her body.

'Can you see it?'

She could feel it.

'Now a little detail,' as he undid the buttons on her blouse

'Can you see the music?'

And she did.

'What do you see?'

The sea at dusk; Jonathon Livingstone Seagull gliding on thermals; diving for the joy of diving; nearing the cliffs, a white streak; faster and faster; a blur; but not pulling out; going with it; going for it; into the cliff; through the rock; out into another plane; gliding on higher thermals; diving again, for the joy of diving . . .

Naked now; Simon gliding above her; then diving; entering her; through her. And how she wanted him; even though it hurt; wanting him through the pain; waiting to break through the other side; trying to get through but failing. Yet it didn't really matter because they were together even after he had ejaculated and roughly rolled off her they were inextricably linked because of where they had been and what they had shared and what . . .
BULLSHIT.

49

Her lip had stopped bleeding but she picked off the 'Newskin' to start it again. She opened the cut and it hurt. Not a pleasant pain, nothing subtle, just a hack open to the winter frost.

Now Pachelbloodybel, slipping into his self-gratifying gigue like a blood-gorged penis. Dee dee dee dee deedle dee dee. Full of it now that he'd had his way. Skipping around, boastful, broadcasting his conquest.

Spray-painting it in six-foot letters. Had her. Rotten ride, but I've had her.

Thefuckpigarsewipebastard.

Simon, who had it all going for him and needed more. He was there now, in her head, and she couldn't shake him out. She was back, seven years back, studying to become a nurse, in her final year, proud, achieving something, escaping from the housing scheme, living in the flat with the two younger nurses and Simon, the junior doctor, in the flat, his daddy's flat, and the girls paying rent which paid the mortgage and Simon living there for nothing and he'd had the other two girls and daddy was going to give him the flat anyway and she was the only one he hadn't shagged and she was holding out and really only because she really fancied him and thought that maybe, well, she hoped that he'd know she was different and . . .

Whatthefuck.

It had changed her. Too easy to say she had become hard. But hardened. Too simple to say that she'd lost her innocence. But definitely wiser. Yet still stupid. Still didn't know how it worked. And Simon acting as if nothing had happened. But sometimes she caught him smirking. The typical middle-class sneer. She didn't know where to go but knew that she didn't want to be here. And she was the only one who could get herself out of it.

Working in the hospital, all hours, studying, saving. Job in a bar three nights a week when she was on dayshift, but weekends better, paid time and a half. Cutting out the few things that brought pleasure, to put the cash away every month. In a deposit account in the bank. Watching it grow, the fruits of her own labour, reaching £5,000. Looking about, finding a flat. Asking a couple of the girls at the hospital if they'd like to share it. Not fixing a price but promising she'd be fair. Then asking the bank manager how to get a mortgage. Watching him look at the digits and seeing everything in his little middle-class smirk even before he told her. And he couldn't just say no, he had to give her the little lecture too and tell her how one day he looked forward to seeing her and her fiancé . . .

Lisa washed her face, patted it dry with the towel and looked at herself in the mirror. She didn't notice that her face was flushed red or that the paper cut was hardly visible. She wasn't looking at her appearance – it was more of an internal inspection, looking through her ice-blue eyes into her soul. It was a cold place.

She went back to the living room and picked up her address book, opened it at B for bastard. She'd kept that bank manager's name and phone number. Maybe she could do a bit of business with him now. What would it be? Something he'd be willing to die for?

Onions frying and death. Unmistakable smells and you got both at the mortuary.

The Hunter's nostrils were being assaulted by the former as he walked past the hamburger van at Paddy's Market. The husband and wife who ran the fast food outlet were known locally as Sam'n'Ella. E. coli U Don't Like. The market, a cousin of the more famous Barras, dealt in third-hand clothes and two-thirds of the stolen goods in Glasgow. If they didn't have it, they could get it. Just place your order and wait until they stole it. The traders' pitches were in a lane which curved down to the Clyde. Same in every city. The flotsam and those jettisoned by society washed up at the river. Historical connections, trade routes, Hunter supposed. Easy access and, more important, ready escape route.

The sickly sweet stench of death and disinfectant was coming out of Hunter's pores.

I've gotta wash that Tosh right outta my hair.

The pathologist had kept the heavy gear till later – the circular saw and the big knives that opened bone and flesh to expose the greys and russet browns that had once made Toshie walk and talk and laugh and . . . live. Hunter hadn't needed to be there. Could have got the pix and the technical data in the morning. But he wanted another look while it was still Toshie, before it became just another cadaver on the same slab.

The pathologist began by removing the tampon, saying, by the by, that it was the first time he had ever had to remove such an item from such an orifice in a male. It was just gallows humour, joking a bit, making light of it to keep himself sane. But Hunter wasn't playing today. So the operation was carried out with a sterile, efficient dignity. The pathologist used strong tweezers to remove the tampon, gripping the string firmly and pulling steadily. It came out smoothly.

He took a ruler and measured the hole.

'The entry is . . . one centimetre, no, one point two centimetres in diameter.'

He probed the wound with a thin implement, then measured it off against the ruler.

'And the depth is three point two centimetres. The wound has been made, on preliminary examination at any rate, by a number of cuts. The flesh appears to have been gouged out – a bit like taking a wormhole out of a potato. This has been done skilfully, economically and with a minimum of fuss.'

Dr Strangelove.

The pathologist picked up the tampon with the tweezers and examined it under a powerful light.

'And it was inserted post-mortem. The cotton material is constructed to absorb blood but,' he held out the tampon, 'as you can see there is very little blood in it or on it for that matter.'

Hunter asked about the time of death.

The pathologist replied, somewhat sniffily, 'Some time between 2 a.m. and 3 a.m. Probably nearer the former.'

The fatal blow, and there had been only one stab wound while Toshie was alive, was deeper. He was reluctant to say how deep. That would be ascertained after the top of the skull had been removed.

'But, Officer, before you press me on this too, it is my initial opinion that the incision is sufficiently deep to have penetrated the brain itself.'

Hunter had already known that. Seen the likes only once before – when a spoke of a motorbike broke off on Duke Street and hit a road-sweeper on the head. Dead before he hit the tarmac.

Hunter had gone to the mortuary to, kind of, pay his last respects to Toshie. He'd be at the funeral – most of the troops would be there – but that would be different. He'd be working, watching, looking for any known faces, seeing who acted strangely, checking for crocodile tears. So he'd gone to say his goodbyes.

He'd brought Digger Burns with him. Good man, Digger. Good copper. And faithful as an old dog. Always got the shitty end of the stick and never mumped about it. It was Digger who told Toshie's wife. Said she'd taken it really hard. Two bairns, a boy, just toddling, his big sister, in primary one, and their mum little more than a lassie herself. Insisted on ID-ing the body herself. Just her and Digger. She'd cried on his shoulder. Hugged the man who told her her husband was dead and her life would never be the same again. All this and she was only twenty-five. Second time round the block for Toshie. Hunter made a mental note to check out his ex. You never know, she might be a darts player or a butterfly collector. Maybe had a daughter in the final year of her doctor's degree at Glasgow Uni.

That was the thing about this job, you had to rule out the obvious ones first. And it changed you, changed how you thought about people. Dictated what people thought about you.

Digger drove Hunter back to the copshop. He didn't go in, though, opting instead to nick round the corner to a tearoom. He ordered a pot of tea and a treacle scone and had a wee think to himself.

Mrs Toshie had told Digger about the Press Fund Ball. Digger had phoned that in right away. It caused a unique problem for Hunter. The procedure, the do-it-by-the-book way, is to trace the victim's last known movements. A saw him at B, then he went on to C with D. Straightforward stuff, retracing his footsteps, zeroing in on who ever stood beside him in the back court in the Merchant City. But sometimes you couldn't do it by the book and this was one of those times. There would be, what, a hundred and fifty folk at the ball. Call it two hundred including the hangers-on. What was he to do, call another press conference and tell them they were all suspects? Anyway, most of them would have been so drunk they wouldn't even know their own last movements.

But he belled Toshie's partner, the guy who drank brandy and port, and put it away as if it was Ribena and he needed the vitamin C. He'd come into the copshop toute de suite and wept like a wean when he heard about Toshie. He'd left the do just after 1 a.m., and Toshie had still been hard at it. He came up with the guest list for Toshie's table and said, in a quiet, conspiratorial voice, that Toshie had told him that he was off the leash for the night and fancied checking out Miss Scotland's vital statistics.

Hunter had put the DC on to it – Murdo, the Islay lad. The boy done good, found out about the Rangers player, an Italian striker who cost more than the gross national product of some small, third world nations. No one had noticed them leaving, either together or apart, but the bint hadn't gone home (she lived with her mum in some godforsaken place in Ayrshire) and the player hadn't shown up for training. Practising his ball control, no doubt. Right team of shaggers at Ibrox these days. The Gers play tomorrow, don't they? Livingston, away, wasn't it? Might be good odds. Yes, Livi might be worth a punt. Now and again being a copper had its advantages. Although, in this instance, perhaps, it could be considered as inside her trading.

Hunter's phone rang. One of the newfangled ones that told you who was calling. Bad news, Bella. No, hang on a sec. He was in the good books,

Brownie points from playing happy families at the Paborsky concert. So he picked up.

She had her posh voice on. What did she think? He was going to put it out on the Tannoy? She hooped she was nott calling at an inopportune momentt. The garage (which rhymed with barrage) had called. The kah had been repaired and was ready for collection. She did nott wantt to hold him back, so goodbye, Dahling.

He had forgotten all about the car, abandoned at the marina, nursing a broken leg beside the Carmichaels' sleek yacht. But the breakdown could yet prove to be a stroke of good luck. The Drouth, God bless his old cotton socks, would provide two bills – one for the parts, it was only fair to pay for that, and the other for Bella's ledger. Jesus H, The Hunter was reduced to that. Skimming a few quid here and a few quid there. And all thanks to a Christmas dance when the loudmouth wife of a henpecked Detective Sergeant told Bella how much a Detective Inspector earned. He'd known, when he came back from the bar and saw her face, that she wasn't a happy badger. He thought it was more of the same – his behaviour/drinking/language/ogling/breathing. He'd got the silent treatment for the rest of the evening. A good night's snoring did nothing to temper her mood and it was Frosties for breakfast. But frankly, My Dear, he didn't give a damn because he was off to the golf.

As he rose from the breakfast bar she had asked, remarkably concisely, 'How much do you earn?'

Just like that. No preamble. Didn't work up to it or anything. It never rains but it pisses down on you.

He'd tried a body swerve, a flippant 'not nearly enough', something like that, but she was not to be deflected.

'How much?'

He had waffled, making his way to the car, but she'd followed.

'How much?'

Hard to say, no two months the same, bare rate one month and some expenses returned the next, maybe a wee bit overtime. It varied. He said, without a word of a lie, that he couldn't honestly say.

He was thinking about it while he took his golf bag out of the old wardrobe in the garage. Somebody must have dropped him in the brown stuff at the dance. Okay, so he creamed a bit off the top. Jesus H, every guy did. That was why the bank statements were directed to his office. All the boys did that. Well, maybe not now, not this bunch of wimps, but the old guys, the real men. Been forced to, what twelve, fifteen years ago, when they stopped handing out the wages every week at the cashier's window.

You gave the missus a handful to buy the messages and stuffed the rest into your sky rocket. And when she was skint, pleading poverty, at Christmas or the kids' birthdays or something like that, then you always came up with the goods. Christ, Bella hadn't starved a winter yet. Come to think of it, she made Buddha look like slimmer of the year.

Yeah, those had been the days. Wages every week, dirty tenners in a brown pay poke. Then the bean counters insisted paying it into the bank, monthly. No vote, no choice, no thought of the matrimonial strife that might be caused if the Mrs Plods found out the cost of making a copper's life worth living and multiplied it by the number of wedding anniversaries. And Bella, clearly, had done that.

He stuffed a towel into the golf bag, zipped the pocket shut. Fished in his pocket for the car keys, turned round and she was in his face. One arse cheek perched precariously on the boot of the car, pink candlewick dressing gown barring entry. And a face like fizz.

He couldn't remember, not exactly, what he said, but he was willing to concede that he might have phrased it better and that unparliamentary language could have been used. It worked at the time, anyway. She fucked off.

For a fortnight.

It did not take a detective to work out where she was. At Celine's, her best pal, in Giffnock. After ten days he decided to get in touch, to make the peace. The freezer was just about empty, he was out of clean shirts and his socks walked to meet him in the morning. It was time to negotiate, to do a deal. Then came the lawyer's letter. A female lawyer's letter, of course, and the firm of Dyke and Dyke was in no doubt how much a police Inspector earned. They were equally knowledgeable about how to divide by two and asked him to please find enclosed (not just marriages they split infinitively) a direct debit form to facilitate the monthly payment of this sum into a new bank account they had opened for Bella. And, now that they had him by the balls, they decided to give them a squeeze. Further claims on estate and property would be forthcoming when a full assessment of same had been completed.

Outfoxed, he had to cut his losses. It was roses for Bella and humble pie for him. A truce was called, but it took three days to work out the treaty. Bella held all the aces and played them well. The first item on the agenda was mental cruelty. It appeared that his fiddle (it turned out to be about four grand a year, though God knows where it went) was nothing short of deceit, deception and duplicity. He'd tried a joke, just to break the tension, asking if Celine had been feeding her *Roget's Thesaurus*. But he agreed, quickly, that it was not a laughing matter.

Bella continued. He had betrayed her trust, which, she said, was like committing adultery. She had paused at this point, waiting for him to flinch but his nerve held.

Then she laid out the new rules. She was to be Chief Executive Officer (Finance). Another bank account was to be opened, a joint one, and his salary paid into it. Bella took on all the fiscal duties. Mortgage, gas, lectric, car bills, the lot. She used the breakfast bar as her boardroom table and noted the outgoings in a ledger she had bought (from joint finances, of course) in Woolworths. He had to provide an annual account of his personal commitments, golf club and bowling club fees; the Masons' meetings; fishing permits; etc.

They retreated to separate rooms for half an hour. He could justify about £800 but he called it a grand, to be on the safe side, just for those unforeseen expenses, and was relieved when she didn't quibble. She just divided it by twelve and entered the sum of £85 (let's round it up, she said) on a left-hand page in her ledger as Allowance (Alexander) A. Then, on the right-hand page, she entered £85 as Allowance (Isabella) A.

And she exposed a sleekit smile he had never seen before.

She might have sold her soul to get it, done a deal with a voodoo witch. Maybe it had been lurking in the pelmet above the dining-room curtains, just waiting to dreep down when his head was bowed. Or perhaps she had ordered it from Celine's club book. Wherever it came from, it gawped at him for the remainder of the negotiations. Chiselled out of stone, a permanent expression of a sneering thing from the island of Sneering.

They had gone on to discuss how much he would require for pocket money: baccy; sandwich at lunchtime; a few pints with the boys. Allowance (Alexander) B was agreed at £100 a month and, what a fucking surprise, so was Allowance (Isabella) B.

She had left him no room for manoeuvre. It wasn't as if he could earn a bob or two on the side, do a homer. Maybe a Saturday nabbing shoplifters for Marks and Spencer or clearing up a murder or two for Lothian and Borders coppers on a week's hols. He knew that he was only getting a dose of his own medicine. Fair dos – he could take that, could even see the fairness in it. But it seemed as if she had passed an indeterminate sentence – at Her Majesty Bella's Pleasure – and no time off for good behaviour. She was putting the knife in but at least she didn't have arsenic on the blade. She could have been spiteful, could have hurt him. She might have told the kids, both of them, making their own way, building up their own homes. Bella could have called a family meeting and given him a right showing up.

At least she'd spared him that. And she did say, too often actually, that he only had to ask if he found himself a bit short. Yeah, sure, like you're four grand a year down and you won't notice.

It had never been a grand love affair, not even in their young days. They'd been happy in the early days when he was a copper on the beat and money was scarce. But even after twenty-four years of marriage (most of the time apart, admittedly, because of the job) he was still . . . fond of her. He was aware now, that he no longer told her, didn't say the words (but then neither did she). And he hadn't been an angel – far from it – but the occasional leg-over had been only that, it had never put his marriage in danger. He had thought of them as, well, solid. That wasn't the right word but he thought of them as okay, comfy – the kind of thing that folk of their age settled for.

He had expected Bella to keep a tight grip on the finances for two or three months, then split the difference, two grand each, that would have been fair, and no hard feelings. He was waiting for that because he had never imagined her as vindictive. But, when it didn't come, as he accepted that this was how it was, his feelings for her changed. At first he merely resented her control but it festered into a bitterness. And the job had given him an understanding of bitterness and the guile to harness it. This he did without any feeling of guilt. He was not the one who had made the rules. But he was the one who went out in all weathers, at all hours of the day and night, taking on the great unwashed in their own backyard and bursting his balls to earn the poppy. So all he had to do was come up with a way of keeping a fair share of it.

The opportunity had arisen after four months AB (Anno Bella) when she announced that she was taking the car to drive the 'Coffee Girls' through to Edinburgh to see a pre-Christmas musical. Now the Montego wasn't much to look at, two-tone, mustard and rust, but it was a reliable old workhorse. Or it was until he had a shoogle at the plug leads. And, God is good, Bella and the biddies made it to the outreaches of darkest Lanarkshire, in the fast lane of the M8, foot flat to the boards, almost breaking 60 mph, when the plug lead slid off. The Montego lost power, coughing and spluttering like a sixty-a-day miner and shaking all over. Mobile phones not commonplace in these days, a mile walk to the emergency phone and, Gird Your Balls With Dicks of Holly, it was blowing a blizzard.

Don't go away, there's more.

As luck would have it, he was working (honest to God!) and could not be contacted. The motorway breakdown truck towed the Montego to Harthill Service Station (must have cost an arm and a leg but she did not discuss such financial matters) from where they had to phone the husband of one of the Coffee Girls who, as luck would have it, was not working and had to drive through to Harthill to collect the entourage. And after that, Bella never felt the same about the Montego.

A couple of days later she convened a board meeting at the breakfast bar. Only one item on the agenda – the acquisition of a reliable car. He milked it for all it was worth. Just unlucky/kind of thing that happens/major expenditure. But Bella, as chairperson had the casting vote and he had to admit that the car, at seven years old, was past its best. It might just be throwing good money after bad repairing it. A new car, a brand new car, would be great. Would the finances run to it? They would not. So he agreed to accept responsibility to identify a replacement. He was to report back after he'd had a look. And he knew exactly where to look.

It so happened that the cops were about to get new cars which meant that the old ones would, as usual, go to auction. James Smith, had a nice Vectra, three years old, and less than 40,000 miles on the clock. Greasy Pete, their head mechanic, had his eye on it for himself, so he kept it in tip-top nick. And Greasy Pete would probably have got it, too, but he reversed his decision at the last minute. The reason for his change of mind was not unrelated to a conversation with The Hunter regarding a gallon of oil which Pete was putting into protective custody in the boot of his own car. Nice guy, Pete. He agreed to fanny about with the mileometer, so the figures looked a wee bit wavy, which made the 40,000 figure a big bit iffy. That would be enough to put off the private bidders. Just to be on the safe side, just to do his pal Sandy a favour, Pete knocked the timing off too, so the car banged and farted like an old hoor. Then The Hunter pulled his masterstroke. He tipped the wink to Dougie The Drouth, who bought the car at auction for £1,050, then sold it back to his polis pal who had buried the chargesheet for his drink-driving offence.

The deal was complex but, in its simplest form, the way The Drouth explained it to Bella, it went something like this. The Vectra (its timing back in order) cost £6,100. The Montego would be taken as a trade-in, valued at £500 (but she beat him up to £600). She had to fork out another £500 to make up the deposit, leaving a balance of £5,000.

Next came the good bit.

The Drouth, out of the kindness of his heart, was offering an apr of 5% over three years. Much better than the bank. So the balance was £5,750, which panned out at £160 a month, near as dammit. But there were others interested in the car. They would have to take it or leave it. They took it.

Next came the really good bit. The Drouth was not an ungrateful man.

He had already agreed to give £1,050 for the Montego. He was a married man, too, and understood the complications which could arise in a household. The £500 which was the rightful property of The Hunter was returned as soon as Bella's back was turned.

Then came the really, really good bit. Every month £160 was transferred from Mr and Mrs Hunter's joint bank account to that of The Drouth's garage. And every month £160 of The Hunter's hard-earned was duly returned to him in cash.

So, from month five AB (Anno Bella) The Hunter's finances went something like this: £160 courtesy of The Drouth; £100 pocket money; and £85 for the gowf, bools, fishing, etc. An annual total of £4,140.

Oh, yes, and the one-off £500 from the Montego deposit scam. Just to prove that there were no hard feelings, to show that he was not vindictive, he bought Bella a present. It was a mug which said The World's Best Banker. Sometimes a man's gotta do what a man's gotta do . . .

He was still smiling at the thought of it all when Digger knocked at the door. He'd played a hunch, gone over the evidence bags from the scene of the Knox murder. One of them held a sanitary towel. It hadn't been anywhere near the Audi, so no attention had been paid to it. A conscientious young SOCO guy had picked it up, no doubt with tweezers and a stout pair of rubber gloves, from the back court of the adjoining building. Digger had remembered it. He'd had it tested and, guess what, they could tell straight off in the lab that the blood wasn't menstrual. Initial tests showed that it was O RH positive, same as Knox, and, pound to a pinch of shit, by the time they had finished burling their centrifuges it would match perfectly. Confirmation, if any were needed, that they were looking for one killer.

She was becoming more elaborate and more obvious. A sanitary towel used to mop up the blood and discarded in the vicinity. But the cops didn't pick up on it. No headlines in the papers. No credit for it. So she sticks it in their faces or in Toshie's face. Probably goes back to do it, too. Risks returning to the murder scene to put her signature on it.

Hunter could recall at least two unsolved stabbing deaths. Strangelove might have killed earlier, leaving more subtle clues. He sent Digger to check them out.

He switched on his computer, checked out BIZDEATH, and renamed it BIZDEATHS. He was working on the similarities in both murders when the Chief Constable came in, a copy of *The Herald* rolled up and carried like a sergeant major's baton under his arm.

Stroke of luck, Digger's discovery; and a bigger stroke of luck that the faithful Sergeant wasn't there. Hunter claimed the credit for himself, updated The Jug on developments on Toshie and sat back to accept the plaudits. Instead, Fastnett dropped the newspaper on to Hunter's desk. He appeared to be searching for the right words and settled for a monotone, 'Good review of the Paborsky concert.'

Hunter didn't bite.

Once The Jug had left, he opened the paper. Page three had a big picture of Paborsky and a review. Hunter read the first three pars. It was the usual crap, the writer so far up the maestro's arse he could have tickled his prostate. There was a cross-reference to 'Leader Comment', so he turned to that. It was more to his liking. The maestro was really getting it up the arse here. He was described as petulant, ungracious, ignorant and downright rude. His crime? He had failed to show for a news conference before his performance. Didn't do to upset the fourth estate. Hunter would never dream of doing that.

Digger Burns was driving and answering questions and taking orders on the five things he had to do first thing in the morning and wondering how he could apologise to his wife for being late home again. It was after 8 p.m. and he'd been out of the house for more than fourteen hours. The best he could expect was to be delayed by another forty minutes. But he'd learned to expect the worst where Hunter was concerned. At least it wasn't raining. The Fiesta's sunroof could stay open as a chimney to suck some of the worst of Hunter's pipe reek out of the car. His new car, Lorna's pride and joy. He had polished the paintwork at the weekend and she had insisted in hoovering the seats and carpets. Wouldn't wait for him to do it. Wanted to do it herself. He smiled gently at the memory. He had asked her to give him the manual from the glovebox then pointedly made a show of flicking through the pages. After an age, Lorna had asked what he was looking for. How to dismantle the seats, he'd said. With a considerable degree of difficulty, she extricated herself from the car and switched off the hoover. He patted her three-months pregnant bump, and told her he would finish it off. She accepted it with good grace but told him to do it properly because, you never know, Wee Digger might be born there.

'Tell me again,' Hunter said, 'about the tampon.'

Burns told it slowly, as if he were giving evidence in court. His mate in forensics had tipped him the wink. Nothing official, and it wasn't gospel, but he reckoned there were two types of blood on the tampon. One Mr Macintosh's and the other menstrual blood.

Hunter said, 'Dr Strangelove.'

He was fiddling with his pipe. He patted his pockets, feeling for his tobacco pouch. Shit. He'd left it in the copshop. He tamped the last remnants of tobacco down with a finger, sparked a match, stuck it deep in the bowl, dragged deeply and sucked in flame.

'Fuckin . . .'

He jumped and spluttered and spat. The pipe dropped from his lips, hit his leg and tumbled into the footwell, disgorging its cargo on the way. Burns grimaced and braked, but Hunter flapped a hand, hurrying him on.

'Not got all night,' he said.

He retrieved his pipe, examining it carefully for damage and was finally satisfied that it had survived unscathed. With the sole of a shoe, he ground the ashes into the carpet.

'Good for the pile,' he said. 'Gie's a fag, Digger.'

'I've stopped.'

'Oh, you're a big help. When?'

'Two years ago.'

Hunter huffed for a bit. Then he said, 'C'mon then, the tampon.'

Burns said, 'Two types of blood, a woman's at the string end and Mr Macintosh's at the other.'

Hunter interrupted him, 'You said that. But the middle. The middle was dry.'

Burns went on, 'Not dry, he said that it did not seem to be saturated. It wasn't swollen. He spoke about absorbency percentages, said they would dissect the tampon, slice it and examine it the way geologists look at rock cores, for the different strata . . .'

Hunter snapped, 'Just cut to the chase, eh?'

Burns showed remarkable composure. He knew that, if he left anything out, he'd be criticised for that, too.

He continued, 'If the tampon had been inserted into Mr Macintosh's wound just after he had been killed, it would have been saturated in his blood, even if the heart stopped pumping immediately. The body was face down when we got there, head on that side – remember it was partially covered by the jacket and we didn't see the tampon at first – and gravity would have taken blood to it. So it must have been done a considerable time after death.'

Hunter said, 'Are you saying that she went back?'

'Or she hung about.'

Burns mentally chastised himself. They didn't know, nothing to prove absolutely, that it was a she.

'How long are we talking about?'

'Don't know.'

'C'mon to fuck, Digger. I'm not asking you to cross your heart and hope to die.'

But Burns would not be pushed into speculating. He was too good a copper for that and he knew that Hunter would hang him out to dry for any guesstimate that proved to be five minutes out.

Hunter said, 'So she dipped it into her fanny then stuck it into Toshie.'

'Or,' Burns said, 'she inserted the tampon then put her blood on it.'

Hunter made a face. He had a bad feeling about Strangelove. Felt she was going to come back to haunt him periodically.

There had been one piece of good news. Well, goodish. There was nothing to link Strangelove with the two unsolved stabbing deaths. Both different knives; no items of women's sanitary equipment.

Digger had volunteered to drive him to East Kilbride to collect the Vectra. Well, volunteered might not be strictly accurate but, hey, who was twisting his arm up his back? They had just gone through Busby and were now passing the Carmichaels' clinics. The Mercs were still in the car park and there was another car there. A big, flashy Bentley. The one he'd seen at the marina, where the Vectra gave up the ghost.

'Ease up, Digger. Do a U. There's a Bentley in there, see if you recognise it.'

Burns slowed but didn't stop. He said, 'Saw it, big silver job. Sir Ranulf Jedburgh's.'

Hunter waved him on again. Good old Sir Ranulf. Old money, shipyard, wasn't it? In the family for yonks, but the ball's burst now. Yard went down the Swannee.

'What's he do now?'

Burns said, 'Nothing, except bend his elbow too often, from what I hear. Cost him his licence – two years – that's why he kept the chauffeur on when the yard shut.'

It was falling into place. Sir Ranulf was the figure he'd seen through a chink in the curtain of the yacht's cabin, side on, half a face and a hand signing a cheque. An anonymous donation to one of the fragrant Zara's charities? Wasn't his style. Liked to see his name in the paper did old Sir Ranulf. So what did Calder Carmichael have that he needed? There was something fishy about the Carmichaels. Hunter was on the point of asking Digger to check them out first thing in the morning but changed his mind. There was power and influence and wealth within those walls. So there must also be corruption. If it was a big fiddle, like a double-bass, it would be a right good collar. And, if it was a wee one, maybe Zara not paying the customs tax on ukuleles made by poor piccaninnies in her bongo-bongo land charities, well, if anyone was to take the responsibility for turning a blind eye, it should be a senior officer. And, if the Carmichaels were grateful and wanted to express it, well, it would be churlish not to accept. And The Hunter could remember doing many things but he could not recall the last time he had churled.

Burns was slowing down, indicating to turn right, across a busy dual carriageway, into the garage which sat halfway down a hill. It wasn't a big business, a workshop that could take two cars at a time; showroom with four shoehorned into it; and another half a dozen cars under an awning in the forecourt. The Drouth would make, what, say a grand off each one. Sell one a fortnight and you kept the wolf from the door. The repairs side did okay, too. One mechanic and a panel beater or metal-oriented beautician or whatever the hell they called themselves nowadays. Both guys working on the side. No stamp, no pension – no show, no dough. Then there was the pick-up truck with the contract to tow breakdowns off the motorway. The house was round the back and a bit to the left. It was a kit home, the kind that looked as if it you picked it up from MFI on Friday and moved in on the Monday. Walls made out of sawdust and glue, breeze blocks thrown up around them and a slavver of white plaster with wee white chuckies thrown at it. Stick on a Lego roof and that'll be £125,000, thank you very muchly.

Burns waited patiently. Vehicles were coming over the hill at a fair skelp. Easy to get halfway over then be hit amidships. He ignored Hunter's offer to carry the effin car across the road. He swithered about going to the roundabout and coming back down. But he knew that would not meet with his boss's liking either. Finally, he took a chance, put the foot down and screeched into the forecourt.

Hunter saw The Drouth waving to him from a conservatory built on to his kitchen. Christ on a bike, that was new. Must have been a sale of greenhouses at B&Q. He got out the car and Burns was giving it wellie as soon as the door was shut. He caught a flash of the badge on the boot – Ghia – that was top of the range, wasn't it? Jesus, was he the only man in the world who had put weedkiller on the money tree? Still, he didn't wish Digger any harm. He was one of the good guys. Good brain. Sharp. He'd make a good DI but that was the last thing The Hunter needed – a double whammy, lose a good Sergeant and get a rival. He hoped that Digger's father had died, left him a bob or two. Better that than looking for extra dosh that promotion would bring. But Digger, God bless 'im, had never shown any ambition. Still, didn't do to be complacent. Hunter made a mental note to give him a mental kicking at the earliest opportunity. To stop him getting ideas above his station. Prevent him from getting too cocky. Confucius, he say man with hole in pocket feel cocky all day; man with hole in two pockets no' feel two cocky all day.

The Drouth had good news and bad news. The good news was the itemised bill for Bella's ledger. It showed that the Vectra had been endowed with more spare parts than a poofter's wedding: master cylinder; brake discs; pipes; couplings (it was a poofter's wedding) – and all for just under £500, cost of course. Didn't want Bella to think they were being ripped off. The real cost, of course, was less, £400 less to be exact. And that was straight profit. No tax, no VAT. What's more, it was upfront. The Drouth slipped him an envelope stuffed with dirty tenners. Hunter palmed it adroitly and took it into the kitchen. Aye, like he was going to count it in a fuckin' hothouse. Smile for the cameras. That'll be shining bright. The envelope contained £560.

The Drouth said, 'The extra's next month's car payment in advance.'

Then came the bad news. It was the last payment. Three years already? Hunter took it bad. It was like a bereavement. A tragic loss. He had known it would happen, one day, but so sudden . . . and without any warning? His first reaction was to berate The Drouth who should, at least, have warned him a few months ago. Given him the chance to make alternative arrangements. A man shouldn't just lose his pocket money, his freedom, his dignity. Not just like that. But he took it on the chin. Didn't blame The Drouth. Even asked about the hothouse. Pretended to look interested.

'Got a great deal,' The Drouth said, 'from a wee fella, just down the road, just started up and desperate to do business.'

He took Hunter on a guided tour, all the way round the circumference of the inside. Pointed out the wee vents that ensured an airflow but prevented condensation. Stroked the cane furniture that gave you skelfs in your arse (though he failed to identify this hazard.) Then skilfully manoeuvred him out, bumping his gums about rhino glass and great security and the genuine plastic window frames. Hunter nodding and smiling, taking it like a man, ready to forgive and forget, despite all, willing to shake The Drouth's hand, to say so long.

Then The Hunter was slighted.

The Drouth said, 'That's us quits.'

Deadpan. Just like that. He'd practised it, that was clear. Delivered his line to the pig like a ham actor. He'd looked forward to it, maybe tried on different expressions in the bathroom mirror. Just to get the feel of them, to see which one he he liked best.

That's us quits. And don't call me, I'll call you.

Like you did when you were caught drunk-driving. We weren't equals

64

then, were we? Not when you were shiting yourself and I had to clear up your mess. Tell the boys that you were a mate, a brother. Know what I mean, nudge, nudge. No need to roll the trouser legs up, let's just shake hands on it. And it's not like the old days when it took a plod with two fingers on a typewriter two hours to fill in the paperwork. Then you could just take forms, screw them into a ball and kick it into touch. A careful man even destroyed the carbon paper, just to be sure. But these days you've got to be a lot more careful. So I ask the boys if they really need to take another breath-test. Mention that some of the wee blow-intae thingmies had been playing up and maybe theirs wasn't one hundred per cent, eh? And say that since it hadn't been written up yet, hadn't entered the system, well as a favour to me . . .

So I stick my neck out and you get off. That's okay. What are mates for? But, if it had gone pear-shaped, who would have got it up the arse? Would it have been (A) me. Or (B) me. Could have lost the job, pension, the whole bloody lot. With Bella waiting at home full of love and understanding. Aye, that'll be shining bright. And you, sunshine, what was your part of the deal, apart from getting half-pished and being caught playing at dodgems in Cathcart Road. You call a brother, drag him into it, to save your own neck. But fair dos, you do your bit later, act as a clearing bank to allow him to withdraw cash once a month. His own cash. And you bail out smucking fartly at the first opperchancity. Or you think you do . . .

The metal concertina doors at the back of the workshop were open. Just a crack. Just enough for a trained observer to catch a glimpse of the big red Rover with a rear end like a bulldog's face and a roof like corrugated iron. Hunter gave the metal door a shove. It slid open easily on well-greased bearings which made a noise like a sharp intake of breath. Or was that The Drouth?

Hunter's eyes zeroed in on the oxyacetylene torch.

'Tut-tut. Nice car too. And only, what? 8,000 miles on the clock. Wee cut and shut here, eh?'

The man who had been his friend tried to look shocked, insulted even. But the expression needed work in front of the bathroom mirror.

He said, 'Oh no, it's not what you're thinking. It's a write-off. The chassis's twisted. Like your English Chief Constable, eh?'

He laughed, left plenty of time for Hunter to join in, but he declined.

'Just stripping it for spare parts.'

Hunter said nothing. Just kicked at the big gas canister and the oxyacetylene torch. But he's not one to bear a grudge. He's back at the boot of the car. Crumpled and squashed.

'Reminds me of the wife,' he said. 'She's a bit rumpled round the arse, too. Mibbe you could do a wee job on her.'

The Drouth laughed loudly.

'Fire up the blowtorch and turn her into a coupé. Still have enough left over for a wee trailer.'

It was the funniest thing The Drouth had ever heard.

Hunter spoke quietly.

'Naw, only joking. And Bella would know it. We're best mates, really, trust each other, you know?'

He lowered his voice to a sinister whisper.

'Naw, the wife's okay, she's got nothing to fear from me. Not like my enemies, if you take my meaning.'

He paused, put on his hard face so the man could not fail to understand. Then he went on, 'Enemies are the ones that really have to watch out for The Hunter. And I don't have crystal balls, so they can't see me coming.'

He turned on his heel. 'See you,' he said. 'Soon.'

And with that he got into the Vectra and drove off, heading for Fintry to see Mary Knox. The Jug had been on his back. It appeared that the widow had friends, powerful friends who had leant on the Chief Constable, put on a wee bit pressure and caused a big flap. Hunter had told him yeah, she'd been his main suspect. And sure, he'd rattled her cage. She had found the body, or said she had found it, after driving all the way from Fintry. There were holes in her story through which one could drive a coach and horses. The Jug had not been impressed, not even with the grammar.

Said she woke up in the wee sma' hours to discover that her man was not giving it zzzs beside her. So what does she do? She worries, well she would, wouldn't she? Then she puts the kettle on and makes cup of tea, eventually phones his office and gets really worried when there's no answer. But then what does she do? She faffs about for half an hour – or was it forty minutes? – she wasn't sure. Then she phones the local bobbies to see if he's been in a car crash. Like the boys wouldn't have been ringing on her fancy doorbell if they'd known. Like they were in the habit of holding back bad news, not wanting to spoil her whole day. Waiting till she'd had her Special K and a bowel movement. Anyway, she's told that he has not wrapped the Audi round a lamp post and she gets really, really worried. Distraught, that was her word. So the widow-to-be drives to his office. Only problem is that it takes her fifty minutes to get distraught and turn the ignition key in her shiny new Volkswagen GTi. Hunter was warming to the task but The Jug headed him off at the pass. Wanted to know if she was the main suspect for Toshie's murder too and, if so, would her daughter be charged as an accomplice because she had been with her mother all night. Hunter had heard the word apology mentioned then and he didn't quibble with it. Didn't commit himself either.

The Jug had never been there, hadn't got his hands dirty with blood and snotters at a domestic murder. Weans screaming or worse, standing silent in the corner, taking it all in, storing it in a dark corner of their memory, never knowing when the replay button would be pressed. And a wee wummin breaking her heart, still holding the smoking knife. She's been duffed up for umpteen years and hit back just this once. So what do you say? You're a naughty girl, you've killed your husband. Don't do it again.

And all the seminars in The Jug's hermetically sealed world, all the role-play scenarios and all the instruction manuals weren't worth a monkey's fuck when you walked into one of those wretched homes. Because none of them could even touch on how you feel. First time's hellish and so was the last one. Next one will be too. You tell the young cops that they're the good guys, they won't be haunted, but you don't believe it yourself. And you try to keep out the suffering and the misery, to develop a protective shell. Detached, dispassionate and disinterested. That's what the manuals say. Written on a day when there was a fire sale of words beginning with D. By an author called Diddy who'd never Done it. But they get you – the ghosts – every one, there's always something that creeps in through your pores when you're not looking and you only know that it's there when the replay button is pressed.

You swear you'll never take it home with you and you know you always do. And in the beginning Bella's good about it, wants to know about it, says she wants to share, to know what you're going through. And the sad thing is that she really thinks that she does. But you know that she doesn't. Really, she doesn't. So you tell her a little, the least of it, because you don't want it to get between you. But you know that it will. And you know that it must. And after a while she doesn't ask again but by that time it's too late because you're a different guy from the one she married. And she doesn't see that most of you is still the same.

Part of you has grown hard and cold. That's the part that Bella sees, and she blames herself for letting it happen and feels inadequate because she was unable to stop it, and it hurts her. So much that she has to let it go. And she's a different woman from the one you married.

And every now and again you get a good murder, when you can nail some right bad bastards. No shades of grey, no doubts or recriminations. You put on the white hat and ride out into the range to bring the baddies back to town and, hey, what's it matter if they're strapped across the saddles of their horses? And your sweetheart is standing on the boardwalk, with a little sad smile on her face, and she's so proud of you and so relieved that you're safe

The bad ones are the easy ones. Take the drug wars. So they're killing each other, say the fellas in the pub, so who gives a shit? They're all bad bastards. Good riddance. Take them out on to Glasgow Green, give them sub-machine guns and let them go for it. Or the paedophiles, dirty old fuckers, cut their balls off and weld them to their ears. They'd do it themselves, the wise guys, honest to Christ they would, just let them finish their pints first.

Digger was good with the bad ones. Tenacious, didn't bend the rules, mind you, but knew when to look the other way. With the others, the domestics, well, Digger wasn't so hot. But that was because he wasn't cold. Maybe that was why he'd stuck at Sergeant. Didn't want to pay the price. Was he that smart? Smarter than The Hunter?

Decision time on the Widow Knox. It was just after 9 p.m., so the timing was right. Take about an hour to drive to Fintry, catch her in her goonie and she'd have to let him in. Hunter could see her now, hands up at her neck, fingers twiddling at the buttons, trying to conceal her wrinkly bosom, a blush and a flush on her cheeks, defensive even on her home turf. Different species entirely to the one who'd gone behind his back and over his head. Vulnerable herself now and eager to make the peace. They could call it quits.

He got a glow of satisfaction at the thought and realised that would take the pleasure off the reality. Besides, he couldn't be arsed driving all the way to Fintry. He decided to leave the widow with the powerful friends till tomorrow-days. Let her stew.

It was a calm, still night, with autumn snuggling up to summer. A few of the leaves were on the turn, a tinge of yellow and a touch of russet warning of the coming winds and frosts that would strip the trees bare. A light rain began to fall, twinkling like little diamonds in the headlights. Hunter went for his pipe and cursed when he remembered that it was empty. He felt about in the plastic pocket of the door and located another, a Falcon which had a metal stem that burned too hot for his taste. He stuck his finger in the bowl. The baccy was all but gone. He stuck the pipe in his mouth and, after a little struggle, got the matches out of his pocket. Next part was the tricky bit. Like patting your head and rubbing your stomach at the same time. Both hands at the bottom of the wheel. Matches in the palm of the left hand. Right index finger gently (gently, mind you, or the whole bloody lot'll fall out) tapping the box open, then extricating a single match, sparking it off the sandpaper and up and into the bowl. A perfect example of what separates homo sapiens from the rest of the animal kingdom. Fire and the power of reason. That's why he pays good money to burn cancinogenic materials, then drags the smoke into his body.

The tobacco was stale and bitter. But it was better than walking to Busby with a nail up your boot.

The pipe was a present from Bella, two Christmases ago. A bit like him buying her tinfoil-lined knickers. Looked okay and the theory was fine.

He'd smoked the pipe a few times in his den, strolled down to the living room with it dangling in his gob, loaded but not cocked because she didn't want the smell of his tobacco all over the house. Then he'd tucked it away in his locker at the bowling club. Of course, Hawkeye had noticed the absence. Mumped on about it. Said he didn't like it, did he? And he told her that, no, he liked it, he liked it a lot. Just keeping it good, that's all. But she said that she knew him and when he liked something he used it a lot like that hideous old brown jumper that she'd tried to throw out and he'd taken it back out of the bin and he was still wearing it and . . . So he'd brought the pipe back from the bools and he smoked it in the garden, making sure to walk past the kitchen window when she was doing the dishes or peeling the totties. He kept it in the car now and would kindle it if she was out of her pit in time to wave goodbye in the morning. He'd played the part of the man who loves the Falcon so well that she bought him another last Christmas.

He was approaching Busby now, at the part of the road where the street lights started, and the little liquid diamonds on the windscreen reflected a million rainbows. There had been a long dry spell (well, long for this part of the world anyway) and a film of filth had built up on the glass. He switched on the wipers, which protested noisily and smeared grime over the wind-screen, further impairing his vision. He flicked on the washers but they yielded only a weak piddle, like a two-day-old baby with his nappy off. He braked, not too hard because he knew that the build-up of rubber and fuel on the road might turn it into a skating rink, and stopped across from the Carmichaels' clinics. The Mercs were still there but the Bentley had gone, not long gone though, for he could see the dryish patch where it had been parked. He wondered if Sir Ranulf's chauffeur got time and a half for night jobs. Or did the bold boy drive himself? Bit daft in that car, but you never know. Once a mug always a mug.

Hunter got out of his car and rubbed the windscreen with an old cloth. Seemed to be really concentrating on it too, but really keeking across the road out the corner of his eye. Saw an image, just for an instant, like the shadow of a black cat. Was it a face at a window? He'd come across that kind of thing often enough. Folk who wanted to see but didn't want to be seen. Especially by the cops. Was it Zara? Couldn't be sure but he felt it was. Peeking through a wee chink in the netting. Ducked when she thought he was looking.

He got back into the Vectra and sat for a bit. Just to let her sweat. That would be a new experience for the fragrant Zara. A gentle glow was more her style. Then, just to test her, to see if her deodorant was up to it, he flicked on the offside indicator and drove into the car park. Opened the car door, so the internal light came on, so she could see it was him. But didn't make any move to get out.

It was an impressive little empire, with the large, two-storey red sandstone building at its heart. Calder's office and consulting rooms had been built on to the left; Zara's fertility clinic to the right. The his'n'hers single-storey extensions were in harmony and had been treated with a facade of red sandstone. There were buildings round the back too. The stables or the servants' quarters, something like that.

Hunter remained in the car for about a minute, then he got out, banged the door shut and marched up the six stairs to the big double doors of the main building. Big on brass, the Carmichaels. Brass coach lamps either side of the doors; brass nameplates, his with more letters after his name than your average sorting office and hers with just three – MBE. Hunter gave the brass bell pull a yank and heard it jangle some distance away. After what he thought was too long a pause, light footsteps approached. She didn't look through the spyglass, just opened the door wide and she gave him a big smile. One that looked as if she'd tried it on in the bathroom mirror.

'Look at you – you're like a stick with boobs – I hate you!'

But, of course, she didn't. Louise loved her big sister dearly. Lisa, the model, the local hero, the one who had escaped. And no bragging about it either; didn't flash the cash (though she was good to Mum.) Probably knew, too, that Mum passed most of it on. Some things were better not discussed.

Lanky Lisa, that's what they'd called her at school. And just look at the swan now, tall and willowy, tummy flat as a pancake and boobs that still passed the pencil test. They'd done it as kids, after Louise read it in a magazine – that you'd started to grow old when you put a pencil under your breast and it didn't fall to the ground. She'd teased her big sister, nearly four years older, said she'd go saggy first, and they did it every Sunday, bath night – Louise first wash one week, Lisa the next. And now Lisa would pass the test with an eyeliner pencil and Louise could hold on to

70

an emulsion paintbrush. That's what two kids did for your figure. And a third on the way. Wouldn't change it for the world, though. But swop Big Sis for just a week, well that was something else . . . Maybe that was why Lisa didn't talk about it – the five-star hotels and chauffeur-driven cars and posh meals.

But she'd been on good form. Mum had got the photos out. Hair in bunches, missing teeth and skint knees. They'd laughed and teased each other just like old times. No pictures of Dad and, of course, no mention of him either. Just like old times. He'd done a runner early, though Lisa could remember him. But she refused to talk about him. Always had, even when Louise had pleaded, as a little girl, said she'd wash the dishes all week.

Louise had met him last month. It was just a day like any other day. She'd put the wee fella into school and was pushing Samantha in her buggy. Going to get pies for the tea, really fancying a strawberry tart but trying to fight it. He must have been following her, stalking her in a way. And he'd come up and said 'Hi, Louise, I'm your dad.' Just like that. Wasn't too clean, either. Not smelly, not like a dosser, but not . . . well not like you wanted your dad to be. And he asked how she was getting on and what about Mum and Lisa, and gave Samantha 50p for her piggy bank. Didn't say where he'd come from or whether he'd be back. And Louise just said, 'Bye then.' and went on to the baker's. Got a strawberry tart, too, and felt guilty about it later, cos that was what was important in her life now. Not wishing him any harm but, really, he was a just a stranger and she didn't have any space for him. That surprised her, pleased her a little. Well, not pleased but it filled in the gaps. She only had to see him alive to lay the ghost.

She'd told Mum and she'd listened to everything but didn't ask any questions. But Louise realised that she wanted to know more – everything – so she kept talking until she was repeating herself. And all Mum had said was 'Don't tell Lisa.' That had intrigued her more than meeting him, more than anything he had said.

The night had passed quickly. Mum had made toasted cheese, toasting both sides of the bread for Louise and only one for Lisa. Sisters, so alike and so different. And later, when Lisa was going home, Louise had gone downstairs to see her into the taxi. And she realised then that, for all her sister's money and excitement, she really didn't want to swop places. Not even for a week. It didn't matter that her husband would be back from the pub soon and he might be okay or might be in a foul mood. But he was better than nothing. And that's what her sister had – nothing. Louise could see it in her eyes. Saw an emptiness in her big sister's life, like she'd lost something along the way and would never be able to replace it.

'Oh, Sandy, what a nice surprise,' Zara said. 'Do come in.'

It was Hunter's first glimpse inside the big house and already he knew Bella would give her eyeteeth for it. B&Q hadn't made any dosh out of the Carmichaels. The walls and ceiling were painted duck-egg blue, with the ornate, foot-deep cornice picked out in white. The doors, skirting boards and wood surrounds had been restored to their original state, the floorboards were sanded, a warm red pine caressed by satin varnish. Not too shiny. That would be vulgar. The dimmer switch controlling the six brass wall lights was turned down low, providing a reassuring glow like a baby's bedroom. The main source of light came from a standard lamp, a penalty kick away at the other end of the hall. It stood behind a big Turkish rug, duck-egg blue with reddish-brown ducks. Hunter made a mental note to lift his feet high, in case he tripped over it and broke an ankle.

Zara was wearing a peach-coloured, turtleneck sweater. Lambswool or cashmere, something like that, soft, nice to stroke. A pair of reading specs dangled on a cord above her small breasts. Her full-length black skirt was thin and shiny. Satin? Hunter wondered. He wasn't that good on materials. But it had daubs of blues and greys and the same peach of the sweater. And it looked nice to stroke.

Zara turned away, leaving him to close the door. By the time he started after her, she was four or five paces ahead, ensuring that he got the full-length view of her slender chassis. She flicked her head, the way the models do in the shampoo ads on the telly, and her expensive coiffeur fanned out briefly, like a halo that had slipped, then fell back into shape. Every hair knew its place.

Hunter had not seen the subtle temptress during any previous meeting. And he would have noticed. He was, after all, a trained observer. She was giving it the chassé, just a tiny turn on the balls of her feet, her boots leaving little squeaks on the floorboards. Interesting. What had he done to deserve this? Or was it what he might do . . . He decided to play along, to let her think that it was working, maybe lure her into over confidence. And, anyway, it was better than driving through Busby with your windscreen covered in shite.

Her wee tight erse led the way, indicating a left turn, no right, no left again. She was wearing boots. Strange, he thought. They passed four doors and she half-turned her head, whispered something, caught him leering.

She turned right at the standard lamp, then sharp left, past a bathroom with a lifting device to ease people in and out of the bath, on a bit then left

72

again into an elegant dining room at the rear of the house. Same simple, classy decoration, but the walls were an orangey red. Bella wouldn't get away with it in her wee room. Be like eating inside a postbox

Zara stopped at a well-stocked cocktail cabinet, lifted a bottle of The Macallan, and raised her eyebrows, seeking approval. Hunter said something smart, and one for yourself, too, something like that, and she smiled a nice smile, nodded to the squat crystal glasses and walked through the room into a conservatory. Jesus H, don't see one for a lifetime then two come along at the same time. You could have put The Drouth's into a corner of this one and still had space to park a couple of rumpled Rovers.

Hunter picked up two glasses and followed Zara.

'Don't sit there,' she said, nodding to a chair with a telltale damp patch on the floral cushion.

Hunter said, 'Somebody have a wee accident?'

'He's about to,' Zara said. 'Bloody builder.'

She pointed to the roof, then to a couple of basins on the floor. They had been lined with sponges to deaden the plink, plink of dripping water.

Zara sat on a two-seater sofa – a comfy bugger, none of your cane crap here – and patted the other seat. He joined her. A wee squeeze, but cosy. She uncorked the whisky and poured two large ones as he held the glasses. She took one, chinked it off his and said cheers. She took a sip, let it tickle her teeth, then swallowed. She repeated the process but increased the quantity. Hunter just went for it big time. Straight down the hatch. The raw spirit hit the stomach with a clatter, then seemed to vaporise and mushroom out, warming the cockles of his heart.

Zara leant her head back, closed her eyes, stretched her legs. She was comfortable. They were a couple, relaxed, having one together at the end of a long day. No small talk, just a deep sigh of satisfaction from her cockles.

Finally she said, 'Heaven.'

Hunter drained his glass and reached for the bottle at her feet. His hand brushed her leg and she returned the pressure. He felt the soft leather of her boot mould into the back of his hand. She put the little smile on again and sighed like a Labrador puppy. He didn't ask, just topped up her glass.

'Ta much,' she said. Getting informal now.

When she sat up her thigh rubbed against his and he thought he heard a crackle of electricity. Then again, it might have been a drip falling from another part of the big greenhouse. She told him to smoke his pipe – her dad had smoked a pipe and she just loved the smell. He explained about the lack of tobacco and she rose quickly, disappeared into the big post box and returned with a cigar. The real McCoy, too – Romeo y Julieta in a metal tube. She took the cigar out and produced a cutter.

'You don't have to watch,' she said, 'especially if you're Jewish.'

She clipped off the end and put the cigar in her mouth. Gave it a good sook, too. Then she sparked a match.

'It's got to be a match, right?' she said.

He said, 'Of course,' though it sounded like bullshit to him.

She kindled up the cigar, going at it with enthusiasm, wee cheeks nearly meeting in the middle. Then she had one last long sook and handed it to him.

He made a mental note never to lumber a rich dame. Couldn't afford the foreplay.

He smoked for a while and drank some more of her whisky. Finally wore her down.

'So,' she said. 'Were you just passing?'

'Kind of.'

She said that was intriguing. And his job must be so interesting. He wasn't working on the murder, was he. Did he know that they knew Phil Macintosh?

But they didn't or she'd have known that it was Philip or Toshie. He hated Phil.

He asked, 'Was that Sir Ranulf's car?'

'Beg pardon?' she said.

But she'd heard perfectly well. It was just a wee device to win a bit of time.

He said, 'Sir Ranulf. His car, in the car park.'

'Oh, Randy,' she said. 'Yes, he was here earlier. You just missed him. You know each other?'

Hunter said no, he didn't really know him and asked about his health. He didn't keep well, did he?

Zara swirled the whisky in her glass. She said, 'There's an old Japanese proverb which says, first the man takes a drink, then the drink takes a drink, then the drink takes the man. But Calder's helping him. Although they're probably at the pub just now. All that is, of course, confidential. Now, I've told you a secret, you must tell me one.'

These kind of games, eh? He said, 'I'll tell you two if you want.'

She said, 'I want,' and leant closer to him.

He said, 'Okay, the first one is I tell lies.'

There was the sound of a vehicle starting up. A diesel. The Mercs were petrol, surely.

Zara rose quickly, hands to her face. Shock. She was good but not good enough. Hunter knew that she wanted him out of there.

'Matthew,' she said. 'I nearly forgot. I must check on him. See that he's all right.'

Hunter didn't flinch.

She said, 'You remember Matthew, from the other day?'

He didn't give her anything back. Definitely a diesel and pretty rough, too.

'The boy who tried to commit suicide.'

It was close. At the extension that housed her clinic.

'Calder's favourite,' she said. 'I promised I would keep an eye on him . . . only I'm a bit afraid. You never know what you'll find. Could you possibly . . .'

How could he refuse?

She'd sent the seductress backstage, though who knows? She might be called back for the bedroom scene. But for now, Zara was the frightened girl. Not a little girl, she gave Hunter too much respect for that, but she led the way along the hallways and kept close to him. All the time getting farther from the diesel engine and whatever secret it held.

She stopped off at an office to get keys from a safe behind a painting. Then they went on to the door marked 'In-patients'. She unlocked it and locked it again behind them. They were in yet another corridor, like a small hospital ward, with the inevitable aroma of antiseptic. Six rooms leading off, two beds to a room. Five rooms full, each with the reassuring glow of small nightlights set high on the walls.

Matthew Whittle was the sole occupant of the last room. It was lit by three table lamps, which Zara did not switch off. The room's dimensions were similar to the others but it looked like a bedsit, more like a permanent home. He had his own things around him. TV, music centre, a hairdryer, still plugged into an electric socket. No pictures – no evidence of an existence outside Chateau Carmichael, but child-like drawings pinned on the walls. A page of his latest efforts – they looked like tadpoles with legs – lay on the bedside cabinet beside an ashtray with two cigarette ends in it, a packet of Golden Virginia hand-rolling tobacco and a book of matches. Even the smell in the room was different. A sickly-sweet smell, not unlike the mortuary.

Matthew was sleeping like a baby. There was something familiar about him. Something about the eyes. Hunter bent down to get a better look and got a fright as the boy's eyes twitched and flickered as if demons were fighting to get out.

75

'REM,' Zara whispered. 'Rapid Eye Movement. Matthew's dreaming. That's him living it out. And the amazing thing is he'll remember it all in the morning.'

Then she gave a yawn. Panto time already. And it's 'Sleeping Beauty', not 'Pussy in Boots'.

The rain was coming down like stair rods, so Hunter drove carefully, keeping within the speed limit. It would be just his Donald Duck to get stopped by a couple of traffic coppers eager to find out how much of the fragrant Zara's whisky he had consumed. Too much to be driving and not enough to dissuade him from taking the risk. It was a few minutes before 10 p.m. Bella would be draping her goonie over the radiator and switching on the electric blanket. She'd bought a new one, with dual controls, that enabled her to warm only her half of the bed because, she'd said, 'There was no point in wasting electricity to heat an empty bed. Or one that was half empty.' He'd said, 'Yeah, great, right enough.' Made a joke of it. Said he could put his half on at regulo seven to get his plates of meat well done. They didn't fight any more, didn't even argue, just performed the occasional act to register discontent and disapproval.

Hunter knew that, if he went straight home, Bella would feel obliged to make him something to eat. He'd spotted a packet of those chicken Kiev things lurking in the back of the fridge. Bella had perfected the art of bunging them in the microwave and zapping them just long enough so the garlic butter filling exploded like Chernobyl when you finally penetrated the breadcrumb fortifications. She'd probably do them for him and he'd say, 'No, no spuds – they'll do just great.' She'd make him a cup of tea, then she'd sit across from him at the kitchen table and ask how his day had gone though she knew he wouldn't really tell her, then she'd say what she had done though she knew he really wasn't listening. Then she'd say she'd better go up to bed before it caught fire and he'd say yeah, okay, be up in a minute and he'd wait a couple of minutes after the loo had been flushed before he went for the whisky bottle.

The rain fell harder as the Vectra dropped down into Busby. Hunter went down to third gear for the S-bend under the railway bridge then, subconsciously, a couple of hundred yards on, took a left and pulled into the hotel car park. He turned the engine off and watched the rain bounce off the bonnet of the car. It was drumming rain, that was what Melanie would call it. His mind drifted back twenty years to the caravan holiday in Anstruther. Maw, paw and the two bairns. Happy days. Alex was five, first year at primary school, and Mel not yet three. They'd just moved into the house in Clarkston and taken on the mortgage that seemed to stretch till doomsday. Didn't think they could afford a holiday until one of the old coppers offered his caravan for the price of the ground rental and a fresh tank of Calor gas. Some of the vans had electricity – tellies too – but theirs was more basic. No lectric, no loo and a flickering light from gas mantles that turned to dust if you sneezed too close. And it had poured with rain every day. They hadn't slept a wink the first night. He'd said it was like being trapped inside a snare drum and Mel had picked up on it. A downpour in their family had been drumming rain ever since. On the third day of the floods, with no respite predicted, he'd driven home alone and collected wellies, anoraks, more towels and the games' compendium Alex had got at Christmas.

The days were spent splashing about the streets, kicking up wet sand, chases into the sea and who cared if the waves cascaded over the wellies because wet was wet and it was always a race back to the caravan and then Alex and Mel were stripped bare and rubbed and tickled dry. Then Mum would kindle up the fire using the coke from the brown paper bags in the bottom of the wardrobe while the kids got into early jammies. Hunter would drive to the chip shop and pick up dinner – special fish supper, black pudding supper, two sausages and one of those wee jars of nippy onions. The van would be warm as toast when he got back and the inside of the windows would be misted with condensation. There would be buttered rolls on the table and four big dauds of kitchen roll for their fingers and he would plonk the newspaper package down and unwrap its steamy contents, Mel shouting, 'Do it, Daddy, do it!' and he'd have to pretend that his fingers were being burned and suck them and yelp like a skewered pig and she would scream with delight and even Alex had been known to laugh. Then they'd all dig in, fighting for the biggest chip, taking a bite of sausage and going huhuhuhu to get some cool air in. Fingers dooking into the onion jar – only one allowed at a time – and Mel complaining because her fingers were too wee to reach once the jar was half-full – it was never half-empty in those days. Alex would take only one onion which he stripped layer by layer, nibbling the thin strand between his front teeth. He would remove the bulb from his mouth, hold it between thumb and forefinger and examine it as if it were one of those little Russian dolls.

The Vetra's windows had steamed up so Hunter started the engine and put the heater fan on full bung. Another five minutes and it would be safe to go. Bella would be in her pit. He could walk upstairs with heavy feet, stick his head round the bedroom door, say still awake, eh? How're you doing? Good, good. Me? Fine, yeah, great. Getting there, y'know. Slowly but surely. Then she'd yawn or he'd rub his stomach, some device like that, and he'd say he'd rustle up a sandwich or something and he'd see her in the morning.

How had it come to this? He could understand it, maybe even accept it, if there had been a barney, if she'd caught him at something, like she'd done with the salary. He could say sorry and mean it. Up to Bella, then, to give him another chance. But there had been nothing, really. Just a succession of wee drips eroding the foundations of their marriage. It was his fault. He knew that. He didn't work on the relationship. That was what the counsellors would say. Tell him that he didn't spend enough time with Bella. That was right enough. Only problem was that she'd already filled in the gaps. Didn't blame her for that. It was fair dos. She had her Coffee Girls and the church and Tuesdays with Alex and his wife and Thursdays with Mel and her man at their big hoose in The Mearns. Sure, he could try to keep Tuesday and Thursday nights free. Play at happy families again. Wheedle his way back in. But . . . there was always a but.

He would tell himself, whisky glass in hand while Bella snored upstairs, that it bored the tits off him listening to the price of curtains and discussing the pros and cons of whether it should be a pelmet or a valance above the curtains on Alex's patio doors, or hearing again how well Mel's man was doing in the IT business and which European city he was going to next week and how, all being well, he was going to set up on his own and all this hard work would pay off in diamonds. And it was true enough, to an extent, but it wasn't what held him back. The real reason was that he didn't like himself. He couldn't remember when that had happened either. Couldn't say it was the thirty-first of February, 1996, or the forty-third of June, 1998. And it hadn't hit him in a blinding flash – hey, Hunter, you're a right shite – but it had drip-dripped itself into his consciousness and he had accepted it as a fait accompli.

'Fuck this for a game of soldiers,' Hunter said and drove off.

The rain was easing as he arrived home. The light in the front porch was still on but the rest of the house was in darkness. The street was deadly still, the Volvos and BMWs and Volkswagens lined up neatly on the grid, ready for the off in the morning. A million quid's worth of metal prestige on the catwalk of their owners' fragile vanity. Hunter knew the faces, but he didn't really talk to any of them. Difficult, mind you, when you hardly ever saw them. They were in their pits by the time his shift was over and in their offices before he was even thinking of surfacing. Bella had said, years ago, that he didn't even try to get to know them. He had to make an effort. 'To integrate,' she said. He could wash the car on a Sunday morning, a lot of the men did that, and they'd kind of mingle, meet up, sit in each others' cars and 'have a chat – find something in common. I've seen you,' she'd said, 'You just walk past them, say "Aye." and do that strange wee nod with your head.'

He'd tried to head her off, said it was a criminal offence to sit in men's cars and twiddle their knobs, but she wouldn't be diverted. Said it was him 'all over the back, coming the copper, trying to joke his way out of it.'

So it had come back to the job again. She didn't do it often, in fairness, cast it up, complain about the hours he spent working and the time in the pub long after he'd finished. He'd promised to wash the Maestro that weekend, adding, with a mischievous glint in his eye, that he wouldn't be held responsible if any bits fell off when the muck was removed. Bella had never liked that car. It had never even been given a name. He'd noticed that. The first time they'd had a car without a name. The kids had made a big deal of it, giving their 'new' second-hand car a nickname, a kind of ritual to mark acceptance into the family. Mel always got her way. Younger than Alex, but tenacious and much louder. 'Her father's daughter,' Bella said. Tina the Cortina had been Mel's first, then Snowy the white Hillman. Gay the Cavalier had been a bit suss, but Winnie the Rover had been Hunter's favourite. Mel had been eight, when he'd bought the Rover. They'd seen it in Arnold Clark's showroom and it appealed to Bella's bourgeoning snobbery. He'd tried to put her off. Said it had seen better days. It would be greedy on the juice and hefty on the insurance, but she wouldn't be put off. Finally, he resorted to women's tactics and said he didn't like the colour. Said it was a shitty brown. Bella had rebuked him, through thin lips, but it was too late. Mel had heard. That night, Mel had told him the joke. About the wee boy being driven home from nursery by his mother and he says, 'Look, Mum, a moo-moo.'

And his mum says, 'You're a big boy now – it's not a moo-moo, it's a cow.'

And they drive on a bit and the boy says, 'Oh Mum, look, a meh-meh.'

And she says, 'It's not a meh-meh, it's a sheep. I've told you, you're a big boy now.'

They went on for a bit and the mother asked what the boy did at nursery. 'Reading,' he said.

'That's interesting,' his mum said. 'What were you reading?'

And the wee boy said, 'Winnie the Shit.'

Hunter had laughed till he cried. Told Mel not to tell Mum the joke. And he'd bought the car the next day. Bella had been delighted. But it wasn't for her. It was for Mel. For her joke. For their secret, their little shared naughtiness.

Alex had a name for the car and Bella liked it.

'The Wraith,' Alex said proudly. 'It's our Wraith Rover.'

Hunter said it was good, very good, but it was such a posh car that it needed a middle name and, right on cue, Mel chipped in with Winnie.

He said, 'That's it then. Wraith Winnie Rover. No, that doesn't sound right. Loses Alex's clever play on words. Doesn't do you justice, eh, Alex?'

So it was Winnie Wraith Rover, for a week or so, and just Winnie for ever after.

Hunter couldn't be bothered putting the Vectra in the garage, so he crawled up the street looking for a space. There was a possibility, about twenty yards from the house, but it looked a tight squeeze so he drove on slowly. It was a solid wall of metal right to the end of the avenue so he turned round and went for the wee gap. Reversed in slowly, God bless power steering, and was about to reverse the lock when he nudged the Volvo at the back. Mercifully, the alarm did not go off, so he drove forward a little and switched the engine off. It wasn't a neat job – arse sticking out to the middle of the road – but he said, 'Bugger it. I'll just walk to the kerb.'

5

The Hunter was in his lair, at the centre of his web. He had woven the gossamer strands, tugged them taut, and now he had to keep watch over them as his coppers rummaged around the perimeter, turning over stones, looking in dark places. The cops would put a fright into someone; panic them into trying to run for cover. Maybe not today, maybe the radius would have to be lengthened, the circumference increased. The systematic search would continue, the strands of the web would hold and the ripples of fear would, eventually, be detected. It was the bread and butter of police work. The gossamer strands were now obsolete, replaced by the fibre optic cables of computers, but the theory remained the same. Tried and trusted. Doing it by the book.

Yeah, sure, and, if your auntie had balls, she'd be your uncle.

But The Jug was playing the big man. Told Hunter to be in the office, 'available for conference and able to respond to diverse developments'. So he'd tried to make the best of it. The guys in the white coats had been on the phone already. They'd been burning the midnight oil, shaking the test tubes and sooking the pipettes big time, testing traces of blood taken from the paving slabs where Toshie's body had been found.

More interesting was that attempts had been made to clean it up. SOCO had retrieved slender cotton strands and they were confident that they had not come from the tampon that had been inserted into Toshie's fatal wound.

The guys had news for him. She had put perfume on the cotton item to wipe up the blood. Hunter had an image of a nurse cleaning up in the operating theatre. Strangelove. The guys in the lab were spinning their centrifuge at the moment. They already had an alcohol base and citrus (weren't they all?) but said that the big manufacturers would have to be leant on heavily to divulge the exact contents and percentages in their potions.

Hunter promised to kick ass. Told them to put it on hold till he got back to them. Same with the hairs they had taken from Toshie's suit. Even though it was new, first time on for the Press Fund Ball. There had been eighty-four females there, thirty-nine of them under the age of forty and a further five a bit older but with big knockers. So that made forty-four possibles for hair. Not to mention Strangelove. He asked them to concentrate on the cotton fibres, to try for a match with the sanitary towel that had been found near Knox's body. He assumed that women stuck with the same brand but, hey, he wasn't an expert.

The boys had done good and in damn good time too. Put him on to her scent. Jesus H Christ, in other circumstances he would be squeezing the balls off the perfume-making woofters. But these weren't normal circumstances. Strangelove didn't do anything normally. So The Jug could take the book and stick it up his arse. Sideways.

Strangelove was talking to The Hunter and she was saying, 'I did this. I killed Knox and I killed Toshie too. And here's my DNA to prove it.'

The snapper had dropped off large, aerial photos of the murder scenes taken from the police helicopter. Hunter stuck them up on a wall. He stared at them, playing the part of the killer.

The Knox site is good. In the heart of a financial area; few residential homes, expensive homes, and good people abed and asleep at 4 a.m. Easy access, easy egress. If you want to kill Knox, this is a good place. But not as good as inside his office. He lets you in his car, so he would have let you in his office. But if it isn't Knox that you want to kill . . . not specifically Knox . . . if you just want to kill . . .

The place where Toshie had breathed his last was different. City centre. Merchant City. Trendy pubs, clubs, eateries. Yuppieland. Always folk coming and going. But you know that you can get into the back court. Specifically that you can get into this back court. So you know the area . . . or does Toshie? This is not a good place to kill. Well, not if getting away is the priority . . . but if you didn't care about that . . . if you liked that . . . if it only added to the excitement . . .

Hunter fired up his computer, making the most of his imprisonment, determined to crystallise what he knew as fact and filter out the unlikeliest speculation. He created two documents on his computer and called them KNOX and TOSHIE. Then, from memory, he typed in everything he knew. Did Knox first. Didn't bother with spelling mistakes or punctuation, just keyed it in, flow of consciousness. Same with Toshie. Then he created a new document, called it KnoxTosh and took great care over it.

KNOX TOSH

stabbed ded thin blade.
one wound expert hand.
killed early morn.
21 days apart.
white, midle-class, married, bizzmen.
well off.
cash taken, other valubles left.
no fingerprints.
toshie a ladies' man.
knox liked prossies.

Murdo, the young tec, had filled in the last bit. He had spoken to the ladies of the night who plied their trade around Anderston. A ten-minute walk from Knox's office. Or seven with a hard-on. Two of them recognised Knox. They spoke out after the laddie promised that they would never be called to give evidence. Showed potential, Murdo. Had come back to base and picked the prossies out from the mugshot books. Just in case they had to give evidence. They had told him that Knox was a nice man, nothing pervy, just straight sex. In his car. So it was a five-minute drive, hard-on optional. They had recognised him from his picture in the papers at the time of the murder. But, it was nothing to do with them, was it? And they didn't know any of the girls who carried a knife.

Hunter created another document, named it KILLER and stopped for a while. He took a pipe from his pocket, the Falcon, dammit, stuck it in his mouth and sucked at it unlit. This bit was important, for it might form part of the chain of evidence. A smart defence lawyer could call for notes, could question his procedure. In the old days you could ad lib, you could finesse it, but now there were electronic records . . .

He changed the filename to

KILLER(S)

Knife; same knife? still has/have it?
Know(s) where to strike to kill; medical knowledge
Kill(s) in city; in the open, but secluded
Know(s) the city well
Killing for thrills?
Or vengeance?

He saved the document and checked it into the system. Then he took a pencil and paper and got on with the real business. He wrote,

Leaves DNA signature.
Cocky – catch me if you can.
Killing for thrills.
Man hater.
Abused, prob sexually.
Brutal to Toshie; she's losing it.
Will take more chances.

The morning had not been wasted, for more reasons than one. Hunter had been blessed with a stroke of good luck. The windows had been cleaned. He had missed the event last month. Where had he been? Was it the drugs murders? No, it was the Widow Knox. The woman with the clocks that couldn't tell the time. Anyway, doing the windows was a major operation, conducted by contract cleaners, in a cradle lowered from the roof. Down a bit, stop. Left a bit, stop. A Moses basket with skyhooks.

Not like the old days, at the old copshops, where a wee fella in a pair of sandshoes just walked along the ledges smearing your windows with a dirty chamois on the way and nobody said anything to him in case he told you to do it yourself. One floor up or three floors up, it didn't make any difference to him. But he'd been banned, made obsolete, because his skill was deemed to be too dangerous. The dialithium insurance policy cannae take it, Captain. The cradle-dreepers had taken his place. Oh, well, that's progress and that'll be £500, plus VAT, thank you very muchly.

And today, this very morning, a little miracle had happened. It was not witnessed – nor should it have been, for miracles are, are they not, a matter of faith? But one fact was beyond dispute, a window in Hunter's office had been cracked. An outer pane, three floors up, on the outside wing of the building. And the windows, Holmes, could not be opened from the inside.

The way Hunter saw it, and the way he told it, was that a gust of wind had taken a fancy to the cradle. Just sooked it out a wee bit then spat it back again, dunting the window. Not enough to cause the cleaner to fart, never mind shit himself.

How else could it have happened? Maybe a pygmy with a big blowpipe, one of the wee fellas in the jungle that David Attenborough was pally with, the kind of guy who could put a dart in a monkey's arse two miles up a tree, well he could have done it. And it was possible, dangerous but just about doable, for a fella out on the emergency stairway to stretch out and, with a long pole, like the one used to burl the wee wheels that open the slat windows up near the ceiling in Conference Room One, well, with a pole like that, a fella could lean way over the safety rail and give the window a skelp. That would probably do it. But what could anyone possibly gain from that?

The window cleaner, when questioned by the bean counters denied responsibility. Made the oft-used Glasgow plea, 'It wiznae me!' sensibly failing to follow it up with 'A big bad boy done it and ran away.' The man insisted that it hadn't happened, couldn't happen. Well, he would, wouldn't he? But Hunter had seen the evidence straight away, when he returned from the canteen after a coffee. Just a hairline crack, tiny, the kind that only a trained observer would notice. And, being a conscientious copper, he had reported it immediately. Well, who was to say that the window wasn't dangerous? Especially with the wind swirling like that. Could shatter any minute, falling on the guy emptying the bins. He might have his kids with him, just showing how their dad earned a living, encouraging them to stick in at school, get their Highers, go on to university. And the binman and his kids would claim on the insurance . . .

No one could quite believe that the window had been replaced within the hour. What a stroke of luck that the firm just down the road had one the right size in stock and that two fellas could fit it right away. And so what if it wasn't a perfect match, if it was hinged and could be opened? Who was complaining? Certainly not the occupant of the office. Not the guy who had just pulled his chair over there, who had put his feet up on the window ledge and was puffing his pipe reek out into God's good fresh air.

A fifteen-minute nicotine injection cleared the cobwebs from his mind. Catching a killer, particularly a clever killer, was a chess game. You sacrificed the pawns early, made some space to get the main players into action. The castles went next – straight down the line and too predictable – and then the bishops, scuttling sideways like crabs. The knights were Hunter's favourites, shuffling two steps sideways to make one forward, coming at the enemy from all angles and causing confusion. But, as in all aspects of nature, the queen was the killer. Goes where she likes and does as she pleases. Just like Strangelove. In her game, all of the pawns were still in play and it was her move. So Hunter decided he would just bide his time.

He returned to his desk to a contest where he had more control. He called up the file named DRUGDEATHS. Three murders and another guy brain-dead in hospital and all because the planners in the City Chambers didn't know their arses from their elbows. The two drugs gangs had kept the peace for more than five years. Not best buddies, sure, but businessmen who knew when they had a good thing going. Jimmy Stone, The Stoneman, controlled the South Side. Danny Boyd ruled the East End. The boundary was clearly defined. A river ran through it at the greyhound track at Shawfield. Or it did until the city council approved the regeneration plan. It took in the razed acres of the Oatlands slum in the South Side to Glasgow Green on the other side of the river. The house builders had swung the deal with the promise of a sports centre. And that had emerged as the flashpoint.

Both gangs made an early pitch for the right to ply their trade at the sports centre. It was the perfect spot. Who could tell if the bags contained Nikes and sweatshirts or £20 wraps of heroin?

Stone gained the upper hand after sending in his main men to trade at the lowest prices in the West of Scotland – below the minimum figure agreed at last year's historic meeting of the city's drugs godfathers. Boyd had decided to play by the rules and called another summit, arguing that there was enough trade for everyone. All that was needed was a little common sense, a business agreement. It was said that Stone, too, was willing to negotiate. And then fate took a hand.

It started with a simple argument between two pushers, but Stone's man lost the rag. He pulled a knife, meaning just to stripe the other guy, but caught him on the neck, puncturing the artery. It was lights out within a couple of minutes.

Boyd was left with no option. He had, after all, made the peace overture. Failure to strike back would be interpreted as weakness. His retaliation was swift, but carried out with considerable restraint. He brought up a pro from the Smoke and paid in readies out of his own pocket. It was a clean hit, one bullet in the back of the head in the young fella's own house. No witnesses, no relatives spattered with blood. The victim was only a bit player in Stone's operation. Just a statement. Payback. No loss to anyone, really. That's what Boyd thought. How was he to know the guy had been boffing Stone's daughter?

And then it got nasty, really serious. Stone sent a team into the East End. They were tooled up. Hit Boyd's pub just before closing time. They trashed the place, left seven seriously injured – the barman in the no-brain unit in the Southern General Hospital. And they took Larry The Laundryman.

Larry was a treasure. Every drug dealer's dream. An accountant who had pissed his own business away. He still hit the bevvy, but Boyd allocated him a minder to ensure that he didn't get into any trouble. Or start to keep bad company – like the cops. Larry knew all the dodges on how to launder money, shove it through so many channels that it returned whiter than white. And, he carried out one stroke of genius. He was the first guy who had seen the possibilities of the surge of building societies converting into public limited companies. He had set up the network of more than two hundred folk – not all of them junkies, there were single-mums and hard-up grannies too – who invested Danny Boyd's dosh in the mutuals to cash in when they turned plc. The lay-out was considerable, almost £700,000 – three grand per investor, £500 in each of six building societies. But it ensured voting rights and thus the acquisition of shares, the sale of which turned in a tidy profit. But that was just a bonus. The real investment was almost one thousand three hundred building society savings' accounts. The passbooks were neatly tucked up in Boyd's lawyer's safe.

You puts it in, you takes it out whenever and wherever you like.

Stone's team had taken The Laundryman out of the pub and bundled him into the back of a stolen Transit. Then they had taken the Transit on to the M8, up to 100 mph, and bundled Larry out the back. The horrific death had stunned the criminal fraternity. Four days had passed and there had been no retribution. The Stoneman had firmly battened down the hatches. But he knew, and The Hunter knew, that it was only a matter of time. Boyd would have to retaliate or he would lose all credibility. It had gone beyond nasty. Now it was personal.

Hunter dialled Danny Boyd's mobile. He wondered what tune it played. Eric Clapton's 'Cocaine'?

Boyd answered with a curt 'Yesss.'

'D'you know who this is?'

There was a pause before Boyd said, 'Ya bastard. Stone?'

'Worse.'

'Hunter?'

'Right. Just to remind you, Danny, just a wee warning.'

'Aye. Right.'

'Aye. Right.'

The line went dead. It was truly wonderful what one could articulate when one spoke the same language.

Now and again it all came together and God was in his heaven and all was well with the world. A welcome change from the norm (well it seemed that way to Zara) when woman had to intercede – or should that be enter seed – His wonders to perform. An egg implanted here, a skoosh of the old testicle tadpole there . . . and I name this child Little Tommy Test-Tube. Yet wee hairy Mary over the hill in Castlemilk only had to drop her drawers for a minute in the bus shelter – didn't even have to put down her fish supper – and Joseph was in there, like a rat up a drainpipe, and, lo and behold, nine months later three wide guys from Barlanark were down at Glasgow Zoo to steal three camels. But half a mile from the clinic, in the tidy bungalow in affluent Carmunnock, the Barons had a chart of her menstrual cycle on the wall, an anal thermometer on the bedside table and, after twenty years of faithful copulation, they were still bundle-of-joyless. Mother Nature could be cruel. Or was she just becoming increasingly selective? Singling out the weakest of the species, splitting them off from the herd, ensuring that their flawed genes did not enter the breeding stock. A compassionate cull, really. But now and again she relented. Rewarded perseverance.

Tired tonight, Darling? Got a headache? Or shall we persevere?

Strange word. Latin root. Through separating. Should be through uniting, coming together, so to speak. But perhaps that was just too . . . vulgar. Like Zara calling her fertility clinic an infertility clinic. She liked words, liked the feel of them in her mouth. Mellifluous was her favourite, sweet sounding. Not sweet, because that would be an indisputable fact, but sweet sounding, which clearly put the sweetness in the ear of the beholder. It was the basis for business. The seller made the deal sound sweet; the buyer then made the commitment; and, after the tasting, it was too late to withdraw. And anyway, a couple desperate for a baby never used the withdrawal method.

Zara knew how to use words. Not only their meaning and where correctly to place them in sentences, but how to project them too. They had taught her in drama college how to breathe properly, to use her mouth to pronounce words in various ways for different affects, and she had mastered the dialects. It had been Eliza Doolittle in reverse. Zara naturally dropped the jaw, propelled the air along the roof of the mouth for her middle-class accent. Pronounced axnt. But go a bit nasal, tighten the lips, keep the bottom jaw firm, say ack sent, and one was transformed, as if by magic, to the heights of Chateau du Lait. But they hadn't taught her how to make a living at it – how to stretch the cash from a four-week run in panto until Butlins opened in the summer. Then Calder came along, brilliant Calder – academically that is – but not, well, not worldly wise. He knew the meaning, but not the power of a mellifluent woman. He was sweet on Zara, a good woman who could point him in the right direction . . . And the direction in which Zara pointed led to the altar.

She went to one of the kitchens in the old house and put a kettle on. Looked out of the window towards the intensive care suite where Clive was keeping watch on Josef Paborsky. The transplant really had gone better than they had dared hope. The old fellow was doing well – still sedated and on the ventilator, but the vital signs were good. Perhaps their luck was changing.

There was a newspaper on the counter, folded over neatly at the crossword puzzle. Calder had completed all but one clue, I, J, K, L, M, N – water (3). Eau? Mais non. Zara took a box of Twinings teabags from a cupboard. Teabags? – accepted generic terminology although these sachets contained not tea but a mixture of raspberry, strawberry and loganberry. Caffeine-free, healthy, but lacking a bit of oomph. Zara been up and about for more than eight hours – six of them in the delivery suite. She put two spoonfuls of honey into a mug, popped in the sachet, poured boiling water on top and stirred. She removed the sticky sachet and looked around for a receptacle – a polythene bag would be ideal, kitchen roll acceptable – but saw nothing suitable. So she dropped the gooey mess into the sink. Was that not, after all, why one employed staff? The brain might be a bit slower, but it was not addled.

She had another look at the crossword. The letters between H and O. H to O. H_2O. Clever. Simple. The best ideas always were. She decided against filling in the answer. She could nudge Calder towards it later or, depending on how she felt, lord it over him. Lady lords (4) – Zara.

She took her drink through to the conservatory and slouched in the comfortable sofa. She kicked off her shoes and put her feet up on the coffee table. It was damp, as if a dew had fallen on it. Her eyes lifted to the roof, but she was not going to dwell on such mundane matters. Not this morning, Good Lord what a morning, just like the old days, in Rottenrow. What a name for a maternity hospital! Zara had heard why it was so called but she had forgotten. A French connection, something like that. It hadn't been a romantic career move, from treading the boards to Rottenrow, and it had taken three years of study. But all the world loves an angel, especially one who delivers babies. And that's what Zara had done this morning. Delivered the baby she had implanted nine months ago. To a forty-five-year-old mother who had been given up as a hopeless case at most of the other facilities in the UK, not to mention one in the good old US of A. The birth had been a natural one – six hours of agony and swearing – and the baby boy appeared one hundred percent normal. The agony and the ecstasy. It was . . . lovely. There were other words to describe it but lovely was the right one. A lovely ending. With five lovely thousand lovely pounds. What a pity Zara wouldn't see any of it. The bank would gobble it up and still be ravenous.

It hadn't started out this way. It wasn't part of the plan. Calder had supported her, academically and financially, during her nursing studies and onwards and upwards through the management ranks. He was fully behind her, too, when she opened the first clinic twelve years ago, in Springburn, not the most salubrious of areas, but . . . worthy. Poor people wanted babies, too, a difficult concept for the wealthy to conceive, but true nonetheless. It had not been a lucrative occupation, but it brought other rewards. They had lived comfortably, Calder working at the psychiatric clinic in Duke Street Hospital during the day and taking private patients at night. Boozers, mainly, who wanted to be told in big words, in medical terms, that they were alcoholic. But special . . .

That's when Zara had got into her charitable work, in the evenings, with refugees and asylum seekers. It had started quite simply, helping out with a soup run, distributing clothing, toys for the kids. Just an act of kindness for the flotsam of the world, washed up on an inhospitable shore. It had been the basis of her first baby deal, too. An act of kindness, a matter of convenience, an arrangement that suited all parties.

The Kosovar girl didn't want the baby. She had been raped somewhere along the road to freedom. She said she was sixteen but she didn't look it. Just a child herself, really. Terrified of authority, terrified that they would send her home. She didn't have a house, not even a place at a hostel. Begged food on the streets; slept in the dark safety of back alleys. She had seen pregnant women come into the clinic and just followed in their waddling footsteps.

'You take,' she said, pointing to her stomach.

She did not know how to say abortion but she knew the actions. She yanked violently at her vagina.

'You take,' she said.

And Zara would have done it. Risky, at about twenty weeks gone. Very risky with a thin, malnourished girl. But Zara would have done it. Then she thought of the rich couple who had everything – except a child. She knew it would be illegal, just as they knew. And she accepted the ramifications even as she was drawing blood from Mrs Rich and the Kosovar girl. Let fate decide, no match, no similarities at all, and there was no deal. But they had the same blood group. Oh, the antibodies would be different, but so what? Questions would not be asked for many years – if ever – and Mr and Mrs Rich were more than willing to say that the child had been conceived in an adulterous relationship. Mr Rich had devised a kind of pregnancy bump, fashioned out of a horsehair cushion from an old settee and firmly buckled at the small of Mrs Rich's back. The lump grew as the months passed.

And Zara helped them all. So it was against the law, so what? The law had done nothing to help the Kosovar, so it was a ass. And who, specifically, was being harmed? The girl lost an encumbrance and got a tidy sum in cash to start her life all over. Mr and Mrs Rich got a baby. And the child got a chance in life. The social workers would call it rehoming.

And Zara got a fee. Mr and Mrs Rich had insisted upon it. She knew that it was their way of binding her to them, of incriminating her. But she accepted the money because she accepted responsibility. She was admitting liability. She held her hand out for the forty pieces of silver. And, if anyone asked, if anyone caught her, someone like Hunter, she would admit it. She would explain it, argue for it. Some things were wrong and it took courage to change them.

Zara took another drink of her fruity concoction and summoned her energy. Two more clients would be arriving soon. A similar arrangement, a drop and swop in a couple of months time. A single girl who did not want the child she was carrying and a well-to-do couple who did. The girl, a daughter of the manse, had come to the city to live her own life, free from the harsh rules of the Free Church. Zara had met her on a late night soup run, hovering on the fringes of the junkies and deadbeats, too proud to ask for help and too lost to go anywhere else. Zara had recruited her, employed her really, to help to dispense the polythene cups of broth and doorsteps of bread. Two nights later, the girl had opened her soul. It took Zara less than a week to fix the girl up with a flat and a week more to implant the thought that the solution to everyone's problems would be to set the baby up in a good home. The girl was both healthy and grateful. She would arrive soon, to go through a battery of checks, to ensure that all was well. The latest Mrs Rich, in an adjoining room, would unstrap her foam rubber lump, her seven-months' pregnant bump, (the neighbours had been telling her how big she was getting!) and put on the eight-month one. Zara had a selection now, perfected over the years, adapted and adjusted. Now they came with backache, varicose veins and a gait like a penguin.

Isn't nature a wonderful thing?

Zara wiped a tear from her eye. It had been happening recently, in emotionless and inexplicable circumstances. Just a chill, probably, caught in a draft in the bloody conservatory, more likely than not. Nothing to worry about and no time to do so anyway. The Ramblers would be back soon, dirty boots and dirty talk, ravenous and thirsty. She always gave them red wine and Clive always proposed the toast, 'The blood of Christ.' Then it would be carry-out curries and gallons of beer.

Zara was almost entirely vegetarian. A bit of fish, for the protein, but even that was infrequent. All things considered, she was really quite good-living. The occasional ciggy, maybe too much alcohol, but it wasn't a problem. Yes, overall, quite good-living. Apart from the murders, of course. But nobody's perfect.

It had started to rain again and Zara could not help but watch the drips fall through conservatory roof and plink into the receptacles below. The water level was up over the sponges. Saturation point and then some, a situation with which she was too well acquainted. A single drip begins a torrent; a pinhole opens a chasm. The Kosovar girl had been the pinhole and the money Zara took was the first fissure of the chasm.

Calder had described the accommodation as outwith the law. She allowed him the euphemism and his taking the role of Robin Hood, romantic and principled. But she had never deluded herself that it was anything other than illegal and, if it ever came to light, it would mean her nursing licence, her clinic and, very probably, a term of imprisonment. She had entered into the deal with her eyes wide open, but she could not see into the future. She could not know that the single step over the edge of the law was the beginning of a march. Nevertheless, when Sørensen, Calder's pal from university days, approached them with his problem, it was Zara who saw the possibilities. It was, she told Calder in bed that night, no different from a drop and swop.

Sørensen, born and raised in Copenhagen, had come to Glasgow to study medicine. He and Calder had been chums during their first four years as students, but had gone their different ways when they specialised – Calder in psychiatry and Sørensen in anaesthesia. Calder had remained in his home city and Sørensen's career had taken him south of the border. The pair, initially, kept in contact but over the years it had been reduced to the occasional telephone call and cards at Christmas. Until the Dane arrived at the big house in Busby with a heart-rending story.

His half-brother, Brian, was dying at home in Copenhagen. One of his kidneys had failed, the other was deteriorating. He was barely kept alive by a dialysis machine. The brothers had different fathers, so Sørensen was not suitable as a donor, nor were any other members of the family. But there was one possibility.

Brian worked in the laboratory of a health centre. One of his responsibilities was screening women in the sex industry for infectious diseases. He had taken a particular interest in the blood samples of one prostitute, a ne'er do well of twenty-three years. She was known to her friends as The Skunk because of her love of the strong cannabis derivative – an indulgence afforded by her nights working in the red light district. But her habits had become more exotic and she was now in the clutches of an expensive crack-cocaine addiction.

Brian, under cover of fears of HIV, ran additional tests on her and confirmed that she was a perfect match for a donor – both blood and tissue. He revealed the discovery to his brother – bitter in the knowledge that the only person who could save his life treated her own with contemptuous indifference.

Sørensen went to see The Skunk on her own territory and paid handsomely for ten minutes of her time. He sat on a hard-backed chair and she lay, uninterested, on an uninviting bed. He explained Brian's plight and begged her to save his brother's life. She laughed at first, said he was crazy, then told him that it was a hard world and she gave nothing for nothing, no donations. Sørensen thanked her anyway, said that he understood and felt better for talking about it.

He was back the next night, paying again, sitting on the same chair, but this time The Skunk was the subject of the conversation. She spoke for twenty minutes, hard luck stories, excuses and how she would not be living like this forever. Eventually Sørensen asked what she wanted – really, really wanted – in all the world. The answer surprised him.

She said, 'I want a normal life. I just want . . . to be ordinary.'

Then she added, with defiance, 'And I want to see beyond the horizon.'

The deal was done on the third night. Sørensen showed her an estate agent's schedule for Brian's Copenhagen house, which had been put on the market that day at a price equivalent to £75,000.

He said, 'It's yours – the house or the money – if you want it. And so is this. He put down an airline slip reserving return flights to Nepal.

He said, 'You can see the whole world from there.'

If The Skunk told anybody about the deal, nobody believed her. Why should they? The crack-cocaine addict had told many stories in the past.

Call it fate, destiny, whatever, but, when Brian told his doctors about a potential donor, they sighed and it was too late. His condition had deteriorated to such an extent that they believed he would not survive a transplant operation.

Sørensen, however, had other ideas. He was well aware that Clive, the brilliant transplant surgeon who had descended into alcoholism, had been suspended from acting in any medical capacity for two years, for being drunk in theatre. Clive didn't know it then, and he didn't know it now, but Sørensen had reported the first drink-related incident for which he was reprimanded by hospital authorities. And, in one of life's peculiar ironies, it was Sørensen who realised that Clive was the only surgeon who could save his brother's life. Because Clive was the only one who might operate outwith the law.

The old stables at the big house had already been converted into an intensive care suite for the fertility clinic. It was too risky to attempt to acquire the equipment necessary for a transplant operation in the UK, but in the countries that had once been part of the Soviet Union everything has a price. Some of the equipment was purchased there, from parties who asked no questions, and transported discreetly to Scotland. Much of the money came from another of Calder's friends, Sir Ranulf Jedburgh, who was to be repaid in a unique way.

The transplant went remarkably smoothly and Sørensen's brother is alive and well to this day. He moved to the south of Spain, under an assumed identity, lest his Lazarus act attracted unwanted attention.

There had only been one problem. The Skunk had not come out of the anaesthetic. Death was nothing new to the members of the medical profession. But murder was. Zara, who had acted as theatre sister during the operation, still remembered vividly the reaction of the three main characters. Sørensen appeared uninterested in the woman's fate. Zara thought then, and had considered it more likely since, that he had actually planned such an end which had, after all, saved £75,000 and the distinct possibility of blackmail in days to come. Calder was quiet, subdued. And Clive went to pieces. She had taken time to calm him, shooshing and cuddling. And, when he was settled, she had collected her Polaroid camera, lined up the men behind the body and taken three photographs. She said they were insurance policies for the musketeers. All for one and one for all.

And later, when it was dark, they had buried the body near the stream at the bottom of the garden, under the weeping willows. It was there to this day.

Zara finished off her fruity drink. The rain had eased and the drips had stopped falling through the conservatory ceiling. She got up, reluctantly, lifted a basin and carried it awkwardly to the sink. Good grief, it had come to this. Changing the nappies of Calder's great white elephant. Zara had never been the kind of woman to say I told you so but she did, she had told him to stop and think three times before embarking on his venture of the empire in Busby, built around the big house, the listed building (listing like the leaning tower of Pisa) where you had to fill in four forms for permission to change a light bulb.

As she replaced the basin, she noticed another wet spot on the floor. Another basin. Another millstone. Another thousand pounds. This was her life now. She was pleased to hear the sound of the approaching vehicle. But not so pleased when the racket from the diesel engine grew louder and the van appeared in view.

The big gold letters on the side advertised the PET CREMATORIUM. He might just as well have added: 'We also take violinists.'

* * * * *

94

Sunday bloody Sunday.

Lisa still in bed, awake for hours, unable to sleep and unwilling to rise. Nothing to get up for. And the urge is still on her. Got a taxi all the way home from Mum's last night. Just in case she met one of them. One of the leerers. One of the middle-class rulers with everything going for them and still they want more. They want her. They want her body. They want to control her life again.

Trying to get back into her dream, into that happy place. But every time she gets to the good bit, puts her hand on her little stiletto, it turns to mercury, drips away and the dream begins to evaporate. She reaches out for it, grabs for its gossamer threads, tries to pull herself back but they snap, sending her hurtling back. To Sunday.

How she hates bloody Sunday. Mum went to church on Sundays. Lisa and Louise left at home. With Dad. Louise just a baby. Too little to remember. Thank God.

Ha! Ha-ha. Lisa laughed aloud. Kicked her heels into the mattress in delight. Thank God! Oh, yeah, thanks God, Great G-man. And if it hadn't been for you, Omnipotent One, All-Seeing All-Singing All-Dancing, Three Into One Does Go Man, if it hadn't been for you, my mum would have been at home. But it must have been part of your great plan. I'll remember that. I'll tell them that. I'll say, 'Oh yes, I did it. I did all those things, but it was part of God's great plan.'

They'll give me a long holiday in Carstairs, in the State Hospital, and I'll get my reward in heaven.

In her dream, she had put the phone down and smiled. A small smile because it had not been a great achievement. In fact, it had been so easy. She was humming a tune, one of Mum's. What was it? By some guy , one of Billy Connolly's pals when they were folk singers. 'Baker Street', that's the name – not the singer, the song. One singer, one song. Rafferty. That was his name. He made a lot of dough out of 'Baker Street', that's what Mum said.

You used to think that it was so easy
But you're crying,
You're crying now.

Or you soon will be.

She'd phoned the bank, in her dream, the one in Duke Street that had refused her the mortgage. Put on a little girl voice, a nithe little lithp, asked for the guy who'd done the refusing. Been told that he'd left two years ago, transferred to Queen Street. Did she want the number?

95

Oh, yeth pleathe.

Phoned Queen Street. Spoke to him in her dream. Made an appointment to see him. At the Royal Infirmary, yes the perfect place, in the mortuary at the Royal in five minutes. Would that be thuitable? She would be tho grateful. And she would do anything to pleathe him.

And she's waiting when he walks in. Three other men there – the first one, the one in Morocco, the dirty old one, and Knox and Dirty Mac. They're all lying down. Not standing up, not erect. Each one lying cold and silent and so peaceful on their slabs.

And she's naked under her long leather coat. And the brooch is in the piping. She can feel its long, slender blade on her breast. She opens the coat to reveal her body to him. And the blade slithers through the lining, pierces her nipple and it bleeds. Blood not milk dropping from her nipple. And she strips him naked, eases him down on to his back, on a fourth marble slab. She lets him lick the blood. Blood and not milk dropping from her nipple. His tongue flicking out, scenting it, tasting the smell of the blood, like a snake. Like the snake that he is. And she takes her long silver tongue from its hiding place in the leather piping and . . .

In the old days, you'd get a body and it would tell you the story. You had to know how to read it but it was there, if you could see through the cold, glazed eyes. If you had learned the language of the dead.

And you said two silent words.

The image consumes you and sustains you on the journey back in time, you and your Sergeant, walking in a dead man's footprints, gathering the evidence, interviewing witnesses, building the case.

You speak to folk along the way, get them to tell you things they didn't know they knew. And you sift their words, allowing the truth to filter through. It can be collected later. What you want is the lie.

And, bit by bit, you built up the picture, working your way back to the body, until you hear the death rattle in the throat and there is just one piece of the jigsaw missing.

All you have to do is slot it in.

You know the killer. You've got his measure. You've looked at him from all angles and you're sure, absolutely certain. So you bring him in, into your place, and you sit him in a hard chair and you leave him for a bit to stew in his own juice. Then you go in and you talk to him, taking him all the way along the route. All the way to the final, empty slot. Then you wait.

Some killers give up before you're halfway there, they leap in, eager to put an end to that part of it.

Others are arrogant, confident. So you turn it back on them and then some. Your Sergeant gives you smug glances, sniggers. It's cat and mouse. Mental judo, get him off balance, use his strength against him. And your Sergeant says, 'Fuck him, he's had his chance.' and you scrape the legs of your chair on the floor, start to rise, put your hands on the desk and you give the killer your look that says, 'You've left me no option . . .'

Some squirm. You nudge these ones, wheedle, wait till they're tired, then lean on them, coax them, threaten them, plead with them. Some coppers put the boot in or lift their hands.

Digger Burns, Hunter's Sergeant, rarely raised even his voice. He asked The Hunter's questions. Digger knew when to keep going, to keep the pressure on, and he knew when silence was a more powerful weapon. The Hunter just watched. Arms folded, like an immortal Buddha, occasionally cracking a smile like a whiplash. He was good at listening, good at watching the body language. And he had one unique talent. He used it sparingly, when the case was weak, when the killer was clever. He would rise up, ever so slowly, Buddha coming to life, lumbering around the table, towering over him, blocking the light. Then slowly Buddha would bend and whisper in his ear. Just a few words. So confident that he whispered it, shared it only with the killer. Their secret. The Hunter's display of absolute power and utter contempt.

Coppers asked what he said and he never told them. But it had never failed him.

It had been like that, it had been so much simpler, in the old days. When a murderer brought dishonour on his entire family. But now there was no shame and no fear either. The deck was stacked against the coppers. And, even if you got your case to court, convinced the jury, the appeal court, the law lords and the European Commission of Human Fuckin Rights, then they'd do their seven years in the BarL and it was time to get out time.

Even so, The Hunter's record was legend. Nine out of ten killers cracked. Told him everything. And then he could make his peace with the victim. Say the two silent words.

God bless.

Then he could let go.

And now his prey was Strangelove. One woman under the scrutiny of the sophisticated, well-oiled machinery of the modern police force. Forensics would subject the items from the crime scenes to the inexorable gaze of modern science. Digger and the teuchter would set about retracing her footsteps. And The Hunter would watch as they pieced together the jigsaw. But he knew that it would not matter a damn. Strangelove was not denying that she had killed Toshie and Knox. She was boasting about it. She had given him the proof. Left her signature, her DNA. And he was no nearer to her today than he'd been yesterday. Than he'd been three weeks ago when she killed Knox. And she was saying, 'It's the world against me. So find me. If you're smart enough. Find me or I'll do it again . . . before I do it again.'

And The Hunter knew that he could not catch Strangelove. She would have to give herself up.

And only then could he exorcise his mate's ghost. For he had not been able to look into Toshie's glazed eyes. They had not communicated in the language of the dead. Instead, Strangelove had spoken to him. Whispered in his ear. Two silent words.

Catch me.

Zara wondered if her hormones were starting to do their own thing. Sure, she was tired after two nights with too little sleep. She was working too hard, too much responsibility for too many matters. And no, Calder wasn't doing all he could to help. And yes, he wasn't well, his heart was not strong. And maybe, just maybe, she was losing it. Not with the big things. At work or in a crisis, she summoned energy from somewhere, focussed her concentration like a laser, just got on with it. But later, when she relaxed, when she was not on guard, she had found herself behaving . . . oddly.

Calder would Catch 22 her if she were to mention it. Oh no, my darling, he would say, the fact that you think you are losing it means that you are not. That kind of thing. Give her his little pawnbroker's smile that said, 'Leave it with me and, if you want it back in six months, we can discuss it then.'

But, after this afternoon's little contretemps, he might consider whether to give her a little more attention. Both personal and professional. Zara had blown a fuse and it had felt simply great. Like setting fire to the summer's old grass to allow the new growth space in the spring. If there was to be a spring . . .

The Pet Crematorium van had been the spark that had ignited her fury. Parked there, in the courtyard, outside the conservatory, and Calder in his suit, leaning on the door, chatting comfortably, passing the time of day with Mr PetCrem, Junkie Jed himself. What was Jed short for anyway? Jeremiah? Or was it his given name, the wastrel son of loony hippies? It had been infuriating to see Calder so easy in his company, in broad daylight, albeit hidden from the road. But, when Calder handed over a bottle of pills, Zara had exploded. Stormed out of the conservatory and gave it to him full volume. She couldn't even remember stopping to take in air.

Jed, snivelling coward that he is, had heard the start of it. He had been the bloody start of it! He had taken off at a rapid rate of knots in his funereal black van. The despicable little man might have a big furnace, which Calder pointed out was the perfect way to hide their mistakes, but the junkie's brain was addled. There was no other explanation. Good God, he had arrived last night, to pick up the dismembered body of Paborsky's donor, and he came in his Pet-bloody-Crem van.

Calder, ever the diplomat, had pointed out that his Shogun with the black tinted windows had broken down. And he just shrugged his shoulders, when it was pointed out that it shouldn't have broken down because we pay him enough and we got the damned thing MoT'd and serviced just a couple of months ago. And she had reminded her darling husband just how close they had come to discovery and disaster by that odious policeman, Hunter, uninvited and unannounced, hands out for everything he could get. Greedy, grasping bastard. And at the arrival of the dogs' hearse last night his ears had cocked like a creature of the night, his nose had lifted to the wind, sniffing the air to check if there might be some carrion to feed off.

Zara knew that Hunter had sensed something. From the moment he had appeared at the door she had been on her guard. He had come to ask questions about poor Randy, expressed concern about his health. Did he know? How could he know? But the damned policeman sensed something. He had not pressed it. Did that mean that he knew a lot and was confident, or just had an inkling and was fishing? Zara did not know and that concerned her. He was well named, a hunter, picking off what ever he wanted when ever he wanted it. Top of the food chain, with no natural predators to fear. He was the law. He had the power. He was a dangerous man. Neanderthal and, she was sure, ruthless.

She had been glad to play up to his base instincts. He had not even attempted to disguise those. He had been undressing her with his eyes from the moment he set foot in the house. Quite brazen about it. She had gone along with it, to play for time, and he had allowed her to do so. Yes, allowed was the right word. He hadn't encouraged it, hadn't made any overt move himself. But he had shown no surprise when she had rubbed her leg against his arm as it stretched out for the whisky bottle. The scene had been quite disconcerting but, she had to admit, exciting, too. It had been a long time since she had flirted seriously – seductively used her feminine wiles – and she had enjoyed the role more than a little.

All in all, she had handled the situation well. Remained in control, despite the fact that, only twenty yards from the conservatory, Paborsky lay still and silent in the intensive care suite, his life reliant on a battery of machines despite the new heart that was beating strongly in his chest. And closer still, in her own clinic, the dismembered body of the young Romanian was stacked in eight black bin liners.

Hunter's ears had pricked up at the sound of the Pet Crem van and she had, momentarily, panicked. Briefly considered pulling down his zip to see what he had in there but, even then, in extremis, her brain was working. What if he declines? she had thought. What if he rejects the advances? Decides to go outside to investigate and questions the contents of the eight black bags.

Her strategy had not been flawless. She would admit, eventually, that taking the policeman to see Matthew, Calder's special patient, had not been without its own risks. Calder had been angry this morning when she had told him. He was on the point of describing her actions as foolish, but stopped at foo . . . and just as well for him. He had yes-my-deared her. Given her the professional nods. God, he had even clasped his hands together on the breakfast table. And she had let it pass.

But this afternoon she had let rip at him. God, she had even told him he could stop leaving his dead bodies in her clinic! He'd smiled at that. Just with his lips. Killed it before it escaped on to his face and just as bloody well. Because she hadn't finished with him. She knew that he was giving Mr PetCrem drugs, it didn't matter what he said, and Clive, he'd have to do something about Clive too. It had been touch and go yesterday, she had seen it in his eyes. The man was on the verge of a nervous breakdown. And that, she had told her darling husband, was clearly his area of expertise. How terribly convenient to have a breakdown whilst one was working at a psychiatric clinic. Calder did not appear to appreciate the irony, so she had told him, ordered him to 'sort Clive out'. She had told him to take him in hand.

Calder's smile had escaped then. Not my type, he had said, perhaps Patrik, Paborsky's boyfriend, is your man for that.

But she had wiped the smile off his face, gone on about the bloody conservatory roof and living inside a colander and how up with it she would not put. Or words to that affect.

It was the comments about the conservatory that caused Zara to consider whether she was losing it. Her life was not without problems and she was worried about a leaky roof. She would apologise to Calder later, once she had savoured the bitter taste of the row. She was entitled to that first. Then she would say sorry, it was the menopause, a surge of hormones that turned Zoë Ball into Lucille Ball overnight.

Calder would smile his knowing smile and promise to keep Clive off the booze so he could give Sir Ranulf Jedburgh a new liver. Randy really, really deserved it.

The little black dress was still a bit damp. Lisa had trickled cold water on it yesterday and laid it out to dry, on top of a towel, on the kitchen work surface. Cold water removed blood. Mum told her that.

'Don't you worry your pretty little head about it,' Mum had said. 'It happens to all girls. It means you're a woman now. Just you take your pants off. We'll put cold water in this bucket. Now you put them in. Just drop them in, that's it. Now we'll put it in the cupboard in the hall where nobody will see it.'

Cold water gets rid of blood.

The dress was dry clean only, the Dior number, and she hoped she hadn't harmed it. That would be a shame. She would take it to the Innocents and they would have it cleaned before putting it in the shop window. The nun might be in the charity shop and she might say, 'Thank you again, my dear. God Bless.'

The Dior might sell for £20 – a tenner would be better if it went to a nice girl from Easterhouse – and she would feel like a million dollars in it. That would be nice.

In cold blood. Lisa had been thinking about that.

She turned the towel, to put the damp patch of the dress on a dry spot. There was a dirty, reddish-brown smear on the work surface. She rubbed it with a finger and it flaked like rust.

Rust in peace.

She remembered Dirty Mac on his knees. She had told him.

'Beg for it.'

And he'd begged.

'Now kissy, kissy.'

He'd hitched the little black dress up above her hips and been really excited to see that she wasn't wearing knickers. Told her she was gagging for it.

She could feel the cold, rough bricks of the bin shelter on her bottom.

His hands behind her thighs.

Her hand on the brooch, taking it from its leather sheath.

His head between her legs.

The slender blade on its way down, like a laser-guided missile, heading for the sweet spot between the vertebrae.

Him looking up, leering.

A sliver of moonlight on the blade.

Fear flashing to his eyes.

Fraction of a second to react. Twist of the wrist, elbow in, all the weight on the left foot. It had been brilliant, really. A brilliant, surgical operation. Got the temple cleanly and in Ms Stiletto went, into the tiny area between the bones, right into the brain. A neat job. Clinical.

There had been a spurt of blood, like a drinking fountain. Fouling the dress and the lining of the coat. He had let out one long sigh of satisfaction. The way you do after the first sip of a nice cup of tea.

She left Ms Stiletto in there. Grabbed his head and lowered it ever so gently. Turned it on the other side. Then removed Ms Stiletto and put her thumb over the wound. Waited till the legs stopped kicking, till she was sure the heart had stopped pumping. Then she got a sanitary towel out of her handbag and dabbed the blood from his temple. Scraped the pad on the paving slabs to leave a clue, then popped the sanitary towel into the nearest bin. They'd find it there.

But they hadn't with Knox. Mum had kept all the papers. Ten days' worth, while she'd been in Corsica shooting the last movie. She'd said there were job adverts coming up that she didn't want to miss. Lisa had looked through all the papers. Two days, that's all Knox had been worth. Two hundred words first day and about fifty the second. And not a mention of the sanitary towel. Maybe they hadn't found it in the adjoining back court. Maybe she'd given them too much credit. So she made it more obvious with Dirty Mac. Left it in the bin, first thing they'd see when they opened it.

Then she had gone home. And discovered the blood between her legs. That was, what, three weeks between periods. It had been worse. Sometimes ten days on and ten days off. A minor operation, a D&C, had helped for a while. But really, it was an occupational hazard, RVI the girls called it. Repetitive Vaginal Injury.

What a fucking way to make a living.

She had cleaned herself with a towel, then popped it in a bucket of cold water. No need to put it in the cupboard. Nobody would see it. Especially not Daddy.

She had put the bucket on top of the coffee table in the living room, then gone back to the kitchen and put the kettle on. But she didn't want tea. She poured a glass of wine, took a little sip and poured the rest down the sink. She had prowled around the flat but she could not get her father out of her head. She could not see him, not the individual features, but the blurred image was trapped there, like an old, faded photograph.

He had left home never to return when she was four. He'd never seen her grow into a woman. And he had taken her childhood.

The very thought had provoked a rage. She had taken it out on her financial statements, torn them to shreds – and, if the £90,000 that they showed had been there in ten pound notes, she would have shredded them too. She could get more. Just lie back, open your legs and moan for the camera. The louder the better. That's why they liked her, the dirty movie makers. It wasn't her boobs or her smile or her eyes. All the girls had boobs and smiles and eyes.

But there was only one Moaner Lisa. She played it for the microphone. No need for dubbing. And all the Dirty Macs all over the world knew who was making her moan. The guy who bought the movie, the one in the dark room, a Kleenex in one hand and his dick in the other, giving it to Lisa big style. Giving her sexual ecstasy, multiple orgasms, and she was begging him to stop and she was begging him to keep going. Because he was the one. The best. The man. The big man.

And in that back court, beside the bin shelter, she had decided to leave a special sign-off for her next audience. She wouldn't see them – she never did – and they wouldn't see her. But they'd know who she was. She'd give them all the evidence they needed. Proof of her RVI. She'd leave her DNA. So she had taken off the little black dress and sprinkled some cold water on the blood stain. Then she'd put the long leather coat over her naked body and gone back.

Strangely enough, she couldn't find the back court at first. She had to rewind her mind, see the old woman fiddling with the security entrance, hear her say that it wasn't working. Then, as dawn was breaking, Lisa had come upon the right place and the body was there. In front of the dustbins. A perfect setting. So who's rubbish now? The birds were singing. It was going to be a beautiful day. The blood, her own blood, was running down her leg. She took her sanitary towel out of the bin and used it to clean herself. Then she popped it in her handbag. And, with Ms Stiletto, she widened the hole in the temple, hardly any blood because gravity had taken it to the lower parts, then she smeared her menstrual fluid on the tampon (the string end, just to play with their minds) and she put it into Dirty Mac's hole.

They should notice that. And they would know that she'd done it in cold blood.

And it had been all the sweeter for it. Dirty Mac had been better than Knox. Maybe (but she wasn't sure) because she knew him. She'd worked for him, spoken to him, rejected his advances all those years ago when he'd hired her as a piece of meat for a couple of his grubby publicity stunts.

He hadn't deserved it any more – it wasn't that. The old guy had got his just deserts, dirty old bastard. A girl strolling home after a night at The Stand, the comedy club in Woodlands Road – nice night. So just walking up towards Park Circus, minding her own business, thinking about going on to The Corinthian in Ingram Street, have a quiet drink, maybe meet a few human beings. Then he appears from nowhere and asks, 'Doing business, Love?'

Yeah, like you looked like a prossie. Like you'd got fed up hanging about Anderston waiting on a punter, so you'd toddled off a mile or so, just for the walk. It's half past one in the morning and you just fancied a change of scenery. And all the prossies are wearing soft Italian leather coats and £200 shoes, aren't they? And suddenly he's there, in front of you, half past one in the morning, blocking the way. And he says, 'The car's round the back, secluded, perfectly safe.'

Tee-hee, that's what you think.

He really wants to do business. 'How much, Dear? Name the price, without a condom.'

Wants to live dangerously, eh?

You walk through the pen, his hand on your bum. He presses his key-ring and the big car beeps twice and the indicators flash orange twice. You open the passenger door but he wants you in the back and you tell him that's for later and you get in. He runs round the front of the car with strange, stiff steps and gets into the driver's seat.

'How much, Love? I'm clean, honest. Come on, without the condom, yes?'

And you ask him how much he wants it and he says lots and he's pawing your breasts and squeezing your nipples as if he were milking a cow.

Then he changes and he tells you that you are a fucking cow. A dirty slut. And he's going to fucking fuck you. And you say yes, yes, yes. But first, it's to be kissy, kissy. You've pulled your knickers down and you're tugging his head to your crotch. And your hand is at your brooch and Ms Stiletto is out. And he gets more than he bargained for.

It's great at the time, a thrill, a real adrenaline rush. It's the ultimate, really. You've taken a life. You're a killer. And so neatly done, too. Ms Stiletto nipped a bit of bone going in – you felt it jar right up your arm – but it didn't stop her, didn't prevent her doing her job. He spluttered for a second or two, and the feet kicked a couple of times, and then he didn't exist any more. The only thing was now he was your victim. And you were more powerful, more important than the middle-aged, middle-class, wanker. And you leave Ms Stiletto in there for a bit because she's so cosy, she fits so neatly, and you keep his head down there because, well, you just do.

And after a bit you get the sanitary pad out of your handbag and take out Ms Stiletto and clean her off, and you dab the wanker's neck then you push him up on to the driver's seat. You're on your period – again – and you put the sanitary towel down there, to get some of your own blood, careful not to mix it with the wanker's just in case he's got something nasty.

Then you get out, close the door, giving it a good bang, too, because you're not scared. And the danger and the risk make it even better. You throw the bloody pad into the back court and you walk away, not too quickly, just out for a stroll, that's all, a change of scenery, and all the time you're listening, wondering if it's your turn now, if you're going to be caught. But every footstep takes you farther away. It takes you over to Morocco, six months ago, and the smelly old man who dragged you into the lane, who doubled up, when you kicked him in the testicles, and died in the dirt after one kiss from Ms Stiletto.

Sunday, 2 p.m., and Conference Room Three is buzzing.

The orange, plastic seats have been stacked up and put around the walls. Two desks placed together, for The Hunter, up on the wee raised stage. This will be the bridge. They'll get their orders here; report back here.

The troops arriving. Denims and baggy jumpers and trainers. Body language different. Half an erse perched on a desk. Half a rugby scrum; one arm draped over a mate's shoulder. Called in on their weekend off. No fixed hols in the polis. Any day that ends in a y is a working day. Come in soonest. Take it back Wednesday. No, not this Wednesday, there's a fitba match on. We'll owe you a day. Give it back around February 30, eh? One PC wearing a shirt and tie and his mates giving him shit. A dozen of them now, no, thirteen. The WPC with the big bazookas. Got 'em out for the boys, too. Jesus H, could hatch a goose egg in there.

The Hunter asks her and the tie guy to lift his desks off the stage, down to their level. The air is electric, crackling with excitement. You could rub a balloon on it, stick it up on the wall. It's the start of a big one. It's anticipation and expectation. Everything possible. Both murders linked now, CR3 the nerve centre. The Jug said they should move in here. Coordinate it from CR3, he had said, asked the switchboard to put him through to HR. Told them to get on to Facilities, they would need IT and he personally would OK all the OT.

Fuckin algebra Pie-arse squared.

Hunter shuffles off to the side as the Information Technology guys lift floor tiles, expose the intestines, yank out yards of liquorice cables.

How many more terminals will be needed?

Hang on, Hunter is tempted to say, I'll give Strangelove a bell. Say, excuse me, I know this is not customary but the IT guys need to know – how many more guys are you going to make terminal?

The blackboard is brought in and put behind his desks. The troops nudging each other, chuckling about it.

The Hunter's board. Naw, The Hunter's never bored! Solved more murders than Sherlock Holmes. But, Murdo knew, not everyone was a fan. Earlier, when the blackboard was in the corridor, someone had chalked on it 'Hunter's a bloody dinosaur'. Another hand had drawn a line through 'bloody' and replaced it with Hunter's own diluted version, 'bliddy'. Murdo had erased the comment. Didn't care who saw him do it, either. In CR3, there are whispers of a serial murderer. Hunter damps it down.

'That's what my missus does to porridge,' he says. 'She's a bliddy cereal murderer, ha-ha-ha.'

The Jug comes in and pulls him aside. The Jug'll open the meeting himself, if that's all right, just to raise morale.

The troops go stiff and silent.

Digger Burns comes in and stands off to the side. Hunter sidles over. Digger whispers, 'We're tracing all women under the age of thirty who live within a radius of a hundred yards from Mr Macintosh's body. Doing it through the voters' roll, cross-checking with plastic card companies and driving licences. She had to live close.'

Hunter nods his approval. But he knows that the radius will increase to one hundred and fifty yards, then two hundred. Toshie, with a good bead in him, would boff any bint on two legs. Pity that Miss Scotland had knocked him back. Hunter goes back to the bridge. His mobile phone goes off. Plays 'The Billy Boys'. He chokes it but not quickly enough. Fastnett pulls him aside. Tells him that he is working for a catholic force, with a small C, and he would be very disappointed if that was a party tune.

Hunter says, 'I'm not an expert, but I believe it is "The Battle Hymn of the Republic". Y'know, while we are marching to Georgia?'

The Jug is not amused. But he is preparing himself for his big performance. Clearing his throat. Taking flashcards, with keywords for the impromptu speech, out of his inside pocket.

Oh, fuck this, Hunter thinks. I'm for the off.

Lisa had been in her secret store, the one behind the false back in the hall cupboard. It was where she kept her working clothes – the usual stuff – tacky outfits for the French maid, the nurse, the schoolgirl, the red and black basques. Men had such shallow fantasies.

She had been looking for the jockey's racing silks and found them, neatly folded in tissue paper, towards the bottom of a drawer. A rich, emerald green top and tight, sheer white breeches. She had used the gear four years ago, for a classy film shoot on a golden beach on Grand Cayman. The pix were stylish – to be used in a calendar for one of the big tyre companies – and the photographer was gay and fun. They had worked hard for two days, then played for four more. Lisa had made Miss October with her all-time favourite picture, sitting on a rocking horse, a warm wind moulding the sensuous silks to her firm body as the ocean was swallowing the crimson sun.

The jockey outfit was to be used one final time. Lisa had broken her promise to herself that she would not take the job under any circumstances. It had been offered last month and the month before. The money had been doubled – to £3,000 for a maximum of two days – and still she had refused. But today, with her mood turning a darker shade of black, she had relented when her agent phoned. She had to get away, even if it meant going back to Morocco, to the memories of the first time she had to kill. Even if it meant working with Abdul.

The plot (that's what they called it, even in porno movies) was a camel race. Lisa, the vulnerable European girl, lost in the desert and rescued by Abdul, a huge, dark-skinned Arab. If she won the race, he would return her to civilisation. If not, she was to be his sex slave. And, surprise, surprise, she would not win.

Lisa had accepted the contract with one stipulation – she was to fly out tonight. So she had looked out the jockey's silks, to allow her to think of better days while her body was being violated. She had packed the black riding crop, too – it would provide pleasure as it raised angry red weals on Abdul's flanks – and there, at the bottom of her secret drawer, she had found the doctor's coat. It was perfectly ordinary, three-quarter length, white cotton, with one breast pocket for pens and two spacious side pockets, one of which contained a stethoscope.

She had thought, instantly, of Simon, and her mind automatically filled with bitterness. Then she had considered revenge and her whole being tingled with excitement. It was like the instant the shower was turned to ice cold and every nerve end became raw and responsive.

Lisa had put on the coat, casually draped the stethoscope around her shoulders and practised her doctor's walk. Long strides, hurrying but not hurried, economic and efficient, head high, purposeful stare. The stethoscope swinging rhythmically, nuzzling one breast then the other.

Kiss, kiss. Kiss, kiss.

So this was how it felt. Dignity and respect. This was how Simon strutted his stuff in the Royal Infirmary. Saw the common people scuttling to the side of the corridor, clearing the way before him, like the parting of the Red Sea.

Power and authority.

Did he even notice it now? Had he ever? He had been born to it, expected no less. It was his birthright, preordained.

Lisa walked in her doctor's coat and savoured the shiver of life and living. Kiss, kiss. Joy, bliss.

She had not thought herself incapable of this emotion, such heady, all-consuming excitement. It had proved to be a true friend, and faithful, for it had not receded, had not threatened to leave her for more than thirty minutes and, in that time, her plan had formed. It was dangerous and all the better for it.

Her mind was spinning. She felt drunk but not a drop had crossed her lips. Mentally drunk and savouring the giddiness. She must retain her focus. She has a target now. She will concentrate on it, accomplish it, to pay for this wonderful feeling. To make Simon pay for it.

She wanted to get it exactly right. He was worth that, he deserved it. Simon the doctor, Simon the son of the Rachman landlord, Simon the abuser, Simon the father of the child she had aborted.

What a change! What . . . maturity. She could see it clearly now. She could confront her pain, harness it, use it as a weapon. She could think about it now. One day she might even be able to talk about it. She hadn't told anyone. Not Louise and especially not her Catholic mother. Lisa tried not to think of it as her baby. It was Simon's and he didn't want her so he certainly didn't want a child. Wouldn't fit in with the middle-class image. So she had the abortion and she bore the guilt. That was okay. That was the price she had to pay.

There were other costs, too. Like dropping out of nursing, in the final year of studies. Mum had been disappointed but never said it. Good old Mum, always seeing the best in folk. She hadn't been happy at the move into the bar full-time but she had been pleased when her daughter won the big brewery's barmaid of the year picture competition, a pleasure which would have been tarnished had she known that her daughter had to let the photographer feel her up along the way. But that was how you got into the modelling business. And now she was going to Morocco, where she would pick up three grand for lying back and thinking of Scotland. She always worked abroad. They were into heavy make-up. Anyway, her face was not her fortune.

The girls refused to work with Abdul and it wasn't just because he was so big. He was cruel, brutal, but that was what the lucrative Arab market wanted. Filthy camels sweating and spitting. Abdul the Bull. And Moaner Lisa. She would do it now because she had a goal, and the spell abroad would give her time to hone the details of her plan. And what if Abdul bruised her and beat her. Her body would heal. What she needed now was her brain and the delicious flavour of vengeance. Lisa had undergone a change. She was no longer the victim, the one who reacted in a random, haphazard fashion. Now she was in pursuit, choosing her target. It would be planned, premeditated. Already, it felt different. The joy starting with the preparation and all the greater because of the increased risk. There was danger, real danger, from now until it was done.

She stroked the stethoscope and said, 'Oh, Simon, what a treat I have in store for you. Now that I have matured from killer to murderer.'

But first, there were things to do. She went to the kitchen and emptied a drawer in the freezer. She took the packages – chicken breasts, asparagus tips, fish fingers, McCain's oven chips – and put them in a bag for the bin. Then she put on the black leather coat, over the doctor's uniform and set off for the Royal Infirmary.

Sandy Hunter screwed the football coupon into a ball, lobbed it up to the ceiling and met it on the volley on the way down. The timing was a wee bit out and it shot off the edge of his Hush Puppy and belted the old guy in the corner on the bunnet.

'Don't give up the night job,' he said, without raising his eyes from the form guide to the three o'clock race.

Hunter tapped his pipe against his heel and a mucky mess of ash and soggy tobacco tumbled on to the carpet tiles. One of the good things about being in a bookie's is that you make yourself at home. Good old William Hill gave you a square go and you didn't have to break a window for a smoke. The shop, below street level, was like the ferry to Arran. Plastic chairs, wee tables with inlayed ashtrays and all secured to the deck with girders left over from the Forth Road Bridge to prevent theft. Nice colours, too, under normal circumstances. Blue and red, same as Rangers.

Hunter took the baccy pouch from his jacket pocket and loaded his pipe. Then he put a match to it and inhaled deeply. The old guy was using a magnifying glass to study the *Sporting Life* form for the racing from Durbanville, South Africa. Maybe Mandela was a relative.

'How y'doin', Nelson. Any whispers for the three o'clock?'

The other punters, a dozen in all, were into the greyhounds. They could think of nothing better to do. Really, no place they'd rather be.

Hunter took another coupon from the blue plastic container. The old guy spoke without looking up. A good communicator but easy on the verbs.

'Him,' he said, nodding towards a young fella in a red polo shirt. 'Mug. Seventy quid, five to one shot, naewhere. Eighty notes, four to one, stone last. Then a winner, ninety quid at six to four. Last race, hundred and ten on the favourite an' it's still running. Mair money than sense.'

The red shirt's face was vaguely familiar. But that didn't mean a lot. Hunter had clapped eyes on thousands of mugshots of Glasgow's great unwashed over the years.

The match was live on Sky, so he waited for the teams to come up on the big screen just to be sure the star striker was playing. Murdo had called on him this morning, in his big house out in Bothwell. Miss Scotland was still with him and, Murdo said, it looked like they'd gone to extra time and then penalties.

The old guy was using the magnifying glass as he wrote down his selections. Five horses picked and still not coming up for air.

The red shirt was filling in another line. Hunter sidled over. Ninety pounds win, trap five, at four to one. Strange bet. Why not a ton? Hunter ran the face through his memory bank. D for drugs flashed up, then D for Danny Boyd, then J for Jamesie. Yes, it was Jamesie Bogie, one of Danny's legmen. The guy turned and Hunter saw that he could have saved the memory bank batteries. Jamesie embroidered in yellow thread on his shirt. The work of his sweetheart, the bidie-in. What was her name?

Jamesie put on his bet and went to stand in front of the large TV screen.

The race lasted forty-four seconds but the punters got their money's worth, shouting on their selections, cursing at their luck. All except Jamesie. Trap five came in a close second, close but no cigar. Jamesie showed no emotion. And then he did a strange thing. He folded the slip and put it in his hip pocket. To confirm to Danny that the money hadn't been squandered. But Jamesie wouldn't be top of the pops. Hunter did a swift reckoning. He was £125 down on the day. Not a dreadful rate for turning over drugs money but not a good one. He'd never fill the shoes of Larry The Laundryman.

The old guy had finished marking out his line. It looked like Einstein's workings on the theory of relativity. Now he was counting out his stake in coppers.

The teams were out on the park. The camera zoomed in on the shagger. Sure enough, he looked as if he'd scored already. Eyes like piss holes in the snow. Hunter peeled ten twenties off the bankroll in his right trouser pocket. It was a skill he had taught himself, a bit like a magician shuffling a pack of cards with one hand. He always kept his wedge in his right trouser pocket (anyone tried to dip him, the old trouser snake would see them off.) Then he went to the counter. At the last minute, he changed his bet. Turned the two into a five. Five hundred gets you three grand. Sounds much better.

The South African commentator was giving the odds for the next race from Durbanville. Bella's Joy, six to four. Great God in Govan, an omen if ever there was one.

The guys in the shop wrote the names of their selections on betting slips. Some filled in the stake but most held off. Stood, open mouthed, as if waiting for communion, seeking guidance from a higher power. The next show would reflect the cash laid at the track. Which horses didn't look the part in the paddock. Where the smart money was going. The trick was to interpret the signs, get in at the right time and bag the best odds.

Hunter took a betting slip from the wee plastic holder on the wall. Paused as a new show of betting went up on the board.

Bella's Joy, only eleven to eight. Four guys went for it but Hunter held off. Just the bookies at the course trying to con the punters. But, as the horses went into the stalls, the odds were cut again. Five to four now.

The old guy stumbled on his way to the counter and dropped his coins.

'Scramble!' one punter shouted.

'Where's the bride?' asked another.

'Shite,' said the old guy, succinctly.

All human life is here.

Hunter filled in the slip quickly. Fifty quid win. Dammit, odds still five to four. But better than fighting Mike Tyson when he was hungry.

Hunter went to the counter. Three fellas in front of him.

'Last one going in,' says the commentator. 'And they're wading into the favourite. It's down to evens.'

Jamesie, punting the favourite too, is waiting in line. Hunter places his bet, turns around and Jamesie recognises him. The new laundryman goes white, chalk white, and tries to make a run for it. But the Hunter's got him, got the belt at the front of his trousers, yanking it up till the crotch bit in, and he's saying, 'It's no' worth it, Jamesie. Your balls are your balls.'

Zara's eye was crying again, the left one. Sinister or should that be sinistra? Latin had been such a struggle. She had not taken it at school deciding, rightly, that Cicero's exploits were meaningless now and, wrongly, that so was the language. As a result, at nursing college she had been at a disadvantage so she had gone to night school and taken her Higher – got a B pass too – in one year. Calder helped – they had been like that in those days – anything was a joy as long as they were together. But he hadn't been able to do anything with her ibles and ables. She'd had a nasty dose of flu in primary school when her class was doing the ibles and rubella during the ables. The result was that her spelling of the words with those endings was terrable – oh, and so were the ovaries. The measles knocks spots off 'em. Never mind, there were dictionaries and a spellchecker on the computer.

And she had seen more than enough shitty nappies.

Zara was in her office. She took the pack of cigarettes from her desk drawer and extracted one. She didn't need it – of course she didn't need it – didn't even really want it – but she lit it anyway and sucked in the smoke greedily. Three deep breaths before she felt anything and, even then, it was a disappointment. She knew how Calder's clients must feel – taking more and more for less and less – but a girl has to take some chances.

She had found out about her own infertility, ironically, soon after opening the clinic in Springburn. Calder wanted babies – joked that it was a bad ad for a fertility clinic if the patron was childless. Zara wasn't so keen but went through the tests anyway. Her initial reaction to the results – that she was barren – had been anger at being on the pill needlessly for ten years. Who knows what it had done to her cardio-vascular system and there were the scares of blood clots, even years later. But, what was it Calder's alcoholics preached? – something about the serenity to accept the things that cannot be changed.

Zara wiped away another meaningless tear. She closed her eyes and sucked on the cigarette. Nothing. No taste or smoke or pleasure. She stubbed it out and let her mind drift back, to the early days in Springburn. Ten minutes in the little Vauxhall Nova from their neat, semi-detached bungalow in Bishopbriggs. Calder up and off bright and early, doing his thing for the NHS during the day then back to the clinic, a change of shirt, better tie and his private work at night. Zara saw him Tuesday and Thursday nights. The other evenings she was with the refugees or on a soup run. Calder called it a fridge door marriage – they communicated via notes left under the magnetic Mercedes on the fridge door. Good Lord, they had argued once (on paper) about there being no milk! Kept the dispute running for three days before Calder yielded and brought in some of that sickly-sweet long-life stuff. Now, on the rare occasions when she took tea or coffee, she had it naked. That was a better ad for the clinic.

Saturdays for the Carmichaels had been sacrosanct. A good meal, lots of wine and taxis both ways. They became a recognised couple about town – young, intelligent and interesting – and the invitations to dinner parties became increasingly frequent. They had taken hols in the sun – three times a year, Greece more often than not – where they had just lounged around and read trashy thrillers. It was a good life with the promise of even better times ahead. But, somewhere along the line, they had lost focus. Lost their way. Ended up on this road.

Who had been driving? Zara blamed Calder but she knew that she had been in the passenger seat. Maybe not navigating, but she could see the way they were going and she could have got out at any time. It was too late now, of course, she was caught up in the momentum. All she could do was navigate a safe passage and to make sure that they got out safely. Or (for the first time she confronted a matter that had been lurking at the back of her mind) that she got out safely.

How she longed to unburden herself of the big house in Busby. It had been the worst decision she had ever made. Or was made for her. They had jumped in, bought at the wrong time, when property prices were at their peak. But Calder had wanted it so much. They put down a £70,000 deposit, £42K profit from the little bungalow and £28K scratched together from their savings. It left them stony-broke but at least, Calder said, they had a mortgage of £200,000 to show for it! They had ignored the surveyor's caution, promised the bank they'd get the faults put right, but they never had. Just papered over the cracks.

It had started so well. The location was ideal – on the outskirts of the city but secluded. Discrete and discreet. Those receiving treatment at Springburn had travelled – and many affluent clients had been attracted – and the fertility clinic had grown.

Calder was in his element, trying all kinds of revolutionary treatments with the abusers. More failures, many more, than successes but changing lives, he said. Saving lives, he said. And to do more, to do better, he needed space. The extensions were his idea. You must speculate to accumulate, he said. And so they accumulated a second mortgage. The bank was delighted to throw another £90K at them. Now they had to bring in £3,000 a month just for possession of the bricks and mortar. The matching Mercs swallowed up £1,200 – and they were only leased. So they needed more than £50,000 a year – after tax – and then there was heating, lighting – oh, yes, and something to eat to keep body and soul together. But, Calder said, they had to look successful. Think big and you'll be big, he said, and left Zara to take care of the little things. Like the bills.

The sums simply did not add up. All of their income came from the clinics. The fertility clinic turned over £220,000 last year. It had two permanent staff – a sister from Rottenrow who had retired early and a thrusting whizz-kid – and they had to be taken care of very well. Each had been happy to receive the week's extra holiday (wouldn't do to allow them a sniff of the extra curricular activities in the theatre and intensive care suite) and the unexpected bonus of double pay. Zara had to keep them sweet. The last thing she wanted was to have to recruit someone new, someone who might ask unanswerable questions or start to look for the wrong things in the right places. Wages, pension contributions, private health plans, etc. gobbled up £60K and running costs doubled that sum. The residue – even after the bloody Chancellor of the Exchequer took his thousands of pounds of flesh – was handsome. As a stand-alone business it was successful and the medium- to long-term outlook was one of solid growth and profitability. But it wasn't stand-alone. It was joined at the hip to Calder's clinic. And last year it had run at a loss of £30,000.

The books didn't show it, of course. Zara made sure of that. Zara and another of Calder's pals, an accountant who had no scruples about copying her fabricated figures into his ledger as long as he was paid £10,000 – untraceable, of course – for doing so. His returns showed a profit of £45K for Zara and a loss of only £5K for Calder. Staffing was the biggest single cost at his clinic. A permanent workforce of nine – four registered psychiatric nurses and five assistants. They worked three eight-hour shifts, one of each on duty. And there was the added costs of bringing in casual labour to cover sickness and holidays. The majority of patients were young addicts – mostly drug addicts and solvent abusers, although there was a sixteen-year-old nymphomaniac there at the moment – and they contributed a big, fat zero. The paying customers were big, fat middle-aged alcoholics, although, fortunately, the number of wealthy drug addicts was increasing. Zara, when she did the figures, reduced the numbers of dependants and inflated those of sad fat cats. But the prognosis for the clinic was bad, terminal, and sooner rather than later.

So the income for the fiscal year ending March, 2003, for Mr and Mrs Carmichael – that well-to-do, highly respected, highly successful couple-about-town – was £70,000. And all this for just twelve hours a day, seven days a week, fifty-two weeks a year before tax, of course. Subtract the mortgages, the accountant's fiddle, the lease of the cars and you were left with £10,000. Or, to put it another way, just about enough to keep the Lady Bloody Zara moored at Loch Lomond. Oh, yes, lest we forget, as an anniversary present in the spring (the anniversary of moving to Busby),

Calder had decided on the conservatory. Another £15K for a see-through colander.

So they now existed by breaking the law. The Kosovar drop and swop – the one-off, principled decision to suit all parties – had been only the first of many deals over the edge of the law.

Mr Rich the Second had made his desire absolutely clear. Mrs Rich wanted a baby and he would pay any price, any price, he emphasised, to get one for her. She was barren and the adoption agencies had rejected them because he was fifty-two years old, had suffered two heart attacks and was unlikely to be around by the time a child started school, never mind university. But he had a lot of money and little morality. He suggested that Zara might know a couple, through her charity work perhaps, who would be happy to think that their new-born would be getting a real chance in life in a loving home . . . And that was how Zara had entered the baby-smuggling business.

Young Master Rich would never know that he was Albanian. There were risks (though they were not great) and the bank was knocking on the door of the big house . . . So it was a straightforward business deal – buy a child for £500 (a sum of money its family could hardly contemplate), pay £2,500 to have it smuggled into the country and sell it for £10,000. While the negotiations were being carried out, Mrs Rich the Second went through the sham with the pregnancy bumps. She had made only one stipulation. She had to have a Caesarian wound. She had to suffer – she needed a scar. Zara had not cut deeply – no sense in tempting fate – and it had proved to be a wise precaution. Infection had set in and the woman had to be detained at the clinic for five days. She had, indeed, experienced pain and her husband had his anxiety – so much so that he had banned anyone from visiting mother and baby. The little boy was at school now and doing well. He would never know his dad, the one who had purchased him, who had died from a heart attack two years ago. Nor would he ever know his history and the fact that he had a biological father – and mother – in Albania. He really was better off without them. The woman scratched a living for her three remaining children. The man had run off as soon as he got the money.

A world apart, Zara scratched a living to maintain the façade of success and respectability in the Busby empire. To do so, she followed the tried and tested principles of the British Empire. She stole and plundered from the needy in poor countries. Her network of charities and contacts with refugees and asylum seekers put her in a unique position of absolute control. There was no shortage of babies for sale. But she had to wait for an approach from suitable buyers. She couldn't very well advertise, could she?

Nevertheless, over the past five years, she had brought eight little bundles of joy into the country. And they in turn had brought – God bless their little cotton socks – a profit not far removed from £100K to help to keep the Carmichael Folly in existence. Zara did not carry out any drop and swops nowadays – they were too risky, too easy for a penitent dropper to kick up a stink – but the four arrangements which she had presided over had been worth just over £20K.

The charity work had opened up a fresh and lucrative field. The possibilities had been raised by Sørensen, the anaesthetist, whose half-brother would die without a kidney transplant. Sørensen had identified and negotiated with the donor. Money for her and a business deal for the Carmichaels. They were to provide and equip the operating theatre. He sought and bought the expertise – medical experts without morals. The transaction had cost him £50,000. Each member of The Ramblers received £5,000, Clive got £7,000 and the Carmichaels collected £28,000. Zara's delivery suite had much of the apparatus necessary to maintain life in an emergency, but more than £18,000 still had to be spent to equip the theatre and a recovery room. As a single enterprise, it was not worthwhile. But, as a starter for ten . . .

Sir Randolf Jedburgh had jumped at the chance. His liver was in a dreadful condition and, because of his rare blood group, the chance of a suitable donor becoming available in the very near future were infinitesmal. And, without one, he would be dead in six months, maybe sooner. Unless . . . Zara's charities abroad, as a matter of course, carried out health checks on the wretched people who sought out help. Blood was drawn from each one and, under the guise of a study into genetic abnormalities, those of Randy's blood group underwent detailed examination. Two years had passed without success but a month ago the perfect match appeared. There was only one problem. The body which held the liver was not a refugee from an impoverished country. It was a Norwegian, an employee, one of Zara's lieutenants currently working in Afghanistan. There was, though, some consolation. The young man was an orphan, an only child too. And so, in Calder's terminology, he was NM_2. Neither missed nor mourned. It was as important a qualification as a perfect match. The donor must leave behind no one to ask awkward questions.

Randy had paid in advance. The last cheque, handed over at the party on the Lady Zara on Thursday, brought the total to £100,000. Payback should begin on Wednesday, the day the young Norwegian was due to visit Busby.

Zara had told him on the phone that she had received good reports about his work and had a special role which only he could fulfil. He was not to tell anyone. It was to be a surprise.

116

Zara had lit a cigarette without realising it. Her eye had stopped weeping but the spiral of smoke aggravated it and started it off again. After four puffs, she stubbed out the cigarette. She was bored, at a loose end. She needed to do something. Not quite sure of what, she rose, left her office by the side door and walked round the perimeter of the building. The bitter autumn wind bit through her blouse making her shiver. Winter was not far off and, she realised, that she welcomed its arrival. A sudden snowfall last year had cut off the clinic from civilisation for three days. A few hours, now, with nothing to do would be welcome. Hibernating for a few months would be heavenly. On a whim, she turned back and headed for the surgical unit. Perhaps a glance at the recuperating Joseph Paborsky would raise her spirits. It had gone well for Josef. They had been pleasantly surprised. His old body had withstood the operation and there was no indication of any trouble. He, too, had paid £100,000.

'But,' he said, 'it is only the deposit. I will pay the price when I die, when I meet my Maker.'

The skipper is at the bridge and the engine room has stoked up a full head of steam. The Jug, the Admiral of the Fleet, had addressed the coppers in Committee Room Three, his flashcards littered with nautical analogies, then, because of the sudden disappearance of Detective Inspector Alexander Hunter, had handed the wheel over to Digger Burns. On Hunter's return, Burns had stood down after giving his gaffer a full explanation of the tasks and duties of the team of thirteen charged with finding the killer of Andrew Knox and Philip Macintosh.

Hunter mingled with his troops, a joke here, a playful punch on an arm there. Their task was damn near hopeless – they would never track or trick Strangelove – but they didn't know that. Murdo watched Hunter's every move, like a doting puppy. He left the lad till last, then put an arm around his shoulders and drew him to the side.

'Been watching you,' Hunter said, 'and I'm impressed. Now, back-slapping's over, it's arse-kicking time.'

He paused, just long enough to share a smile, then pressed on. 'Tell me, the Press Fund Ball, how're you getting on there?'

He knew how difficult a job it would be to track down all those who had been present. He had been at the ball two years ago – at Toshie's table in fact – and had seen the amount of the hard stuff that was put away. It had cost a fortune. To go for a pee you had to pass the bar. And all the hacks leaning on it. Including effin raffle tickets, the night had cost him about £40. He had claimed it on expenses but he had to kick up stink to get it.

117

Networking, he had told The Jug. Could have stung him for £35 for the ticket, too, but the bugger would probably have asked for a receipt and that could have been a bit embarrassing since Toshie had paid for it.

Murdo and a Woman Police Constable had been left to their own devices. It was a daunting task – to conduct preliminary interviews with those who attended the function and report to Burns anyone of interest. They had carried out the operation with efficiency and economy, so much so that, within thirty hours, they had been in contact with one hundred and eighty-two of the one hundred and eighty-five people who had attended the function. Two were on holiday – in Gran Canaria and were due to telephone at any moment – and the body of Philip Macintosh was still on a marble slab in the mortuary. The coppers had obtained the guest list and broken it down to eight groups. Six media groups, Toshie's PR company and 'others'. They had prepared a number of questions and taken about two hundred photostats. Then they had arranged interviews with the guests at their place of work. Hunter knew that they must have been particularly persuasive to get shift workers, especially in the dailies, out of their beds and into their offices, but they had done so.

The result, when the wheat was separated from the chaff, was that Toshie had left the ball alone.

Murdo said, 'He was seen leaving alone by . . .' He went for his notebook.

Hunter said, 'We'll get down to details later. Just the broad brush at the moment, lad.

Murdo continued, 'Well, three people saw him leave alone at 2 a.m., give or take ten minutes.'

The young cop paused, wondering he was entitled to offer an opinion. Hunter said, 'And your thoughts?'

Enthused, Murdo went on, 'It's possible that he had a pre-arranged meeting, a rendezvous, with a woman, the woman. So he would have known her, but not wanted to be seen with her. An affair, you know?'

Good lad, Hunter thought. He had expected Burns to be on to that first. Toshie's partner, the guy who downed brandy and port as if it was Ribena, was adamant that there was no one, 'well, no one special', in Toshie's life. He was more a man for one-night stands – or one-night lays. Once bitten, twice shy, the guy had said, reminding Hunter that Toshie had been married before and had the aliment to prove it. Besides, he said, Toshie didn't mind a bit of the other but, apart from that little weakness, he was a happily married man.

Murdo had collected photographs taken at the ball, Toshie in some of them, everyone identified and accounted for, but nothing unusual. He also had the film from a camcorder. Again, a sweeping array of the cast but no indication of a villain.

Hunter said, 'All the women accounted for? Paired off or there with pals kind of thing?'

Murdo said, 'Yes, the ticket holders anyway, all accounted for. But at one stage, six young women got in. Well, they were invited in. They'd been at a hen night – one of them getting married on Friday. They were on their way home – singing and larking about in the street. Two young reporters heard them and brought them in. I've tracked down the bride-to-be – seems she was sober – and she says that they all left together after about ten minutes. I don't see why she should lie but I can follow it up, speak to them all, if you like.'

Hunter told him to leave it for now.

The young cop went on, 'I've seen one bouncer, one to interview yet – gone to Aberdeen to see a sick father and due back in Glasgow tomorrow. We could get the police up there to see him, though . . .'

Hunter shook his head. 'Naw, they're just a bunch of sheep-shaggers anyway.'

He paused, to allow the young islander to enjoy the irony, then continued, 'You're doing fine. Good work. Now, tell me this. Behind you, the bird with the big bazookas – don't turn around, they'll have your eye out! – what's her name.'

Murdo said, 'Jet black hair, shoulder-length, deep brown eyes?'

'Christ I don't know. I never got above her boobs.'

Murdo showed a remarkable talent for sideways keeking. Then he said, 'It's WPC O'Shaunnessey, Aine. Like 'on yer' bike. It's Irish.'

Hunter said, 'Naw, you're pulling my plonker.'

The young cop smiled again. Hunter told him to concentrate on the fancy woman theory. Then he thanked the lad and allowed him to return to his duties.

Hunter went back to the bridge. Burns, who had known him a long time, had never seen him so hands-off, so distant. He told Hunter about Macintosh's ex-wife. The divorce, she had volunteered, had been bitter. But that was eight years ago. There were no children, the aliment was paid into the bank on time and there was a new man in her life. They had been to a dinner party on the night of the ball and had stayed overnight with their hosts. Six witnesses to prove it.

Hunter was there but not really listening.

Burns asked, 'Everything okay?'

Hunter thought of lying but decided only to be economical with the truth.

He said, 'It's a strange one, Digger. This time you walk in the dead men's footprints.'

Burns was visibly surprised. It was Hunter's way of telling him he was in charge.

Hunter paused, to ensure that his meaning was understood, then he went on, 'The new lad – Murdo – he's good. Give him his head. Never mind the Knox case. It's stone cold. Concentrate on Toshie. I'm . . . I'll be around.'

That said, he left the bridge. He said a few words to Aine and she followed him out of the room.

'I'll never remember O'Thingesy, so it can be Constable or Aine. You pick?' Hunter said.

'No, Sir, you pick.'

Jesus H, another bright one. And ballsy too. Even when he tried to get along with women he kept effin it up.

He said, 'One–nil, to you, Aine.'

She had smiled to let him know that he was forgiven. They had gone into the general office, which was quiet on this Sunday evening, and she had logged on to HOLMES, the computer database which collated information from police forces throughout the UK. It had no listings for similar Strangelove killings or stabbings. Hunter knew this because he had checked already. But he needed someone with expertise and time to carry out another task. He could not get the Carmichaels out of his mind. Aine had taken an electronic peek at them already, after his evening on their yacht, and she had found some interesting stuff about Zara's charity work. But he needed more. He needed a loose thread so he could pick at it to see what lay underneath when the fabric unravelled.

He thought of Calder Carmichael's favourite patient, the boy who can remember his dreams.

She asked Hunter to log on under his own name, said he had higher-level access, skeleton keys to open more doors.

He said, 'Matthew Whittle, W-H-I-T-T-L-E, unusual name. Aged, roughly, sixteen. A patient at The Carmichael Clinic, Busby, for about two years. I want a parent, relative, his GP – somebody from his past. Think you can do that?'

'I can try, Sir,' she said and her tone told him that he'd effed it up again without trying. It also told him that she was confident of turning something up.

Something about Strangelove had been bothering him. A woman's thing. He'd thought about asking Bella but it was difficult. They didn't discuss such matters. But he decided that, since he was getting on so well with Aine, he'd ask her.

He said, 'The murders were twenty-one days apart, right?'

She realised that she was meant to say right and said it.

Hunter went on, 'But she was carrying sanitary things, towels, both times. Is that . . .' he searched for the right word and settled for 'normal'.

Aine told him about the menstrual cycle, and how some women could set their watches by it. Hunter looked so earnest that she tried a joke.

'It's the only way we can have sex without having babies.'

He was baffled and she wished that she had not started. But she had so she was forced to continue. 'Catholics, you know, there are days when conception is less likely? That's the rhythm method.'

'Oh,' he said, 'I see.'

But he didn't. He got his contraception at the barbers. 'Something for the weekend, Sir?' The last packet of three he'd put in the bedside cabinet had best before the millennium stamped on it.

Aine decided to explain it slowly and without all the laughs.

'It's possible that the murders took place when the killer was having a period. If the curse had just finished but she wasn't sure, not absolutely sure, when Knox was killed on September 21st she would have been carrying a towel with her. But she shouldn't be back on until October 19th, five days after the second murder.

'But she might not be regular. A lot of women aren't.'

She stopped and did not speak again until she was happy with the idea which had sprung into her mind.

'Maybe she was having her period when she killed Knox. Used a spare towel to mop up, that's all. And she liked the idea and decided it would be her trademark. Like the Yorkshire Ripper, you know – contemptuous. So she kept a tampon, a soiled one, at the ready for her next victim. You know, here's one I made earlier.'

Hunter was pondering the possibilities when his mobile phone went off. 'The Billy Boys' and no mistake. He had Aine and not Georgia on his mind.

It was Boyson on the phone, *The Herald*'s crime reporter, except he wasn't called that nowadays. He was Home Affairs Correspondent. 'Just ask me if you want to know who's shagging who,' Boyson said when the grand title was thrust upon him. Okay guy, Boyson. He was the one who had first used the nickname of The Hunter. The other hacks had adopted it quickly and this had done no harm at all during Sergeant Hunter's bid for

121

promotion to Inspector. Boyson boasted about it, bless him, and he had forgotten, either conveniently or genuinely, that the seed of the idea had been sown in his mind over seven or eight pints with – The Hunter.

Hunter said, 'How're you doin, you old bugger you.'

Sarcasm dripped from every word that Boyson spoke. 'Working on the big story, the one they'll all be talking about tomorrow. No, not the murder – much bigger than that – well, it is to the wankers who run this place now. I'm on the case of the missing violinist, Josef Paborsky. Apparently he is treating his public with contempt and *The Herald*'s going to bring him to book.'

Boyson had been trying to track him down and kept hitting brick walls. Until this afternoon.

He said, 'I shared about a bottle of vodka with his agent – wee poofy guy – in the Hilton. Cost a bloody fortune, too. And he said – he was well-pished, mind you – but he said that they had been betrayed. Somebody called Sarah had betrayed them. And the poor wee pooftah cried his eyes out.'

Hunter was intrigued. Sarah or Zara? He said that he would make a few calls and get back to Boyson.

Aine was busy on the computer. She had accessed the Health Ministry records. But no sign of a Matthew Whittle anywhere. No medical card number, no general practitioner, no details of any medical treatment. And no record that he was a patient at Carmichael's clinic. She was not surprised. He would be floating in the ether, perhaps doing laps between The Mound and Holyrood, waiting for someone to call him into his electronic blocks. But for now, the boy, to all intents and purposes, did not exist. He had no past and no present.

But it was his future that worried The Hunter. There was something about the boy's eyes.

Aine was trying to get in to the Education Department.

Hunter's phone went again but he killed it. 'Sorry about that', he said.

She said, 'It's okay – mine plays 'The Fields of Athenry'.'

He said, 'Call it a draw, then? One–all.'

She said, 'That's better than your mob are doing today.'

'Eh?' he said.

'Livi are winning one–nil.'

'Beauty.'

'Eh?' Her turn.

'Some things are more important than football.'

He left her to get on with her work. He did not know why but he knew that he had to go to Busby, to the strange set-up that was the Carmichaels' empire. He did not know what was going on there but he knew it was something. And he also knew, as sure as God made little green apples, that he would find out. The dark cloud that had hung over him was not exactly disappearing but there were hints of light at the edges. The face of the fragrant Zara flashed into his mind and he mouthed three words.

I'll catch you.

As he was leaving the office, a constable was taking a report on a missing person. An agitated young man, an asylum seeker living in Sighthill, was explaining in broken English that his friend's brother was missing. He had been gone for five days and they were worried.

'Dead worried,' he said.

The man, quite obviously, was a linguist.

Hunter changed his mind as left the copshop and pointed the Vectra out on to the motorway, heading east. He wasn't up to a contest with Zara Carmichael or her smarmy husband, Calder. He was off form but still fit enough to settle a score with another woman, Mary Knox. He would take her right out of the game. Bitch. Getting her influential friends to lean on The Jug. And he had rolled over, kicked his legs in the air, asked her to tickle his tummy. And he had promised her that he would delay, for as long as possible, linking her husband's death with Toshie's.

'No need to add to her suffering,' The Jug had said.

He added that there was no need to show all their cards to the killer. Keep an ace up the sleeve. He was right about that but wrong about the Widow Knox. She was not snow white – Hunter felt it in his water. She was hiding something, telling porkies, and she was vulnerable because of it.

The Vectra was in the slow lane of the motorway, which appeared to have been constructed by a sadist with shares in car repair companies. Traffic, quite naturally, joined from left at Charing Cross but, within a couple of hundred yards, there was a fresh influx, this time from the right. Vehicles jockeyed for position, some having to cross four lanes within half a mile to leave at the right, for the Royal Infirmary and the High Street, and at the left, for Springburn and the commuter belt of Bishopbriggs and Lenzie. It was Le Mans without the skill. Hunter took his pipe from his mouth and sat it in the pocket at the driver's door. He'd need all his wits about him to negotiate this lunacy. He sat behind a petrol tanker judging, rightly, that no-one would mess with it. A mile farther on, he took the Springburn exit, on to a good dual carriageway, sat at a steady 50 mph and allowed his mind to wander.

Until the astonishing emergence of Strangelove, Mary Knox had been number one suspect for killing her husband. And a good shout it had been, too. She had the opportunity, the time and, he was sure that if he delved deeply enough, he would uncover a motive. It had been a loveless marriage. Hunter knew that because it was like his own. By her own admission, the last time she had seen her husband alive was on the morning of Thursday, September 19th. She had found his body, in his car behind his office in Glasgow, just after 4 a.m. on the Saturday. Now even Bella would be on the blower if he was AWOL for more than twenty-four hours.

Hunter skirted Kirkintilloch and turned the Vectra up into the foothills of the Campsies. Jesus H, he had forgotten about the game. He turned the radio on. It took three long minutes before the commentator told him that Livingston were still leading one–nil, bossing the game and only fifteen minutes left. Hunter fished his pipe out of the door pocket and did his trick with the matches. Tapped the box open, extricated a match, then, with deft hands, brought it to life off the sandpaper and put the flame to the tobacco. He puffed three times, like an old steam engine, then clamped his teeth on the pipe stem. The Lord smiles on the righteous and helps them that help themselves. Mr William Hill was looking after three thousand pound for him. American Express – that'll do nicely. Life was not all bad. It would be a nice wee hump – £3K – at least he would not have to exercise the old grey matter on how to extort some of his own money from Bella's clutches. He remembered, too, that he had £50 on Bella's Joy, the favourite, at Durbanville, at evens. It seemed small potatoes now but, hey, he wasn't proud. The dame at the counter wasn't bad looking. Not great but not half-bad. He'd collect the dosh from the fitba and give her the cuddy line to herself. Provided she agreed to take him out for a drink. Seemed reasonable, eh? And a pretty safe bet that he'd score, too.

Hunter opened the sunroof – Bella called it his chimney – and settled down to enjoy the drive. He was into the hills now, climbing, narrow road, and sharp bends. Livi still in charge, keeping possession and defending in numbers. The Teddy Bears huffing and puffing but getting nowhere. A bird rose from the long, wild grass at the roadside, a pheasant or a partridge – some big brown bugger anyway – and went off to do whatever big birds do. It's okay, really, the countryside. To drive through with your chimney open and your pipe going. But not to live in. Leave it to the birds.

Hunter becomes aware of a change. It's the radio commentator, shouting over the cheering crowd. An equalising goal. And, just to rub salt in the wound, scored by Miss Scotland's Italian paramour.

* * * * *

124

Lisa had seen his kids tonight on the telly. A still picture, grainy, because it was blown up, the big little faces had no definition. They looked like something off the *X Files*.

Lisa was intrigued about her reaction. Guilt? No, but perhaps she should feel guilty. A killer should, really. But she didn't and that was that. She certainly didn't feel sorry. Well, maybe a little, for the kids. It was nothing to do with them. It wasn't their fault. They didn't pick their father. She had that in common with them. Come to think of it, she had quite a lot in common with them. Dirty Mac had been in charge of them all. Or he thought that he was. He'd let the kids down but they were too young to know it. And he had treated Lisa like a plaything. Or he'd tried to, anyway.

Dirty Mac must have taken the photograph himself, in the back garden of his posh house. The wee boy, in Pampers, crawling towards his mum who was pushing his big sister on a swing.

Lisa was in the airport, waiting for the call to board the shuttle for Heathrow. She had been passing the time, playing her departure game. Who are they and where are they going? There was the old dear, the blue rinse granny, who had shoved her husband under a bus to get the insurance money and was going down to Harley Street for a sex change operation. She'd turned away from the telly when the picture was flashed up on the screen. Couldn't look at it, couldn't handle it. She'd turned her head quickly, to the side a bit, as if she'd been slapped on the face. Lisa saw her hand come up a little, to ward it off, to push away reality. As if the image she feared so much wasn't already burned into her memory bank. As if her reaction would make any diff to anybody. Who the fuck did she think she was? She wasn't a player, not even a spectator. But now she was wringing her hands, washing the blood from them.

The priest had done that with his hands when Lisa started to tell him. Only three, younger than Dirty Mac's girl, and Lisa had tried to explain why she didn't want her mother to go to church. And it wasn't for herself, it was for Louise. But it didn't make any diff. The priest has done his Pontius Pilate.

The young couple in the departure lounge, they had been interesting. Brother and sister, on their way to the deep south of America to get married. When the picture had appeared on the telly, the young woman had snuggled up close. Gripped her brother's hand – oh, help me, save me and deliver us from evil. The brother, at least, had the good grace to look embarrassed, helpless even. Lisa liked that. It showed an honesty. Maybe he didn't realise what was going on. Come to think of it, he did look a bit daft. The result of inbreeding, perhaps? But at least he didn't pretend to be something he was not.

125

Lisa couldn't be bothered making up a story for the face in the suit. Nothing could be more outrageous than the truth. A union man, up the workers, right up them – now he was an MP, obsessed by his own self-importance. He was telling everyone with earshot that the TV station was in trouble. He would make sure that it paid for it. Take it up with the authorities himself, he would.

Lisa had been surprised that there had been no mention of the other guy. Not a dickie bird about Knox. Strange – she had left her signature. Surely the cops couldn't be that thick. Or was it just another middle-class mafia cover-up? Had they closed ranks to protect one of their own?

It was strange seeing the picture of the two kids, fatherless now, and their mum, a widow and younger than Lisa. But you will understand, in time, Mrs Mac, that you're better off without him. He didn't love you. He merely deceived you. Kept you and the kids as accessories to match his lifestyle. And you might not have lasted. He'd ditched the first wife when she went out of fashion. Just cut his losses and taken out a new model.

And Dirty Mac's wife, younger than Lisa. But she'd do all right. He'd have plenty of insurance. The big house would be paid off and, after what was not an indecent interval, there would be another rich bastard who'd marry her and take on the ready-made family. The kids would be okay.

Lisa knew what it was like when your dad disappeared. There one night when you went to bed and gone in the morning, never to return. And they'd be able to ask about him. Their mum wouldn't say, 'Look he's away, that's all. Don't ask again. We won't talk about it again. Ever'.

Dirty Mac's kids would survive. Folk would say to them, too, 'You're young, you'll survive.'

It would be better for them than it had been for Lisa and Louise. No shortage of dosh in their family. No shared baths because Mum couldn't afford to put the water heater on twice. And, when they were old enough, they'd be told that their dad had been killed. He loved them very much and would have given them the world. He hadn't left them. He didn't chose to be someplace else. He just got killed, that's all.

It wasn't that easy with Lisa's father. And she had been his special one. More than Louise, who was just a baby. Dad loved Lisa. He told her, said she was special and he loved her more than anything in the world. But he'd gone away and never returned. Lisa had heard something that night, not a row, not a big fight anyway when they yelled, Mum and Dad. It was more loud whispers, angry secrets.

Lisa had tried to tell the priest what happened when Mum went to church. It had started just with Sundays. Then it was Tuesdays and Thursdays too, when Mum was at the women's group. Dad would come into the bedroom and wake her up and touch her and she'd have to do it to his thing. And not to tell anyone. Nobody in the whole world. It was their secret. Because he loved her more than anything in the world. But he didn't because he went away. And she didn't know what she'd done wrong. But it must have been something because Mum looked at her funny. And now Dad didn't love her and Mum didn't either. So she must be bad . . .

That's what she thought then and that's what she knew now. But at least now she could do something about it. Now it wasn't the little girls who were punished. Now it was the dads.

Zara fingered the cigarette packet again but decided against it. She determined to kick the habit for good. At least she would have something on which to blame her moods. Not that she needed anything. Not after Paborsky's death.

She had seen it with her own eyes, got to the surgical unit seconds earlier, looked through the window and marvelled at how peaceful the maestro looked and then – mayhem. Flashing lights. Buzzers. Hubner almost breaking the door off its hinges to get into the room. Zara stock still, transfixed, then her professionalism kicked in. Preparing a syringe of adrenaline. Hubner putting it straight into the heart. Nothing. Clive arriving, trying to kick-start the old boy with the paddles. Nothing. No chance. No hope.

Nothing.

He had just stopped breathing. That's what they said – the so-called experts – he took one breath and failed to take another. No warning, no indication of any deterioration in his condition. Off the ventilator, apparently doing well, for four hours. One moment he was alive and the next he was dead. Nothing could change that. Now it was a case of covering their tracks.

Clive had stayed behind in theatre to dismember the body for collection tonight by Junkie Jed, Mr PetCrem himself. And the world's most brilliant violinist would be reduced to ashes with Shep the labrador and bunny rabbits.

The Ramblers had been notified of the loss in a phone call. They were on their way back from the Campsies.

Calder and Hubner had gone to the Hilton Hotel to break the news Patrik. And to keep tabs on him. Poor Patrik. He would be heartbroken. He had lost his lover and his hero. It was Calder who had put into words what they had all feared – said that Patrik might 'do something silly'.

Like go to the police.

127

Hubner had packed his bags. His immediate task was to make sure that Patrik left the UK. He had a sister in Paris and that would do for starters, but anywhere abroad was good. And there would still be more than enough to deal with in this country.

There would be Sir Ranulf Jedburgh for starters. Poor Randy. His cirrhotic liver would take another alcoholic pounding when he heard that his transplant would probably have to be cancelled. He would have to be told about Paborsky and that would not exactly inspire confidence. But Zara thought that Randy would risk it. Not much of a risk, really. What did he have to lose? Six months of continuing deterioration and an agonising death against a new life with a new liver. Or to go to sleep on the operating table. To sleep, perchance to dream.

But it all depended on Patrik. If he wasn't too troublesome – not too much of a risk – Hubner might be able to return to the clinic. Randy would need his skills. The Ramblers had three more days before they had to return to their various hospitals.

6

''Sup wi' your face?'

Joe put a fresh mug of sweet, milky tea in front of Hunter. Not his favourite customer at 9 a.m. Not his favourite customer at any time. The cafe owner knew that all was not well when the cop put £1 on the table, but he lifted the coin smartly and made a beeline for his kitchen whistling 'Money Makes the World Go Round'.

Hunter had phoned Digger Burns to say he would be late. Digger, sotto voce, had said that the Chief Constable was looking for him, expecting him. Digger, good man that he was, had told The Jug that he believed his gaffer was visiting Toshie's widow. Horseshit, of course, because Hunter doesn't talk to the victim's relatives. The other gaffers do. All of them younger than Hunter, the new breed, Superintendents and DCIs setting the pace and the programme. They say that it's important to see the victims – to hear the sobs and dry their tears. It gives them focus – helps them to go that extra mile – reminds them why they must apprehend the perpetrator. And they get Brownie points for it in the new caring-sharing, touchy-feely police force.

The Jug, in one of the meetings that Hunter had been forced to attend, said that it 'was a vital element in setting the tone and texture for members of the public and junior police persons'.

Jesus H, he had actually said police persons. It was no longer enough, in Jugspeak, to turn up at a funeral in uniform. They had to be seen to be part of the grieving process, to be 'good human beings'. He had gone on to bump his gums about compassion, professionalism and motivation. Hunter had his own way of motivating coppers who needed to be reminded why they had to catch the bad guys – he kicked their arses till their noses bled. He didn't need any of The Jug's crap. He just needed to stay hard. It's the way he does it – the old-fashioned way.

Bella had asked him on Saturday night if he was 'all right'. She had noticed the change in him. She was waiting up for him, even made him toast and scrambled egg. Didn't quibble about The Drouth's inflated bill for the

Vectra. But she asked if he was all right and said that he was not his usual 'grumpy self'. She'd tried to make it an affectionate joke. He had wanted to respond to her, like the old days, but he just couldn't. And he heard himself apologising, giving her bullshit about the pressure of work.

But the truth was that the fun, the joy, had gone from their marriage. He was to blame for it – well mostly, anyway. Hadn't worked at it, wasn't that what they said? But that didn't mean that he still wasn't fond of Bella. Fond of her? What would Calder Carmichael, the shrink, make of that? But the sad fact was that the Hunters' marriage had changed, perhaps irretrievably, while the partners had been busy doing their own thing. They put a face on it – especially when the kids were about – but they remained together because that was the easier option. It was now an arrangement – I'll do this and you do that and when we have to we'll do it together.

The police force had changed, too. And Hunter had been too busy to change with it. The new breed had been doing meetings, going to the seminars and he'd thought it was bullshit. He'd been getting on with finding the bad guys. That was what he was paid for. That was the job. But they'd changed it. The Toby Jugs of this world, the ones who couldn't lace The Hunter's drinks when it came to solving a murder, they'd changed the rules. And nobody had told him. They must have sat one morning in The Jug's office, nibbling Belgian biscuits and drinking decaffeinated coffee out of china cups, and agreed the new order. Probably the same day that they decided that the copshop didn't smoke – that it was a no-smoking building.

And you went in to do a shift after a night in Castlemilk, where you'd watched your feet for junkies' needles and your head for baseball bats, and you kindled up your pipe and the alarms went off and everyone looked at you and probably had a snigger behind your back because you were one of the old fogies and they saw you as yesterday's man, unwilling to adapt, unable to change.

The young ones could be forgiven. They didn't know that you'd changed already. Before they were on solid foods. Years ago, when you were the age that they are now, and you were sent out on the streets with a hairy-arsed constable who'd been told to knock you into shape. You watched him give a snotty-nosed wee kid a clip round the ear for giving up cheek. You saw him dent a skull or two with his truncheon to break up a street fight. And you listened when he told you that the guy would have a sore head for a day or so but everyone who had watched would remember for ever who had done it. And they'd respect you for it. Big on respect, the cops, in those days. Had to have it and had to earn it. Not just from your mates but from the neds. Had to talk their language and they had to know it. So you became fluent. Went for it big time, with the shoulders back and the chest out.

And it wasn't like *Z Cars* or anything like that where the actors learned their lines and acted tough. This was not a case of putting on greasepaint. It was more like having a tattoo on your heart. Your mother saw the change. Told you to mind your language – you weren't in the Gallowgate now and you'd been brought up to know better, no matter what your new friends were like. And Bella, only nineteen then, noticed it too and she made it known that she was interested in you now, though she'd knocked you back at school. She liked the uniform and the strength and confidence. And so did you because you were one of Glasgow's finest and you could feel the force was with you.

And then you went into places where weak men couldn't go. Where The Jug would have to call in reinforcements and helicopters and more horses than trooping the colour. But you went into the pubs at closing time, waded into the battles on the pavements after it and it was just you in there. You and your reputation. And you went in to break up the gang fights – just you and your mates and your baton and your guts against superior numbers of neds with razors and chains and bottles – you went in without fear or hesitation because you knew that you were in the right and that you would win. You had to – you were the law. And you might not win tonight but you would win next week or next month, with one guy singled out from the herd, up a back close, just him and you and your mate and you knew you would win because you were the law and they had to know that.

And they did.

You became a hardman, because that's what the force wanted, that's what you did to get the job done. And your sister told you you were 'coarse' and that hurt because you were doing the job for her and, if she couldn't see that, then neither could anybody else you were doing it for. But that made it easier to come to terms with what you had become. You were superior. Above it. And they might think that the decency had been knocked out of you but you knew it was okay because it was how it had always been, it was what your gaffer did and you were law and order, the glue that holds society together.

Then the likes of The Jug go and turn it all on its arse. And they don't have to change back because they'd never had the balls for it in the first place. But you had and they know it. And they know they've got to knock you down, better still to get rid of you, in case you tell someone what they were like. How they still are. And you know that it's not just your pipe they want to extinguish.

131

But The Jugs have been in charge for a while now and they're getting a bit lazy, a bit cocky. And The Hunter's still there. They know that it's not an inability to adapt but a refusal and, just because everyone got into the new step, it didn't mean that it was the right step, the only step. But they'd taken all the . . . individuality out of the job. All the brains. Now they are all clones, they could all look good and talk their new jargon and they could all fit in. They would shape the new ones too, paying particular attention to the good ones, snuffing out the sparks and brightness that had attracted them to be cops in the first place. Murdo would be singled out for special attention. And Aine, she'd get it in the neck for 'The Fields of Athenry'. Too bright by half those two. Too likely to show the others up. They would have to conform, to be part of it. But what? The clones could recite the rules back to front. They could catch the guys who'd done the crimes by the book. But that was always the way. Digger could catch them. That wasn't a problem. But what about the Strangeloves? They wouldn't have a clue. Mind you, The Hunter might have something in common with them after all.

''S on the house,' Joe said, putting a mug of sweet, milky tea on the table. ''S up wi' you anyway? You look . . . discontent.'

Hunter rebuked him with a glower.

Joe said, ''Spect you're just killin time till the funeral.'

He turned and walked away, then slowed and said, over his shoulder, 'No' bad, eh? Dead funny, me.'

Funeral, whose funeral? Hunter wanted to call him back but couldn't bring himself to do it. Couldn't show a weakness, a need for help. Not The Hunter. He worked alone. And, increasingly, he was feeling alone. Or maybe that should be lonely . . . He pondered who he might ask. Who could he trust with his vulnerability? Bella? Maybe, well, probably. They'd never get back what they had but it would be better than it is now. It would depend on how much she wanted it. Or if she was willing to settle for what she had now. She had known the demands of his job – the awkward hours, the phone call from the copshop on Christmas Day – but she seemed happy enough. She'd filled in the gaps when he had started to drift away. And he had, he accepted that, he had been the drifter. Now she had her pals – her 'Coffee Girls', as she called them, caffeine and calories twice a week at each other's houses – and the church, the Woman's Institute, the WRVS and the kids, of course, grown and off on their own now. She saw them every week – Alex in Kilmaurs, under the thumb of his schoolmistress wife, and Melanie with her posh bloke in the big house in The Mearns.

He could say to Bella that he was unhappy, well, not exactly unhappy, but certainly not happy. She would listen – the strong, silent one in the interview – forcing him to ramble on, to make admissions, to admit failings, to apologise. Then she'd want to unpick him, to take apart the sections of his life, like some bloody Lego set, throw some of the bits away, and put the remainder together again a different way. In her way. It occurred to him, for the first time, that Bella could be doing a Mary Knox. Playing away from home. He'd never thought of Bella with a fancy man but, well, you never know . . .

Aye, Mary Knox, the merry widow, he'd put her gas at a peep last night. Her and her fancy man, the lawyer. Probably the bugger that had shopped him to The Jug, too, sitting in her front room with his shoes off and a wedding ring on and a glass of red wine in his hand and an incriminating rosé flush on his chops. The widow blushing, too, hands at her tousled hair, then down to her blouse buttons, making sure she'd done them all up again, but at least having the decency to stutter a bit, knowing they'd been captured, knowing that The Hunter knew.

He'd let them off lightly. Said that it need go no further but he had to know the facts. Their relationship, he took it, preceded her husband's death. And the flushes turned from to rosé to claret . . . Wonder how strong their relationship is now? Could they work their way through it? Or throw themselves on friends. Take a second opinion.

The Hunter wondered who he would share his worries with. A pal who would listen, sympathise, not want anything for himself. Toshie was dead. But Toshie hadn't been a mate anyway. Just a free drink, a weekend away. A good lad, a good laugh, but just another guy off the leash and on the bevvy. Digger then. Good man, Digger. Damn good legman. He could trust Digger but not with his weaknesses. He was a colleague, a subordinate, and that was how it must stay. Anyway, he didn't know much about Digger. Not since he went off the drink, signed the pledge, what, eight years ago. Hadn't met his new wife. Hadn't even been invited to the wedding. That had hurt a bit. He'd noticed the wedding ring and chivvied Digger about it. Felt a bit embarrassed, too, when Digger said it had been there for four months. The Drouth? No way. He was a taker. Wouldn't piss on you if you were on fire.

Joe? Jesus H, was it that bad? Bare you soul to Joe? It didn't bear thinking about.

Hunter stretched to the next table and lifted a discarded copy of the *Daily Record*. The front of the sports section had a picture of Rangers equalising goal under the banner headline 'Mama Mia!'. It appeared that the goal scorer wanted to go home to Italy because he was missing his mammy. Hunter wondered why he couldn't have gone on Saturday.

133

Bastard had cost him three grand. Now he was pink lint. He took his wallet from his tail. No wedge now in his right trouser pocket. Hardly worth putting the trouser snake on guard duty. Yesterday, he had almost £600 – £560 of it from The Drouth for the Vectra repairs' fiddle and the last batch of money returned from the direct debit scam. Now the wallet held two dirty tenners and two blue bookies' slips. He took them out and unfolded them. Livingston win, five-to-one, £500. Oh well, that's the way the big ball crumbles. At least he'd had the gonads to go for it. He balled the slip and lobbed it, backhand, towards the ashtray in the adjoining table. It hit the rim, hovered for an instant, then fell on to the table. Close but no cigar. He held the other blue slip, reluctant to open it. The bet was only £50 – only fifty quid yesterday, today it was his life savings. And it was riding on some cuddy – the favourite, which had been heavily gambled, admittedly – called Bella's Joy or some bliddy thing in some bliddy race in Durbanville. And you could write everything he knew about South African racing on the back of a postage stamp and have space left over for his Christmas card list.

He thumbed through the paper and past a dozen pages of fitba, until he got to the racing section. His intention was to tease it out, to peep and keek. Cover the results with his hand, slide it down slowly to the three o'clock, get his money's worth. But the headline caught his eye, Boy puts paid to Bella's Joy. Oh, well, that's the way the cookie rolls. He crumpled up the blue slip, thought of having another attempt at the ashtray but couldn't be arsed.

He turned to the main section of the newspaper. No escape from the horsemen – the apocalypse variety here. Death from fire (two bairns and their mum); car crash (couple celebrating, Jesus H it actually said celebrating, their golden wedding anniversary); and leukaemia tot loses fight for life. Page seven was no cheerier but it did resolve a problem for Hunter. A single column article at the foot of the page said,

Police will throw a cordon of steel around Glasgow's Daldowie Crematorium at eleven o'clock today for the funeral of drug dealer Larry O'Hare, better known as Larry The Laundryman. O'Hare, an associate of businessman Danny Boyd, was killed last week when he was thrown from a speeding vehicle on the M8. It is the third murder in recent weeks in Glasgow's drug wars. Some of the leading figures in the city's underworld are expected to attend the service at the crematorium, and police are concerned about the potential for violence.

So that was the funeral. Hunter had forgotten all about it. How could that be? Normally he would be involved in the security arrangements. Jimmy Stone's drugs gang operated from his patch, so he should've been working with the uniformed guys, calling on The Stoneman, warning that he'd break his balls if he stepped out of line. Normally. But these were not normal days. Not with a loony serial killer on the loose. Not with The Hunter loosing the place. He glanced at his watch. Just before eleven. Put the foot down, he could make the crem for the last verse of 'Abide With Me'. Meet some honest-to-god crooks. He got up from the table. On a whim, he lifted the betting slip and smoothed it out. Three o'clock, Durbanville, £50 win, Bella's Boy. He searched through the sports section, found the racing report and read the opening para.

Bella won the feature race at Durbanville yesterday but it was her boy and not the favourite, her joy, that brought home the money. Bella's Boy won comfortably at 10-1.

You dancer. Back in the game, £550 to collect. And a job to do, a real job, with real bad guys. American Express – that'll do nicely.

Chief Constable Tobias Fastnett had set himself on the fast track to the Met and now he was within touching distance of it. Another six months, all being well, and the Metropolitan Police Force was his for the taking. The Home Secretary – that is *the* Home Secretary, not the puppet at the parish pump government in Edinburgh – had as much as said so last month at the Queen's Garden Party at the Palace. And now Fastnett could almost taste it – power, real power, and influence.

He had come north of the border against sound advice. Wise counsel urged him to take the Assistant Chief Constable's job on offer in the Midlands. A sideways step, admittedly, from the post he held in Bristol, but with a larger police force, in a high-profile area. It was, they argued, the perfect opportunity for him to excel and to do so quickly. The unit was running over budget. Fastnett's organisational skills and fiscal prudence, recognised as among the finest in the land, would certainly put that right. Weak leadership had fractured the force. The heads of CID, the Drug Squad and Vice were expending as much energy on fighting each other as they did on crime. A strong man who banged heads together would be noted. The area suffered from all the usual problems, guns, gore and drugs. But the real attraction there was the opportunity to focus on the biggest single problem of the twenty-first century – racism.

Officially, it could be discussed only in the most sensitive of tones. It was an offence, like any other offence, and offenders would be treated like any

135

other offender. But, in the corridors of power, it was top priority. And it was recognised that the lid was barely being kept on a boiling cauldron of hatred and bitterness. The divisions in Her Majesty's realm had come to the surface after the murder of Stephen Lawrence, an innocent London school-boy from a decent family. A black family. The murder, carried out by a gang of white youths, was appalling. The apathy (some said reluctance) of the predominantly white police force to carry out a proper investigation was shocking. The tenacity of the Lawrence family had kept the police failings on the front pages of the newspapers and burned the issue of racism into the public consciousness. The white-black divide had to be recognised and condemned. And followed quickly by the admission that relations with other ethnic communities were tainted, too. Almost inevit-ably, the far right flexed its Nazi-like muscle, recruiting and rebelling. And the police were caught in the middle. Damned if they did and damned if they didn't. So far, the sporadic violence which had had broken out in flashpoints areas had been quickly quelled with minimal loss of life and damage to property. The fever had been damped down and public panic calmed, by strategic operations against ringleaders. But the very real fear was that, one day, the blue touch paper would be lit and every corner of the land would tremble under the explosive fall-out.

Even the men who had nurtured and laid out Fastnett's career passage could not possibly have foreseen how swiftly and spectacularly the issue of racism would become the focus of attention for planet Earth. The stakes had been raised by Osama bin Laden on September 11, 2001, when his al Qaeda forces brought down the epitome of capitalism, the twin towers of the World Trade Center in New York, and dealt a wound to the Pentagon, the spiritual home of the strongest military force in the world. But Fastnett's mentors had told him that the copper who could make a start on healing the wounds that racism inflicted on society (or even won sufficient time to allow a scab to build on its festering sore) would emerge as the strongest contender for the main police job in the United Kingdom. But, for the first time in his life, Tobias Fastnett had gone against their advice. He had done so partly because the Strathclyde post was the top job, enabling him to skip a rung on the promotion ladder. But the main reason was to show that he was his own man. It was a move fired solely by ambition. And Tobias Fastnett could write a thesis on that subject.

He had always played the promotion game. The rules were straightfor-ward. Pass the exams and please your immediate superiors. Curiously, the first step, promotion from Constable to Sergeant, had been the most difficult because youth was an unassailable hurdle. But, after overcoming that, his career had advanced smoothly. He had become an assistant chief constable in Bristol at the age of forty-six, elevated because of his managerial skills which had, of course, been fully utilised. Those same talents, three years on, were spoken of in whispered tones as his weaknesses. He was said to be a pen-pusher, not a copper for the streets, for the sharp-end. So, when the Strathclyde job came up, he acted completely out of character. He took a gamble.

And that was where he learned the most important lesson on ambition. He had thought that he would be in charge of his own destiny. He was wrong. For the first time in his career his destiny lay in the hands of his junior officers. Men like Inspector Sandy Hunter.

Fastnett's appointment had not been popular with the Jocks. He was an outsider, a foreigner. What was it they called him? A Sassenach. But that was okay. Popularity and success do not go together. Still, in the first few months, he had doubts over whether it had been wise to ignore the advice of his mentors who had told him to avoid Strathclyde, so often a career copper's graveyard. The area was vast, taking in a huge area on the craggy, west coast that was a drug smuggler's dream – tiny, rural hamlets, a vast conurbation of towns, built on dead industries, and the sprawling city, riven by violence and sophisticated crime. It wasn't just that the Scots had their own legal system, he had been warned, they were a race apart. Two years on and he thought of them as an entirely different species. Epitomised by Inspector Sandy Hunter. No, that wasn't entirely fair on the Scots. Hunter's Machiavellian character and unpleasantness would have disgraced any nation unfortunate enough to have been the land of his birth.

In the individual staff reports Fastnett had received from his predecessor, Hunter's had been the most damning and the most accurate. It read, 'This man has one redeeming feature, he gets results.'

Two years on, Tobias Fastnett was looking forward to leaving those same words for the next incumbent of the office. However, he knew that he would not be elevated to the Met with a serial murderer on the loose in Glasgow. But he could book a single ticket to New Scotland Yard as soon as an arrest was made. So his future lay in the hands of a man who scorned him and, if the truth be told, a man he hated with a passion which he did believe he possessed.

Hunter made the crem in twenty minutes. The Vectra was stopped at the gates by a young, uniformed cop with a guest list on a clipboard. Hunter pressed the button but the electric window refused to go down. Effin thing. He got out and flashed his ID card.

'Popular place, eh, son?'

'Yessir, they're dying to get in here.'

Hunter laughed, maybe a bit too heartily. He said, 'Did they check their guns in at the sheriff's?'

The young man's turn to laugh too much.

Hunter walked on a bit. The young cop hesitated, then followed him. There was a dozen marked police cars on prominent display around the crem. Jimmy Stone, The Stoneman, the rival drug dealer whose gang had murdered Larry The Laundryman, wasn't going to make a move here. And, if he did, one cop on foot couldn't do a lot to stop him.

The big chapel was packed, with about two hundred folk standing outside. The car park was full and a rainbow of shiny vehicles snaked up the drive.

Hunter said, 'We're in the wrong job, eh? What's your name, by the way?'

'Constable Thomas Ferrie, Sir.'

Two cops with cameras were taking pix of each car, fore and aft. Hunter knew that there would be others with camcorders who had filmed the mourners on arrival and would be ready to zoom in on the faces as they emerged from the chapel. See who had bleary eyes. Who was playing at the Mafia, hairy-arsed men hugging each other.

Hunter asked, 'How many turned up, Tom?'

The cop answered quickly, 'Three hundred and forty-six. Only two didn't show.'

'And all for Larry The Laundryman. Did you ever meet him?'

Ferrie shook his head.

'Wee, insignificant guy – you'd shove him out your way to get to the bar – but he knew all the dodges and invented a few more. Made millions for Boyd. That's why they're all here – for Danny Boyd, see if they can win a few Brownie points with Danny. They couldn't give a shit for Larry. Helluva way to go though. Wasn't two bits of him hanging the same way.'

Hunter pointed to the clipboard. 'You have to check them all off?'

The lad nodded. 'They had invitations. Numbered.'

He held out the list. Hunter noticed that one of the no-shows was a prominent advocate, pal of The Jug. Probably out on the course together at this very moment.

Hunter tapped the name with a finger and said, 'Bloody hypocrite. He's happy enough to take Danny Boyd's money though, eh?'

Ferrie nodded in agreement. He'd heard about The Hunter, of course, didn't suffer fools gladly but he was decent with the boys.

Hunter said, 'Your gaffer work on the guest list with Boyd?'

Ferrie's antennae twitched. He said, 'I wouldn't know about that, Sir.'

'Good lad, Tom. Good answer, son.'

Hunter walked back to the car and Ferrie followed, wondering if he'd just passed a test.

'I wasn't playing silly buggers, though. Just pissed off that we've got to wet-nurse this shower of shit.'

He put on his forlorn look. Then said, 'You know, Tom, coupla sticksa Semtex, just lob 'em into the crem, we could cut the crime rate by fifty per cent.'

The lad smiled.

Hunter said, 'D'you know what they do with the ashes, Tom?'

A frown replaced the smile.

'Sell them to the cannibals as Readybrek!'

It was an old one but the smile returned.

Hunter got back into the Vectra and said, 'I'll just park over there. Mosey on down. Let 'em see that The Hunter's on their case, eh? When you've finished with that list, Tom, just pop it in my sun visor. Catch you later.'

He was off before the lad could explain his dilemma. His Sergeant had told him to take the sheet back to the station.

Hunter stopped the car after one hundred yards. He opened the glove compartment and took out the binoculars he used for the horseracing at Ayr. He got out of the car and walked through the copse of mature trees until he reached a point where he had a good view of the chapel. He made a rough count of the cars parked there. About one hundred and fifty. Mainly four-wheel drives, Mercs and Beamers. Big buggers, strong enough to take a clout from another vehicle and still get off their arses. Just in case The Stoneman got wind of an incoming consignment of drugs and tried a ram raid. He spotted Danny Boyd's dark green Bentley in pole position. What would it cost? If you had to ask you couldn't afford it. Ain't that a fact. What was the average price of the others? Say fifteen grand. Times one hundred and fifty. Way over two million quid and all of it sucked out of the veins of Glasgow's great unwashed. Some of them financing their habit by tanning four or five houses a week, the lassies nicking in Marks and Sparks, the wee guys mugging school kids for their mobile phones. And more cops here than at an Old Firm match. What was it the *Record* had said? 'Throwing a cordon of steel around the crem' – to protect the bastards who benefited from it all. The world had gone mad.

139

The crowd outside the chapel parted like the Red Sea to allow the big boys to come out. Hunter adjusted the bins to zero in on them. It was like a gyppo's wedding. Gold necklaces, rings, earrings, bracelets. And that was just the men. He scanned the faces until he found the one he wanted. Jamesie, the guy from the bookies, had been one of the chosen few. One of the first dozen or so out. Good. That meant he had a front row seat. One of the inner circle. Hunter fished out his mobile and punched out Jamesie's number. He kept the bins on his man, saw his dive to the pocket of his overcoat. The phone was answered on the second ring.

'Christ, Jamesie, that's some coat.'

'Who is it?'

'You know who it is, Jamesie. I've got you by the balls.'

Jamesie knew now, all right, and he didn't like it one wee bit. He turned around, trying to find a quiet place, but he was caught up in the throng.

Hunter said, 'You cannae talk the now, Jamesie. I understand that. So just answer yes or no.'

Jamesie's answer was two words, the first one Anglo-Saxon.

Hunter said, 'Turn to your right, Jamesie. No, your right. Think of your wanking hand. That's it. Right a bit. Right a bit. Stop. Look up.'

Jamesie did, saw The Hunter waving to him from the trees and quickly turned away. He whispered, 'Fuck sake, you'll get me killed.'

'Two choices, Jamesie. Talk to me or I'll come down and give you a big cuddle.'

Jamesie's voice was barely audible. 'What do you want?'

'Anything planned for the night, Jamesie?'

'Naw.'

'Tomorrow, then?'

'Might be.'

'And would it involve guns, Jamesie?'

'Aye.'

'That's all for now, Jamesie. Enjoy the funeral.'

Hunter was driving on the M74, doing the trick with the matches, kindling up his pipe. He pressed the button to lower the window, so he could flick the spent match out, but nothing happened. Bugger it. He tossed the match into the passenger footwell, at Bella's side. Give her something to mump about. He reached up and turned the handle thingy that opened the sunroof. At least the chimney still worked. Just as well, too, because it was getting smokier than the crem. He had the meerschaum today, a grand wee pipe, a present Bella brought from Turkey after one of her weeks away with her Coffee Girls.

'My little treat to myself,' was how she described the hols, paid for by the cash she allocated herself in her capacity as Chief Executive Officer (Finance) of Sandy Hunter Ltd.

Very effin limited actually and actuarially.

He had hinted a couple of months ago – not come right out and said it, as a refusal often offends – just wondered if she fancied getting a wee job herself. She had got on her high horse, then launched herself into the old favourite which started with 'and who do you think does all the wee jobs around the house?'

She had recently acquired the habit of picking up one or two of his words and giving him them back smeared with shite. She ticked the wee jobs off on her fingers (made them sound like bliddy rocket science, too) and finished with a two-hour huff because she had a headache.

For richer, for poorer, in sickness and in stealth.

Anyhow, he had taken the answer to his question as a no.

The cock-up with the cuddies had been a blessing. Mr William Hill promised to pay the bearer of the magic blue slip £550, which would put him back to where he started. But that hadn't exactly been a great place, the very reason why he had waded into Livi. So once again there was only £550 between him and the poor house. And now that the Vectra was paid, an extra £160 a month would be going into the coffers of Sandy Hunter Finances Limited and Bella would clutch it to her ample bosom. Unless he could come up with a way of keeping a hold of it. But that was for after. Just now, there was police work to be done. Good, honest-to-god work, involving thugs and drugs rather than wraiths in petticoats.

The thought cheered him. He had turned on to the motorway, heading south, because he could not bring himself to go back to the copshop. Back to the fruitless search for Strangelove and the futility of routine and regimentation of Fastnett. But he felt a tinge of guilt and left the road at Bothwell, then swung up the dual carriageway towards East Kilbride. The meerschaum was puffing good style, might as well enjoy a leisurely drive back to base.

Without realising it, he found himself heading for Busby and Chateau Carmichael. He wondered if Aine had made any headway in the trawl of official records on Matthew Whittle. What was it the fragrant Zara had called him? The dream boy? No, it was the boy who could remember his dreams. More like the boy who doesn't exist. Hunter's mobile played 'The Billy Boys' again. Must get that changed. Had been a laugh at first but questionable taste in mixed company (or maybe that should be Micks' company). Leave it for a couple of days, though, just in case The Jug

141

thought he'd won a victory. Dangerous things, these mobiles. Nearly went up the arse of a lorry looking to see who was calling. The wee screen said it was Digger so Hunter stopped in a lay-by near the old Philipshill Hospital and phoned him back. Digger was formal and put-offish. Said he would phone back. So The Jug was with him . . .

Hunter drove into the Carmichaels' forecourt as if it had been his destination all along. Only one silver Merc there. He parked beside it, got out and approached the door of the big house. But at the last moment he had second thoughts and turned to his right, off the monoblocks, and over the grass. A flower bed in the middle, a couple of dandelions in full bloom and petunias, well past their best and crawling with greenfly. Could do with a good skoosh of the toxic stuff. His father could never be persuaded to use it in his garden. Said it was against the balance of Mother Nature. So he ran his fingers over the plants, squashing the larvae. Aye, Dad was right green-fingered. Why couldn't the scientists faffing about with genetics and DNA not invent a weedfly? Now that, in The Hunter's book, was a Nobel prize-winner. How many back-breaking hours would that save? Would that not be of greater benefit to mankind than making a sheep out of its own arsehole? Give the lentil-eaters something else to protest about, too.

He followed a pathway of red granite chips around the building towards Zara's lean-to clinic. The coarse gravel crunched under his shoes. Not very practical for women. Bella had walked through some at a garden centre in the summer and said that the chips had chewed the leather off her high heels. It had sounded like a rare excuse to get a new pair but he'd had a shufti after she'd gone to bed and, sure enough, the heels had been nibbled a bit. Maybe pregnant women didn't wear high heels. Maybe he'd better clip the wings of his butterfly brain. What was he here for anyway?

Because he didn't want to be other places.

The grass border at the end of the big house had been scarred by a vehicle's tyre. The passage down the side was flanked by a two-metre high hawthorn hedge and wide enough to take a car with wee wing mirrors. The door to the clinic was locked so he walked along the building. He startled a blackbird, which rose from the hedge, squawking. Better alarm than the chips, actually. Nature's own security system. He peered through a window into an office. Comfy seats, two sofas, desk, computer, nothing out of the ordinary. The guttering to the right of the window was choked and stinking water had overflowed and trickled down the wall. It was not a recent problem. There was a residue of reddish sand on the path and, two-thirds of the way up the wall, the bare brickwork was visible. So it was just a façade. One of Bella's Coffee Girls had paid more than nine grand to have something similar done to her bungalow. Three navvies there for a month, one pretending to work and two to lean on the shovels. They had hacked at the original harling, stuck on some glue, then blasted the walls with sand. It was like the Sahara without the sun. Then a guy came along, cut out pretend blocks and daubed some cement in. Made the wee house a bit like an old slapper – looked the bizzo in a poor light but the plooks and wrinkles were still there under the make-up.

Hunter walked on. More windows, half a dozen, three rooms. Six rooms in total, same as Calder's across the way. But any chance of a peep inside here was thwarted by blinds, vertical plastic strips pulled together by the kind of chains that usually have bath plugs attached to them. He did get a look inside one room at the rear, where the blinds were open, but it was nothing more sinister than a kitchenette.

The gardens at the rear were about forty metres square, tall hawthorn hedges on both sides sloping down to a stream. The grass at the top was neatly trimmed, with half a dozen benches dotted around. There were raised flower beds of perennials and heathers. A pleasant place to sit, even today when the air had a chill in it. About halfway down, the garden had been allowed to grow wild and a spindly army of meadow flowers peered this way and that, bending their heads in the wind. A few willows had sunk their thirsty roots in the marshy ground beside the stream and, beyond them, the view was superb. Dairy cattle grazed in rolling fields, oblivious of the city three or four miles away. The Campsie Hills loftily surveying the vista.

Hunter continued his anticlockwise reconnoitre to a substantial building that had been the stables when the old house had been in all its glory. Zara had told him that it was her delivery room, 'the place where the stork lands'. Once more the windows were shrouded with blinds.

The path widened into a roadway here – covered in the same red granite chips and wide enough to take three cars. Hunter turned to his left, back up towards the main road and Calder Carmichael's clinic. He paused, looking over at the conservatory. An image flashed into his mind, the fragrant Zara, giving a blowjob to a cigar, giving him the come-on. What was it about him that she found sexually irresistible? The grime under his finger-nails? The two surplus stones around his waist? Or had she wanted to distract him? That was possibly just the favourite. She had lost her cool later, wheeched him away quickly enough, through the maze of corridors in the old house and on to Calder's clinic on the pretext of checking on Matthew Whittle. And then the flames of passion had gone out like a match in a thunderstorm.

Hunter took himself back to that night. He had lost his sense of direction winding his way through the rabbit warren of corridors in the old house. But he recalled seeing the lights of tower blocks in the city. So he must have been facing the stream. He turned that way again, Now, what had alarmed her? Oh yes, it was a car starting up. No, bigger than that, a van, an old one, or a clapped-out engine at any rate, diesel, coughing and farting into life. He closed his eyes and listened for that old engine. It came from the right, definitely right, so it over there. He opened his eyes and his arm was pointing behind the delivery suite. So, from the conservatory, that would be at her clinic.

She had taken him through the house, to the left and then further back right, but surely the more direct route to Calder's clinic was just across the courtyard? He walked into the centre of it and there, lo and behold, was a door to the psychiatrist's empire. Interestinger and interestinger.

A figure appeared in the conservatory. The philanthropic shrink himself.

Hunter waved and said, 'Just the man I want to see.'

If Calder Carmichael was surprised, and he had every right to be, he masked it well. Started with 'To what do I owe the pleasure?', went on to the party on the Lady Zara and skilfully brought the conversation back to the here and now.

'Do you have a conservatory?' he asked, turning his eyes to the leaky roof and then down to the array of buckets and basins.

Hunter said that he was thinking about it. He took a sip of the whisky his new friend had so generously poured. Carmichael had settled for Perrier water, with a twist of lemon.

'Then think again,' Carmichael said. 'This,' he raised both arms, 'has brought nothing but grief. Sounded great, too. The freedom of being outside with all the comforts of inside. I think I must have had my brain inside out!'

They blethered about it for a while. He'd bought it from the same guy The Drouth had used. Nice fella, he seemed. New business, just down the road. Now he was washing his hands of the problems. Something to do with cash-flow problems, Carmichael suspected.

They sat quietly for a bit, then Carmichael came right out and asked.

'And what can I do for you? Sandy.'

He added the name somewhat reluctantly.

Hunter said that he was looking for assistance – professional guidance. The psychiatrist looked relieved and intrigued at the same time. He had read about Toshie's murder and said that he'd known him, not well, 'but their social circles occasionally overlapped around the circumferences'.

He knew nothing of Knox – not even that he'd been killed – and his eyes lit up when Hunter said that the murders were linked. Both men killed by single blows from the same knife.

'But,' he added, 'that's strictly entre nous.'

Wee bit of French. Not too shabby, eh?

'So,' Carmichael said with a professional confidence, 'you want a profile of the killer or killers?'

Hunter said, 'Profile? Well, yes, anything actually. Anything at all. Because so far we've got sweet Fanny Adams.'

Carmichael fetched the whisky, Johnnie Walker's Black Label, and topped up Hunter's glass. Maybe Zara had emptied The Macallan the other night.

Carmichael leaned back in his chair. He put his hands together and raised them to his lips, as if about to pray. Hunter noticed that his index finger was about the same length as his ring finger. He'd seen a programme about it on the telly. Too much oestrogen in the womb, Mr Carmichael, that's what happened to you. Your mammy gave you too much oestrogen and not enough testosterone. Just a ba' hair off being a woofter.

Carmichael took his time and, when he spoke, it was in a flat, quiet voice, so Hunter had to lean forward to make out the words. The psychiatrist repeated the facts, entering them into his brain now for assimilation and interpretation.

'No struggle. No physical force. One wound.'

He paused, to give his observation impact.

'Medical knowledge.'

He looked up and Hunter nodded. He had taken a gamble. Decided to feed the guy's ego, get him off guard. Maybe get a different perspective on Strangelove, too.

Carmichael mumbled, 'One killer. No need for two . . . or more. No need for help. Important to do this alone. Sex? There would have been sex.'

Hunter said that there was ejaculate on the underpants of both men. But no evidence of intercourse. The Jug would have a hairy fit if he knew he was giving out evidence like this.

Carmichael went on, almost thinking out loud, 'Foreplay. Maybe just excitement, anticipation. We rule out homosexual activity?'

Hunter said, 'I think so.'

'Be sure of it.'

Cocky little bugger.

Carmichael went on, 'So, one woman kills two men. Uses her sex as bait. She's attractive, desirable. Intelligent. Both blows from above, you say?'

Hunter nodded again. He was beginning to feel like one of those wee dogs on the back window ledges of cars.

'Interesting,' Carmichael noted. He was staring into the middle distance, like some wise mystic.

'Might be that she feels safer, physically stronger, above them. Little chance to defend themselves. She wants everything in her favour. Leaves nothing to chance.'

'So why did she do it outdoors?' Hunter asked and was instantly angry with himself. The last thing he wanted at the moment was to challenge the man. But he need not have fretted. Carmichael was too wrapped up in himself to notice.

He continued, as if he had heard nothing. 'Danger is important to her. Shows that she's fearless. Risk is part of it. The men are beneath her, metaphorically. Not worthy. They don't touch her life. Don't get into her house. They're nothing to her.'

He paused, turned to Hunter and smiled his reassuring smile.

He said, 'Are you still with me?'

Hunter fawned. 'Yes, yesss.'

Carmichael said, 'One man was on his knees. Do we know why?'

Hunter said that he believed Toshie was performing, or about to perform, a sex act.

Carmichael said, 'Cunnilingus. Was there was vaginal fluid on his lips, in his mouth?'

Hunter bluffed it, said no, but Jesus H, he hadn't thought of that. Better check. No, forersics would have done that. Better ask though. But it didn't matter a damn. They had Strangelove's blood. And that was one piece of evidence the shrink was not getting.

Carmichael said, 'Thought not. There's no sexual pleasure for her. The other chap, Knox, was it the same? Cunnilingus?'

Hunter said yes – another bluff.

The psychiatrist was so far into himself he didn't notice.

He said, 'It's power and control. He has to do all the work while she just lies there and thinks of England – or should that be stands there and thinks of Scotland. Could be that she was taking the moral high ground. Comprendez?'

Hunter was genuinely interested now. He said, 'I think so but . . .'

Carmichael explained it slowly, in small words.

'Well, she's not forcing them to do it, is she? Not physical force, eh? She's not paying them. Neither man was on the game, so to speak. Nor is she blackmailing them, using emotional force. But they chose to go down on

146

her. And she's above them, looking down on them. Not doing anything herself. She has the moral high ground.'

'Yes,' Hunter said, 'I see that now.'

Carmichael liked the reply. He was warming to this. 'There's another possibility, an extra dimension. Two, really.'

He raised the forefinger of his left hand and said, 'One – you'll know this – with a stabbing, a normal stabbing, you don't see the blade enter the body. You move in close and just thrust . . .' – he mimicked the action – 'then pull back. But this little madam did not want to miss one little bit of it. She picks her spot, steadies her grip and watches the blade do the deadly deed. It's partly to kill cleanly. No struggle; no shouting. But she's planned it so she can see it all. And two . . .' – he raised the middle finger of his left hand – 'she doesn't want to see their faces. Because she isn't murdering Knox or Macintosh. It's someone else. Some memory. Or she's trying to. She's been abused, of course. Sexually, probably as a child. Father, step-father, mother's boyfriend . . . someone who should have been taking care of her. She's trying to kill him, to lay his ghost. But it didn't go away after the first death – I assume that it is the first – so she tries to make it go away by killing Macintosh. If she has succeeded, we'll never see her work again. If she hasn't, the compulsion to kill will be even stronger. She'll do it again. Sooner rather than later.'

He was good, Hunter had to give him that. Better than good, as his next comment proved.

Carmichael said, 'Was she menstruating?'

Hunter could not hide his surprise.

Carmichael did not even try to conceal his pleasure. 'Thought so. Hormones all to cock, so to speak. Sisterhood and feminism. Intercourse doesn't take place – well, not normally, anyway – during menstruation. So she's been humiliating the men. And showing her power. You know, "I'll bloodywell show them!"'

He laughed loudly. 'That's rather good, actually.'

He looked Hunter in the eye and said in a clear voice, 'That's her message to you. It's mainly about power. She's saying, "Look at me. See how much they want me How they'll do anything to have me. Even die." She wants you to be stronger than her. She wants you to catch her.'

Hunter was impressed and he laid it on with a trowel. Carmichael was used to praise but still he lapped it up.

He said, 'You'll want to know what she looks like?'

He didn't wait for an answer.

'Attractive, of course, that's a given. Not young, not teens – that would not be possible – she's too intelligent, no, too mature, that's it. She's about thirty, minimum twenty-five, max forty, maybe a tad older if she's well preserved. Strong, not butch, but fit. Athlete – possibly, but I don't see it. More likely to work out in a gymnasium. With other women. Hates men, of course. Oh yes, she is certainly a man hater. No husband or boyfriend. Well dressed but not flashy. And she's a professional. And with her medical knowledge, well, a doctor, nurse. A vet, maybe . . .'

He offered Hunter another opportunity for praise. This time, the cop didn't take it. He swirled the remaining mouthful of whisky around in the glass. Carmichael reached for the bottle but Hunter stopped him with a slight gesture of his hand.

Finally, Hunter said, 'But a murderer? I don't get it. Why would a woman like that be a killer? A quantum leap, I know, but I just don't see it.'

Carmichael almost snorted, 'But we're all killers. Surely you see that? We kill or at least we condone it. We all make moral judgments. The steaks we eat come from a dead cow, eh? And what do you do if your dog has a painful, terminal illness?'

Hunter said, 'I take it to the vet and have it put to sleep?'

'And you use the euphemism. But in truth, you are unable or unwilling to kill it yourself – a good whack on the head with a hammer does it, you know – so you get someone to do it for you. So, the issue is not the killing, it's the morals. Yes?'

Now it was really getting interesting.

Carmichael went on, 'So, let's take it a step farther. Some countries have capital punishment – the US to name but one. Now that is killing, legal killing, so it is no longer about morals but about legality. Other countries have legalised euthanasia – killing – so legality goes out the window and it's now about the individual's judgment. Your father has a painful, terminal illness. You can't very well hit him with a hammer but you could take him to a doctor to get a painless injection. You can do it with your dog – could you bring your dad to me? Ask me to do it for you?'

Hunter looked suitably impressed. He said, 'I'm sure there's an argument against you, but you're too sharp for me.'

He drained the whisky glass and got up. Carmichael held out his hand for a professional handshake. Hunter gave him one, limp, two waggles, pretty woofterish, really.

Carmichael said, nice as you like, 'And will there be a fee . . .'

What for, Hunter wondered, killing my father?

'for the professional profile of your killer?' Should I submit an invoice?'

Jesus H, he was serious.

148

Hunter said, 'Oh, yeah, sure. Send it to the wife. She handles all my financial affairs.'

He didn't know what to make of that.

Hunter said, 'Tell you what, double or quits. Since you're solving my problems, here's another – help to get the Chief Constable off my back – where's Paborsky?'

Well, well . . . he didn't like that one. Didn't like it one little bit. The look had only been on his face for a second but Hunter had read lots in it. Surprise, for sure, and was that fear?

Carmichael said, 'Paborsky?'

Playing for time and not very well. Hunter let him have it. See how long it would take.

Mr Smoothie returned pretty quickly, smiling and coming up with a clever out.

'Correct me if I'm wrong, Sandy, but somehow I can't imagine you being overly concerned about the Chief Constable.'

Hunter let him off the hook. Then asked, matter of fact, 'How's Matthew?'

Carmichael taken aback. Couldn't think of a smart answer. Tried a 'Matthew?' With the question mark.

Hunter didn't answer it.

'Matthew.'

No question mark this time but still no answer.

Finally, 'You mean Matthew Whittle?'

Hunter said yeah and put some surprise in it.

'He's fine. Fine. Why?'

'Tried to kill himself.'

Carmichael was visibly relieved. 'Oh, yes. No, he's fine, honestly. No ill effects, none at all.'

Hunter turned his back. He walked away as he spoke and the words went with him, so the psychiatrist had to follow him to hear them. Even so, he only caught a few.

'We . . . look into it . . . against the law . . .'

Carmichael was struggling to keep control of himself. They were out of the conservatory and Hunter was walking towards the psychiatrist's clinic. Carmichael was mumbling about my patient, my responsibility.

Hunter stopped suddenly. 'Least said, soonest mended, eh?'

Carmichael was really relieved. Moved to shake the policeman's hand again but stopped himself just in time.

Hunter asked, 'Where's he from?'

'Matthew?'

'Who'd you think? The guy that's willing to put my dad down?'

He'd meant it as a joke. Trying to wrong-foot Carmichael. Make him worry, make him laugh. But he flushed red, then sweaty pale. His hand up to his chest, to his heart, then down into his pocket. Out with an inhaler, skooshed it into his mouth. His legs weak, buckling, and Hunter stepping forward, arms out, under his armpits, taking his weight. Then easing him down on the conservatory step. Another spray with the inhaler. Taking some in, some coming out, droplets in the air, like used-up breath on a frosty morning.

Hunter thinking, I did that. I did that to him. Planned it. Set him up. Meant to frighten him. Christ, I did that all right. Might have killed him. Just doing my job. Yeah, sure. Blame the job. But I did that.

Carmichael's breathing getting easier. A tinge of pink returning to his cheeks. Not saying anything yet but giving Hunter a reassuring smile. He made to get up, then decided against it.

He said, 'Matthew is well. No-one could . . . look after him better. Please . . . take my word for that. Where is he from? I don't know.'

He got up slowly and opened the door to the conservatory. Hunter kept a step behind him, ready to help if needed, but not knowing whether he should offer. Carmichael skirted two buckets on the floor and sank into the sofa. Hunter, too, sat down again.

Carmichael laid his head back, took two deep breaths, then went on with his story. 'We've taken care of Matthew for . . . sixteen months. Before that he was in a psychiatric ward in . . . no, I'll start again. A year past June, Matthew presented at a GP's surgery. In Gorbals. Didn't say much, but complained of stomach pains. The doctor – a friend of mine – couldn't treat him. He wasn't a patient. Ethics and that. But he sent him to the Victoria Infirmary. End of chapter one.'

Carmichael stretched out and took a sip of Perrier, then he continued. 'About six weeks later, the GP found Matthew, barely conscious, on the steps of his surgery. He had a crisp bag with glue in it. Well, what can I tell you about that? He had three choices. Ignore the boy, like everyone else. Call for an ambulance. Or ring me. You know, don't you, that substance abuse is my speciality?'

Hunter nodded.

Carmichael said, 'Matthew has a mental age of ten. Doesn't know where he comes from. No one has reported him missing. He's eighteen, nineteen maybe, so an adult in the eyes of the law. What should I do with him? Put him out on the streets?'

'You can't do that,' Hunter said.

They sat quietly for a while, then Hunter asked, 'The GP, he must have found out something.'

Carmichael's strength had returned. He went on, with more conviction.

'A little. The Vicky had kept Matthew for observation but could find nothing physically wrong with him. But they identified mental health problems and passed him on to the Southern General. They held on to him for a few days and then, well, there's such a shortage of beds . . .'

Hunter said, 'No medical records?'

'None. Don't even know if his name really is Whittle. There was a kid with him, first time at the Gorbals surgery. That's what he said it was.'

Hunter asked, 'The GP, he must have asked about.'

'He did but he got nowhere.'

Hunter said, 'So, officially, he doesn't exist?'

Carmichael said, 'Oh he'll have records, files, but there's no way of marrying him to them. I wish there was. I could get something towards his keep.'

'So who pays.'

'I do or rather the rich alcoholics and drug addicts do. From each according to his means to each according to his needs, eh?'

Hunter had a thought. 'What if I take his fingerprints. See if he has a record?'

That look returned again. Definitely fear there. It was covered quickly with a sweet smile but it had guilt written all over it. Carmichael's breathing became tighter again and he was wiping sweaty palms on his trousers. And Hunter, to his astonishment, found that he was doing exactly the same thing.

'Simon? No, it's not a good line. Sorry, I didn't catch that. Oh, that's funny – I am a thousand miles away.'

Lisa stretched out on the big bed, trying to find a position that didn't hurt.

'Well, Simon, do you know who this is? Eh? Oh, I'm in Morocco, getting a nice tan. But my cheeky bits are still white. Now that's a clue. Or do you say that to all the girls?'

She laughed, trying to put him at ease. She didn't want to challenge him, to frighten him off. She could picture Simon in his white coat, stethoscope draped around his shoulders, leaning into the clear plastic bubble on the wall in Glasgow Royal Infirmary. The phone pressed to his ear, a finger in the other to block out the noise of the ward.

'What size are my cheeky bits?'

She gave him another laugh, a naughty one this time.

'Well, they're just about the same size but more experienced now. Oh dear, does that make me sound . . . promiscuous?'

She pronounced the word slowly, enjoying the sound of it. Then she chuckled and said, 'Yes, you're right, there's nothing wrong with a little bit of promiscuity between consenting adults. What? Another clue? Okay. You were my first lover. Now that must narrow the search but maybe not a lot.'

She was enjoying this. She could sense his macho pride in the acknow-ledgement of his many conquests. But she feared that he might say some-thing, perhaps the wrong name, that would break the spell. So she told him.

'It's Lisa, from the flat, when we were students? Remember, Lanky Lisa? Yes, that Lisa! Oh, Simon, you never change, do you?'

She turned painfully on the bed and lay full-length on her front. Simon was talking ten to the dozen, asking questions without waiting for answers, comfortable, confident now that he knew it was only Lanky Lisa. He really hadn't changed. That was good.

Eventually, he allowed her to talk again.

'Well, I followed you today – at least I thought it was you – in the souk. And, when it wasn't you, well, I . . . oh dear, I'm not making a very good job of this, am I?'

Simon knew that she was about to say things that he wanted to hear so he urged her to continue.

'Well, I guess I was disappointed. And I realised that I'd really like to see you again. There, I've said it now. Are you going to hang up on me? Good. That's good. Well, after a couple of glasses of wine, I decided to take the bull by the horns. What? No, the horns, not horny.'

But she laughed again so he would think that was a lie.

'How did I know where you'd be? Oh, okay, you've got me there. I keep in touch with some of the girls. No, I have not been stalking you.'

He had taken the hook. She didn't even have to reel him in. He was swimming for the shore. He wanted to know when she would be home. She told him it might be Wednesday, maybe even tomorrow. He had assumed that she was on holiday and was impressed when she said that, no, she was here on business. 'What business?' he had asked, then told her not to answer. It would give him something to think about. That and her suntan, oh, and her white cheeky bits. He had given her his phone number, his mobile, and told her to call. Then he said that he had to dash. Lives to save and all that.

Lisa stretched to return the phone to its cradle. The movement caused her to grimace in pain. She considered taking another bath but the very thought of the exertion was just too daunting. She was sore inside and she was bleeding. It wasn't just menstrual blood. It was coming from an injury.

She lay perfectly still and did her breathing exercises, filling her lungs, big breaths, slowly, in through the nose and out through the mouth. The rhythmic repetition brought a reassuring calmness, relaxing muscle and sinew, soothing the flesh. In her mind, she visited a safe place, the city, Glasgow, in winter, lots of people, wrapped up warm against the elements, and Lisa walking among them, one of them, safe among them, one of the crowd, secure and protected. It's Argyle Street, broad, long, little traffic, and a cool, low sun glinting off the frost on the pavement. Brisk, long strides, nestling her chin down into the scarf, snug, secure.

She had known that Abdul would be rough with her – that was the reason the other girls had turned down such a lucrative job – but he had been fierce and cruel. He was a big man, more than sixteen stone, six foot four and endowed proportionately. But it was not so much the length and girth of his penis as the thrusting and pummelling which did the damage.

She had known that he would take delight in hurting her, so why had she done it? Why had she come here to be brutalised and humiliated? Not for the cash – not for £3,000, that was for sure. It was because it was the last time, because it would serve as a constant reminder of all the men she had known in her life. And why she hated them.

She had only had a couple of hours' sleep after the flight from Heathrow. Then it was up with the sun and on with the make-up. All the indoor scenes with Abdul had been shot. They were in the can. They did them first, when her body was at its best, so the camera would not capture any bruises. Still, she was sore but what could he do to her? What more could be done to her? The pain would pass. The physical pain. The emotional pain would always be there. And so would the emptiness – the space in her womb. That was Simon's responsibility. He really hadn't changed. Still the same selfish, arrogant bastard. But this time he wasn't in charge. This time Lisa was calling the shots and he had fallen for it.

And it had been easy. Easy-peasy. Dead easy.

'It's no' up, Douglas.'

Old Douglas's eyesight was not the greatest but he could see that his bowl had finished some four feet short of its target. The green baize carpet was down on the dance floor at Queens Park Bowling Club and the short rink players were locked in competition. Douglas shook his head, then appeared to identify the problem. His eyes fastened on an imaginary bump three yards down the carpet and, as swiftly as his artificial hip allowed, he ambled towards it and gave it a wee dunt with the sole of his shoe. His opponents remonstrated, making allegations of gamesmanship and likening Douglas to parts of the male anatomy, just below the waist, front and rear. Douglas, undaunted, made his way back up the carpet, John Wayne without the spurs. The delay appeared only to inspire his opposite number who proceeded to put his bowl right on the jack and posed the difficult-to-answer question, 'How d'you like them apples?'

Hunter had been on his way back to the copshop and, on a whim, had turned the Vectra into the booling club. It was a bit like the geriatric Olympics. Wall-to-wall grey beards and baldies on the short rink, in the snooker hall, at the dartboard and, for the less energetic, a posse in the sun lounge playing dominoes.

Sadly, Douglas's second bowl could not better his first.

'You're still no' up.'

Douglas acknowledged the fact, mumbling that he could see that, he'd heard about it and so had everyone else.

Hunter offered a word or two of advice. 'Have you tried Viagra, Douglas?'

The old guy looked puzzled.

Hunter explained, 'Viagra – it'll help you get it up.'

Douglas said, 'I take it already – just a tenth of a tablet a day.'

Hunter's turn to look puzzled.

'Just so I don't splash my shoes when I go to the lavvy.'

That said, he moseyed off to join his pardners.

Hunter looked longingly at the bar. The two generous whiskies in Busby had put him in the mood. A pint of lager would go down well. Touch of lime, to oil the tubes. Just one, don't get caught up in company, forced to buy a round, get into a session and pretty soon it's early dark.

A waving hand caught his attention in the sun lounge, beckoning him over. About a dozen guys, four of them ex-cops, deep in conversation. That settled it. No way to have a swift one. It would have to be none. Hunter gave the guy a thumbs up and followed his nose to the kitchen where a massive pot of Scotch broth was bubbling away. Tried to bum a plate off the women but they would have none of it. They compromised on a coffee.

On the way to the sun lounge, he was headed off at the pass by Haig, the club secretary. Small matter of unpaid fees. Hunter expressed astonishment. Not paid? He'd left it to Bella. He fished his cheque book from his inside jacket pocket and wrote one immediately. Swithered over doing the thing with the date, making it a year behind, hoping that some shrewdie in the bank would spot it and return it. Thought better of it since, after all, it is October. He should know the year by now. And, come to think of it, he'd done that a couple of years ago. The bank did bounce the cheque, and he won a few weeks out of it, but it only deferred the pain. He gave Haig the cheque, got stung for £1 to nominate the bonus ball on Saturday's lottery and £2 for raffle tickets. Who knows? Might win the gallon bottle of Chivas Regal 12-year-old whisky. Not a bad prize but better still would be a year's exemption from buying raffle tickets.

As he was entering the sun lounge his phone played 'The Billy Boys'. It was Digger – again. He looked around for a quiet spot. Haig read the situation and pointed towards the boardroom, said it was empty. Hunter went in there and sat on the big seat at the end of the long table. Digger passed on the personal information first. The Chief Constable had been looking for him all day and he was not a happy bunny. Hunter was to report to his office, ASAP. Not a good sign. The Jug became a man of letters when he was uptight. Hunter wanted to ask Digger to pass on a message – tell him to GTF – but decided against it. Instead he asked for an update on Strangelove.

The first piece of information – and almost certainly the least important – was that The Jug had a prime suspect. A man who had walked into the copshop at lunchtime and said that he and a mate had killed Toshie. Digger had sat in while the guy was interviewed by James Smith, the Assistant Chief Constable (Crime). His story had changed a bit – he hadn't actually committed the murder, hadn't been there at the time – but his mate had followed Toshie into the back court. The guy was not a serial confessor (though God knows there were enough of them) and anything he had said could have been gleaned from the newspaper reports. He did not volunteer any telling information and clearly did not know about the tampon. He had simply told his story and then he had clammed up. Smith did not believe a word of it but The Jug had decreed that the confession had to be treated seriously.

The next development was much more valuable. Murdo had traced a dosser (a homeless man, Digger called him) who had seen Toshie and Strangelove. He had recognised Toshie, or thought he did, from the picture in the papers. He hadn't thought they were together at first. They were, he said, walking in Indian file. A nice description but probably against the Race Relations Act. The dosser had given a description of Strangelove. Not exactly enough for an e-fit (his vision had been impaired by the effects of a bottle of Buckfast) but a start. Enough to put flesh and blood on a wraith. The guy was in a hostel as they spoke, being hosed down, ready for fresh clothes, a meal, a wee glass of wine and a session with a sketch artist.

Digger also told Hunter that Aine wanted him. She said that she had a development in the electronic search for her dream boy.

The final piece of news was intriguing but, on the face of it, unconnected with the hunt for Strangelove. Four phone calls from a man calling himself Shooey to tell The Hunter that he had 'vital information. Said it was something about . . .'

The Sergeant's voice went quiet and Hunter assumed that an alien force was in his presence. The Jug.

Digger said, 'Thank you, Constable, keep in touch.' And he hung up.

Hunter sat for a minute or two, going over the Shooeys in his memory bank. Three Hughs, two Hughies and a Shug. Might be any of them. He sipped his coffee and looked at the silverware on the boardroom table. The cups and trophies had been polished till they gleamed, the names of this year's winners newly inscribed, waiting for the presentation ceremony on Friday. His name was on a couple of them, too, from another lifetime when he had been dead keen on the bools. So maybe he had gone full circle. Maybe it was time to jack in the job, take the pension, join the other four ex-cops in the sun lounge. Hunter picked up a shield and scanned the little discs denoting the winners. When was it? Jesus H, 1978, twenty-five years, a lifetime ago. And what did he have to show for it? The dark clouds of his maudlin mood were descending when there were a couple of knocks on the door and old Douglas poked his head round it.

He said, 'Trying it out for size? The chair – are you thinking of running for president?'

Hunter said, 'Why not – mibbe in another twenty years.'

Douglas smiled, then sat down. Something was troubling him. When he spoke, there was sadness in his voice.

'Tell me to mind my own business if you like . . .' He stopped, trying to find the right way to say it, '. . . but are you looking for the ones that killed Philip Macintosh?'

Hunter nodded.

Douglas said, 'Good. That's good. I know him – knew him – his daughter goes to school with my grandson. Nice guy, Philip. Doted on his wee one, you could see that. Got a boy, too. It's . . . dreadful. But you'll get them, Sandy, I know that. I feel a wee bit better now. Thanks.'

The old guy added, 'You've got a rotten job, Sandy. But it's got to be done, eh? You're a good man.'

With that, Douglas opened the door and left Hunter with the two words he said after he had walked in all the footsteps of the dead.

God bless.

Hunter couldn't get a parking space so he pulled the Vectra in to the kerb about five doors down from his own house. The area really was getting quite well-to-do. He didn't know a lot about cars but, as he walked back to the house, he could see that they were new, or newish, shiny and expensive. He'd decided to drop in on Bella – off the cuff, a wee surprise, maybe have a coffee and a blether. She was always complaining that they didn't spend time together, not 'one-to-one, quality time'.

He used the side gate and, Bella was right, it was in a bit of a state. He had to force it open because the hinges were almost locked with rust. He decided that he'd bin it at the weekend, get a new one. Better still, make one. How hard could that be? Buy some wood at B&Q, hammer a few nails into it, screw on a couple of hinges and Robert's your father's brother.

The paving stones on the path were cracked and crooked. No shame to them. Must be best part of fifteen years since he'd laid them and they'd been the cheapest he could find. All he could afford, then. Come to think of it, all he could afford now. There were weeds growing through the cracks – the dandelions and buttercups were particularly healthy. The frosts would nip them soon, cut them down to size, but they'd be back next year, when the ground warmed up, around July.

He kicked at a big, yellow dandelion head, caught it perfectly and watched it loop high in the air and settle neatly at the foot of Bella's favourite rose bush. Sweet memories, that's what it was called. He bent to retrieve the dandelion, caught the back of his hand of a thorn and drew blood. He sucked the wound then spat out, remembering from somewhere that the thorns were dirty and harboured infections. He'd let Bella bathe the wound, then put on a plaster. He would yelp and feign agony and she would scold him and tell him not to be a crybaby. Quality time.

The back door was open and he could hear clearly that the Coffee Girls were in town. That explained the cars. He stopped in his tracks, like a housebreaker who feared being caught. They were discussing an acquaintance who had just had a conservatory built on to her house. The comments were less than charitable. The proud owner, allegedly, was up to her ears in debt so another £10,000 or so wouldn't make any difference.

Fur coat and no drawers. You know what they say about people in glasshouses . . . Pause. They shouldn't have inside toilets.

It didn't make any sense to Hunter, but the Coffee Girls thought it hilarious. Must be giving the sherry big licks.

Then Bella said, 'That wouldn't be Sandy, then. He pees in the garden.'

They laughed louder and it inspired her.

'He does and he thinks I don't know. He whistles to cover the splashing.'

This nearly cracked them up. Then one of them boasted that her man had peed in the snow at New Year. On the pavement and know what it said? 'Nookie'.

They were almost wetting themselves now. Someone wanted to know why she hadn't stopped the pavement artist.

'Oh, I didn't actually see him doing it.'

'Then how do you know it was him?'

'I recognised the handwriting!'

Hunter carefully retraced his steps. He closed the gate carefully. It would last a few years yet.

Digger Burns made a beeline for Hunter as his Inspector entered Committee Room Three.

'A word, Sir. Please, Sir.'

He was already guiding his boss out of the room. The troops were doing their best to pretend not to notice. Hunter was not best pleased. Digger better have a good reason. He had.

Outside, in the corridor, he whispered that The Jug was spitting blood. He wanted to see the Inspector immediately. He was just off the phone – again – and this time he knew that Hunter was in the building. The front office had been told to report his arrival and Digger was under orders to tell his boss to report to the Chief Constable immediately.

Digger said, 'He's been in and out of there,' he nodded to CR3, 'all day. Thinks you should be here. Mentioned . . .' he dropped his voice even lower 'dereliction of duty.'

Hunter went back into the room. He said, loudly, 'Oh he did, did he?'

There was total silence. Everyone had heard him.

Hunter said, even louder, 'And "diddy" is the operative word.'

A chuckle – from Murdo, he fancied. For an instant, all eyes were on him then everyone suddenly found something urgent to do. All except Murdo and Aine, who gave him knowing smiles.

The best of the whole bunch and they were his. He wouldn't forget it.

He said, 'Notepad. I need a thick notepad.'

Aine threw one to him. He caught it one-handed, turned to the corridor and paused to stuff the pad down the seat of his trousers.

Then he said, 'If anybody's looking for me, I'm upstairs. Getting my arse kicked.'

It was a disciplinary hearing. Fastnett had said that he wanted that understood clearly . He had not asked Hunter to sit down and he had not looked up from his notes.

James Smith was in attendance, looking sheepish. He asked Hunter if he wanted to have 'a representative present'.

He did not.

Hunter had let Fastnett huff and puff and now he had all but blown out his storm. He was repeating, again, the principal charges – Hunter had left the bridge and he had been AWOL.

In fairness, there was a degree of truth in what was said and Hunter would have accepted the criticism. But he had been boxed into a corner, his future in the force on the line, so he waited his chance to hit back. It came when Fastnett lifted his head, departing from his prepared speech, becoming cocky and even more vindictive. He had barely glanced at Hunter throughout the entire proceedings and, even now, he addressed his comments to his Assistant Chief Constable.

'And when Mr Hunter is off doing whatever Mr Hunter does, who does he leave in charge of a double murder investigation? A sergeant, that's who. Makes one wonder whether he feels that an officer of rank might do better than the famous Hunter, eh?'

Hunter, too, spoke to Smith.

He said, 'I am sorry, Sir, to put you in this difficult position. But I must cite you as a witness.'

Both of his superior officers stared at him in amazement.

He went on, 'First and foremost, I will not have Sergeant Burns's name or reputation maligned. He is a first-class policeman and deserves better than this. Second, the Chief Constable will recollect that I considered it unwise that I should take charge of both murder inquiries. But I obeyed his instruction to do so.'

Fastnett did not contradict him.

'And, third, Danny Boyd is about to hit Jimmy Stone's gang with more guns than the Royal Artillery. If you want the names of his shooters, try this for starters.'

He took the guest list from Daldowie Crematorium from his jacket pocket and laid it on Fastnett's desk. Then he turned on his heel and stormed out, banging the door behind him.

* * * * *

159

Even the camels hated him and that had made the past two hours less unbearable.

Lisa had insisted on forging ahead with the filming, challenging him, taunting him, saying if the stud needed time to recover, if he wasn't up to it, well . . . And Abdul had bitten, promising through gritted teeth that she would find out what a real man could do to her. So they had set out in the 4x4s, well off the beaten track, into the desert. This was the location the director really wanted. This was to be the money shot. Abdul as the Nomad, Superarab, riding his camel over the sand dune and coming on the little white girl. Literally.

The preliminary shots were in the can – Lisa gradually shedding her jockey's silks, using the riding crop on Abdul as he ripped off her flimsy underwear and, naked, with Lisa bent forwards over the bonnet of the 4x4 as he sodomised her. But she had shown no pain. She had amazed them, insisting that they make full use of the daylight, helping to polish the sweat and stains off the bonnet of the vehicle so they could film her expression of mounting sexual pleasure reflected in the sheen. Abdul had been subdued, performing his role professionally but without any great vigour. She was sore never the less, still suffering from the abuse he had inflicted during the indoor shots.

The ground was filthy – hard, brown and rutted – and a wicked little breeze whipped up some surface sand that bit the flesh like a thousand insects. The fierce heat was out of the sun but still it burned her pale skin. The baby oil they insisted she smeared on her body magnified the rays and soon she was covered in grit, so that when their bodies touched it felt like sandpaper. Abdul noticed this and laughed. And he promised, as they brought the camels, that she was about to suffer as she had never done in her life.

The female camel refused to be anywhere near him. It could smell the sex and, when Abdul came near, it would create a fearful noise, bare its filthy teeth and spit out a foul, noxious stream. It had to be taken more than one hundred yards from the cameras. The male was more manageable but still succeeded in throwing Abdul from its back. He landed awkwardly on his shoulder, cursing and showing his pain.

Pity is wasn't your dick, Lisa thought.

They got about a minute's worth of filming on the beast's back. The cameraman on the roof of the 4x4 and the Arab producer asking them to perform impossible tasks. The camel curtailed his plans. It got down on its knees and refused to rise, even when they beat it with sticks. The sun sank lower, basting a rosy glow in the sky, and the cameraman fussed over his light meter and cautioned that they had less than half an hour left. The producer was ready to call it a day and return in the morning.

Lisa got on the camel's back, goading them. So these were the men of the dessert, the great and strong Arabs, beaten by a girl and a camel.

The producer remained calm. He could not film from only one angle. Lisa told him to dig a trench, then shoot up. She would give him a show, even if the Arab stallion wasn't up to it.

It was an insult too far for Abdul and he grabbed a spade himself and began to dig in fury. Lisa was happy to see him drain some strength but, all too quickly, the trench had been dug and Abdul thrust his sweating body upon her. Her began to pound her and insult her in a language she did not understand.

She closed her eyes and went to another place. She blotted out the pain and it was not Abdul's face that she saw. Her body, for so long the flesh and bone puppet for the cruel marionette, began to respond to invisible caresses. Her mind took her to a different world, a different time.

The cameraman was the first to notice the change in her, even before Abdul who was wrapped up in his own sexual athleticism. The lens saw her body begin to respond, the nipples pout in arousal, the muscles, under the milky skin of her tummy, ripple like soft waves lapping up a gentle shore.

She sees strong hands, feels them stroke her hair, neck, across her shoulders, down to her chest. Big hands, powerful yet gentle, light as butterfly wings, and Lisa is giving herself to them – willingly, eagerly, desperately casting off her grasp on reality. Depending, trusting everything to those hands and the face way up there just out of sight. She raises her head to see better but it is just out of sight. She knows that it is smiling. She sees the smile, the white teeth, but the features are too fuzzy to put a name to it. But he is smiling down on her and she loses herself in that radiance. She pulls up her legs, digging her toes into the camel's wiry hair for more purchase.

The producer, too, spots her enthusiasm and stops barking his banal commands to the cameraman. And even Abdul realises that he is no longer in command of this coupling.

Lisa increases the tempo, thrusting her pelvis up and down, swivelling her hips. Her white teeth bite down on her bottom lip, hard, and a tear of blood forms and trickles on to her chin. She is in her own little world, moving quickly now, oblivious to the heat, the flies, the leering men around her. She is intent on one thing and one thing only. And when she reaches that place, when she achieves climax, it is not the usual Moaner Lisa, it is a different person – pure, innocent – and the noise which escapes her lips in

161

not the feigned sexual ecstasy. It is much more real, almost primordial. It is a long, high-pitched yell, like a ululation.

Daddydaddydaddy.

Tobias Fastnett was still furious with himself. He had blown the disciplinary hearing with Hunter and now the infernal man would consider himself bulletproof.

The Chief Constable knew that he had acted – not without cause – in haste and anger. Rage, really, brought on by the phone call from his opposite number in the Midlands. The Chief Constable there, Fastnett's biggest rival for the top job in the Met, had heard about the middle-class murders and was offering assistance. Damn cheek! The bugger also knew that Hunter was leading inquiries and said that, of course, Fastnett knew his men best. During the course of the brief conversation, he managed to go from Jack the Ripper to Jill the Sticker. Fastnett had remained cool (ice-cold would be more accurate) and actually managed to score a point by promising that he would remember the offer of help, and the spirit in which it was made, in the months and years to come. But never in his life had he been so dependant on one man and, as the day's events clearly showed, never had a police officer been less dependable.

Fastnett had been right – even James Smith, ACC (Crime), admitted that – to call in the Inspector. They had differed on the nature of the meeting – Smith suggesting that Hunter be given a sharp reminder, a 'ticking-off' was the phrase he used – but Fastnett was adamant that nothing less than an official, disciplinary warning would suffice. He had wanted to make an example of Hunter, to let it be known both within and outwith the force that he ran a tight ship.

It had gone well, too, according to plan, until he had got sucked into a bit of street-fighting. And Hunter, quite simply, had been too good for him. Too sleekit, that was the word the Jocks used to describe how only they could behave. Hunter had used a perceived slight on his Sergeant to take the moral high ground. Then he had left in high dudgeon, playing the ace from up his sleeve. The list of names turned out to be those who had attended the funeral service of a man who laundered drugs money.

Fastnett had despatched Smith to get a full explanation from Hunter. This was, admittedly, a shitty job but that was why they were called number twos.

It really did appear that the city was about to see a full-blown drugs war, with the most recently-wronged gang planning bloody revenge for the murder of their colourfully-named colleague, Larry The Laundryman.

Hunter, in his own inimitable style, said that he would handle it. Did he want help? Yes, he had told Smith, he wanted a WPC seconded to plain-clothes. The arrogance of the man was limitless. And Fastnett could only wish Hunter the very best of luck in everything that he did and pray for his success. For Fastnett knew that his elevation to the top police job in the United Kingdom now rested solely on the shoulders of the sleekit Scot.

Aine O'Shaunessy knew that she was in a minority – quite possibly of one – but she actually liked the man. Part of it was his power, of course, and how comfortable he was with it. An aphrodisiac as potent as money to a certain type of woman. But not Aine. What drew her to Hunter was the vulner-ability just under the surface of the hard shell. To the boys, he was The Hunter, one of a kind, a loose cannon tolerated by the head of the house because he always got the bad guys in the end. But The Hunter had shown her the boy in him but that, too, she reckoned, was part of the act. And that was sad and really why she had warmed to him. Because he didn't like himself.

He'd spent so long playing the roles, getting into the characters, that he was not comfortable in himself. Everyone had a story to tell about The Hunter but nobody knew anything about the man. Sergeant Burns was the exception. He'd known the Inspector longer than anyone, but he did not contribute to any conversation about the myth or the man.

Aine put her thoughts away for another time and returned to the matter in hand, though she was not sure of its nature. She was driving to Busby, that much was straightforward, but that was about all.

An elderly woman stepped off the pavement without looking, forcing Aine to step on the anchors. She gave the old dear a colourful mouthful. Her passenger showed no reaction. He was a Croat or a Serb or a Slovene or something. No speaka da anyway. And that, naturally, was why she was driving him to the fertility clinic.

It was, of course, at Hunter's request. And it was that, a request, not an order.

'How'd you like a wee jaunt?' he had asked.

She had hesitated, unsure of his meaning, and he had said, defensively, 'Up to you.'

The refugee, whose brother had been missing for six days, had set up camp in the front office. His mate, who did speaka da a wee bit, had come in with the guy yesterday. But today the bloke arrived himself, with a photo of his brother and a piece of paper on which was written, 'Find my brother. I will not leave.'.

This was Hunter's jaunt. She was to see what 'the fragrant Zara' could make of it. The approach would be made to her in her capacity as expert in affairs concerning refugees and asylum seekers. Her guidance could easily be sought on the phone but Aine knew that it was not hers to reason why. And she did want a peep at the Carmichaels' empire, the home of the boy who could remember his dreams.

'And while you're there,' Hunter said, 'see what you make of her. There's something about that place that's not kosher.'

He had gone a bit awkward, vaguely conscious that the comment might not be pc, and wondering if he had offended the WPC. She had tried to reassure him with a smile, then turned to leave, but he had not been finished with her.

'By the way,' he had said, 'you've been transferred to plain clothes. Con-gratulations, Detective.

She was about to thank him but he stifled it. Instead, he told her to take a marked police car and park it on the lawn, in full view of the neighbours.

'Then we'll see how fragrant she is . . .'

The guy had been on the phone six times. He wouldn't say what it was about, just that it was 'dead, dead important' and to tell Mr Hunter that it was Shooey and he would understand.

It was the last thing that Hunter needed but Digger had taken two of the calls himself and said that there was a desperation in the voice.

Not the brightest crayon in the box, Shooey, but doing his best now. And he had a nice wee mammy who didn't need any more hassle. She had turned in her own man – what? – must be twenty years ago now, for a string of indecency offences against children. Hunter reckoned they'd send him to Carstairs, let the white coats look inside his head and try to rearrange his marbles, but they'd put him in Peterhead with the really bad bastards and he'd come out in a pine box.

Shooey hadn't been the most popular wee laddie in the Gorbals before his old man's hobby became known and, after it, his life was a misery. He had made it all the way through List D schools to Barlinnie and all for stealing cars. He was known as Shooey after Formula One racing driver Michael Schumacher. He was a piss-poor car thief. Not for him the Ford Escorts of this world that you could open with a paper-clip and flog to shady dealers down the side alleys. Oh, no. Shooey only went for big, expensive cars, the ones with the big, expensive alarms that attracted the mee-maw coppers like wasps to your can of beer. He said the buzz was better than drugs. For as long as it lasts, 'I'm the man. Top of the world, Ma. You know what I mean, Mr Hunter?'

Problem was that the last car he took belonged to his lawyer. Nice shiny BMW, personalised number plate and all. Shooey had worked it out. 'It was only a wee loan, really, and I was due that. I've made him a lot of money, when you get right down to it.'

Shooey was off his head – no question about it – but another spell in pokey would not put him back on it. So Hunter had got him a job and his lawyer (his new, legal aid lawyer) had got him a year's suspended sentence.

The job at the mortuary at the Royal Infirmary involved tagging dead bodies and severed limbs. Shooey had been there for nearly two years. Said it 'wasn't the best job in the world, but it's important, and it's no' everybody that can do it. Know what I mean?'

The corridor was about twelve yards long. Chipped, dark green lino, dark green glossy walls and a ceiling that had been white when there was a king on the throne. Hunter paused at the double-swing doors at the end of it, taking a deep breath, as if it would last for the time he would spend behind them. Toshie's face flashed into his mind. Toshie laughing, knocking back a swig of whisky, Black Label, by the neck and passing the bottle on to the other fishermen. Toshie's face at the bin shelter, a tampon inserted in the temple. Toshie's face, already turning a bluish black where the blood had settled at the lowest point, on the pathologist's marble slab.

And the sickly-sweet smell of death and decay.

Shooey spotted him before the swing doors had come to rest.

'It's no' right, Sir, stealing a wean. Even a dead wean. It's just . . .' he searched for the right words, '. . . not on.'

He had reported the incident but insisted that they 'were covering it up'. So he had called The Hunter.

'This'll do me no good at all, Mr Hunter. They might even try to get rid of me. Cos they all stick together, don't they? But it has to be investigated. That doctor stole a dead wean. It's the God's honest truth, Sir. Cross my heart and hope to die.'

Jamesie continued to decline to take Hunter's phone calls. That was the thing about mobile phones. They gave the worst of people advantages. Hunter had left his number with the answering service and realised, almost immediately, that it had been a mistake. Jamesie could programme the effin thingie, put his number into it and know whenever he was calling. Snigger his defiance, pretend to wipe his arse with the phone. But his victory would be short-lived. Two could play at that game, play it dirty.

Hunter had dropped in on Alma, Jamesie's sweetheart, or, in the vernacular, his bidie-in, although she preferred to be referred to as his common-law wife. She had lived with Jamesie, on and off, for twenty years but still kept her maiden name. She was Alma Rogan, Jamesie's housekeeper. And she ruled him with a rod of iron. When Alma said jump, Jamesie asked, 'How high?' So Hunter gave Alma a call, on his mobile, from his car parked across from her house. Said long time no see, Alma, how're you doing? Oh, and by the way, he was hoping to hear from Jamesie. He had a wee message to do – it would only take ten minutes or so – then he would come back. Pop in for a cuppa, wait for the man of the house to return.

Jamesie called him in two minutes flat. Whispering because he couldn't talk. Said that Hunter could get him killed. Hunter agreed and said that Jamesie should never forget it. Then he arranged their meeting place. Jamesie said that he couldn't go there. Hunter told him that he would, one way or another, and hung up.

The receptionist had left Aine and her refugee standing on the doorstep of the old house in Busby while she had gone to find out if it would be possible for Mrs Carmichael to see them at all this evening, though she doubted it, doubted it very much, since Mrs Carmichael was particularly busy and they hadn't even telephoned first and what was it about anyway?

Aine had told her it was about police business.

But what, the receptionist said, looking at her watch and then squinting at the marked police car which was blocking the entrance to the clinics, should she tell Mrs Carmichael?

Tell her it's about police business, Aine had said quite slowly, very quietly and definitely finally. Her refugee – she had found out that his name was Radovan and nothing else – watched the exchange with little more than disdain.

The door had been shut in their faces so they stood on the doorstep, examining the impressive credentials of the Carmichaels on the ostentatious metal plates. Radovan rubbed his thumb and forefinger together in the international recognition of money. A lot of it. A couple of minutes later, Aine spotted the telltale chink in the curtains on the window to their right. It appeared that Mrs Carmichael had found a window in her busy schedule to take a peek at her visitors. She would also have noticed the marked police car.

Aine heard the receptionist clip-clopping along the hall. When she opened the door she had a nice, big smile on her frosty face. Mrs Carmichael would be only too happy to help. If they wouldn't mind going to the back of the house. Just round the drive. They could take the car.

They could but they didn't. They walked past Calder's clinic and around the old stables with their hidden secrets.

Zara was waiting for them at the little kitchen. She greeted them cordially and led them to a reception room, all the way to the front of the building. She asked, out of politeness, if they would have time for a cuppa or were they too busy?

Aine accepted, partly because she was not expected to do so but mainly because she knew that it guaranteed a hearing of at least fifteen minutes. Zara used the internal phone to enlist the receptionist's assistance. If she could just make a pot of tea, maybe some biscuits, and that would be all for the day. Zara put the phone down and made a point of tidying some papers on her desk. Aine fancied that the receptionist's approaching clip-clops on the wooden floor were just a little petulant. Hunter would be proud of her.

'Now,' Zara said, all polite efficiency, 'how might I help?'

Everything directed at Aine. Zara had given Radovan a cursory glance – the cheap clothing, square face and demeanour – and had labelled him immediately. Aine told the story – how Radovan had refused to leave the police station until steps were taken to trace his relative.

Zara said, 'And the nationality is?'

Aine said that she didn't know.

'But surely . . .' Zara started, then quickly regained her composure. 'Could the interpreters not communicate with him?'

Aine said simply that she did not have interpreters.

Zara's smile dimmed but her perfect teeth were still on show. She said, 'You're not from Sighthill Police Station?'

'No.' Aine was not helping. The opposite, in fact.

Zara was forced to ask her, 'Where are you from?'

'HQ,' Aine said.

The receptionist arrived with the tea and Zara was glad of the interruption. While the milk and sugar were going the rounds, she tried a few words on Radovan until she got a response. The sound of his own language brought the refugee to life and he spoke animatedly, arms flapping, eager to relate the whole sorry tale. He could have saved his breath because, even if Zara could have understood, she was not listening. She was tapping at her computer, calling up a list of names and phone numbers. When she found the one that she wanted, she punched out the numbers on the phone. It was answered on the second ring and Zara was not overly polite.

'This is Zara Carmichael. I have one of your people here. He has been bothering the police. Talk to him.'

She handed the phone to Radovan, who started to speak but shut up quickly.

Aine could hear the angry voice on the other end. Radovan paled, then nodded obediently. He gave the phone to Zara, got up and beckoned to Aine to do so too. She shook her head and he took her by the arm and physically lifted her. A smirk crept into Zara's smile. She was enjoying this now. Aine let the show go on a little longer. Then she bent back Radovan's thumb, taming him in an instant, putting him back in his chair. She felt bad when he put on his sad face again but she would deal with that later. Right now, she had other fish to fry. But she would do it slowly. She took a sip of tea, then lifted a biscuit, a ginger nut, and effortlessly snapped it in two.

Zara appeared to have recognised a challenge and determined that she would not blink first.

It was Calder who broke the deadlock. He burst into the room. 'There's a bloody police car . . .'

Then he saw that his wife had company.

Zara said, 'This is my husband, Calder.'

She smiled sweetly, then added, 'And this is . . . oh dear, I've forgotten your name.'

'Yes,' Murdo said, 'it's Strangelove.'

He had taken the tape to his bedsit in Dennistoun, locked the door and watched it on his VCR. He'd dared to use the pause button once, and then only briefly, because the old machine had developed a tendency to chew up tapes. It had done it on Saturday night, when he was sure Rangers should have been awarded a penalty rather than a free kick on the edge of the box. The matter remained unresolved because, as he was examining the late tackle frame by frame, the tape had snapped. He'd had to unscrew the cover of the VCR and gently pull both halves of the tape from the heads. It was like trying to hold on to a dream, retaining a balance between imagination and reality and then splicing them together for a memory. But the join showed, an awkward step, between then and now, and the moment was gone forever.

He'd had to create to get this tape in the first place. The guy in charge of security at the Royal Infirmary was an ex-cop, chief inspector no less, and he'd tried to pull rank. He said that a full internal inquiry was under way and, if – only if, mind you – police involvement was deemed necessary he would get in contact 'through the appropriate channels'.

Murdo decided to play it slow. He pointed out that he had been asked to request the tape from the CCTV camera which covered the passageway leading to the mortuary. But, if the security officer was refusing, he would have to report to his superior officer. The guy had told him to be careful, very careful indeed, with the allegations. Nobody was refusing anything. Then he had become all Chief Inspector-ish. Murdo pointed out that Constable (serving) outgunned Chief Inspector (retired) and the procurator fiscal would know it. The tape would, no question about it, be taken by the police intact. What the guy had to ask himself was how did he want to be known to his mates on the force. Did he want his reputation intact or in tatters? The outcome had been decided at that moment but Murdo allowed him five minutes of bullshit, to let him save face. He'd got what he wanted, no sense in making an enemy.

Hunter had been surprised that it had gone so smoothly. He knew the guy of old. Said he was 'a bit of an arse who hates my guts'.

Murdo didn't say that he hadn't mentioned Hunter's name. But he'd sussed that, if his boss had thought it would have smoothed things along, he would have been there in person.

The star of the film appeared for a total of eighteen seconds, equally divided into a back view and full frontal. The tape was of poor quality – fuzzy was the young cop's description to Hunter – because it had been used time and again in the CCTV camera. The young woman (a defence counsel would rip this to shreds but Murdo felt that she was young) looked every inch the doctor. White coat, stethoscope around the neck, flat, sensible shoes and a no-nonsense haircut. She had a purposeful stride, along the middle of the corridor which would make anyone of inferior rank give way. Murdo assimilated all of this information immediately and then little else. The biggest single impression he had arrived at was – good legs, though he decided not to pass this on to Hunter.

She was inside the mortuary for two minutes and twenty-eight seconds. Then she reappeared, backing out of the swing doors like a gunfighter leaving a saloon. When she turned round, it took a conscious effort of mind to look any place other than the little white bundle that she cradled in her arms. Murdo decided that, even if he had not known that the sheet contained the body of a stillborn child, his eyes would still have been fixed there. It was as if the film director had studied all the angles to ensure that the viewer's attention was drawn to that one place and the eyes followed it all the way along that grim passage. It was something to do with a life being snuffed out before it even began and then, in a macabre twist, being spirited back to the land of the living.

Murdo watched the front view seven times. The woman was looking down at her little bundle so that only the top of her head was visible. Her hands were crossed over the body of the child, left over right, and no rings were visible. She raised her head at the end of the corridor as she took the last stride. Murdo initially thought that she was looking at the doors, which she bumped open with her right hip. But, on the seventh viewing, he saw that it was done for a different reason. The action was carried out so quickly that the face was a blur. You knew that there were features there – eyes, nose, mouth – but the quality of the film was so poor and she moved her head so quickly that you could not gain any perspective. But the lips were moving. He was sure of that. She was talking to them.

Hunter had asked just one question and Murdo had glanced at the sketch drawn from the description given by the homeless man. Then he had said the words Hunter wanted to hear.

'Yes, it's Strangelove.'

'I'd just love to make her smile on the other side of her face.'

Hunter chuckled, a strange, contagious sound, a high-pitched laugh like a boy having his toes tickled. It took the edge off Aine's anger. She had been seething ever since the visit to Busby.

Hunter said, 'Didn't like the fragrant Zara, eh?'

Aine went all professional, started to tell him how Mistress (that was how she pronounced it) Carmichael had used her interpreter to threaten Radovan, to terrify him, but Hunter cut her off.

He said, 'We'll do the run-of-play later. Tell me what you think about her.'

Aine's face told it before her words. Hunter noted that he'd have to work on that with her. Teach her to mask her feelings.

She said, 'Mistress Carmichael is a cold, calculating, cruel, ruthless bitch. You asked me, you'll get it. She treated that poor guy like he was a piece of shit on her shoe and she took a twisted pleasure in it. She took an instant dislike to me and she'd decided to put me in my place, too. And I don't know what you're smirking at because it was when she found out that I worked for you that she turned into Dr Jekyll or Mrs Hyde or whatever one it was that was the bad one.'

Hunter killed his smile. 'Doesn't sound like the woman who makes babies.'

Aine said, 'I wouldn't let my niece take her dog there. And I'll tell you something for nothing – her husband's a weirdo, too.'

Hunter said, 'So it's Mr and Mrs Weird, eh?'

'Well, you asked for what I feel but I can give you the facts any time you like.'

She suddenly felt that she had gone too far, forgotten that she was reporting to a superior officer and one who was opening doors for her, too. But she need not have worried. Hunter's silence was not a rebuke but an indication that an idea was germinating. He'd had an inkling about Mr Weird. Why not the missus, too? But how – babies, refugees, both? He hoped that it would keep. He had a serial killer on the loose, an impending slaughter in the drugs war and a Chief Constable who didn't know his arse from his elbow but wanted The Hunter fired.

And, for my next trick . . .

He said, 'Your man, wotsisname, Transit Van, he okay?'

'Radovan,' she corrected him, 'and he is, okay, actually.'

She was still angry. A lot of passion there, Hunter noted. Firey. Some young man would have his hands full. Never a dull moment there.

Aine went on, 'Zara is only fragrant when Zara is in charge. When she is ruling the roost. She said that Sighthill was a "melting pot for the disenfranchised of the world". That was her description. Impressed? Neither was I. She said they all had their own cliques – now there's a surprise – you talk to the folk who understand you – so, once she found out where Radovan was from, all she had to do was contact his leader – she called him his godfather, made it sound like the Mafia – and get him to sort it out. But she did it in such a . . . cruel way. Frightened Radovan. Treated him like shit.'

She came up for air, then added, 'Did I mention that I don't like her?'

Hunter noted that she had not said 'didn't'. The matter, quite clearly, was not closed. Zara's name was in her notebook with a black spot beside it. One day . . .

Hunter said, 'So Transit Van's not going to park, permanently, in the front office.

Aine said, 'No. I took him back to Sighthill. He's twenty-eight storeys up, living in the clouds, but that's another matter. It turned out that his brother had just done a runner. Got in a fight with an uncle and bogged off. He's in Manchester, safe and well. Radovan spoke to him on the phone.'

She recalled another observation from Castle Carmichael. 'Zara assumed that I was from Sighthill Station but Calder immediately associated me with you. I don't know what that means but there it is anyway. His eyes almost popped out of his head when I asked how Matthew Whittle was keeping. He said fine but quickly added that he was sleeping. I thought it was a joke, you know, about the dreams and all, but he said no, he was asleep. Then he said that he had to rush. But I thought he was spooked.'

171

Hunter said, 'Okay, you've got two choices. Write up a full report or take me for a drink.'

She hesitated, pretending to weigh up the pros and cons, then said, 'You buying the crisps?'

'Maybe,' he said, 'but after the drink. I don't like to eat on an empty stomach. But first, we've got to see a man about a bitch.'

He had seen Hunter there, all too often. At the centre of the spider's web, a finger on each strand, taking the pulse. He had sat in, briefly, when the webmaster darted off to examine an interesting vibration, so he had an idea of how it all worked. But Digger Burns had never been in overall charge. He had not wanted it – not until recently, anyway. And now that he was getting a taste of it, he was having doubts that it was the way to go.

His major motivation to seek promotion, if the truth be told, was money. And he had always thought that a wrong reason. He had enough to get by – even after the aliment was taken away – so who needed all the hassle? That was how he had always thought. But that was before he had remarried – and she was a great kid. Best decision of his life, no question about it. Lorna took him for what he was, didn't buy into the basic model then set about trying to upgrade it. Said she didn't need, or want, to change him. But now there was a baby on the way. Now Lorna was on maternity leave and neither of them wanted her to go back to work after the birth.

Digger had raised the matter – maybe he should go for his Inspector's ticket – a few months ago.

'If you want to,' she'd said. 'If you really want to, do it. But not for the money. That would change us.'

He had asked how, in what ways, but she wouldn't elaborate. Just said that they'd manage. Added that they hadn't starved a winter yet.

He'd mentioned it again last night, said he was already doing the job anyway because Hunter had gone walkabout again.

'And?' Lorna said.

'And,' he told her, 'it's a lonely job. Being in charge, depending on the other cops to do the job for you. Trusting them but watching their faces when you tell them to do something they disagree with. When you pull them off one line of inquiry and put them on to another. And, I suppose, it's a bit scary.'

She'd said that was okay then, he should go for it, if it was a bit scary. But not for the money. He'd said that was fine because there wouldn't be any extra dosh, not for a while anyway. Oh, and incidentally, he'd need clean underpants. Often.

She'd laughed and they had gone on seamlessly to discuss the important things in their life. Like wee Digger practising for Murrayfield. Lorna had rolled down her trousers and he could actually see the lumps in her big tummy as the wee man kicked for touch. She was sure it was a boy. Her gran had done the test with the wedding ring on a piece of thread over her stomach and it had gone back and forth, or in circles, or whatever Gran said was the boy way.

Digger put a Polo mint into his mouth. He'd stopped smoking two years ago but recently the craving had returned. He had looked at the fags in the newsagents this morning. Wondered if he could buy one packet, just one pack of ten, and use them like medication. But he knew, if he did that, he was back on them again. He didn't do it. And the main reason was the money.

Committee Room Three was dead, apart from two young cops keying the Strangelove data into the computers and manning the phones. It was like that, sometimes, in the biggest cases. There were always occasions when nothing was happening and taking a long time to do it. Digger usually made himself scarce, found a place he had to be – any place, as long as it was far from the deafening silence, the feeling of helplessness which frayed tempers and turned good cop against good cop. But tonight he didn't have that luxury. He had to remain at the centre of the web, going over the vibrations, praying that he was not misinterpreting them.

Hunter had told him not to try too hard. To pretend that he was watching the telly. 'Morse, Frost, that type of crap. The good bits, the important stuff'll be obvious. You won't miss it. It'll jump up and bite you on the balls.'

So far he'd only had a few nibbles. The best had produced the artist's impression of their killer. It had been Murdo who had found the vagrant who claimed to have seen her walking in front of Mr Macintosh along St Vincent Street. The young cop had walked the route from the venue of the Press Fund Ball to the scene of the murder exactly twenty-four hours on. Did it off his own bat, unpaid, of course. He'd found the bloke dossing in the doorway of an empty shop.

'Yeah,' he said, 'I saw them. Together, but apart.'

Problem was that bottle of Buckfast he'd seen them through. But, then again, Digger reckoned, that was pretty normal for the guy.

The artist had been reluctant. Come over all temperamental. There was little to go on, the witness was not reliable and he had no confidence in the job. Digger took him aside and left him in no doubt that the task was not a request, it was an order. The troops didn't hear a word but they saw another side to the Sergeant. The artist pouted a little but he did his job. The outcome was, well, sketchy but they had produced an image. It was more an abstract work than still life and, although pencil drawn, it looked as if it had been roughed out using an inch paintbrush. It was all lines – Digger could make out five different noses – but some of the strokes were darker than the others and somewhere in the middle of it all was the image. The really spooky thing was – and Hunter had used the same word, spooky – it looked just as they had imagined her. Somewhere in the middle of all those lines and curves was the face of their killer.

Strangelove.

Digger tried to remember when Hunter had named her. It was soon after the second murder, at the bin shelter, he reckoned, when they had found the tampon inserted in the expertly cut wound in Mr Macintosh's temple. Hunter had actually called her 'Dr' Strangelove and every scrap of evidence to date had fitted in. Not *been* fitted in – Digger had been careful about that, ensuring that he had not given priority to the information which backed up the theory – but all the solid pointers showed that Hunter had been spot on.

There had been nothing at first to prove that the killer was a woman. Then the lab team had found the menstrual blood and it had matched that on the sanitary towel she had left near Mr Knox's body. The fatal blows had been delivered by a knowledgeable hand – and they were becoming increasingly confident that they were looking for a doctor or a nurse, past or present. And, of course, sex had been the lure.

Strange love.

Digger had always respected the Inspector – his rank and the fact that he got the right result. But he did not like the man, either as a person or a policeman, though the two were indistinguishable. He was too selfish, too manipulative. Everything had to be done when and how it suited The Hunter. Even the nickname, which Digger suspected he had given himself, said me, me, me.

But now, at the centre of the web, Digger had a different perspective. Hunter might be a bit of a joke with the top brass but nobody was laughing on the streets, where it mattered. He was treated with respect there, from the Jimmy Stones and Danny Boyds all the way down to the young tearaways sent before the Children's Panel. Nobody messed with The Hunter. He knew the city and its lowlife like a bad penny. If he didn't know who had done the crime, he knew a man who did. And he wasn't too bothered about what he had to do to find out. He said it came under the overriding, fundamental Hunter's Law – bad guys have no rights.

Digger could see now that Hunter had put himself in the firing line. He took on the toughest cases before he was given them. And he resolved them the only way he knew how. He had set himself up and now he was isolated. Not one of the Indians – though he played at it when it suited him – and certainly not one of the chiefs.

He was one of a kind.

There had been a few occasions over the years – not many, thank God, but more than Digger cared to remember – when he had blundered. Hunter had been hauled upstairs for them – got it in the neck, too – but he never passed it on. He'd kicked Digger's backside, of course, kept him on his toes, but the Sergeant had never been rebuked by another superior officer. Hunter had acted as a buffer, protected him from that. He could see that now.

Just as he could see that his gaffer was giving him the chance to shine in what looked like becoming the biggest murder hunt the force had seen in many a long day. Digger wondered if Hunter knew that he was finally thinking about his Inspector's ticket. Was this Hunter's way of helping him? He would never know. But he did know that his gaffer was still keeping a watchful eye on him.

Hunter had dropped in to CR3 earlier – 'just a pit stop, new pipe and a piddle' – and asked what was doing. But he had already known. Aine had been despatched on a trip with a refugee. That had puzzled Digger and he was on the point of questioning this use of the limited resources but thought better of it.

Then Murdo, Hunter's other protégé, had appeared briefly at the door. Now you see him, now you don't. Hunter had delayed his own exit. Gone over to a couple of the coppers, shook one guy's hand. A fellow Mason, probably – have to count your fingers afterwards – then teased the other guy about St Mirren, his football team, a 'bunch of J Arthur Rankers', then drifted out.

Murdo had appeared back five minutes later. Ten minutes after that, Digger's phone rang. It was Hunter, asking him to pop down to his office. It was a decent act, a kindness from a man who didn't want the Constables to think that Digger was getting instructions, that he wasn't in charge.

But there were no niceties in Hunter's office. There was no time for that. A window was open (How did he manage that?) but there was already a thick fug of pipe smoke in the room. Digger hadn't even time to cough when Hunter started. There was a drugs war looming but he needn't bother about that. There was something really fishy about a health centre in Busby but that wasn't his concern, either. But this was . . .

A television and video had been set up in the corner. Hunter pressed the remote control and ran the CCTV tape from the Royal Infirmary. The face on the film was fuzzy but it was the face the artist had drawn. It was Strangelove.

And Hunter said that now she was stealing dead babies. Then he went on to tell Digger about the hundred and one things that he had to worry about.

Digger listened and watched The Hunter in full flow. He was like a circus act, the guy who takes a dozen folk out of the audience and gets them to spin plates on sticks then keeps them all going himself. They begin to wobble at the same time but he knows which needs attention first. Then he catches them, individually, until only one is left.

Lisa pressed the silver button on the armrest and the aircraft seat eased back to reclining position. She closed her eyes and tried to sleep. She blended in well with the passengers on the holiday charter flight. She had been on stand-by and was delighted to get a seat. She wore a powder-blue tracksuit – hastily purchased at the souk – that covered the bruises which were appearing in black-blues all over her body. As she had dressed, she had noticed Abdul's fingermarks, five to each hip, where he had held her aloft and pummelled her with his penis at the end of the film shoot in the studio in the morning. The cameras had not been running – they had run out of film – but that didn't matter to him. He was just ramming home his control over her. Or so he thought.

Lisa shifted on the seat, sliding down, taking the weight off her hips, but she succeeded only in shifting the pain to another area. It didn't matter. She would heal. She always had. The bruises would turn to autumnal russets and yellows before fading, leaving only wintry memories.

The fasten seatbelt sign is on and the captain has said that the plane had begun its descent into Glasgow airport. Two babies were crying and a little girl in the row of seats behind Lisa was becoming increasingly fractious. She wanted to know why she couldn't see the sun. She was nearer to it, so surely she should see it. Her mother said it had gone to bed but the explanation was not satisfactory. Mum explained that the big, dark cloud was its duvet and the sun had popped its head under it. That was acceptable to the girl.

Lisa was suddenly envious of both mother and daughter. She never had such a childhood. Never had wonderment or make-believe; never had a relationship with a parent where trust was such that reality could be suspended and her imagination allowed to roam free. For her, it was straight from fairy tales to the father grim. She had also been robbed of the chance to experience that age of innocence through the eyes of her own child. Another man she had trusted had stolen that from her. Dr Simon. It was not only his unwanted baby that had been sucked from her womb. It was her ability – no, her right – to conceive another child.

Lisa moved again on the seat, redistributing the pain. There were some things that she couldn't change. But she could get mad – and she could get even. Dr Simon would discover that very soon. He had not been quite so pleased to hear from her when she'd called his mobile. But he said that he could probably squeeze in a drink tomorrow night. Told her to call at lunchtime to confirm it.

She said that she was really looking forward to it – and so were her cheeky bits! That aroused his interest and he said he was looking forward to seeing them too.

But he would see much more than that. He would see something to die for.

'You're really sick, d'you know that? I mean, there's something wrong in there.'

Jamesie tapped his temple with a forefinger. He was still shaking – from fear and anger.

Hunter opened the door of the smart cabriolet and lowered himself into the passenger's seat. He had watched the car crawl down the dark, tree-lined avenue to Daldowie Crematorium. Jamesie had kept the lights off, afraid of drawing attention to himself, and Hunter had seen him stop twice and ignite his cigarette lighter. As if that would help him see better. Or maybe it was in prayer to the great god Embassy.

Hunter had arrived at twenty minutes to midnight, parked the Vectra at the rear of the west chapel, well out of sight, and walked to the meeting place at the east chapel. He leaned against the lavvy and kindled up his pipe. Ban smoking here and they'd go out of business. He was not sure of Jamesie. The guy respected him, no doubt about that, but he was also afraid of Danny Boyd. And he couldn't serve two masters. Well, he could but not for long.

Jamesie had arrived bang on time and, when his wee puddle-jumper of a car stopped, Hunter sneaked up from the back, banged on the driver's window and pulled a funny face. Jamesie nearly shit himself. He told Hunter to get in quickly, shut the door quickly. He was worried about the piddling wee bulb in the courtesy light.

That was good, Hunter thought. He wanted the man scared. Needed him to know his place. He got right down to business.

'Well, Jamesie, here at the crem we're doing a bit of forward planning. It's a busy time for us y'see – first cold snap'll snuff out quite a lot of muppets who escaped last winter. So, Jamesie, my man, what we need to know is this. When're you planning some more work for us?'

And James trotted it out, chapter and verse. The names of those who were going to hit Jimmy Stone's team, the weapons they had, where they would gather and when.

Hunter thought it almost too good to be true. And almost too bad to be bullshit. Jamesie gripped the steering wheel tight. Hunter noticed that he was wearing a knuckleduster – a big, ostentatious job, heavy gold, that spanned the middle and third fingers of his right hand. It might be a trick of the light but Hunter thought that it spelled out Jamsie. He looked at the ring for a while, to allow the silence to become uncomfortable.

Finally, Jamesie said, 'It's the truth. I'll swear it on Alma's life. And I'll tell you something else but you've got to promise me first that that's it. We're quits. Okay? Promise?'

Hunter reined him back. 'Hold on to your horses, Jamesie. What's the rush? It's not as if we're on a parking meter or anything, eh?'

And he took Jamesie through it all again, slowly, backtracking, at some points deliberately changing some of the data, pretending to be confused. But Jamesie picked up on the traps immediately, corrected the errors, told exactly the same story.

And Hunter believed him. So much so that he said, 'Jamesie, my old son, Danny would have your guts for garters for this. You know I've got to stop this hit. Not that I give a shit for The Stoneman and his neds any more than I do for Danny and yours. But the noise from all those guns might disturb some decent folk. Now, Jamesie, I'm going to be straight with you.'

Jamesie snorted in derision and turned his head away. A cloud rolled over the moon and the chimney of the incinerator disappeared.

Hunter continued, 'Just tell me this. All this stuff you've told me – now think before you answer – could Danny know it was you?'

Jamesie turned on him in a flash. 'D'you think I'm fuckin daft? D'you think I'd be here if he could. No. No way. There's too many involved – and I'm the last one he'd suspect.'

Hunter nodded, then said, 'Okay. Fine. That's good. Just checking, Jamesie. And thanks. I mean it. I owe you one.'

He opened the door, but Jamesie reacted as the light flickered.

'Hang on,' he said, 'I've not finished yet. There's another thing. But first you've got to promise. After this, we're quits. Give me your word.'

178

It would have been easy to lie. Hunter's Law – bad guys have no rights. But Hunter closed the door and told the truth.

'Sorry, Jamesie, no can do. You live in your world and I live in mine. But I will promise you this – if there's another way of doing my job, I won't call on you again.'

Jamesie thought about this for a long time and seemed to consider it fair.

He said, 'Okay, then, Mr Hunter. I'll tell you anyway. There's a contract out on you.'

7

They passed in the hall and he dropped her a little smile, the kind he gave people he once knew. She pulled her dressing gown tighter across her chest, an expression of curiosity on her face, as if she couldn't quite place him. Strangers in the morning.

She went into the kitchen and saw that he had poured the dregs of his cup of tea into the sink. It was lying there staining the stainless steel. Little boy's tea, that's what he drank, sweet, weak and milky. But he took his coffee strong and black, without sugar. One of his many contradictions.

She had been in bed when he'd come home last night, well this morning, just after 1 a.m. There had been no phone call to say he'd be late and, if she asked why not, he'd say that it hadn't been possible or, when it was, it was late and he thought she'd be in bed and he didn't want to wake her. He'd come straight upstairs – no nightcaps, she had noted – and, when he got into bed, she could hardly detect the smell of whisky. It was there, as ever, but barely discernible under the reek of pipe tobacco. They both lay utterly still and she wondered if he knew she was awake. She had considered saying something but couldn't decide whether to be nice or ask him where he'd been. Again. So she said nothing. At least he was home and she didn't have to worry about him. Not till tonight, anyway.

She ran the cold tap and rinsed the sink. The kettle was empty so she filled it and switched it on. Maybe he'd want another cuppa. He didn't eat in the mornings. Truth be told, he rarely had a meal in the house full stop. Except Sundays, if he wasn't on a case. He'd make brunch – a fry-up, about a million calories – but she'd eat it and they'd read the papers. At night she'd have a roast or steak or stew. Now and again she'd give him chicken or salmon, a nice bit of pork. Something different. And he'd eat it and say that was good, now where's my dinner? Bits off a dead cow, that's what I like, he would say. Bits off a dead cow.

She went to the front door, took the newspaper from the letterbox. Must be a new delivery boy, he'd left the wrong one. No matter. She could hear the tap running in the bathroom upstairs.

He'd be brushing his teeth. Must have shaved when she was still asleep – run the water gently so he wouldn't wake her. But it was gushing now. She knew she'd have to wipe the splashes off the floor tiles later.

She laid the paper on the kitchen table and scanned the headlines. Nothing or the front page. Two and three were clear, too. So nothing big had happened. If he had been involved in anything big, it would be on the first three pages. She checked the next four, just to be sure.

The water stopped. Then she heard him spit out the toothpaste. It would leave a white rim around the sink, two inches up from the plughole. She put on the grill, sat the loaf on the breadboard and got the big knife out of the drawer. When he came down, if he wanted to talk, fine. That would be good. If not, she'd have something to do. Cut a couple of slices off the loaf. Put it in the grill. Get out the sunflower spread. A knife.

She heard him coming down the stairs. At the kitchen door. She had her back to it but she could feel him there. She cut one slice off the loaf. Sneaked a look in the kettle. He looked as if he was in the hall of mirrors at the fair. Tiny legs. Big, fat waist. Tiny head. And he had his jacket on. The kettle was nearly boiling, making a noise, so she could pretend she didn't hear him. She cut the second slice, slowly, sneaked another look. He was still there but she couldn't tell if he was looking at her. She wanted the kettle to boil, to click off. Then she could reach up to the cupboard, take out a cup. Get a teabag from the stainless steel caddy. The kettle hissed but didn't boil. She had to turn round to put the bread in the grill. And recognise that he was there.

But, before she could do that, he said, 'I'm for the off then. I might be late.'

Then he was gone.

Hunter had been awake most of the night, listening to Bella snoring. She'd heard him come in, she hadn't been asleep then, because she was still and stiff as a corpse when he'd got into bed and she had lain like that, well over in her own side of the bed, for a long time. He was going to talk to her – he wanted to talk – just had to say, 'Are you awake?', something like that. But what next? I came home specially to see you at lunchtime and heard you tell your pals that I peed in the garden. Or I nearly got the sack today. Or somebody's hired a guy to kill me.

He took a bite out of the bacon roll and washed it down with a swig of tea. He was at his favourite table in Joe's Cafe off Victoria Road. Couldn't remember driving there – must have done it on autopilot – didn't even think consciously of going. One minute he was looking at the back of

Bella's candlewick dressing gown and next was parked outside Joe's Cafe. The driver's door window had been open a couple of inches and the wee electric button wouldn't move it. Bugger it. He wished that was all of his current problems.

The small cafe was busy. Real working people, too. A team of road workers, wellies and tarry overalls, were steaming into fry-ups. A couple of bus drivers up at the counter waiting for a carry-out. A postie, half-full bag on his back, standing at the door and shoving a roll on sausage into his face. Two guys waiting for Joe to impregnate perfectly good food with lard. They looked like lorry drivers. Or were they hired killers?

That's the kind of thing he had been thinking about when he should have been sleeping. The number of crooks who would want him out of the way would run into three figures. So he had refined the search. That's what they did on the computer to reduce the possibilities, refined the search, to make the list manageable. He'd decided just to go back ten years and work forward. Anybody he had put away in 1993, even for murder, would be out now.

One guy sprang to mind immediately. Snotty Wyllie, released in August, no July, when Bella was in the Algarve with the Coffee Girls. Hunter remembered that he was washing a week's teacups and whisky glasses when the phone rang. He'd taken the call in the kitchen. It was a mate in the parole board, to let him know that Wyllie was getting out, 'just because there's a history'.

Wyllie had robbed the building society and made a good job of it. Worn a hallowe'en mask, had a motorbike parked round the corner and disappeared like snow off a dyke. But it was him, no question about it. He had the form, two previous, and a total of seven years in pokey to prove it. Hunter's informants had told him that he was planning a job. They didn't know exactly when, but it would be on the south side of the city and he would have a gun. He was bragging about it. Afterwards, Wyllie was seen to flash the cash. Paid off the loan sharks, bought rounds in pubs owned by folk with selective memories. But the main reason Hunter knew it was him was the interview. He'd hauled Wyllie in, a week after the robbery, just when he would be thinking that he was home free. He'd been worried – but not a lot – when Digger had picked him up and he was edgy when Hunter walked into the interview room. But, as time wore on, as he realised that they had nothing on him, he became as smug as a eunuch with a dildo. He didn't just want to get away with it. He wanted them to know that he'd done it and was getting away with it. Wanted to put one over on The Hunter.

So Hunter had helped his case. Just a wee bit.

182

Wyllie had a sinus problem. He'd been called Snotty at school because of his runny nose. The woman in the building society said the guy who held up the building society had a cold, 'you know, spoke through his nose'. SOCO had picked up a paper tissue outside the building society. Could have been dropped by anyone but they had bagged it nevertheless. But that's as far as it had gone.

They'd held Snotty as long as they could. Then he'd walked. He knew Hunter was watching as he left the copshop. He'd turned around and given a cheeky wee wave. Then he blew his nose and dropped the tissue.

And, well, one paper tissue looks much like another . . .

It had been Digger's idea – at least he thought it was – to go back over the evidence from the scene of the crime. And – surprise, surprise – the DNA boys said the snotters on the bagged tissue were Snotty's. A billion per cent certain, they were. And so was the jury. As they took Snotty down from the dock, Hunter had given him a cheeky wee wave. Snotty had screamed blue murder. He'd been set up and he'd get even if it was the last thing he did. It had been no big deal. Just anger and bravado, the usual. Worry about that kind of thing and a copper might as well put his papers in.

Snotty had done his time – he'd got nine years and was out in five – and it had all been uneventful. He had protested his innocence of course – he'd been set up – the usual. Not a hint, not a cheep from any of his fellow inmates that he had meant what he had said. And anyway, Snotty didn't have the balls for a murder.

Hunter took a mouthful of cold tea. The postie had gone, so had the bus drivers, and the navvies were just about finished their fry-up. One guy was wiping runny egg off his plate with a slice of bread. Hunter put his hand in his pocket for a couple of quid. Nothing there. Not a sausage. All his change was sitting beside his chair, where he'd put it when he got home last night. Or this morning. He took his wallet out of his tail-pocket. Fifteen quid. He slipped the fiver under the mug and got up to leave.

The lorry drivers were shouting for another mug of tea. Not the act of contract killers.

So who, then?

Digger Burns was seriously thinking about enrolling in his wife's amateur dramatic society. He'd taken charge of the hunt for Strangelove on Sunday and done more acting than police work. His role was complex. He had to pretend that he knew what he was doing – gee up the troops and ensure them that they were making good progress and that he was about to lead them on to the next, and very possibly the final, stage of the investigation.

Digger took comfort, though, from knowing that Hunter was offstage, directing the players.

Digger had been out of the house since 6.30 a.m. and Lord knows when he would get back. Lorna had been in bed, fast asleep, when he'd got home last night. She'd left a note under the stork magnet on the fridge door – 'Your dinner's in the oven. PS – it's a salad! Love, Lorna and Digger Jr xx.'

The salad, actually, had been in the fridge – along with a note which said 'Only kidding!'. He'd picked at the food but put most of it into an Asda carrier bag, tied the neck and put it under her rubbish at the bottom of the dustbin lest he hurt her feelings. He had tiptoed across the red granite chips, placing his feet slowly, like a thief in the night, careful not to wake her. As he climbed the stairs, he had heard her snoring gently. She was sleeping on her back. The duvet formed a big mound on her tummy. He had slipped into bed and done the trick with his head – bumped it six times on the pillow – impressing on his brain that he wanted to wake at 6 a.m. – and it had worked. He got up quietly, had a wash in the sink – didn't want to risk waking her with the shower clanking the water pipes – and dressed quickly. He spent a while trying to compile a note for the fridge door but settled for 'Sorry (again). I love you (both). Digger Sr.'.

He had entered Committee Room Three just before 7 a.m., an hour before starting time. His intention was to gather his thoughts, prepare for the troops coming in, practise his lines. But Murdo was already there, poring over a front-page story in *The Herald*. He had handed over the paper, without comment. The headline said it all – 'Woman Linked to Two Murders'. Digger nodded his head – as if he had read it already – but he hadn't. In fact, he had forgotten all about it.

He asked, playing for time, 'What do you reckon?'

Murdo took his time, then said, 'Actually, I reckon it's not too bad for us. I wasn't sure why we didn't release it – the link – before. She killed them. It's not as if we're telling her something she didn't know. I suppose it might cause some worry among the punters, the public, you know. But that's not necessarily a bad thing. Increase awareness and that. And it might jolt a few memories – bring up some witnesses.'

Murdo paused, a look of puzzlement on his face.

Aine came into CR3, a copy of *The Herald* under her arm.

Digger nodded to her, then said to Murdo, 'There's something else, eh?'

Murdo said, 'It's nothing, really, nothing important. But the story wasn't in their first edition. I picked one up on the way home last night.'

Digger said that they did that – held back some stories, the exclusives, so rival papers wouldn't have time to follow them up. He didn't mention that they had also done it to avoid having to ask for a police comment.

The young cop appeared to accept the explanation. Or most of it.

Digger said, 'C'mon, lad, before the rest of the rabble drift in. Spit it out.'

Murdo spoke very softly. 'It seems that there's a leak in the team.'

'Well then,' Digger said, 'woe betide him.'

'Or her,' Aine said. 'Let's not be sexist.'

There was a twinkle in her eye as she added, 'But they'll never hunt 'er down.'

The rest of the troops arrived in ones and twos and everyone was in place well before 8 a.m. Digger, seated at the top table, writing some notes, never lifted his head. The newspaper story was all the buzz. Most had read it and the others caught up fast. Digger waited until it had all gone quiet before he rose and gave his first Oscar performance of the day.

He picked up Aine's copy of *The Herald* and said, 'It might help, it might not. I've got one thing to say about it. This,' he held the paper above his head, 'came from a leak.'

There was total silence. Digger dropped the paper into a waste bin.

Digger went on, 'And I know it didn't come from any member of this team. Now, we've got work to do.'

It was a bit of amateur dramatics and it did the trick. Any doubts about whether a mere Sergeant could lead this inquiry were dispelled.

Digger lifted the video remote control and switched on a copy of the tape from the mortuary corridor at the Royal Infirmary. The original was so fragile, potentially so precious, that he did not dare use it. They saw the woman in the doctor's white coat walking confidently away from them, along the passageway, through the double swing doors of the mortuary. Then a pause, the doors opening and she is striding out, a little white bundle in her arms, checking her pace a little to glance at the camera before disappearing. She was visible for a total of eighteen seconds. They watched her five times and left her image on-screen, freeze-frame, looking up at them.

Digger went to the top table and lifted half a dozen copies of the artist's impression of Strangelove, drawn from the description produced by Murdo's homeless man. He laid the pictures down before his troops.

'What do you reckon?' he asked. 'Strangelove?'

'Christ, I hope so,' one voice said. 'I hope there's not two of them.'

*   *   *   *   *

Where are the parents? Do they know it's missing? How was it born? Where? In theatre? Did they know it was going to be born dead or that it would be a difficult birth? Who was there when it was born? Who knew about it being taken to the mortuary?'

The questions were on everybody's lips, each one a lead, every answer having the potential to lead them to Strangelove's door.

Aine stopped the flow. She said, 'It? Is it a boy or is it a girl? Because we're talking about a human being here and I don't think we should forget it.'

Digger winced. He of all people should have known better. Lorna didn't know the sex of Digger Jr but she certainly wouldn't call her baby it.

'You're right,' he said. 'I'm sorry, I should have said. The baby's a little girl. We'll call her Laura.'

Good lord, he had been about to say Lorna. He had allowed them to discuss the CCTV tape and how it would help their inquiries until just before nine o'clock. Then he had stepped in again. He really wanted Aine to sit at the computer, to pull things together, but he knew that Hunter might come in and steal her at any moment. Murdo had already been despatched to the Royal Infirmary to collect every tape from every CCTV camera to cover the time when the baby had been taken into the mortuary.

'Back to work,' Digger said. 'We need a time line on Laura. From the time her mum went into the hospital until the moment Strangelove took her out of it. Oh, and check if an undertaker had been informed. Now, Strangelove. Thoughts.'

They came thick and fast. How did she get away with it? Somebody must have seen her. How did she get there? In a car? It's a hell of a place to park. Did she drive herself? Are there cameras on the parking spaces at the mortuary? At the entrances and exits? What about the gatemen or ambulance drivers – did they see her? Or the porters. Did she park outside, maybe illegally? Might have got a ticket. Check with the traffic wardens. Did somebody drive her there? An accomplice, waiting for her. She might have taken a taxi. Two taxis, one there, one home. Check with the Taxi Owners' Association. She might have taken the bus there.

Dear God, Digger thought. She might have taken the bus back, snuggled Laura to her chest, pretended the wee soul was sleeping. She could have walked home if she lives close. And Mr Macintosh was killed just down the road . . .

What was she wearing, apart from the white coat? Dark dress and light, but not white, blouse. No coat. What was the weather like on Sunday? Was it raining? Showery. Around 2.30 p.m., what was it like at 2.30 p.m., when

Laura was taken? She might have left Laura in the hospital. She seems to know the layout, knows all about the morgue, she could have hidden the baby, in a cupboard or something, gone back for her later.

Aine said, 'Why the Royal? Why not the Queen Mother's or the Southern General? They handle difficult births. So why the Royal?'

Because she knows it, knows the layout. She's been a patient there. She lost a baby there. She had a stillbirth in the Royal. She knows somebody who works there, her sister or her boyfriend. She knows the guy in the mortuary – he's involved, too. She works there. She really is a doctor or a nurse. Or she was. It's close to her home. She can take the bus or walk. Hide the baby, go back for her later.

They were repeating themselves, so Digger called a halt. Told them all – except Aine and a young cop – to go to the canteen for ten or fifteen minutes. They were reluctant to leave, but he insisted, said, 'I'm new at this, remember. My head's full of broken bottles. Let me gather my thoughts.'

They liked that. A boss who admitted a weakness. He was one of them.

As they left, Digger stared at the frozen face on the TV screen. He began to pace the room, turning to look at her from different angles, as if to catch her off guard. The eyes were always on him, following him. Like Mona Lisa. She was watching him but he couldn't touch her. He started to talk out loud, unaware that he was doing it.

'What do I know about you? What did I know before this morning? You kill men. The first one could be your dad. The next one, the ladies' man . . . maybe your lover. You get them to go down on you when you're bleeding. Cos you want to humiliate them. Leave them shamed. And you kill them with your long, thin blade. Outside, in the open, in the city. When? In the wee small hours.'

He walked right up to the television, put out a hand but couldn't bring himself to touch her.

'And what have you told me this morning? You've told me about the baby. And the Royal – but why the Royal? And why not a living baby? Eh? Why didn't you take a child you could feed and cuddle? Who would cuddle you back.'

He turned away and paced again. Then, suddenly, he stopped. Looked back at Strangelove.

He said, 'I know. I understand, now. It's your baby, isn't it? You're trying to get your baby back. How did you lose her? Was she stillborn or a miscarriage? An abortion? But what are your plans for her? What are you doing with that wee mite?'

*　*　*　*　*

187

Tobias Fastnett hesitated even as his hand went out to the door handle. He stepped to the side, just in case he could be recognised through the frosted-glass panel. This was not good – skulking in his own corridors – this was not how it should be.

Damn the man. He hadn't even had the decency to bring the plan to him. Hunter had gone to James Smith, used him as a go-between. Boyd's attack on the rival drug gang was planned for tonight. Fourteen men with firearms and six targets – two public houses and four dwelling houses, including James Stone's. And Hunter was using the situation as a club with which to beat him over the head. How did the man get such information? He mixed with them, thought like them. He had so much in common. A lowlife.

The report in *The Herald*, written by that boor Boyson, one of Hunter's pals, confirmed it. No question about the source of the exclusive information. And nothing that could be done about it. Well, nothing now. But things change . . . And, when they did, Fastnett would not forget the treachery. But, now, he knew the number one priority was to head off a drugs war, the bloodshed it would bring and the stain that would be indelibly etched on his reputation – not to mention his future.

Give Hunter his due, his plan was sound. He was going to swoop simultaneously at the known haunts of Boyd's hoodlums. No guarantee that they would all be there, he said, but that was his information. And, if one or two got away, he said, the word would soon get to them.

He had insisted that the plan go no further. And he wanted forty-eight men.

Fastnett had decided what he was going to say to Hunter – it was okay, fine, anything you need – but that was before Smith had pointed out the report in *The Herald*. The Chief Constable had been incandescent with rage. If only he had not tried to discipline Hunter yesterday he could, without question, have done it today. Smith pointed out that it was because he had failed yesterday that Hunter had been able to pull the stroke today. And Fastnett had accepted that. Agreed that preventing bloodshed was the priority and said that he would personally give Hunter approval for his plan. It might not heal the wound but at least it was a basis for a decent working relationship.

It had been a morning of acceding to the requests of his staff. Hunter's arrogance and impertinence was contagious. Burns was at it now, not directly, of course. Like his mentor, he moved like a sidewinder viper, slithered at angles and struck when it was least expected. Smith, again, had been the conduit. Burns needed the cooperation of the General Medical

188

Council, the Royal College of Nurses and sundry other medical groupings. And he knew that a mere Sergeant would not be able to exert the necessary pressure on such august bodies. So, again, Fastnett had agreed to do the legwork.

The Chief Constable stretched, actually put his hand on the Hunter's door.

Then he drew back. He couldn't do it, just couldn't bring himself to give the man the victory. He would sign the forms, approve the costs but he wouldn't give him the satisfaction of lording it again. Fastnett turned on his heel and marched off.

If it all went pear-shaped, it would be clear who was to blame.

Zara is in the office, in her clinic, where she has promised never to smoke again, and she is lighting yet another cigarette. A scene from *Airplane*, the movie, flashed into her mind – I picked the wrong day to give up smoking/ drinking/glue-sniffing/drugs – and she laughed. It was loud, high-pitched and didn't sound like her laugh but, hey, this wasn't the day to give up laughing. No time for that. Still work to do,

Her eyes were gritty and she rubbed them with her knuckles even though she knew it was the worst thing she could do. She had been on the go since 6 a.m. after five hours' fitful sleep. She hadn't taken a bath, just put on the same clothes – knickers and all – and her skivvy's apron. Tiptoed along the hall in case she disturbed Calder. She knew that he would be sleeping like a baby – a clear conscience, he said – but she didn't bother checking his room. God bless separate rooms. Best invention since spinsterhood. Happy days. Now it was sinisterhood or should that be sinistrahood? Interesting word, spinsterhood, invented by a man, of course – compounded by a man. The condition of an unmarried woman who spins, sits at home alone, her old head covered to hide the shame of being unable to attract a man. Which word would a woman hatch? Zara had no problem with spinster, come to think of it she liked it. Had it been created today its meaning would be: 'One who spins; one who presents data in a favourable light.

The hood would have to go. Hooded would be better, as in hooded cobra, which rears up when provoked, gives fair warning of the danger and needs only one deadly kiss to end it. Spinsterhooded – certainly sinistra – Zara liked it. There was no word, though, for a woman who had had a man/men, who had tried it and said no thank you, not for me. Goodbye. Divorcée for women – divorcé for men. No sex.

Zara heard herself laughing again. That was good, no sex. If that was the criterion, then she'd been a divorcée for some years now. A married

189

divorcée. But it was no great loss. The passion in her relationship with Calder had cooled considerably when they found out the extent of his heart problem. The horizontal jogging was not actually banned but strenuous exercise was not recommended for a man with an aorta which functioned at only forty per cent and whose lungs were caving in to boot. It didn't bother Zara, being celibate, she didn't miss the sweaty, bouncy stuff and she had become quite adroit at self-assistance at the times when a physical release was desirable. There had been times – good lord, the other night with that odious creature Hunter had been one – when she had found herself reacting physically to a man but she had not yielded to temptation. Life was so much simpler without sexual encounters. She remembered an old joke, 'What's the definition of a spinster?' 'A woman who doesn't make the same mistake once.'

But what about the woman who had been there and done it? What word would she put on the T-shirt to show that she didn't want it anymore. Divorcée displeased her. She tried spinsterfree. Spinsterjoy. Closer but still not right. She would give it some thought. When she had more time. She took one last, long drag on the cigarette, sucking the burning tobacco close to the filter tip, then stubbed it out in the ashtray. The nicotine injection was working. Her energy was returning.

The kitchen had been a mess but she'd known it would be. She'd heard The Ramblers letting off steam into the wee small hours. Their way of handling it, she supposed. Each to his own. They had made a snack. Might even have eaten some, too. But most of it – soup, baked beans, toast, cheese, appeared to have been smeared on the cooker, worktops, walls and floor. And there was, of course, the usual array of alcohol cans and bottles.

Seven bottles of Miller's Lite lay in a pile in a corner of the dining room. An orange in the middle of them. So that was the clanking during the night. Some of the best brains in British medicine having a game of skittles.

Zara suppressed her anger. Nothing she could do about it now, except tidy up. She filled a black bin liner with their debris. She'd seen worse. Saturday night, for example, after Josef Paborsky's transplant, when everything had gone so well and everyone was so happy. Then Sunday, when it all went to hell in a handcart.

Zara put the beer bottles into the bin bag then put it outside the door. One of the buckets of dirty rainwater had been overturned and no attempt made to mop up the mess on the conservatory floor, so that was the next task.

She emptied all of the receptacles, mopped the floor and left the door open to allow the air to dry it. The dining room carpet and the dark staining of Miller's Lite was next. Then on to the kitchen.

It took a little under three hours to complete the chores. Get the place shipshape, as Calder would say. She did it on autopilot and, although it was not a pleasant job, it was not without satisfaction. There was a definite sense of achievement.

One of the wall cupboards in the kitchen had been damaged. A corner of the glossy, white finish chipped off revealing two ugly inches of wood shavings. C'est la vie. Cheap crap. Accept the things you can't change. Until the time you can.

Zara was pleased to complete the skivvying before anyone got out of bed. She knew that, as soon as they appeared, they would expect breakfast to be cooked for them. But not today, too busy, too much to do. She had gone to the office just after 9 a.m., made some green tea and had a cigarette.

She had one hundred and one things to do and no one to help, no one to depend on. So she made a little list. The butcher, the baker and she thanked God for electricity. She picked up the phone, called the local butcher and ordered enough meat to feed her regiment. Like the baker, who was the next call, he could deliver and put it on the tab. The booze was more difficult, a little matter of an unpaid bill. Zara decided that she would go into town, pick up the alcohol herself.

Cash, today, was not a problem, thanks to Calder's two latest admissions to the abuse clinic. Well, to one of them anyway, the Manchester criminal who paid for a fortnight upfront, in dirty twenty pound notes. He said, if he couldn't last the pace, money would be the least of his troubles. He had come up north to protect his anonymity while he got the booze out of his system and allowed Calder to look inside his head to find a way of keeping it like that. The man had arrived, as arranged, on Sunday morning, wearing a tracksuit but with a pinstripe suit, white shirt and tie in a suitcase. There was no smell of drink from him but he volunteered that he had been 'hammered' on Saturday. He had agreed to take the injections to ward off damage to the old grey matter but had refused tranquillisers and sleeping tablets. He said that he wanted to face his demons alone. He was through the worst of the DTs, but his hands still trembled. He had been given Calder's name by an Edinburgh gangster. He was a criminal, no doubt about it, but there was something likeable about his honest vulnerability.

The other new client was a different kettle of fish. An arrogant young shit, a lawyer sent for treatment for his cocaine habit by his boss, who just happened to be the procurator fiscal in a neighbouring county. This raised some interesting questions. Would the taxpayers ever be made aware that they were footing the bill for his treatment? Well, maybe not. But the account would be paid, eventually, from the public purse. The sums properly noted and accounted for, although a certain economy with the truth would be exercised when explaining the precise nature of the medical treatment. The legal aspect could also be guessed at with a fair degree of certainly. Had he fingered his dealers? And, in so doing, implicated himself, leading to a trial in open court and questions from a defence counsel, one of which would be – 'And what is your job?'

Zara pondered the interesting exercise in morality and legality. The little shit proved one thing – there were two sides to the legal line. You could step over it and, much more interesting, you could step back.

Zara had been giving that a lot of thought recently – how to get back on to the right side of the law – to become the prodigal daughter. And she reckoned that she knew how to do it. There was a word to explain the process – 'connections'.

Hunter opened the window and patted his jacket pockets. No pipe. Unheard of, a historic occasion. He realised that he hadn't had a smoke all morning. He'd left the pipe, the nice meerschaum, on the coffee table at home. Baccy and matches too. Put them there when he got home, went to get the whisky bottle, then decided against it and went straight to bed.

There was a spare in the car, in the pocket in the driver's door. Fat lot of good that would do. He'd left the car outside Joe's Cafe. Caught the train, then walked to the copshop, just to clear his head. The Falcon was in a drawer in his desk. So was his emergency tobacco, about half a pack, old and brittle, and a book of matches. Awkward buggers, just stuck-together paper, bendy and too wee. Good for lighting your fingers. He shut the drawer and looked again at his computer.

He'd been working on the file for the best part of an hour, ever since he'd left James Smith. He'd decided to approach it like a case, just like any other inquiry, to take himself out of it. Depersonalise it, that was how The Jug would put it. Hunter had racked his brains for suspects, folk who had a grudge, either real or perceived. He was a bit surprised that there were only five. The task was made easier because he could eliminate Danny Boyd and all of his gang and, of course, Jimmy Stone and his team.

The names of four of the suspects were typed into the file, duly considered and dismissed with a good degree of confidence. No guarantees, of course, but ninety per cent. Good odds for a polis inquiry. For the fifth, he made a phone call to the State Hospital at Carstairs. The guy was still there and it was highly unlikely that he would ever leave. He never got visitors – no one who cared enough to buy revenge for him.

So the file ended, as it had started, with only three lines.

Contract killer.

Danny Boyd.

Me.

Lisa hadn't expected him to drop everything, hang up his stethoscope, just leave his patients and run down the road from the Royal Infirmary to her flat. She wasn't anticipating flowers and intimate confessions about how much he'd missed her and what a mistake it had been allowing her to leave all those years ago and there had been butterflies in his tummy since she'd phoned from Morocco yesterday and now that he'd found her again he would never let her go.

But the bastard could have taken a phone call. Simon's mobile was still switched off (but it would be, wouldn't it?) so it wouldn't interfere with the electronic equipment in the hospital. One of the nurses had answered the phone in the ward and said that the doctor was busy and he would be doing his rounds next and he was not able to come to the phone. Yes, of course, she said, she could take a message, she would tell him to call Lisa but she couldn't keep the snigger out of her voice.

Lisa had rushed home from Morocco. She could have stayed, lain on the beach, rested her battered body, allowed time for her bruises to fade and the sun to soothe her weary flesh. God knows, she deserved it and she could afford it. She had £3,000 in cash. But what had she done? Rushed home, that's what, with undue haste. And why? So she could sit by the phone, a prisoner in her own flat, afraid that the butcher would have sold his best fillet before Simon called. She wanted to buy fillet steak, a whole one, and it had to be from the butcher. The supermarket would be open later, but Mum always bought meat from the butcher. It was dearer there, she said, but then you got what you paid for. And you never knew what you were getting at the supermarket. They had special lights to make the meat look good and they painted it with a red dye. You could tell if you fried it, then scraped the pan. A red dye. Only showed at a certain temperature, their scientists had not been able to disguise that.

Lisa knew this was crap but still, for special occasions, she went to the butcher.

This wasn't how she had planned the day. But, she told herself, she was stepping up a grade, from random killer to premeditated murderer so, inevitably, there would be problems. No, not problems, situations, challenges requiring extra skills and disciplines. Patience would be one. But, today, that virtue was in short supply.

Lisa had awakened shortly before 10 a.m., disorientated, surprised to find herself in the familiar surroundings of her own flat. She had lain motionless for a spell then, gently, extended her limbs, first one arm then the other, to ascertain the extent of her pain. It was as if she had been struck by a car and was assessing the extent of the damage. The collisions with Abdul had left her bruised and wounded – she saw that the sheets were stained where she had bled from her vagina during the night – but she was okay. Nothing that would not heal. Or deflect her from her mission. She had taken a bath and planned the entire day. Worked it out from the phone call, to the visit, to the deed. Gone over the plan, time and again, considering the options, preparing alternative strategies, until she was confident that she had covered every contingency. And now she couldn't throw a double six to start. Simon was not taking her calls.

She knew exactly what she would say, how she'd flirt, turn on the provocative giggle. He'd liked that yesterday, oh yes he bloodywell had, he'd been intrigued, fascinated by the sassy woman who had metamorphosed from Lanky Lisa. He'd wanted to see more of her – he'd wanted to see all of her. But that was then and this is now.

Lisa was fighting the urge to go up the High Street to the hospital, just drop in on him, say, 'Oh, there you are. Have you been trying to get a hold of me?' But it was too risky. He might feel cornered, threatened, and wriggle free. So she waited for the phone call. She took the sheets from the bed, put them in the bath and ran the water.

Cold water. Cold water gets rid of blood. Mum said that.

There was a wry smile on Hunter's face as he put the phone down. Funny how you react in strange situations. This lark would be interesting if it wasn't so serious. He was broke because Bella was keeping all his money and here he was, trying to get her another fifty grand. She couldn't collect right away, of course. Have to wait (maybe not too long) till he was dead.

The guy in the Masons had been surprised to hear from him. Well, he would be, wouldn't he? Who in his right mind phones up for a life insurance policy? Hunter had mistakenly believed that it would be simple. He already had cover – needed it for the mortgage vultures – so he thought it would be just a case of topping it up. All he really wanted to know was how much it would cost. The guy's gaffer must have been standing beside him because he had launched himself into the full spiel which, when it was all boiled

194

down, meant that Hunter would have to go through a medical. Compulsory at his age.

No, he said, he had no problem with them getting in touch with his GP and, yes, he would be happy to go to see their quack.

Bliddy insurance. Good God in Govan, he'd be going to church next. Same thing, really, bit more selfish, a bet on eternity. What would it be – twenty pieces of silver each way? Where's the pay-out window – up or down?

The GP's notes would bring up the thing about the enchondroma. Jesus H, that had been a laugh. Not. He'd been getting a bit of bother with his gut. Indigestion, heartburn, the fish supper coming back on him in bed at night, that kind of thing. Anyway, he'd been watching the telly – must have been a Sunday night – and one of the adverts had described his symptoms to a T, so he'd asked Bella to pick up some of the wonder tablets from the chemist. Next day she told him – phoned him in the bliddy office to tell him – that she'd made an appointment for him with the quack. There was a new GP at the practice, an 'exceptionally caring young woman', and she'd see him at 5.40 that evening. And Bella would be checking up to make sure that he went. One of the Coffee Girls knew the receptionist.

The doc was a doll. Good body, great legs, long, black hair and take-me-to-your-sickbed eyes. She listened to him, she sounded his chest, she asked how much he drank, how much he smoked and multiplied the replies by two. She said that it might be angina, just a possibility, but better safe than sorry. Then she made a phone call – said are you busy? Good, excellent, I'll send Mr Hunter down right away. So he went to the Vicky – to the bliddy geriatric department – for chest X-rays. Six of them, three front and three rear, because the machine had been playing up. Aye, he thought, pull the other one, it's got bells on.

The doc phoned the next morning. Bella was in the bath and he took the call himself. She wanted to see him at the surgery. Yes, it was important. His constipation was cured instantly.

Afterwards, he couldn't remember what she had said. He knew that she had black tights on and a tight jumper and was doing the thing with the eye contact. But he couldn't recall anything about the start of the consultation. He must simply have switched off. It was her tone that frightened him. Soft, caring, breaking it to him gently. He remembered saying that she had a terrible job. And thanks. Thanks for your kindness.

She had written it down. In capital letters. ENCHONDROMA. It was rare but, if it was that – enchondroma and she had to tell him that it looked like it – well, she said, let's take one step at a time. What she meant was that he could put his head between his knees and kiss his arse goodbye. She would arrange an appointment with a consultant. Should be in the next couple of days. He told her to phone him at the copshop and she gave him the number of a helpline – a cancer helpline.

The X-rays had shown up holes in his bones. Two ribs above his ticker and in the top one at the right. The consultant offered him two options. He could operate, have to go in from the back, through the big muscle, take a sample of bone for testing. It would hurt like hell and, if it was bone cancer, there was nothing they could do about it. Well, they could give him drugs to make his hair fall out, help him to shit through the eye of a needle but they couldn't cure it. The second option was to do nothing. Go back in a month for more X-rays. See how it looked. He went back in a month, then a month after that. Three sets of pix and no change, no deterioration. The consultant was smiling as he checked them. Said they would keep an eye on things – three-monthly X-rays for the next year – but it looked as if it was a false alarm. Seemed that it was congenital.

Hunter could have told him that – he had been born with bad bits in him. He went out and got rat-arsed to celebrate.

He'd told Bella about it – the enchondroma – a couple of years later and that had been another bliddy row. She'd been mumping on about pains in her kidneys. The doc – the looker who was too conscientious by far – had checked it out and given Bella a new MOT certificate. But still it wasn't enough. Her mother had died after pains in the kidneys (actually, it was pneumonia and she was ninety-four, for God's sake) but Bella said that things like that ran in the family. Hunter had said that so did diarrhoea and that not been appreciated.

It was, Bella had told him, typical of him. Just typical.

So he'd tried to reassure her. Said the doc was really thorough. Told her about the enchondroma thing. And she'd hit the roof. Seems that he'd done the wrong thing, protecting her from all that needless worry. She had gone through her entire repertoire. He had just taken it on the chin. And that was another thing about him, she said, when she'd run out of other things to say. He didn't even care enough to argue.

Hunter's phone rang. It was the insurance guy to tell him that the company doctor could see him on Friday, would that be okay?

Sure, Hunter said, yeah, no probs. Oh, one thing. He'd have to tell his wife about it because she'd be paying the instalments. Was that the right word? Whatever. But he'd have to tell her anyway. If she asked, phoned or anything, could he say that it's a good deal, a special offer for cops, something like that. What? Yes, his wife was the beneficiary. She'd get the dosh. Right, ta. Yeah, Friday, one o'clock. Cheers.

Hunter had learned his lesson. No secrets from Bella. Well, not a lot anyway. He'd tell her but not until after the medical. No need to get her agitated, to have to go through the twenty questions routine. And, who knows, he might not pass. The quack might find that he was full of bad bits. He had a wee chuckle to himself. He might be deemed a bad risk. So what's new? The notion, in a weird way, amused him. The contract killer could do him a favour. Eradicate months of suffering. And, at least, he wouldn't die healthy.

He went to his desk, took out the Falcon and the book of matches. He sparked one carefully. Didn't want to get his fingers burned.

Lisa lifted the phone, started to punch out the numbers, then put it down again. Bloody thing was like a life-support machine today. The last thing anyone wanted but the equipment needed most. Stay with it, stay connected, and there was hope. She had been dependent on it, needed it to keep her going. Take it away and I'll die, she'd thought at the lowest point. So she'd stayed with it – left the doors open when she went to the loo – and clung on to hope. And it had rung.

'Lisa, Darling! You're home. Why didn't you phone me?'

It was Mum. 'You know how I miss you. I worry about you, you know that. You should have phoned. You promised . . .'

The fusion of emotions – disappointment, humiliation, rage – had been too much and Lisa had . . . overreacted. She could see that now. She would concede it. Make an excuse, stress, difficult job.

She had been abrupt with Mum. Said she was waiting for an important call. But Mum had interrupted, said she only wanted a minute. And Lisa had told her, again, that the call was very important to her. But Mum hadn't listened, said just a minute, that was all she wanted and was that too much to ask?

Yes, it was, Lisa told her. And she said other things, too, hurtful things (though she couldn't remember exactly what they were) but she was willing to admit that she had been curt and she would say sorry, ask Mum to forgive her. And she would, of course, because mums did that. They understood that sometimes daughters became overwrought and said stupid things they didn't mean.

But Lisa did. She meant every word she said and much, much more. She could remember what Mum had said, how she'd been provoked, why she'd gone over the top.

Mum had called her selfish.

Now that was good. That was very fucking good. And Lisa had hung up.

197

She had stormed around the house. Throwing things. Broke some stuff, just things – the coffee table for one, smashed the glass, with the big, crystal unicorn, must have hit her hand because it was hurting now and her wrist was swollen and the strap of the Cartier watch was broken.

And all because of Simon. The bastard. The fucking bastard. How dare he? How fucking dare he run her life like this, dominate her, treat her like shit. He had ruined her life then, way back then, and now he had returned to finish it off. But first he would humiliate her, again. Have her running after him, again. Then he would cast her off like an old boot, again.

He had already turned her against her own mother. But that's what men do. That's what they do to Lisa. It had always happened to Lisa.

She picked up the phone again, to call Mum, then decided against it. No, let her stew. Mums are meant to look after daughters, after all. And what had Mum done for Lisa, to protect Lisa, when men were degrading Lisa, abusing Lisa. Mum had gone to church, that's what. Said her Hail Marys and prayed to the Virgin. Left a virgin at home, a three-year-old virgin at home. But she hadn't come back to one. And never a word said about it. Except one night, Mum and Dad, shameful whispers. Couldn't be said out loud. And in the morning Dad was gone.

Lisa began to pick up the broken pieces of her furniture. Tears falling from her eyes and dropping little rainbows on to the broken glass and shattered crystal. The unicorn's metal horn embedded in the leather sofa.

The phone rang then. A few sentences – not enough to call it a conversation. But all she needed to hear. Oh, thank you, Simon. It's going to be all right. Thank you for phoning. It's good again. Not exactly as she wanted but that was okay. Lisa back in charge again. Already drawing up Plan B.

B for bastard.

Lisa grovelled, Lisa begged and Lisa said she was so sorry. So, so sorry, Mum. Can you forgive me? Of course, I didn't mean it, not a word of it. I was just . . . no, no excuses, Mum, I was out of order. Well, that's up to you, Mum. You decide. You're entitled to tell Louise, I know that, but no, I won't tell her either. Yes, you're right, no sense in upsetting her, especially in her condition. No, I don't want to upset her, Mum. How is she, Mum? And her bump, the baby, still well? Good. That's good. And you, Mum, how're you? Good. That's good, Mum. Me? I'm okay, fine. No, honestly. Yes, Mum, I did get the phone call. Yeah, everything's fine. It was just a bit of boyfriend trouble. Yes, Mum, that's what I said. A boyfriend. Yes, he is new, well, newish. Look, I'd rather tell you all about him when I see you.

It'll be tomorrow, Mum. No, I'm sorry, I can't manage tonight. Yes, I am seeing him. No! I am not. Mum! I am not pregnant.

Mum said, 'That's good. There's a proper time for everything, you know.'

It was getting to Hunter. Not that he was a target, might be killed as soon as he stuck his face out of the office. He was trying to accept that, was working on getting used to it. But what he really hated was the helplessness, the impotence, the inability to do anything about it. He felt like a character in a movie who hadn't been given any lines. He remembered the feeling from the time the good-looking doc had told him they thought he had bone cancer. In his body, his life, and they were about to tell him how much of it he had left. Nothing he could do about it. Couldn't cut it out, couldn't will it away. As much chance of that as he had of teaching his arse to shit sugar-covered doughnuts.

Some faceless guy could be sitting round the corner at this very moment, waiting patiently to rub him out, and there was bugger all he could do about it.

He wondered how it would happen. A shooter was the obvious. Could be worse, really. One bullet, he might hear the bang, then it's goodnight Vienna. A shooting was the favourite, an even-money shot. A knifing was less likely – less chance of putting his lights out and a greater possibility of the assailant being caught. A pro wouldn't risk that. No way. A stabbing was a five-to-one job. A car, a hit-and-run, ten-to-one, no, twenties. It was too risky. He might hear it, see it coming, jump out the way and be forewarned. And forearmed? He'd thought about it. Just go down to the armoury, sign out a pistol and a bulletproof vest, use the Danny Boyd thing as an excuse. Then say he was going after Stone so he'd hold on to the gun for a couple of days. Just an insurance policy. And he hadn't rejected the idea.

He was sitting at his desk, where he had been working for the past hour or so. A street map of Glasgow lay open. It was marked with green crosses, for the addresses and known haunts of Boyd's neds, and red crosses, for their targets – the two pubs, used by The Stoneman's team, and four houses, including Stone's.

There was a knock at the door. He said come in and, when he saw that it was Aine – added lass 'Come in, lass.'

She noticed an open window but the smell of tobacco filled the room. He told her all about Boyd's plans. The phone rang on three occasions and each time he ignored it. Made her feel important. They were interrupted once, when a couple of guys brought in a photocopier. She didn't ask any questions. She didn't have to – he went through it all, from A to Z, like a good teacher, pausing until she nodded that she understood. He picked up his pipe at one point and put it in his mouth. He lifted a book of matches, then put it down to represent one of the pubs frequented by Boyd's shooters. The pipe dangled from his mouth and he spoke with a little lisp which made him seem vulnerable. He told her clearly what she had to do. She felt privileged to be invited into The Hunter's web, to see how he worked, to watch as the brain ticked over. He was different, somehow. Quieter. None of the patter. This was the man behind the myth. She spotted an idiosyncrasy, a little nervous habit. His hand occasionally flicking up to his head, fingers running through the wispy hair, patting it over his bald spot.

When he had outlined his plans, he asked what she thought.

'Spot any flaws?'

She pointed to the book of matches – the pub – then to the place he had identified for the unmarked police van to wait until the time was right for its six occupants to carry out their raid.

She said, 'The map's out of date. These tenements here,' she prodded the page with a finger, 'were knocked down last month. And Boyd's man, wotisname, McCafferty, lives . . .'

'In the next street,' Hunter interrupted her. 'In full view of a van load of coppers hanging about like spare pricks at . . . Aye, well spotted.'

He did the nervous thing again with his hair.

She said, 'There's a bowling club . . . here.' She pointed it out. 'Seems like a reasonable place for spare pricks, eh?'

Digger Burns criss-crossed Committee Room Three, like a hawk quartering its territory, hoping its prey would be startled and take fright. He would pause occasionally, glancing over the shoulder of a guy working at a computer, giving a reassuring nod to the WPC on the phones. Aine had looked up once and he had winked at her. He missed out no one, encouraging, coaxing, keeping them going. He thought he was Mr Cool but, really, he was pacing. No one mentioned it, though. It was just his way. He was uptight, too. He wanted a breakthrough as much as anyone.

He had told them that the net was tightening. They couldn't be sure what would be left wriggling and squirming, when they hauled it in, but that was why they were trawling – to see what stirred in the murky depths.

The CCTV footage from the Royal Infirmary had been an extraordinary breakthrough. The police artist had been given a copy. He had gone up to the hospital, been filmed himself from the same camera, walking in Strangelove's footsteps, partly to get her measure, but also to get a feel for her. He had returned to the police station and, remarkably swiftly, produced two new, improved sketches. The first was full-length, side-on, showing a slender, well-proportioned woman, youngish, five-foot eight and around nine stone. The other, the portrait, bore a remarkable resemblance to the original facial image. There was still little detail (the poor quality of the film did not allow such a luxury) but it was drawn in charcoal, rather than pencil, and the effect was more authoritative. The quality was not good enough to be released as an e-fit, but it did instil a confidence in the team.

Murdo, too, had been up to the Royal, to see his new pal who was in charge of security there. The ex-Chief Inspector was expecting a visit and had anticipated three of Murdo's four requests. Charles – he insisted that Murdo call him Charles – had ready and waiting twelve video cassettes, one from each of the hospital's CCTV cameras, each rewound to 2.20 p.m. on Sunday, ten minutes before Strangelove was captured on film entering the mortuary.

He also provided a biography – that's what he called it – of Baby Jenkins. The birth had been complicated, very difficult and very taxing on the poor woman who was still in the intensive care unit. She was aware, of course, that the baby was dead, had been born dead.

Charles had stopped there and put on his thinking face, wondering if that was the correct expression. Born dead. He thought it sounded wrong. But it was so sad, tragic. He'd seen it many times, of course, tragedy, and the one thing he'd learned was to think of those who were grieving the loss, to show compassion for those left behind.

'The truth of the matter is,' he said, 'she knew her baby was dead. And it has been considered unwise to tell her that the wee one is . . . missing.'

The mother really was quite seriously ill and there was quite enough tragedy in her life already. Single parent, two children, not yet at school, and one . . . he looked at his notes . . . yes, one other perinatal loss. Foetus, nineteen weeks gestation, buried in a communal grave owned by the hospital.

'It's all here,' he said, handing Murdo the notes, 'but I would ask you to exercise discretion in your inquiries.'

Charles then turned his attention to a disk, and hard copy print-out of the entire staff list at the hospital. The names of those on duty, at the time the baby's body had been taken, had been neatly highlighted in pink and details of five others – three agency nurses, one locum doctor and a porter, who had only recently been appointed – were handwritten on the last page.

Charles had not expected to be asked for two separate lists, of female doctors and nurses. He had said that there might be difficulties, mentioned the data protection act, how he was overstepping the mark already, personal intrusion, not to mention that some very important, influential people might feel that they were being singled out without just cause. Murdo reassured him that such concerns could be overcome if, and when, they arose. But he failed to see how anyone could reasonably complain about proper action being taken to secure the return of the baby's body and, in so doing, minimise the hospital's responsibility. His argument won the promise that the refined lists would be available before the day was out. Murdo thanked him for his understanding and asked if he could beg another favour. Lists – female nurses and doctors, from the other hospitals in the city – could Charles possibly use his influence?.

It was the first request which he could reasonably refuse but he didn't. He would do all that he could to help and he had a request of his own. It was, he said, an embarrassing situation and the hospital would, of course, do all in its power to assist the police to resolve it. If the police artist could provide him with an e-fit, a sketch even, he would personally show it to responsible people who might help point the finger at the perpetrator.

Murdo knew that Charles's priority was to avoid three or four uniform officers doing exactly the same thing but, perhaps, with a lesser degree of subtlety. But he thanked Charles for the generous offer and promised that he would ensure that their best image was delivered as soon as possible. Then he raised another matter. The registration of the death of the missing baby. When would that take place?

Charles shuffled the folders on his desk and produced a document entitled 'Perinatal Loss, Legal Requirements'. It declared that the 'legal age of viability is twenty-four completed weeks of gestation'. Pregnancies ending after this period were classified as stillbirth. A doctor was obliged to complete a Stillbirth Certificate and a midwife had to fill in a Stillbirth Registration Card which had to be taken by the parent/parents to the Registrar in Martha Street where the baby's name would be entered on the Certificate of Registration of Stillbirth.

Charles read on, drawing his finger across the small, tight print. Then he found it.

'Twenty-one days,' he said. 'It says here the death must be registered by a parent within twenty-one days. So we're okay, a bit of breathing space, eh?'

He went on to tell Murdo that, when a pregnancy ended before twenty-four weeks, the foetus was officially classified as a spontaneous abortion. Registration was not required but, if parents wished to make arrangements for burial or cremation, the undertaker would require a Certificate of Non Viable Foetus which would be completed by a doctor or midwife. However, this was not an official document. Most parents in these circumstances agreed to allow the hospital to carry out 'a sensitive disposal', which was generally done in the crematorium.

Murdo had returned to the office, given Digger the Royal staff list, then gone to a quiet room to examine the tapes. One image had sent his pulse racing. A woman, not unlike Strangelove, a white bundle clutched to her chest, being driven out of the main gate in a Jaguar. But, rewinding, checking the accident and emergency department tape, showed nothing more sinister than an arm in a sling. After almost two hours, Murdo had to admit that he had come up with the square root of nothing.

Digger's lines of enquiry had produced similar results. The taxi rank at the infirmary was used by all council-approved cabs but it was used mainly those registered with the Taxi Owners' Association. There were Freephones in the hospital linked directly to the TOA. It was a long shot but two coppers had been despatched with copies of the artist's latest work to the TOA office. A message had been put out on their radios, giving a description of Strangelove and her baby, wrapped in a little white sheet. So far, it had drawn a blank. So, too, did checks with the traffic department. But Digger had harboured no hopes on that one. Laura's body had been taken on Sunday, when parking restrictions were eased. No tickets had been in written in the streets around the hospital that day.

Why the Royal Infirmary? Why did Strangelove go to the Royal for a baby?

The question kept niggling at Digger. Why not the Queen Mother's Hospital, the specialist hospital? More babies, dead and alive, there. Had she lost a baby in the Royal? A stillbirth, maybe. Blamed the doctors. Or was it simply that it was closer to her home.

Digger had checked the weather. It had been dry on Sunday. Chilly but no rain. She could have walked or taken a bus. Snuggled the wee bundle into her neck, the way mothers do. Was that why she went to the Royal? Because it was more convenient. He could not come up with an answer but he knew it was important. So he put most of his team to work on the Royal connection.

The first job was running the names from the staff list through HOLMES, the national database of criminal convictions. This produced two results – neither of any significance. A doctor who had been given a suspended sentence two years ago in Bradford for credit card fraud and one of the mortuary assistants (whose name was vaguely familiar) with a passion for other people's cars.

As they were drawing to an end of these checks, the e-mail on the computer went crazy. The Chief Constable had exerted pressure on the General Medical Council and the Royal College of Nurses and they were sending, simultaneously it seemed, a list of their entire membership in the United Kingdom.

The teaching hospitals and the universities in Glasgow had also been persuaded to provide names of those who had dropped out of medical courses. The information was being faxed piecemeal. Priority was being given to final-year students, those certain to have the expertise to kill with a single blow using a thin blade.

Four members of the team had gone to see the city's Chief Registrar in Martha Street. They had learned that a baby that had gone full-term had to be given both birth and death certificates. And these documents included the occupations of the parents. The entries were recorded on computer – but it was not the most reliable system. It was, nevertheless, one of the best leads today.

The troops had been hard at it for five hours. Digger wandered amongst them. Each glimmer of light was almost instantly snuffed out but he praised them. Good. That's good work. The net's tightening. Getting down to the fine mesh now.

It was Aine who spotted it, after she returned to Committee Room Three. She'd been away for two hours, with Hunter, but Digger had not enquired about what had gone on. That was their business. He had put her on to the computer, at the heart of the operation, alongside Murdo, logging names, cross-checking, hoping that the identity of a bereaved mother on one list would ring bells on another. Two blown-up versions of the artist's new sketches – three feet tall and two feet wide – had been pinned to the wall behind the top table. Aine had wandered up to scrutinise them, laying hands on them, as if hoping for a message from another world. She returned to her desk and lifted the grainy photograph taken off the CCTV film from the mortuary corridor. Her eyes narrowed in concentration. Something was not right but she couldn't quite put her finger on it. Then she did. She rose quickly, holding a corner of the photo between her thumb and forefinger, as if she was afraid of contaminating evidence. A few heads were raised in response to the sudden movement. Digger had offered a break a while back, said they could go for a bite to eat, maybe a walk outside to blow the cobwebs away. There were no takers so he'd ordered sandwiches, from the canteen, and metal flasks of tea and coffee. The drinks had been consumed but most of the sandwiches were untouched. Some were becoming soggy under the clingfilm and the corners of those exposed to the air were beginning to curl.

Aine asked, 'Anybody got a measuring tape?'

One of the guys offered a ruler.

'No,' she said petulantly, 'it's got to be . . . stretchy.'

There was a brief silence, then a WPC murmured something about pinking shears, French chalk and there were a few chuckles. Even Digger smiled.

But not Aine.

'A piece of string, then?' she said.

It was break time.

'How long?' a young cop asked.

It was fun time.

'How thick?'

'How come?'

Only Aine now was serious, looking around for something to make do. Her eyes rested on an older copper, a twenty-year Constable, whose girth would see him struggle to pass the next fitness test.

She said, 'Your belt. Give me your belt.'

'My belt?' he said, pained.

Everyone laughing now.

'I'll give you a belt, all right. I'll belt your lug.'

But Aine was insistent. She looked at Digger, seeking authorisation, and he nodded to the old copper and told him to get it off for the girls.

Dada da da

Dada da da.

Dada da da da da da da.

The troops were giving it 'The Stripper' and even Aine cracked a smile. She took the belt and offered the photo to the old copper. But his hands were firmly on his waistband and he refused to take it. Digger stepped in.

She took him by the shoulders and turned him round so he was facing the troops. Then she gave him the photo, got him to hold it in front of his chest and made sure that his fingers did not obscure the image.

The room fell silent, every eye on her.

She said, 'We know, from the guys who examined the CCTV, that Strangelove's about five foot seven, five eight. Same as me. Now this,' she held up the belt, 'is my stethoscope.'

She draped the belt around her neck. The ends came down to her waist.

She went on, 'So tell me when my stethoscope is the same length as hers.'

She began to roll up the belt, inch by inch, and the buckle end crept up towards her left breast. The troops drew closer, watching Aine, then the photo, then back to the belt.

That's it.

No, a bit more.

Too much. Yes, there. That's it.

She removed the belt slowly, careful to keep her mark, then laid it out on the top table. She called for the ruler.

One of the cops had pulled off one of his trainers and was extracting the lace.

Aine measured the length of Strangelove's stethoscope. Thirty centimetres. Two feet.

The lace was laid on the desk to be measured. Thirty centimetres. Aine draped it around her neck, adjusted it a little so the ends were equal, touching her breasts.

Digger looked at her, looked at the photo.

'See,' she said excitedly. 'What do you see? Come on, look, can't you see it? It's too wee – it's a toy! It's not real – she's using a kid's toy.'

Digger saw the significance.

And so did Murdo. He said, 'She's not a real doctor. A real doctor would have a . . . real one.'

And the net was drawn tighter still. No need to check doctors, working or otherwise. Digger ruled out working nurses too. They would have access to stethoscopes. If Strangelove was a working nurse, she would steal one. The trawl was halved. Only two teams now, nurses who were idle – not in work at the moment or struck off the nursing register – and drop-outs from nursing courses. And the troops went back to their work with a renewed vigour.

Digger waited twenty minutes, then quietly left the room. He went along the corridors, to Hunter's office. It was empty, except for the smell of pipe tobacco.

He wasn't the type for the boutique. Oxfam was more his style. But he had flashed a wad of notes that would choke a horse and gone to a changing room with a bundle of clothes over his his arm. He didn't know his size, neither waist nor chest, so could she measure him? His wife must have bought his clothes – the tweed jacket and twill trousers he had on, too – for the past twenty-odd years. So she went to get a tape and Joanne – told her to cast an eye – just in case the old guy tried to feel her up. But he was okay.

He took the tape from her, said, 'Thanks, lass.' and tried to measure himself. Thought his waist was around his hips and nearly dislocated a shoulder faffing about at his chest. So she had measured him, put the thirty-two inch waist trousers back on the rack and gave him the thirty-sixes. Replaced the thirty-eight inch jacket with a forty-four. He was right about the shirt, well, the size anyway – XL.

Sad old drongo, wife probably left him and this was to be the big transformation to attract women. It might appeal to a certain type, too – blind ones who had lost their sense of touch. And what would it tell them? End of the season sale. Final reductions. Pair of drain-pipes that went out of fashion two years ago, orange shirt that was never really in and silk blouson more suited to his daughter.

He'd left the curtain open a crack and she saw him trying to recognise himself in the mirror. Kept running his hand over his shaven head. At least he was right about that. No sense in trying to hide the bald spot. Joanne's dad did that, combed it over, took it up from his oxter. Plonker.

She went back to the racks and picked out a few items. Had to go to the bottom of the pile of shirts on the table for the sky-blue one. He had big, blue eyes. She'd noticed that. Nice, Mills and Boon sad eyes. He was out of the dressing room, shoulders drooped a bit, arms outstretched asking what she thought. She said it was okay – for the panto at the Pavilion – and gave him her selections. When he emerged from the changing room the shoulders were back and he didn't look too terrible. And the shirt really did something for him. He liked the effect, too. Asked for a carrier bag and stuffed his old gear in it. Spoiled the new look by buying a baseball cap. Cheeky bugger even asked for a discount because of the misspelling. He smiled, and those eyes twinkled, as he was told no, 'FCUK' was actually a designer label.

He wondered if they had one for his boss – 'ASRE'.

The half-pint of real ale had gone down and stayed down so Boyson risked another. He wouldn't have dreamed about half-pints in *The Herald*'s regular pub, wouldn't have given the bears the chance to question his sexuality. The TSB was a man's pub. Boyson had given the place its nickname. The editor had been on the warpath, out of his office for the third time, looking for one of the boys. Boyson had defused the situation, confided that the guy had been called down to the TSB. And The Station Bar had been referred to by its initials ever since. You didn't do things by half measures in the TSB. But none of the merchant bankers in this flash place gave him a second glance.

Boyson thought about a packet of crisps, just as a late lunch, but decided against it. Too soon to risk food. Later, perhaps, once there was a lining on the stomach and if one of the guys would lend him some money. He had really tied one on last night, celebrating the front-page story about the mental woman killing city businessmen. Cracking good piece it had been too – even the editor said so. Made a pleasant change from the usual crap the news desk handed him. Boyson had been happy to get his teeth into a real story – and it was all down to The Hunter. But, as ever with the cop, there was a price to pay.

So Boyson had hauled himself out of his scratcher at one o'clock on his day off, had an Alka Seltzer for breakfast and set off for Busby. Didn't dare risk taking the car. It would be just his Donald Duck to get hauled over by a couple of plods and have to blow into the say-goodbye-to-your-licence thingy. He'd hailed a taxi, failed to notice that the bugger was taking the pretty road, too, and had received six quid back out of the only £20 note between him and pay day. He wasn't at his best as he pressed the fancy doorbell at the fancy big house. He couldn't see what they could tell him about Josef Paborsky. And he didn't have a scooby-doo about why Hunter wanted him to ask questions. But, as the homosexual fiddlers say, one good turn deserves another.

Maybe if he hadn't been so hung-over it would all have gone differently. He might just have turned on his heel when the snotty receptionist said that Mrs Carmichael was not in. Did he have an appointment? Well, did he want to make one? And who should she say had called?

Boyson's years of doorstepping experience had kicked in. He'd made a living out of asking people questions they didn't want to answer. So he'd just barged his way in. She didn't like that, screamed blue murder, and that's when they'd come running. Within twenty seconds there were four guys in front of him – two that looked as if they could take care of themselves, too. Then Calder Carmichael, the thinking man's shrink, turned up, wheezing like an old miner, but he took control. Boyson flashed his press card and Carmichael called off the hounds.

Zara, honestly, was not at home. But perhaps he could help. He led Boyson through a warren of passageways and sat him down in a leaky conservatory.

Fair dos to the guy, though, he produced a bottle – nice malt, too – but Boyson didn't have the stomach for it. He got right down to business.

'Josef Paborsky,' he said, 'you were the last one to see him alive.'

Might as well have kicked the guy in the balls. He doubled up in his chair, giving out the wheezing again, overdoing it, Boyson fancied. The guy was flapping at his pockets, bringing out an inhaler. Asthma or something. But Boyson didn't give a shit. He had his own problems. The fucking seat was wet. He could feel it now, seeping through his Ys. He stood up quickly, pulling his strides out of his arse crack. Oh, Jesus, it'd look as if he'd pissed himself. And only enough money left for a bus fare.

Carmichael had sucked at the inhaler as if his life depended on it. When he looked as if he was taking in enough air to talk, Boyson hit him with another question.

'What did you do with him?'

Carmichael had held up the palms of his hands, like a boxer giving up.

Boyson made for the conservatory door, reaching for the handle. He stopped, half turned, said you had your chance. Put you down for no comment. Read it and weep.

Carmichael forcing himself to his feet. Saying no, no, please. Then keeling over.

Boyson had counted to ten, then shouted for the cavalry.

He was nursing an inch of beer in his glass when the horse's hoof came into the posh bar. Baseball cap, navy-blue blouson jacket, over a sky-blue shirt, and sprayed-on stone-coloured chinos. A bit sad but it takes all kinds. He sat down at Boyson's table. No probs. Then he shoved over a pint. Boyson didn't look up, just pushed the pint back over the table.

Checkmate. Now fuck off.

'You must've been well pissed last night.'

It was The Hunter, baseball cap and all.

Boyson said, 'FCUK me.'

'Not as long as there are sheep in the fields,' Hunter said.

Boyson wanted to know if it was an undercover operation, 'a crackdown on rentboys.'

But Hunter wasn't playing. He said, all business now, 'How'd it go at Busby?'

Boyson took him through it. How the four guys had breathed life into Calder Carmichael.

'I'll tell you, if it hadn't been for them, your man would've been a deader. These guys were pros. Dead cool, talking in polysyllabic Latin shit. Pumping hands on his left tit, then the kiss of life. He'd a face like a Rangers strip. Then he coughed and, all of a sudden, he'd signed for the Hearts. Honest to God, it was as quick as that.'

Boyson took a drink, draining three inches from the pint. Not bad stuff, not bad at all. He was beginning to feel human again.

'So,' he said, 'when I saw he was back in the land of the living, I decided it was time for the off. And he was desperate to stop me. Two of the guys restraining him but he was trying to get up. I'll tell you, he's shit scared about something. The guys were trying to calm him but he was determined.'

Hunter took the baseball cap off and rubbed his hand over his shaven head. Boyson smiled but thought it wise not to comment. But the beer really was quite good. He couldn't resist just a little fun.

He said, 'I expect you'd like to know what he said to me.'

'And I expect,' Hunter said, 'you wouldn't like a size 10 rammed up your arse.'

Boyson was enjoying this now. He glanced under the table at Hunter's shoes and said, 'The Hush Puppies really don't go with that outfit. But keep your hair on.'

Hunter told him to cut the crap.

Boyson said, 'It was Paborsky. He told me . . .' he paused, took his notebook out of a pocket and flicked it open. 'I took a note of it while I was waiting for the bus. It's here, right, yeah, he told me, "It's lies. I took him to the Hilton. To Partick."'

Boyson closed his notebook. 'He kind of lost it there. The Hilton's not in Partick, though he made it sound posh. Came out more like Parteek.'

Hunter really wanted another pint, fancied one strongly, but he knew he daren't risk it. Maybe, if he'd been at the top of his game, but not today. He'd need all his wits about him to brief his troops on tonight's operation. It would all be down to the timing. Timing and planning, and he was happy with that now. But he knew that he needed to arrange his mind. He'd found a useful tool on the computer this morning, a thingy that sorted files in different orders. Just needed to ding the wee thingy (a pop-up, Aine called it) and the articles appeared alphabetically or in order of creation or length. He'd gone for alphabetically, though it didn't make a great deal of difference. The five items were now arranged from BIZDEATHS to STRANGELOVE.

Hunter didn't have a pop-up in his head. More of a pop-out. Used it every night, bevvied or not, to empty his brain. Last thing he did. Just after he took his watch off and put it on the bedside cabinet, he sorted his brain out. Then he mentally replaced the files, in reverse order, most important replaced last. So he'd go to sleep with it on top of the pile and wake up thinking about it. He'd tried doing it in a kind of chronological fashion, going from the kick-off to the final whistle. Lift the meerschaum, buy petrol, baccy, quiet word with Digger, that kind of thing. But it never worked. The most important thing wriggled its way to the top and effed up the system. That's why he ran out of petrol and baccy so often.

Jesus H, this time last week how'd he sorted his brain out? Skint – high up the list (was it ever anything else?) but not top. Knox would be top. Yeah, the first Strangelove victim. The lack of progress had been worrying him. He had been planning a midnight visit to Anderston. Pick up a prossie, two if he got lucky, the ones who had told Murdo that Knox was partial to a wee bit rough. Hunter wouldn't nick the girls himself – that's what the vice squad was for – but he'd pop down to visit them, individually, in the cells, see if they'd anything else to tell him. Strangelove wasn't one of them – he knew that – but maybe she was a five-star hooker. Hilton class, grand a night from filthy-rich fuckers. Maybe the girls knew more than they'd told the young copper. Could be their memories would be jogged if he could do them a favour, get the charges dropped, allow them back on to the streets to make their living. He didn't really know any of the girls nowadays. It had all changed. All wee lassies now, taking a quick meat injection so they could convert the dosh into drugs and stick it in their arms.

Boyson's visit to Busby had been interesting. Carmichael nearly a goner, eh? So the stuff about the dodgy ticker was for real and the physician could not heal himself. Maybe it was the same with every profession. The banker or accountant who couldn't balance his own books and dipped into the till. The bookie who punted too much. Or the copper incapable of nabbing the guy who was about to kill him. And still couldn't get it out of his newly-shaven head.

He'd told himself, promised, threatened that the daft clothes and the baldie would be the end of it. He hadn't been taking care of business. No two ways about it. Christ on a bike, Aine had bailed him out this morning. Spotted his blunder. He'd been lazy – planned the raids from memory – hadn't known that those tenements near the bowling club had been demolished last month. Could've sent a team practically into the back garden of one of Danny Boyd's heavies, tipped them off and they'd all have scarpered. Hit The Stoneman's team another time.

So Hunter had checked out a car from the pool, a souped up wee Peugeot soft-top, and taken a skite out to look at each of the waiting points. They'd all passed muster, and it had reassured him, but he knew that he'd have to put the contract out of his head, if only for tonight. He decided to change his image – to make it as hard as possible for the hit man – and he'd stopped off at a wee barber's shop near Parkhead Cross, told him to rump it, right into the wood. The guy had plonked a wee plastic thing on to his zizzer and two minutes later he was holding up the mirror at that funny angle. They always did that. As if you could say no, I don't like it, thanks for your trouble but I think I'll just stick with how it was. Hunter could see the two-inch scar where he'd been hit with the beer bottle, what? – twenty-odd years ago. Westmoreland Street, outside the Clada Club, closing time and the Irish guys a bit boisterous. Nothing new, no big deal. Just take the steam out of it, maybe have a joke, let them disperse with their dignity intact. Going okay, too, until one of the women cracked him on the skull, from the back, with a full bottle of Newcastle Brown Ale. Split him like a kipper. Blood right down to his ankles. They'd shaved it at the Vicky before they'd stitched it, keeping him in for a few hours 'just to be on the safe side'. Then one of the boys giving him a lift home. Cracking a joke, so Bella wouldn't worry. Asking her hold up a mirror so he could see the damage. And she gets her wee powder compact and they're both wriggling and twisting, trying to get the right angle in the bathroom mirror. The back of his noggin looking like a baboon's bum but Bella kissing it better, then tucking him up in bed with a big toddy.

Hunter emptied his beer glass. Then, subconsciously, lifted his hand to the scar. A reminder of the last time he'd been careless, the time when he'd taken his eye off the real target. He knew what he should do – what the rule book said. He had reason to believe that his safety was threatened so he was obliged to report it to superior officer. And what then? Removed, for his own safety and that of fellow officers. Given compassionate leave? Sent to Auchterarder, to a police federation rest home, well out of the way, so that operations were not put in jeopardy. Or given a couple of minders, two big guys to watch his back and cramp his style. The Jug would take great delight in that. Call in a couple of plods from Edinburgh or someplace to have a good poke about in his business. Make sure they found what he wanted, too. Aye, that'll be shining bright. And anyway, he wasn't about to give Fastnett the satisfaction.

Hunter thought that it would be good to have a blether with a mate, somebody who knew the Hampden Roar. He drew up a list of one, then discarded it. Digger had enough on his plate.

Jesus H, he'd nearly told Boyson. Okay guy, Boyson, wouldn't do you a bad turn, but not the man to bare your soul to. So Hunter had packed him off. Slipped him twenty quid, too. Said he'd had a lift at the bookies which, in a way, was true. There was a healthy bulge in the right-hand pocket of the chinos.

The oldest-swinger-in-town gear had fooled Boyson so it was fair to assume that it would dupe a hit man. Especially a freelance, a guy working from a photo. Kind of levelled it out a bit. He wouldn't recognise his killer. It had happened again. Didn't matter what order he sorted the files, the important one squirmed to the top.

Who wants me dead?

He thought he might have said it out loud but not a head was raised in the posh pub.

It's someone who doesn't have the balls to do it himself. But he does have the money. What's it costing? What's the bounty on my head?

He had a mental picture of his face, complete with wispy hair, tacked on to a big cactus. WANTED, DEAD. REWARD???

How much? What was the going rate?

Hunter remembered one hit in the city where a sixteen-year-old had been paid £200. He'd have done it for nothing, just to get a reputation as a hard man and a place at the gang's top table. They'd given him a shooter – big bugger of a thing it was too – and told him the target would be coming out of a pub in Maryhill Road around eleven at night. He could do it then – just walk up to the guy and blast him with the cannon, then disappear into the crowd. And the boy had done it. Draped a couple of *Daily Records* over his left arm and shot the bloke through them. Took half his head off. Didn't make it away, though – the target's pals had blown him away with the big gun.

The latest hit was commissioned by Danny Boyd himself. The scuttlebutt was that the pro, who had come up from London to off the young fella who was shagging The Stoneman's lassie, had been paid £5,000. Of course, that was nothing to Boyd. Five hundred tenner bags. Do that on a wet weekend. But that was the going rate for a pro. It would be more, surely, to top a cop. Jamesie said his boss had knocked the job back. Too risky, he said. Or was Boyd just playing hard to get. Considered it just a first bid, open to negotiation? It would be £10,000, surely, for a cop. Even then, Hunter couldn't see Boyd biting. It would bring too much heat on him. Killing a cop, well, that could seriously damage your business. And there would be no way of keeping it quiet. Somebody would talk. Be made to talk. There would be a reward, too. The papers, they'd put up the dosh. Not Boyson's mob – too tight-fisted – but the *Record*, the *Sun* – they'd up the ante. Twenty grand, easy. Fifty, maybe. Jesus H, if he could find out in advance he could tell Bella. Save on the insurance payments.

So Boyd was the key. At last, he spotted a weakness. Danny Boy was vulnerable. And pretty soon The Hunter would have him just where he wanted him. In a cell, alone. Then he could start to play with Danny Boy's brains. He'd find a scab and pick at it till it bled. Then, maybe, call in Digger.

No, he had enough on his plate. Aine, yeah, she could do it. That would annoy the shit out of Danny. The lassie asking all the questions. And Hunter just sitting there. Schtum. Wee smirk now and then. Not too many. Doing his Buddha. Then, when the time was right, getting up slowly. Scratching the chair legs on the lino. Over to Danny and whispering in his ear.

And Danny would tell him. The Hunter would have Danny Boy singing like a lintie.

> 'Tis you, 'tis you must go,
> and I must bide . . .

The prospect cheered Hunter considerably. He sat for another couple of minutes, sorting out his brain. Lowest priority in first. Strangelove. Danny Boyd. Heilan hardmen. Buy new pipe and baccy.

The press conference was to take place in five minutes, at 4 p.m. The timing was partly to suit the guys on the dailies, the big-hitters, and mainly to win some breathing space, to gauge the response to the front-page piece in *The Herald*.

The TV and radio journos were not best pleased and, as they shuffled into CR2, they made it known. The crime correspondent from the *Evening Times* was still smarting from the arse-kicking he'd got for missing the story. They had been playing catch-up all day, trying to get a new angle and getting little help from the cops. An official statement had been released over the Presswire, saying that inquiries into both deaths were continuing and there would be no further comment at this stage. In response to phone calls, the old Press Officer did say, off the record, of course, that there was evidence that the murders of Andrew Knox and Philip Macintosh were linked. They were looking for one killer – a woman.

The *Evening Times* had led on 'The Kiss Of Death'. The guy from the *Sun* said he was thinking of going with 'The Shag of Shame'. One of the guys asked him what was wrong with 'Last Tango At Barras'. He pointed out that none of the killings had happened at the Barras and was told that that wouldn't bother the *Sun*. They never let the facts get in the way of a good story.

One journo was conspicuous by his absence – Boyson, the man who had broken the story in the first place.

Just along the corridor, Digger Burns was in the office of James Smith, to bring him up to date with the investigation and to offer advice on what scraps of information could be cast before the newshounds.

Smith was still intrigued by the removal of the body of the baby from the Royal Infirmary. He'd never heard the likes, said he wasn't even sure what the charge would be. Unlawful something or other; preventing the burial . . . something like that. He was concerned, too, that the mother was not aware of the situation. They had a legal obligation to tell her.

Digger explained that he had taken the advice of the medical profession and they considered that she was not well enough to receive another shock.

Smith appeared to be relieved. The one thing they didn't need just now was the papers carrying stories of some demented woman walking about the streets with a dead baby.

He said, 'Are you sure? No, that's not fair. How can you be sure? But, you believe, you're as certain as you can be, that it's her? Our killer. She took the baby?'

Digger said confidently, 'It's her all right. It's what she'd do. It's twisted, sick. It's her. It just feels like her.'

Smith said, 'Feels like her, eh? You even sound like Hunter now.'

Digger said, 'I'm not sure if that's a compliment.'

'Nor am I,' Smith said. 'Do you, by any chance, know where he is?'

Digger answered, honestly, that he did not. Smith did not seem concerned about this so he ventured another question.

'Can I ask, Sir, what you're going to tell the press?'

Smith smiled, then said, 'Absolutely nothing, because I won't be there. Good luck, Sergeant. Hurry along – your audience awaits you.'

It didn't take a rocket scientist to figure out that the guys had been brought to Glasgow for a rumble. They were big lads – all forty-eight of them – a bent nose here and there, a few scars, but mostly the bruises were on their knuckles. They wore the gear – denims, boots that could do a bit of damage and dark sweaters, not too baggy to allow anyone to get a hold of them. Not men to mess with but good guys to have on your side. Sixteen of them had flown in from Inverness and nineteen from Aberdeen. They had been met at the airport by no less a figure than James Smith – evidence, if any were needed, that it was a big deal. They had picked up six rental vehicles – two minivans and four cars – and followed Smith to Rangers football stadium at Ibrox where thirteen cops from Tayside were waiting for them. They had been told they would be away from home for a couple of days tops. It went without saying that they were sworn to secrecy. No outside contact, no mobile phone calls. Smith left and a couple of the ex-players, who now worked as ambassadors for the club, had given them a tour of the stadium and taken part in some good natured banter. Then the cops ate a light meal.

215

One young lad from Inverness asked for fish. His Sergeant told him he was at the wrong end of the city for that – fish was only available here on Fridays – to be exact, every fifth Friday in February. After they had eaten, they were shown into the Waddell Suite where Hunter was waiting.

Showtime.

He gave them a brief floorshow, just to settle the nerves.

'Thanks for coming, lads. I want to tell you right off that you were specially selected for this job. The minimum requirement was an IQ of 110.'

He stopped, made a show of counting the heads, then said, 'Think we just make it.'

He told them that they were here so the sheep could get a wee rest and got a few choice replies. Then said that it was a research project, so they could see how real coppers did the job, and almost everyone shouted him down.

He took out his pipe, a new briar, nice bit of wood, and kindled it up. By the time he was satisfied with it the room was silent and every eye was on him. He took forty-eight packages from under the desk, then they got down to business.

Zara was keeping it simple. She finished buttering the toast, just three slices, just as the kettle boiled. There were four mugs on a tray, sugar and milk, three Penguin biscuits and two pieces of special shortbread. She put four teabags in the teapot and poured in the boiling water. Then she put the teapot on the heatproof mat on the tray, lifted the lot and began to wind her way through the house to Calder's clinic. Planning and prioritising, that was the secret. One crisis at a time, Sweet Jesus.

She had shut up her clinic. All appointments cancelled (there were only three and none important), no new admissions till next week and, if all went to plan, not ever. It had not been possible to lock the door on Calder's clinic but she had done the next best thing and discharged all but two clients. That had always been the plan – to clear the decks for Ranulf's operation. But that would not happen now and that had been the most difficult task of the Zara's demanding day. It really was – it was not a word she used often – but it really was a bastard. Telling Randy it was off again. The staff had been given the remainder of the week off – even the housekeeper – but she had retained Old Hugh, just to keep an eye on the nice crook and the uppity druggie lawyer. It meant extra skivvying for Zara but everything had its price. Besides, it wasn't exactly mentally taxing. In a way, it was quite therapeutic.

Stefan, the Norwegian lad, Randy's unwitting donor, had also been sent packing. He had arrived on the dot at two o'clock, all bright tailed and bushy eyed. Handsome lad, big and strong, with a dreadful stutter and a permanent flush of embarrassment. She had given him a glass of wine and some old chat about the good reports, the very good reports, she had received about his work, how well he was doing and how she had plans for him. She had given him £500 and phoned a taxi to take him to Queen Street railway station in Glasgow. From there, he was to go to Inverness. Zara confided that there was a proposal to build a reception centre for refugees there and she wanted his opinion on how the locals might receive the idea. He had to spend a week there, mix and mingle, just chat and suss, but not give any specific information. And she had taken a Polaroid picture of him to keep, she said, in her files. But it was for Randy, to give him hope, to let him see with his own eyes that his donor was in place, alive and well. Just a heartbeat away. Randy had taken the setback so very well, expressed genuine concern for Calder, then he reached for the whisky bottle. She had asked him not to, said he must preserve his strength but he had given her the saddest of little smiles.

Zara selected a key from a bunch like a jailer's, unlocked the bottom door leading to Calder's clinic and climbed the stairs. Old Hugh had heard the security buzzer and was waiting to unlock the top door. The young lawyer was strutting his stuff and, as soon as she got inside, he launched himself on another tirade of abuse. How he had seen no one today, received no help and no medication, and how up with this he was not prepared to put. Zara considered, but only for a moment, upsetting the tray, allowing the teapot to dispense its boiling water down the front of his designer denims and then say, 'Oops, so sorry.' The nice criminal must have read her mind because he stepped in, drew the young man aside and whispered in his ear. The words had an immediate effect. The lawyer turned on his heel and disappeared into his room.

Zara poured tea and took a mug and the special shortbread, neatly baked with cannabis, through to Matthew Whittle, the boy who could remember his dreams. He was, as ever, lying on his bed. He tried to smile when he saw double rations tonight, two pieces of shortbread, but his eyes remained cold. Enjoy, Zara told him, thinking that it might be his last. It all depended on Calder. How well or how unwell Calder was.

Zara stopped on the way out to thank the crim. He raised a hand – to show that it was nothing. She thought of Caesar – thumbs up to allow the gladiator life to fight and suffer another day, thumbs down to order death and the end of his misery. He had told Calder that he had killed – with a gun and with his hands. He had thought nothing of it at the time. It was something he had to do to gain respect, to get to the top of his trade, and something he had to do to stay there, to stay alive. But he had acquired a conscience, allowed the indulgence of remorse to take root and flourish. Then tried to drown it with alcohol. Did it in style, too, with champagne. And tonight the withdrawal left Caesar's hands trembling. Et tu, Brute.

Calder's slender grasp on life had nothing to do with indulgence. A weakness, yes, but not self-inflicted. Congenital heart disease – no sin greater than being his father's son. No male Carmichael surviving beyond the age of fifty. It was what had drawn Calder to medicine. A little knowledge, he had hoped, would bring a lot of years. He had lived 'properly', taken all the precautions, watched his diet. Butter, literally, did not melt in his mouth. But it didn't make a blind bit of difference. The Carmichaels had built-in obsolescence.

Zara decided against retracing her steps through the old house and, instead, left the clinic by the side door. She walked down past the conservatory towards the building which, in another life, had been the stables. She pulled her long, thin cardigan across her chest to try to ward off the chill of the autumn evening. Her breath went before her in little spurts of mist. Oxygen and water, the stuff of life. A sliver of dull light had broken through a crooked slat in a Venetian blind in the high-dependency unit. Zara made a mental note to stroke it back into place, to prevent its secrets from escaping.

She selected the appropriate key from her jailer's bunch, unlocked the door and stepped into the antiseptic hall. A shiver ran over her flesh. She put it down to fatigue, then put it out of her mind. No time for weaknesses or self-pity. Things to do. She gently eased open the inner door. Sørensen was on sentry duty, on a chair beside the bed. He got up and came to her. He stepped into the hall, half-closed the door before speaking and, even then, he did so in a whisper.

'No change,' he said, then added quickly, 'That's good. Every hour's a battle won and more strength to face the next. We'll watch over him – we have a roster – we'll take care of everything.'

He took Zara's hand is both of his, indulging himself in his guilt. His half-brother was alive today because of the Carmichaels. It had been their first transplant – and their first murder. The donor, the young woman they referred to as The Skunk – had died. Her body still lay in the boggy ground under the willows at the foot of the garden. Fortunately, she was NM_2 – neither missed nor mourned. The anaesthetist had sworn life-long loyalty. But his memory was short. He had become a thoroughly unpleasant person. And he had warned them that the next transplant was his last. Yet here he was, holding her hand like a priest, trying to repay his debt and assuming that he could go some way towards that by offering her – what? Comfort? Platitudes? The fool had a conscience after all so she let it pass.

She knew that Calder had suffered a heart attack and, without the skills of the Ramblers, it would have been his first and last. She knew, too, that the first twenty-four hours were of paramount importance. If he survived, it didn't mean that he would live. It just meant that the likelihood of him dying was reduced. She had thought it through very carefully and she really didn't have a position on it. If he survived, that was fine. She was comfortable with that. And if he popped his clogs, well, that was okay too. A decision made.

Sørensen was squeezing her hand, gently, doing the macho thing, presuming that the testosterone was seeping through his pores, permeating her frail, female flesh and acting as a tranquilliser. It was all perfectly . . . ridiculous. So she continued the farce, stretching on tiptoe to kiss him full on the lips. She might as well have slashed him with a razor. He pulled back in horror (even wiped his lips with the back of his hand) and turned his back on her.

What fun! So she still had the ability to shock. What joy. Maybe she did have a position on Calder's lifespan after all.

She went to the bed and looked down on his waxy face. He was sedated, connected to an ECG machine which monitored his vital signs. He was perfectly still, his skin almost translucent, and he looked younger than she could ever remember. He seemed content in this half-life, half-death, as if he, too, had no preference for what the next few hours might bring. Zara remembered, vaguely, that there was something she had to do. Then it came back to her and her eyes scanned the blinds. She had difficulty in identifying the buckled slat (strange, she thought, how the darkness does not creep in) then she spotted it and smoothed it back into line. She returned to her husband, left a little kiss on his forehead and said two silent words.

Sweet dreams.

Sørensen gingerly made way for her to leave. The notion flashed into her mind that she could brush against his thigh, maybe let a hand drop to his groin, but she quickly discarded it.

She left him to lock up and walked back towards the old house. The wind was gaining strength, unravelling clouds, stretching them under a waxy moon, and whipping spent, brittle leaves from the trees. Mother Nature's cull. Zara's cardigan flapped half a pace behind her and the cold bit through her blouse, pinching her nipples erect, and she was suddenly acutely aware of the reawakening of her sexuality. She had been conscious of a need for some time but she had suppressed it, although she had been tempted with Hunter. It had started as she toyed with him, sucking his cigar, so to speak. His apparent disinterest had been a challenge and she had wanted to sap his seed, to see him spent, under her spell. And that was the heart of the matter. She wanted to be in control.

But there were other pressing matters tonight, priorities, part of her plans. One more trip to the Pet Crematorium. Hunter could wait.

If only Calder had spoken to her, asked for her view or, better still, left it all to her. But no, his testosterone must have been overflowing, too. And he had gone to Junkie Jed, asked him to arrange with some of his junkie contacts to have the policeman killed.

It wouldn't happen. Zara had made sure of that. Hadn't taken a great deal of imagination, either. Just a few ampoules of morphine, hand delivered to Mr PetCrem this afternoon before she had driven on to see Randy.

She could still see Jed slouched in an armchair, already high on something but greedy for more. As she charged up the syringe, he wrestled with his old school tie, using it as a tourniquet around his upper arm, one end clutched in a scrawny hand, the other clenched in his teeth. But the veins were shy and flaccid. Not coming out to play. Zara had knelt before him, pulled down his trousers and pants, taken his penis in her mouth and breathed life into it. Not much of a specimen, really, but it had swelled slowly, as the surge of blood awakened long-unused erectile tissues. He did not get a full erection but, when she set it free, her saliva glistened on the big blue vein which was pumping his lifeblood. She had lifted the syringe, depressed the plunger to expel air bubbles and a thin spurt of death from the needle. She had paused then, giving Jed the opportunity to do it to himself but he declined. He had looked at her with pitiful eyes and said, 'Do it for me. Please.'

Afterwards, she had kissed him on the forehead and said, 'Sweet dreams.'

Digger Burns was ashamed of himself. He could have been home, should be sitting beside the fire with his heavily pregnant wife and here he was prowling around Committee Room Three, looking for something to do. He had reached Lorna on the phone earlier, on the third attempt. She was fine, she'd just popped round to a pal's house, for a blether, she said, a bit of company. Digger was relieved and felt a bit less guilty. They made idle chat, like two ex-lovers, meeting on the street, keeping it light and avoiding promises.

Digger found himself again thinking about Hunter, wondering if this was how he had become the man he was. It was a solitary job, had to be, stuck in the middle, between the cops and the top brass. Had to stay apart from the former and kept at a distance by the latter. Hunter handled it, well, Hunter's way. He was a chameleon, able to slip into any crowd, then disappear just as easily and never be missed. It worked for him, got him through the day, got the job done, but, somehow, he seemed to have lost himself. Forgotten who he was. He'd become the character. And Digger swore to himself that he would never do that.

There were four officers on duty – two due off shift at midnight (but he knew they would stay longer) and the two who had turned up a couple of hours early. He had been particularly pleased about that because it had given him the opportunity to get a feel of the mood as their colleagues brought them up to date on the case. He hadn't liked what he had seen but he had known already from the quiet tones that were being used in CR3. The drooped shoulders were more from disappointment than fatigue. And he felt the same himself. He had thought about giving them a pep talk, saying how well they were doing, how much progress had been made. But he had decided against it. That was something you did only once. And he had to keep it up his sleeve. He had also considered asking them how they thought it was going. Nudging them towards the accomplishments of the day. But he rejected that, too, fearing the failures that might be raised.

He was discovering that this was a lonely job, where decisions had to be made in grey areas in a bad light.

He had called the troops together, clapped his hands to get their attention, hauled Aine off the computer, saying it would wait. He was careful not to sound insincere or patronising and he thanked them for their work and promised more of the same tomorrow. Said that a suspect list which had included half the women in the western hemisphere had been whittled down. And they would get to a list of one.

Their target was a nurse – not working or a drop-out.

A single woman who had lost a baby.

She had a link with the Royal Infirmary – had worked there or lost her baby there

Finally, he had held up the artist's sketch and said, 'This is her.'

Then he said the taxpayers had got value for money today, twelve hours was more than enough. And he sent them home. Told them to have a beer – just one though – and to keep their mobiles switched on. Just to give them hope, to let them think they were getting close to the endgame. But they weren't. They were stuck in the middle. And it was a lonely place.

221

When they had gone, he briefed the new arrivals and looked on while their colleagues showed them how to carry out the checks on stillbirths and abortions. Aine had spent around an hour with the IT guys, setting up a programme to match the names of nurses and midwives with those on the Certificate of Registration of Stillbirth at Martha Street Register Office, and lists of Certified Non Viable Foetuses which had been provided by the Royal Infirmary and the maternity hospitals in and around Glasgow. Search name; search employment record; search addresses.

Search next name.

They concentrated on the Royal Infirmary but, even on the computer, it was a mammoth task, tedious and time-consuming. The bad news had been admitted just before 7 p.m. No name, no link with any female doctor, registered nurse or midwife who had worked there in the past five years.

Digger had seen it coming, as they worked their way through the Macs. He had gone to see James Smith, persuaded him to stick his head into CR3, say he was confident that the universities and teaching hospitals would cough up soon on the names of medical drop-outs.

But everyone knew that the Royal was the prime suspect. And, when it produced nothing, the heads went down.

Aine did her bit to try to perk them up. Said she always thought it was a drop-out, cited the toy stethoscope around Strangelove's neck in the corridor outside the mortuary, insisted that a doctor or nurse in employment would have a real one. And Digger had told them they would get there, they would get the match, all it needed was time.

But he hadn't told them that was one commodity they did not have. He hadn't told them what had happened at the press conference. How a couple of the guys had held back, said they'd had their own conference earlier in the pub and agreed a timescale. And the two journos, good guys, had said, 'Sorry, Digger, but we want to be straight with you. You've got a day, one more day, then we're going for the jugular. Botched investigation. How many more must die? You know, that kind of thing. Sorry, mate, but that's how it is.'

'Can I get you something, ma'am?'

The waiter startled Lisa. She had been lost in her own little world and it wasn't a nice one. She had teased her drink out to forty minutes, her anger rising all the time.

She said, 'Another Campari. Lots of soda.'

The waiter nodded politely and headed for the bar. Simon was thirty minutes late. It was so inconsiderate, so fucking annoying. Yet, even now, she could imagine him coming in hurriedly, his hair tousled, breathing heavily because he had been running. He would start to apologise, explain about the emergency that had arisen in the ward, start to go into details . . . and she would hush him with a little kiss. Tell him not to worry, Darling. I understand. They would order a drink, chat easily, old times, new times, then step outside and hail a cab. She would tell the driver to go to her flat. She had a present there for Simon, a surprise. Neatly wrapped up in her freezer . . .

The waiter returned with the drink and she lifted her purse. But he told her that it had already been paid. The gentleman at the bar.

He tilted his glass of malt whisky towards her and flashed a smile. She just knew that he would follow it over. His aftershave lotion arrived a few seconds before him.

'On your own, Doll? Me too. D'you mind?'

He sat beside her before she could object. Lisa took a sip of Campari, said thanks, then buried her head in a magazine.

He had kept an eye on her for the past twenty minutes and assessed the situation accurately. The body language made it obvious – she'd been stood up. She wasn't half-bad looking. Not bad at all, even close up. He was out and about, making sure he was seen. He would need an alibi for tonight and why not a pretty one? Easy to believe that he'd spent the night chasing his Nat King Cole. He cleared his throat to get Lisa's attention.

'So,' he said 'hungry, Doll? Fancy a wee Ruby Murray?'

Boyson turned up the collar of his jacket, then stamped his feet to keep the blood flowing, to try to get warm. A bitter wind scythed its way through the ugly, concrete buildings on the way up from the Clyde and whistled around the Hilton Hotel. Boyson set off again, pacing up and down in the car park, always keeping the main entrance in sight.

Good God, it was 8.50 p.m. Five more minutes, he promised himself, then I'm going in.

The wind rattled his ribs but at least the jacket, his only jacket, was getting a good airing. That had to be a plus. The chill was biting through the fibres, blowing away the smoke and smell of stale beer. There were usually three or four of the troops in the pub when Boyson went in and, sometimes, one or two others when he left. But he was a constant. Like air. Though, one of the girls had whispered, not so fresh, recently. Good on her, made a bit of a joke of it, said she only mentioned it because he did not seem to have a best friend.

So it appeared that he was a bit stinky – on the way to becoming a dirty old man. He'd seen them – just didn't know that he looked at one while he shaved each morning. Well, most mornings anyway. He'd taken to walloping on aftershave, splashing it all over his body. He'd taken a toothbrush and one of those wee free samples of toothpaste in the office.

But it went deeper than that. He needed, as they said in the features pages, a complete change of lifestyle. The flat needed to be gutted for a start. Not good enough just tilting the furniture till the dust dropped off, then sprinting around with the Hoover. He'd have to do it like a woman – the way his mother and his wife used to do it – empty one room at a time and give it a right seeing to. Have to go to the supermarket first, try to find the aisle with the cleaning products and stock up on hospital smells. Dettol, TCP, that kind of stuff. Then he'd have to think about new clothes, two jackets, one for wearing and one for airing. Damn the expense. Even get two socks!

Jesus, he could do with two pairs tonight. His feet were like lumps of lead. This was a bad idea. No, it was okay, just taking too long to happen. Then it did.

A people carrier drew up to the main entrance and disgorged six Japanese and about ten hundredweight of suitcases.

Boyson timed his arrival perfectly, nicked in behind the tourists and followed them into the foyer. He'd sneaked a look at the woman on the reception desk earlier and didn't rate his chances. Stern, that had been the impression from a distance, and nothing he saw up close changed it. Fiftyish, probably divorced and a man-hater.

She cracked a smile for the paying customers and took an age to lead the first couple through the rigmarole of registering before handing over the key to a room. She did it all by the book.

The other Japs – fair play to them – turned to Boyson, bowed politely, offered to step aside, to allow the man with no luggage a minute to do his business.

'Thank you, no,' Boyson said. 'You've come a long way. Please, I insist.'

He thought he saw the frosty face melt a little but she was still too efficient, too clinical for his liking. That meant Plan A was a non-starter. It was his nutty professor routine – not sophisticated but it had a surprisingly high success rate. It would involve asking for Paborsky, fumbling with his notebook, pretending not to listen to the answer, saying that . . . who was it? the other chap, the one with Paborsky, asked him to call; what was his name? it was here . . . then dropping the notebook, picking it up slowly, flicking through the pages again, hoping that she'd offer a name he could seize on.

But Plan A wouldn't work with this one. Nor would Plans B or C. And all of the tourists had their room keys now and were turning towards the lifts. Desperate times call for desperate measures. Boyson decided on honesty. Well, nearly.

He took his press card from a pocket, showed it shamefully and said, 'I'm sorry to have to ask . . . I've been sent down to . . . well, it's about Josef Paborsky.'

She didn't answer immediately and he thought that was a good sign.

Then she said, 'A bit late, aren't you?'

He said, 'Couple of days, yeah,' and gave her a sad little smile.

She said, 'More like three or four.'

A dialogue, this was good.

'Well,' he said, 'time flies, you know.'

'When you're in the pub?'

He smiled again and said, 'You've been reading my mail. Look, I really am sorry but it's important . . . to me.'

She tutted, then tutted again and he knew that he'd cracked it. She told him the truth but he didn't like it. Paborsky hadn't shown after the concert on Friday. But they hadn't expected him. He'd only been booked in for a couple of nights.

Boyson sighed and shook his head a couple of times. She thought that this kind of thing had happened to him before. Maybe it happened all the time. He half-turned, about to leave, then faced up to her again.

He said, 'I don't suppose he said anything about a pot of brown paint?'

Now he had lost her.

He said, 'There's this bloke and he hasn't seen Tam, one of his drinking pals, for a couple of weeks, so he goes round to his house and knocks on the door. It's answered by a guy wearing a suit, shirt and black tie. So the bloke says to him, "Is Tam in?" But, before the guy can say anything, a woman comes to the door, black dress on, eyes red with crying, and asks what's happening. The black tie tells her the bloke hasn't heard about Tam, then says, "I'm sorry, but Tam died this morning. This is his widow." And the bloke says to her, "Did he say anything about a pot of brown paint?"'

She laughed, looked around quickly to check that no-one had heard, then whispered, conspiratorially, 'That's sick.'

Boyson said, 'Yeah, story of my life. But you've got to laugh, eh?'

She had another furtive look around then, satisfied that she could never be quoted, leant forward and told him what he wanted to hear.

'Mr Paborsky did not return to the hotel after his concert . . . but his friend did.'

She dropped her voice lower still. 'His boyfriend, Patrik.'

Partick Hilton. It was what Carmichael had said. No it wasn't. He'd said Patrik. Hilton.

'Patrik stayed until Sunday night. Then two men had called – one of them a foreigner – to take him to the airport. One of the men paid the bill . . .'

She stopped there, teasing him.

'. . . with his credit card . . .'

He noticed that she wasn't wearing a wedding ring. He had no money but he could offer his body.

The main door opened and a couple walked in. The man made his way to the reception desk and the woman, clad in a full-length black leather coat, seemed to melt into the shadows.

Boyson moved quickly. He said, 'Could you be persuaded to tell me more if I were to take you to someplace less . . .'

She offered, 'Expensive?'

'Yeah,' he said, 'that too.'

She said, 'On one condition.'

He said, 'Name it.'

She said, 'You wash off the aftershave.'

Then she turned her attention to the paying guest and said, 'Good evening, Sir. How can I help you?'

The operation had gone as well as could be expected. Eleven teams of cops in hired vehicles arrived at their targets at 8.14 p.m. Each man had been given a separate sheet of instructions which clearly stated his specific role. At 8.15 p.m. they had moved in with military precision. Twenty-seven of Danny Boyd's henchmen had been arrested. Fifteen were safely locked up in cells spread throughout the city. Six, who had suffered injuries while resisting arrest, were under police guard in the Royal Infirmary. A further six had been released without charge on Hunter's instructions. He did not want Boyd's little empire to be left totally devoid of muscle lest any rival be tempted to move in, to seize control. A vacuum was a dangerous thing. It could suck in so many undesirables. Better to keep a balance among the undesirables – opposites repelling.

The most dangerous of Danny Boyd's thugs would be taken to Glasgow Sheriff Court over the next few days. The charges would include, conspiracy to murder; possession of firearms and other weapons; assault- ing police officers; resisting arrest; and possession of drugs with intent to supply. Bail would, no doubt, be requested and would, without question,

226

be refused. And men who had murder in mind would be remanded in custody.

There had been a brawl in one of the pubs where a call to a mobile phone had alerted those inside of the police raid on Boyd's house. It had been bloody and brief. The policemen had obeyed their orders. They had retaliated first. Four of Boyd's men were removed by ambulance. Two had suffered concussion, one had a fractured skull and facial injuries and the other had broken ribs one of which, possibly, had punctured a lung. Given the fact that the six police officers had been attacked by much greater numbers, many of them in possession of handguns and bladed instruments, it was fair to assume that a jury would consider the damage inflicted to be minimal force to protect life and limb.

The raid on the second pub had gone by the book.

There were nine other teams of cops, each with four members. They had battered down the doors of their target houses. This took some time (more than six minutes at Boyd's home) because of the panzer-like armour protection favoured by drug dealers. But, once the noise was over, most of the occupants saw the sense of assisting the police with their inquiries. However, the skulls of four dogs – three Rottweilers and one pit bull terrier – had been cracked by baseball bats. A total of thirteen arrests were made. Two teams detained three each; one team made two arrests; five teams each made one arrest; and one team drew a blank. Two of Boyd's men were admitted to the Victoria Infirmary. One suffered a dislocated arm in a struggle and the other broke both legs after jumping from a second-storey balcony. One cop got a tetanus jag after being nipped by the pit bull, six others had bumps and bruises, the worst being a broken nose. The last cell door was banged shut at 9.14 p.m. and the booze began to flow in the Waddell Suite at Rangers' stadium about twenty minutes later.

Hunter gave them an hour to celebrate then joined the party. A porn tape was on the video. Noisy wee bint, too, he could hear her begging for more even above the coppers' lewd comments. Nice eyes, though, kind of sad. And empty.

Then one of the coppers spotted him. The porno was switched off and all eyes turned to The Hunter.

He lifted a bottle of whisky and drank from the neck. Then he raised the bottle and gave the toast.

'To the heilan hardmen.'

'Heilan hardmen,' they echoed.

Glasses were drained, then refilled.

Hunter walked among them, one of the boys, quick with the patter.

227

He threw a short jab at the young cop with the broken nose.

'Good job, kid, good job. Just one thing. Hit them with your fists next time.'

One of the Dundee guys showed a nine-inch slash in his denim shirt. Hunter said he hoped that the body armour hadn't been damaged. Then he singled out one of the Aberdeen guys.

''Sup with you? You going soft, big poof or something? No charges of police cruelty laid against you.'

The troops loved it.

The bloke said that he had dislocated the guy's arm.

'Yeah,' Hunter said. 'Only one, though.'

He listened to their stories. Feigned pain when they showed their bumps and bruises. After half an hour, he banged a bottle on a table for a bit of hush.

When it fell silent, he said, 'I've got to go, lads, There's a bliddy mountain of paper work thanks to you lot.'

They shouted and cheered.

He went on, 'Well done, lads, a right good night's work. The bad news is you've to be in HQ to do your own paper work in the morning. The good news is you've got the rest of the night to play.'

Another roar.

He told them that they were booked in across the way in the Swallow Hotel. Enjoy and put it on the tab.

'A word of warning, though. Avoid the seafood. Don't want you going back up north with crabs, eh?

Then he raised the whisky bottle by the neck and proposed another toast.

'To Hunter's heilan hardmen.'

'Hunter's heilan hardmen.'

Zara sparked a match and it fizzed into a phosphorous flame before the wind snuffed it out. She took out another, then paused. There really was a delicious irony about not being able to make fire at a crematorium. She lit another match, cupped her latex-gloved hands around the flame but again the wind extinguished it. Was this a warning? An omen? Strange word, cremate. Two syllables, making no sense together. She had never thought about it before. And now, really, was not the time for such nonsense. She would look it up in the big dictionary when she got home.

It was strange, too, that, no matter how carefully one planned an exercise, there was always something unforeseen which could go wrong. And Zara had given considerable thought to the disposal of Jed's body. She did not trust the man alive, nor did she trust him dead. So she had decided to incinerate his cadaver and any incriminating evidence he might have tucked away in the dark corners of this hovel he called home.

She was wearing a tracksuit and trainers, 'borrowed' from Matthew Whittle. A fitting touch, she thought, with a certain sinister symmetry. Matthew's way of saying goodbye and good luck to the man who had kept him supplied with cannabis resin. There was an ample supply in the shortbread tin to keep Matthew happy for a couple of weeks. After that, one way or another, he would no longer be a consideration.

She had told Sørensen that Jed was dead – an overdose – and she had found his body in the afternoon. Said that she was not unhappy about it either, because Jed had been threatening to go to the police, to tell them everything. And, she had said, the worry of that had been a major contributory factor in Calder's heart attack. So Sørensen had agreed to drive her but said he would have nothing to do 'with any other business'. They had taken Calder's car, stayed on the back roads, seen only one other car and he had parked in a passing place. Said he would go no farther – would not drive up the rutted hill to the house. So she had walked. Very pleasant it had been too, in a *Wuthering Heights* kind of way. Windswept and interesting.

Jed had put his penis away, zipped up too. Good boy, that was nice of him. He was sitting in an armchair, perfectly calm. Really quite at peace. Zara had turned on two rings of the gas cooker, popped two dirty pans on them too, just to make it look good. She had opened up Jed's old newspapers, scattered them around – under the curtains, by the furniture – any place they would spread the blaze. Then she had splashed around the gallon of petrol. It seemed the perfect recipe for a fire, leading to an explosion. But she couldn't keep a damned match alight.

She went back into the house. She could smell the gas, even over the petrol, but she just ignored it. Lit a match and held it under the front page of *The Herald*. Today's, as luck would have it. One headline caught her eye – 'Woman Linked to Two Murders'. One of them was Philip Macintosh. She read as much as she could while the flame consumed the story.

Police are hunting a woman who has killed two Glasgow businessmen in the past four weeks, *The Herald* can reveal.
Both were killed by a single blow from a knife, and senior officers are concerned that the murderer will strike again.
The first victim was Andrew Knox, an architect, who was killed on 21 September outside his office in Park Circus. The other was Philip

Macintosh, whose body was found on Sunday morning in the Merchant City.

The flame had risen too high and Zara was forced to drop the page. It landed on a trail of petrol and a tongue of fire licked across the room. She walked out, with a song in her heart. The police had more to worry about than poor old Junkie Jed, Mr PetCrem, who was about to incinerate himself. Zara closed the door behind her, to keep the gas in. Jed would go out with a bang.

He draped his Givenchy shirt over a hanger and placed it in the wardrobe beside his Armani suit. The shower in the lavvy was on full bung and he could hear his lumber singing over it. An old number, from the sixties, maybe early seventies, surprised that she could remember it. Maybe it had been re-released. They were doing that more and more. Covers they called it – a cover version from the golden age.

Simple Simon says
Put your hands in the air,
Da da da dada dada da

He slipped off his Y-fronts and socks and bunged them in the wardrobe as well. A night in the Hilton Hotel with a young bint. Danny Boyd could think of worse ways to spend the night. He went to the bed and jumped in. He spent some time moving the sheet up and down on his chest. How much naked flesh should he show her? He settled on a bare chest and covered-up belly. But it didn't really matter. She was a goer – a randy wee bitch. Had her tongue in his ear as soon as they were out of that posh pub. And some numpty had stood her up. Well, that was his loss. Danny had decided that he would stand her up too, then lie her down, then do it doggie-style.

He thought about making a quick phone call to check that the hit on The Stoneman's team had gone as planned. His mobile was on the blink – bloody batteries again – and stretched for the phone on the bedside cabinet then changed his mind. The cops might have the phones tapped. That bastard Hunter. Wouldn't put it past him. Bastard knew the moby number. Had the cheek to phone to try to put the frighteners on, warning against getting revenge for Larry The Laundryman. Aye, that'll be shining bright. And The Hunter would know it by now. But he wouldn't pin it on Danny Boyd. No, Sir, couldn't pin anything on a naked man. Danny chuckled to himself. It really was a great alibi.

And where were you, Mr Boyd, between the hours of 8 p.m. and 10 p.m.

I was chatting up a bird, then shagging my brains out. In the Hilton Hotel, by the way.

And can you prove it, Mr Boyd?

Well, I can, actually. You'll find these used Johnnies in the wee bin in the lavvy. Feel free to test them for DNA. They'll still be warm. Kinda Johnny come lately – no, make that Danny come lately. That's better. Oh, by the way, DNA stands for Do Not Apprehend. Goodbye, officer. Oh, and wasn't that a terrible thing that happened to Mr Stone and his friends. Tut-tut.

The splashing in the lavvy had stopped. The bird had got herself nice and clean. Danny liked that in a woman. Oh, he'd boffed some right dogs in his day – didn't deny it, some proper wee hairies – but he could afford to be fussy nowadays. Yes, sir, nowadays he could afford just about anything. Like the champagne chilling in the ice-bucket. Big crest and Hilton on the outside. He had swithered about checking in under another name – Nathaniel K. Cole – but had resisted the temptation and flashed the gold card. American Express – that'll do nicely, Sir. Especially when the cops check up on it.

The bint had body-swerved reception. Maybe she was a known face, a professional, but Danny didn't give a shit. It was her body he wanted.

The bathroom door opened and she came into the bedroom. The wee bird really had a bit of style. She was wearing the full-length leather coat and, he hoped, nothing else. He was instantly aroused. His penis began to raise a bulge in the crisp, linen bed sheet.

He said, 'Are you shy, Doll, or a wee bit kinky?'

Lisa twirled around quickly, arms out and the coat flapped open, giving him a tantalising glimpse of her naked body. She strode to the bottom of the bed and stopped. Then she began to stroke her body outside her coat.

'Nice,' Danny said, 'go on yerself, Hen.'

The bed sheet began to rise. Lisa moved to the side of the bed and shimmied and swayed like a belly dancer. She had performed the routine for a movie in Turkey, earlier in the year, so she knew the movements well. After a minute or so, Boyd tried to grab her but she stepped back. She thrust her pelvis towards him, a promise of what was to come, but drew back every time his hand reached out.

Boyd, on his side now, lay back to enjoy the performance – and bide his time.

Lisa's hands returned to caress her black leather skin. She spent some time on her breasts, cupping them, stroking, emphasising the outline,

231

circling the nipples slowly and seductively. Then she lowered a hand to her vagina and began to simulate masturbation.

Boyd's hands moved under the sheet. Two could play at that game.

If he noticed Lisa's right hand move up to her left breast, he thought nothing of it. Not even when it continued on its journey up to the collar to the silver cross there. And, if he saw that cross being removed, had he realised what it really was or seen a glint of light as it flashed towards him, it was already too late. The single blow pierced his heart before he could take his hand off his penis.

But, Lisa chided herself later, the wound did not kill him. Not instantly.

Boyd, initially, did not react to the pain. Even managed another pull on his plonker, she thought. Then he yanked Ms Stiletto from his chest, stared at her in incredulity, rose from the bed, as if merely pricked by a pin, and went for her. His lips moved but no sounds emerged.

Lisa backtracked, thinking of the bathroom. Could she make it in time, slam the door, bolt it? But it wasn't necessary. Boyd managed only one step before keeling over, face first. She knew that he was dead but she left him there for a full minute and, when she did approach, she kicked at him, at his head, just to be sure.

He was heavy and she struggled to turn him over. She had to get Ms Stiletto back. She was nowhere to be seen at first, then Lisa saw her embedded deep in Boyd's throat. Her silver tongue had given him one last lick as he fell. The wound was about two inches long and jagged. Lisa didn't like it. It looked amateurish, untidy, as if she had panicked. She grabbed the knife firmly and pulled it up towards his mouth. It cut cleanly. A much neater job. But still it did not please her. Then she had a thought, an idea. Brilliant! It would really annoy the police.

She laughed aloud as she fetched her handbag. She had been paid in cash for the Morocco shoot, and she had brought the money with her, just to impress Simon. She took the £3,000 and began to stuff it into the gaping wound in Boyd's throat. When she was finished, she opened the champagne, poured a glass and sat back to admire her work. She sipped slowly, savouring the moment, appreciating the study in still life. It would be better if it was Simon but nothing's perfect. She had improvised, made the best of a bad job. And this cocky, arrogant bastard had deserved all he had got.

She drained the glass, went to the bathroom and had another shower. She was sore, battered and bruised by Abdul, but she ignored the pain, dried herself briskly, then dressed.

She poured another glass of champagne – shame to see it going to waste – then went to the wardrobe and took out the dead man's clothes. She laid them on the bed, curious to see if she could guess what he had been, what he had done for a living. The gear was expensive but flashy. He was a crook – she was sure of that – probably drugs. His wallet was in the hip pocket of his trousers. She removed the AmEx card. Danny (not Daniel, she noted) Boyd. She slipped the card into her purse but left the cash, more than £700. From his right jacket pocket she took a packet of condoms, with two still in it. The inside pocket held a neat little box which opened into a cocaine-user's kit, complete with mirror, a silver straw and a packet of the drug. She looked again at the body. It was, as Mum would say, good riddance to bad rubbish. So long, Danny Boyd, missed only by a few thousand junkies.

She looked around the room, checking that she hadn't left anything too incriminating. She didn't want to make it too easy for the police. There were fingerprints all over the place, especially the champagne glass, but she did not have a criminal record so it didn't make a blind bit of difference. It would give the police something to do, though, running them through their computers.

Boyd's mouth had popped open and Lisa felt that it spoiled the aesthetics of her sculpture. Her eyes fell on the condom he had placed on the bedside cabinet. She picked it up, carefully tore open the foil and unrolled the sheath. She used the foil to scoop some of Boyd's congealing blood into the condom – not a lot, just about a loving spoonful. Then she knotted the end of the Durex and dropped it into his mouth. That would give the psychiatrists something to chew over.

Hunter tilted his head to the left, jamming the phone between chin and shoulder, and reached out with his right hand for the whisky bottle. Just out of reach, dammit. He thought about taking his feet down off his desk but decided it was too much trouble. There was a silence at the other end of the line while the guy stopped to draw breath.

Hunter said, 'You're right, of course. Out of order, completely, I said that.'

He frowned as the voice started up again, going over the same ground.

Hunter knew that making the call to the Superintendent whose turf he had invaded earlier was a good idea. Sore on the ears, pain in the arse, but better in the long term. Like lancing a boil. Take the pain, get it over and done with.

The guy, understandably, was livid. Hunter had come on to his patch, arrested his crooks and brought in officers from three other forces to do it. The inference was clear – the Superintendent couldn't be trusted. Neither to do the job properly nor to prevent his coppers tipping off Danny Boyd. But the old sweetiewife, didn't have the balls to say it.

Hunter said, 'You're quite right, you're entitled, I would feel the same myself in your shoes.'

The Superintendent mumped on and Hunter sprinkled in yeahs and I knows. But he was getting a bit pissed off. So he cut to the chase. 'That's what I told him,' he said. 'That . . . and how it would look as if you weren't to be trusted.'

That did the trick. Hunter put the Hush Puppies back on the floor, laid the phone on the desk, grabbed the Black Bottle and poured an inch into the coffee mug. Couple of slugs later, he lifted the phone again just as the volume was going down.

'Who?' the Superintendent said. 'Who did you say it to?'

Hunter said, 'You've lost me. Who what?'

'You said that you told him it'd look as if I couldn't be trusted. Right? Well I'm asking you right out who's the him?'

Hunter said, 'You know I can't . . . Look, I'm phoning just to square things with us, a call to a mate, just to let you know that I had no choice. Ours is not to reason why and all that.'

But the guy wouldn't let go. Jesus H, what did he want? A postcard? He was going on about mates and how mates could be trusted, right. Right?

Hunter took another sip of whisky, just to let him think that he was making a moral decision. Then he said, 'Okay. Let me put it this way. He wouldn't even let me use our own vehicles. Insisted on hiring them at the airport. I didn't sign for them. Now, I've said too much so don't you say anything. See you soon, eh? Buy you a pint. Bye now.'

He hung up. The Superintendent would chase the paperwork, find Fastnett's name on it and do one of two things. Tell the other sweetiewives that it was the Chief Constable's operation, hint that he knew about it all along. Or, more probably, he'd do nothing.

That was the one awkward call out of the way. Hunter made two easy ones – to the *Press and Journal* in Aberdeen and the *Courier* in Dundee – telling them how their cops had been specially drafted in to Glasgow to head off a drugs war. Not much they could say about it just now, a lot of charges pending – police assault, right up to conspiracy to murder – it would make right good copy when it got to court. Told them they could run with the charges. Did they have the Press Officer's home number? No, hold on, it was here somewhere. Oh, and by the way, don't say where you heard about it, okay?

The heilan hardmen had done a good job. No reason why they shouldn't be heroes in their own land.

Then he called Jimmy Stone. Took great pleasure in it, actually.

'D'you know who this is, Jimmy? Yeah, right first time. You owe me. You know why but I'll tell you anyway. I watched your back, Jimmy.'

The Stoneman was still listening. The Stoneman was worried.

'Danny Boy upped the ante but he didn't bet on me. Nobody does that on my turf. You're vulnerable, Jimmy, so watch your own back from now on. Oh, and by the way, I've got a new team, a heavy team. Trust me on this, Jimmy, you don't want to meet them. Night, night, don't let the bugs bite.'

That would give him something to think about. Just in case he was thinking of making a move on Boyd. Talking of which, where was he? Hunter tried his moby for the fourth time that night. It rang out again. No mug, Danny Boy. He'd made himself scarce, set up a good alibi. Spent the whole evening in a convent or something. Arranged plenty of witnesses who would be happy to say, 'He was with us all the time, honest to God.'

It was almost midnight. The end of a productive day. Hunter poured another inch of whisky into his mug and kindled up his pipe, the new briar. Not a bad wee pipe, actually. Should give it a rest, break it in gently, but what the hell. Live dangerously, eh?

He put the Hush Puppies back up on the desk. The Black Bottle was starting to warm the cockles of his heart.

This is the biz. This is what polis work is all about, what Robert Peel did after he got the bad guys. Puffed his pipe and had a dram. Nowadays it's karaoke and a kebab. That's what the young heilanmen were talking about, anyway. Their idea of a good time. Ah, well, each to his own. The older guys would have put the porno back on. Tucked the memory away for a J Arthur Rank in the hotel later.

Hunter thought about phoning Bella, wondered if she'd seen the news about the arrests on the telly. It had mentioned something about officers being injured. Maybe she was worried about him? But he'd told her long ago that no news was good news and she'd hear the bad plenty soon enough. No, she'd be tucked up in bed, dreaming about how to spend his money.

Blondie flashed into his mind. The dame from the Carmichaels' yacht with nipples like organ stops. He had her phone number some place. Could give her a bell, pop round to her smart wee bungalow in Milngavie. Give her a night of passion. Maybe not. Might not be up to it. Drunk too many stiff ones. He had a wee laugh to himself. Not bad that. Can't get a stiffy because of the stiff ones. He hadn't done much for Blondie last time either. Well, first time. No, he decided, it was last time. He'd got away with it once, it would be just his luck to get captured. That, after all, was how Blondie got the bungalow. Caught her man playing away from home. Just be his Donald Duck if Bella had the divorce police on him. Take half of everything. Half of the house (would she go for upstairs or downstairs?) also demand one eyebrow, one ball. Might explain Bella's favourite expression – used it a lot, on the phone, talking to the Coffee Girls. Wee wicked whispers. And they'd tell her secrets about their men – how they pissed in the back garden. How they were screwing their men for cash. And Bella would say, good, have a ball.

Hunter made a mental note to ask Digger how much the divorce had cost him. It had been a bit of a shocker, that wee mousy woman giving him the boot. Okay, Digger had been hitting the sauce. Not on duty, not that it spilled over on to his work, but she'd used it against him. Used the law against a copper. She'd had a ball.

Hunter lifted the bottle again, then decided that he'd had enough. He put it back in his desk drawer, opened the window wide to let the pipe reek out, then left his office. He walked along the corridors, a bit unsteady on his pins, towards Committee Room Three, to see how the Strangelove team were doing, see if there was any progress. He paused at the door, peeped through the wee glass panel. Four guys there and he only recognised one of them. Jesus H, can you lose touch so quickly? He thought about phoning Digger at home and realised that he didn't have his number. It would be in the computer, somewhere. Under fones or phoney or some phuckin thing. The Duty Sergeant would have it. Get it from the Duty Sergeant.

Hunter caught a glimpse of his own reflection in a dark window. The pale trousers already a bit worse for wear, pipe ash staining the right leg, and the trendy blue shirt had more wrinkles than an old hoor. Good disguise, though. Decent hitman might decide that he wasn't worth the price of a bullet.

The Duty Sergeant was an old hand. He pretended not to recognise Hunter at first, then asked who did it, who did that to his hair? Offered to send a couple of the lads to sort him out.

Hunter told him that he was very fucking funny. He forgot about Digger's address and the whisky began to talk about the arrests of Boyd's gang. He was on good form, some of the lads came out to listen and he put on a show. Then the Sergeant chased the troops and asked, nicely, how he was getting home. Did he want a lift?

That killed the good mood. Hunter asked what was happening, what else was doing in the dear green place?

The Sergeant said there was a suspicious death in a fire outside East Kilbride. The local cops were there and the fire guys didn't like the look of it. Smell of petrol. The gas had gone up and they couldn't find the thingy to turn it off.

He said, 'Oh, and you'll like this. It's at a crem. A pet crematorium. Have you heard of it?'

Hunter said, 'I've seen the film. *Revenge of the Labradors*. Or was it *Hamsters with Matches*?'

And, as he walked out into the night, the warm glow returned.

8

Hunter was trying to whistle, smile and have a hangover at the same time. He was at the top of the big tree-lined avenue, fighting with the soft-top of the wee Peugeot. One long line of cars slowly snaking out and another crawling in behind the hearse. Doing the Daldowie dawdle.

Rotten place to meet. What do you put on the eccies? Black tie, packet of Handy Andies, really chance your hand and try for a wreath? Jamesie had chosen the venue. He'd phoned early doors. Hunter was busy conning James Smith, talking ten to the dozen, busybusybusy, making a big thing of the pressure. It had taken Hunter a few seconds to realise that it was his own mobile because it was playing a different tune. One of the young heilanmen had been faffing about with it last night. 'Not The Billy Boys', but vaguely familiar.

'Like to trade some information?' Jamesie had asked. 'Same place as last time. Ten o'clock.'

Perfect, Jamesie, Old Son. It enabled him to finesse a body-swerve of the paperwork for the charges on Danny Boyd's gang.

Hunter finally managed to fasten the studs to tuck away the soft top, got back in the car and drove off. Not for very far, though. Stopped at the traffic lights at the top of the road. Big queue to get out here and no one waiting to get in. Seems about right. There was quite a blow here, a nip in the wind too, so he slapped on the baseball cap, tugged it down firmly so it wouldn't take wings. Hunter looked at himself in the interior mirror. FCUK it, not entirely apt for the crem. The hat looked welded to his head and his lugs were sticking out. Looked a bit like the Scottish Cup. Mouth felt like a goalie's jockstrap and tom-toms were pounding in his temples. Still, it was better than coming out in an urn. The lights changed to green and he gunned the zippy wee Peugeot on to the M74.

Jamesie had wanted to know if Boyle was in custody. Now that spoke volumes. Hunter told him no, much to his regret, Danny Boy was not enjoying a mug of tea and a roll on sausage at the taxpayers' expense.

Jamesie had asked him to swear it was true, made him say cross my heart and hope to die. Jamesie's information was interesting, too. He had produced today's *Daily Record*, ignored the front page coverage of last night's swoop on the Boyd gang and pointed out the story on page five – headlined 'Burned Alive at the Crem' – and said, 'That's your man. Or it was, anyway.'

Hunter didn't get it.

Jamesie said, 'That's the guy – the one that wanted to take out the contract on you.'

Hunter couldn't believe it.

Jamesie said, 'Honest to God.'

So Hunter's driving, towards East Kilbride, to the scene of the incineration. Crem à la crem. And he's whistling, the tune from the moby. The name escapes him, but a few words spring to mind.

When dada da da meets Yogi Bear . . .

The Pet Crem guy wouldn't toast any more terriers. What was his name? He'd read it in the paper and it had meant nothing to him. Jed something or other. Didn't know him from Adam. Certainly wouldn't recognise him now. Suspicious death, that's what the Duty Sergeant had said last night. Copspeak for murder. Be a bugger of a crime scene for evidence. Gas blast would take the roof off. Place would burn like bloody hell. Fire brigade had said something about accelerants. Usually meant they'd found a can marked 'Petrol', a box of Swan Vestas and maybe a letter addressed to Molotov.

And this was the guy – Jed Somebody, Jed Nobody – who wanted him dead. Willing to pay for it, too. And he had – with his life. Hunter hoped that he hadn't suffered too much, that the body wasn't badly burned. That it had some secrets to tell him.

Had Jed found a hit man, then had a fall-out? Over money, probably. Had Jed reneged on the deal, tried to barter him down? Or did the killer try to squeeze him for more? Lose the place, top him, then start the fire?

Unlikely. No point in that. No profit in it.

Then an idea occurred to Hunter. Maybe it wasn't Jed. Not Jed dead. Maybe Jed was the guy with the matches and the charred stiff was the killer, the hit man that is. Or maybe somebody completely different. Like Danny Boyle.

It was getting too much like Monty Python.

Hunter had cut off the motorway at Bothwell and started to climb the dual carriageway towards East Kilbride. The wind was starting to blow away the cobwebs. Fine day to have a hangover, good day to be alive. He couldn't tell, no way to be sure, but he reckoned that he was a free man again. Felt it in his water. It was a new start, really. All kinds of opportunities. A second coming.

It takes you all night to do what you used to do all night.

Another line from the song. What was the next bit? It was the title. The hook, repeated time and again.

Da da dada dada da da.

Dammit, it was annoying him now. Think on something else. Like the rest of his life. And, how much in his tail? It had been almost £600 yesterday and now it was little more than half of that. At this rate he'd be skint by Friday.

Might be able to claim back the cost of the hotel room, though. But what was the point in that. The eccies went straight into the bank and Bella claimed them. Pokey hotel room it had been too. He'd tried to haggle on the price, pointed out to the smarmy young guy on reception that he'd get nobody else at that time of night, half was better than nothing. But he wouldn't budge. Hunter had thought of bringing out his warrant card (he'd also thought of sticking one on the guy), then he realised that the establishment didn't want him at any price. He'd left quietly. Decided to hail a cab and go home. Saw two black hacks, lights on the buggers, too, but they gave him a wide berth. Too pissed even for a Glasgow cabbie to risk. He had considered walking back down to the copshop but he couldn't be arsed. So he'd gone back in to see the smarmy young guy, paid upfront, taken the lift to the pokey wee room, then found that he couldn't sleep.

For some strange reason he couldn't get the Vectra out of his mind. Where was it? The wee Peugeot was at the copshop but he was buggered if he could remember where he'd left the Vectra. Bloody typical. Just paid for and now he'd lost it. Might work out okay, though. Might be pinched. It was starting to play up again, anyway. Window was cream crackered. So, better really if it was half-inched, get the dosh from the insurance company for it. Have to buy another. But that was a bummer, too. Bella had been talking about a new car – brand new, with the wrapper still on. She'd seen the ads in the papers – three years to pay it up and no interest. And no profit in it for The Hunter. A new car never broke down. And, if it did – if he was lucky enough to get a bad one – a Friday one – they fixed it under warranty. No fiddle there. Bella had even been talking about taking out an extended warranty – three bloody years. No, the car enterprise had been good, it had kept some of his own money in his pocket, but it was yesterday's idea.

No probs for Bella, though. She was doing nicely, thank you, out of her job as Chief Executive Officer (Finance) of Alexander Hunter Ltd. He'd phoned earlier, from the hotel, just to let her know he was in the land of the living. Staying out all night without a pass had been no problem. Was that a good thing? He decided not to think about it too deeply. But Bella had made nothing of it, been quite chatty, actually, then slipped in that she was thinking of going to Hawaii. And he couldn't afford a Friday night at Hamilton Racecourse.

Jesus H, Hawaii, it was the other side of the effin world. Going there, no doubt, with the Coffee Girls. Now that would be a sight to make the eyes sore. They wouldn't hire a car at the airport – they'd get a combine harvester, do the grass skirts at the same time.

Nothing else for it, he'd have to make economies. Haircuts could go for starters. Wouldn't need another one of those. Just give the noggin a rub down with wet and dry sandpaper once a week. And the fancy clothes. No more trendy gear. The new shirt was creased and crumpled and the white chinos grubby and covered in pipe ash. He'd just paid a year's subscription for the bools and it was a cheap pint. But the golf might get a three-wood into the rough. Would Bella just give him the cash? She should, she's not short of a bob or two herself. How to get a few quid. It was a recurrent problem, now.

He'd lain awake last night thinking about it. Central heating was a distinct possibility. Always a copper talking about it, saying how much the estimates varied. It wasn't rocket science, either. Big kettle thingy to heat up the water and a pump to chase it round about the house. What could be easier than that? One of the guys in the Masons was a gas board man and he did homers. Said to be pretty reasonable, too. But it had to be cash on the nail. Half up front (which presumably was his skin) and pay for the copper piping as you go along. Says he can get it cost though, nudge, nudge. Hunter had half-mentioned to him that he was thinking about it. Maybe not entirely new but an update kind of thing. Said he'd like the guy to come to the house – size up the job. But first, step for a hint, how much. Just ballpark, nothing binding. And the guy starts with the questions – reasonable at first, like is there an upstairs and how many rooms. Then he wants to know how big they are, the ceilings and all, bloody volume or something. And he keeps talking and Hunter realises how he's always talking and, if he managed by some bloody miracle not to let slip the scam to Bella, he'd be sure to blab it at the Masons meetings. Boast how he'd done this big favour for The Hunter and how he helped him to fiddle some money, just a few hundred, maybe a grand, out of his wife.

It always got back to that. Putting one over on Bella. Now, surely, that's ironic. Boyd and The Stoneman turning over millions and The Hunter scrabbling about, desperate for a grand of his own dosh. The two filthy rich crooks afraid of the impoverished copper. The same one who couldn't sleep and had got up at 2 a.m. to scan the ads in the *Evening Times*. Even looked through Yellow Bloody Pages. Stopped at double glazing and gave it serious consideration.

The windows in the house had been put in what? – must be fifteen years ago. Well past their best. Kitchen one effed, seal burst or something and a permanent mist trapped between the panes. Bella constantly mumping about it. And those guys were always doing deals – 115% off and nothing to pay until the second coming of Christ. Now these people, surely he could do business with. Parts would cost, say, £15,000. Get the guy to write it up to £18,000. Take Bella along to the bank and borrow £18K, give the salesman a bung for his understanding and cooperation. It was a possible.

Hunter had cut off the dual carriageway and was climbing into the hills to head for the Pet Crematorium. Then, as he slowed to take a sweeping left-hand bend, he saw the businessman's sign. Not very professional, hand-painted and at least one misspelling. Hunter hammered the brakes and the wee Peugeot stood on its nose. He reversed, then drove up the rutted drive. He had a good feeling about this one. This guy could see him all right.

The buzz of activity never failed to surprise Hunter. He didn't get the adrenaline rush any more, not like he used to, the surge that sharpened the brain and had the nerve ends tingling. There was still excitement – like the start of a holiday – the thrill of anticipation. And the fear was there, of course. The fear of making a mistake, of missing a vital clue, of failing to read the runes correctly. But Hunter had seen it all before. Life – and death – held no surprises for him.

He had parked the Peugeot about twenty yards down the pitted, single-file track and started to walk up. Halted after a few steps and went back for his jacket. The day's early caress of warmth had gone. Dirty grey clouds hid the sun and there was a damp chill in the air. The first thing he had seen as he neared the crest of the hill was the chimney. About thirty feet tall, looming over the small outbuilding that had been untouched by the fire. That could be the *Daily Record*'s follow-up – 'Crem Not Damaged in Fire'. Hunter had gone past four police cars, a white Transit van favoured by Scene of Crime Officers, the firemaster's car and a fire engine.

242

Just one death – that's all it took – and the place was alive. Doesn't matter if it's a low-life, a lord or a sad wee man like Jed. Murder is a great leveller. A body is a corpse is a cadaver. And then it's first-class treatment for all because, if the truth be told, the full might of the law is not activated for the victim – he is dead and nothing can be done about that. The investigation is for the living. And not just for grieving relatives and friends. It is for the old man who lives in the next street, the girl who works on the supermarket checkout counter, the mechanic who serviced his van. And equally, it is for those who had never seen the victim. Murder is a crime against everybody – the biggest affront to society – and the terror and outrage generated is not dependent on the amount of violence involved. The Jimmy Stones and Danny Boyds of this world could mass their troops, have a go at each other with sub-machine guns and Chieftain tanks in Queens Park, and it would not raise the fear and alarm of the lieges any more than the murder of the woman in the cul-de-sac down the road.

One match and a litre of petrol or one small knife wound was more of a threat to fabric of society. Danny Boyle did not touch the lives of the vast majority. But, if the guy up the hill could be burned alive, well, it makes people think, makes them feel vulnerable. If it could happen to him . . . ?

Hunter surveyed the crime scene from a safe distance. He lit his pipe and put the spent match back in the box. There was no police tape cordoning off the shell of Jed's house. Shoddy work. Okay, so it was up the hill and PC Plod was stopping cars at the main road. And there wasn't much left of the house. Some interesting items might have survived. And other pieces would be left in the sieve after the black, watery gunge had been filtered through. But there should be tape. First thing Hunter did. Get the blue and white plastic stuff round the crime scene, make sure the photographer gets good shots of it. Only takes a couple of minutes and spikes the guns of the lawyer who likes to go along the road of contaminated evidence.

The coppers, six of them, were huddled around a black van, 'Pet Crematorium' painted on its side, about ten yards away. He recognised the gaffer, a Superintendent, what was his name? Crabbit old sod.

One of the SOCO guys was coming out of the house, ducking his head to avoid the charred door lintel which was hanging at an angle, secured only by a couple of shoogly nails.

I'd have that off, too, Hunter said to himself. And, if the wall comes down, it comes down. But not on anyone's napper.

The SOCO guy's blue coveralls were smeared with the filth and grime. Wellies covered in a black lumpy mess up to the ankle. But he emerged with his treasures, safely secured in clear evidence bags, cradled in his gloved hands. White gloves, in a bliddy fire. Crime scene black as the Earl of Hell's waistcoat and white gloves on. Creature of habit and no bad thing. A guy who does things by the book. You'd know where you were with him. The guy took off the mask which had been covering his nose and mouth. Hunter didn't recognise him but he filed the face away for future reference.

The Superintendent – what was his bliddy name? – spotted Hunter. Made a beeline for him. Big strides, chest out, fists for fingers.

Not much chance of a swig at his hip flask.

'Can I help you?' he snapped.

Hunter decided to play it straight down the line. Maybe the guy hadn't recognised him with the new hairdo. He produced his warrant card. Arsehole didn't even look at it.

Hunter said, 'Just passing, Sir. Thought I'd have a look.'

'You've had it then.'

Four of the coppers were looking at him, sniggering. The other was getting into the black van.

Hunter said, 'Yes, Sir.'

No sense in making an issue of it. Let him look the big man. It was no big deal. Hunter turned on his heel, walked away, then stopped suddenly. The copper was trying to coax the black van into life. The engine would start, then miss a beat and die. A diesel engine, poorly maintained. The man who wanted Hunter dead was talking to him from beyond the grave.

Start, miss, die. Start, miss, die.

Now where had he heard that before?

Then he remembered the Superintendent's name. Pollock. More commonly known as Pillock or was it Bollocks?

He nearly got it, approaching one of the roundabouts on the dual carriageway, wee Peugeot in fourth gear and his mind in neutral, driving by instinct, memory in rewind, searching out an iffy diesel engine. Then the mobile played its new tune.

Digger to say that Boyson was looking for him. Wouldn't say what it was but said it was important, about the Partick Hilton. There was something else, Digger said, about Strangelove.

Hunter pulled off the road, into one of the big lay-bys which had a directory of the businesses in the area. Digger told him that the technical guys had broken down the video from the Royal Infirmary mortuary, frame by frame. The final second or so, where she had looked up at the CCTV camera, had intrigued them and they had called in a lip reader. Strangelove had been talking to them. Two words.

244

'Catch me.'

The cars coming up the hill from Busby had their wipers on. Hunter retrieved his roof from its hidey-hole, taking his time, working methodically, stretching and studding, until the black lining was securely fastened. Not a minute too soon, either, for the heavens opened and the rain came down in sheets.

Hunter put a match to his pipe and sucked in the smoke. He thought about Digger. There was something in his voice. He had sounded . . . efficient. A bit clinical. Maybe even a bit pissed off. He had every right to be. He was getting a bum deal but still playing his cards well. Smith had noticed it. Not much the Assistant Chief Constable missed, really. They could do worse, an awful lot worse, than step him up if The Jug got the job he lusted after in the Met. Smith had said that Digger was ready for a step up. He'd done a right good job, that was for sure. And, if he got a decent break – maybe the stillborn baby and the drop-out nurse – he might actually be able to ring Strangelove's bell. But that was one sentence with a maybe and a might in it. And two into one doesn't go.

The pipe reek was filling up the wee car, so Hunter opened a window an inch. The traffic scudded by. Seemed to travel in threes. Start, miss, die. The Pet Crem van. Hearse black. Black as death.

Start, miss, die.

Where had he heard it before? He tried to empty his mind, to return to where he had been, but was unable to do so. The memory had returned to its audio library. Refused to come out to play.

I was here, I came to you and you spurned me. You'd something better to do. If you want me, if you really, really want me, you must woo me again. And then, if I'm in the mood, I will come.

Boyson, then, Boyson had something for The Hunter. He phoned *The Herald*. Boyson was not there. He had been in but he had gone. No, the voice did not know where he was. Or when he might be back. Hunter called directory inquiries, almost asked for the number for the TSB, changed it to the Station Bar. No joy there, either. Boyson was not there and, although way above the clouds the sun was over the yardarm, he had not been in either.

The hangover had not gone away, just been relegated in importance to the developments of the day. Now a couple of wee fellas with rubber mallets were playing the tom-toms again inside his temples. The downpour had eased and he watched the little rivulets snake down the windscreen. An insect, a mayfly or the like, was trapped in one droplet, wings flattened on the glass, legs buckled, trying to gain purchase to break free. It was like a

245

nature documentary, just lacking the whispering commentary of David Attenborough.

Jesus H, it had happened again. Where had he heard that before? It was turning into a day of déjà vu and nothing nailed down. But this one did come back to him. He remembered Aine, after her visit to Zara Carmichael with the asylum seeker. A weirdo, that was Aine's verdict on the fragrant Zara. And Calder, too. Mr and Mrs Weird, she had called them. Calder had come into his wife's office and taken great pride in pointing out the strange drawings that were pinned on the wall. They were like beasties, Aine had said, wee creepy-crawlies, the kind David Attenborough whispers about. But Calder had said that they were some kind of acid. What was it? Aine had looked it up. Three letters – MNA, that was it. Mononucleic acid. And Calder said Matthew had drawn them. Matthew had said it's me, its my mononucleic acid.

Hunter remembered his first meeting with Calder, in his office, with the priest and the rich bitch, desperate to bung him some taxpayers' dosh to continue his work at the abuse clinic. That was when Matthew Whittle had tried to kill himself. Swallowed half a bog roll. Calder had said that the boy was his favourite patient. A poor soul, he had said. Learning difficulties, he had said. A mental age of ten. Now Hunter prided himself on being a reasonable man. He was perfectly willing to admit that his experience of ten-year-olds was limited. But he was willing to bet, pound to a pinch of shit, that there were not many who knew about mononucleic acid. And none that was Dolly Dimple.

He started up the wee Peugeot. The Carmichaels' empire was only a couple of miles away. Be there in five minutes. Sort it out once and for all. Then the phone played its wee tune again. It was Digger. There had been a murder at the Hilton Hotel. Danny Boyd. And Strangelove had done it.

The big, black, chauffeur-driven Rover purred along the dual carriageway towards East Kilbride leaving behind it a very, very happy Ms Carmichael.

She had said that was how she wanted to be addressed. The newspapers, the television too, of course, would refer to her as the tsar. Or maybe tsarina. Ms Zara Carmichael MBE, the Prime Minister's Refugees' Tsarina. A bit of a mouthful but it did have a nice ring to it. A ring of confidence and the protection of Her Majesty's Government.

The nice man from the Cabinet Office had asked when she could take up her duties and she had told him immediately. She accepted the burden and responsibility with immediate effect, she said.

246

He had liked that, smiled and said that the Prime Minister would be pleased. But there were formalities to be concluded, details to be finalised. Such as her salary. An incidental, she had said and he had liked that too. It would look good on the press release. And the title, he had said, how would she like to be addressed? She had told him that was unimportant, it was the work which mattered and 'Ms Carmichael' would serve well until the minutiae was formalised. And would he be kind enough to pass on her gratitude to the Prime Minister for bestowing upon her the honour and privilege of serving her country. The nice man had said that she could do that herself. He had telephoned Downing Street, gone through a couple of minions.

Then he said, 'Prime Minister, I have Ms Carmichael for you.'

And she had spoken to the PM himself. Said yes, no, and thank you in all the right places. Listened obediently as he had outlined the magnitude of the task. Then he thanked her and hung up.

He really was a pompous, smarmy little shit. Praise be to the Lord and all the saints in heaven.

Zara was in her office, emptying the filing cabinets, dumping the contents into black, plastic bags. Cleaning up her past, erasing any link with the drop and swop babies, destroying any possible evidence of refugees' waifs who had been rehomed.

Where was Jed when you needed him? She would take the black bags to the bottom of the garden later, down to the willows, and put a match to them. Ms Carmichael would do it herself. She would cremate the evidence. Cremate, from the Latin, *cremare*, meaning 'burn'. Had to be Latin, didn't it? Her weakness, the gap in her education. She'd looked it up in the dictionary and there it was, just below cremaster. She knew that one – the muscle of the spermatic cord by which the testicle can be partially raised – but she didn't know that it came from the Greek, *krema*, meaning 'hang'. Greek, another weakness.

Beware of Greeks baring balls.

And an entry on the next page had been interesting, too. Cremona – the name applied to any of the superior violins made in Verona in the 16th–17th century, including those made by Stradivari, Amati and Guarneri. Zara thought of Paborsky. What had happened to his Stradivarius? Had Patrik taken it? She hoped so. She must ask Hubner. He had returned last night after concluding his escort duties. He had gone with Patrik to Paris, found the sister and united the pair. No, that had not been the verb. Introduced, that was not right, either. He had put them together. Blood relatives with nothing in common. But he had forced them together, like the same poles of two magnets. Poor Patrik, he had lost his hero, his lover and his meal ticket. The least he deserved was the fiddle.

Poor Josef, it was an ignominious end. The last of Mr PetCrem's dispatches. And now Jed's dead and so are his secrets.

He hadn't even merited a line in *The Herald* this morning. She had been pleased about that. He wasn't worth it. Maybe the redtops, the gutter press, had something about it. But, Zara thought, 'Frankly, my dear, I don't give a damn.'

It had been a good day, marred by one dark cloud that had blackened during the visit of the Prime Minister's man. Calder, the man with the waxy face in the high-dependency unit, had had another heart attack and was now hovering in the half-world between life and death. Clive had come in to tell her. The smell of whisky on his breath. Not a lot, just enough to steady his hands and his nerve. He had been ever so kind. He really was a gentle man. Calder had not suffered any pain, Clive had said, just slept through it, but it had damaged his weakened heart further still. They wanted to wait a bit, not impose any more trauma, and then carry out the transplant. There would be a great risk – because Calder really was weak – that he would not survive the operation. But without it he had no chance at all.

Clive had been to check up on the donor. He was well. Sleeping peacefully. No surprise there. Matthew Whittle did little else.

The Ramblers were preparing the theatre. They wanted, ideally, to wait another forty-eight hours, to see Calder a little stronger. But they had to be prepared, just in case. But one way or another, Clive had said, the transplant must go ahead. There was no choice.

He was wrong there. Ms Carmichael had not got to where she was today without making difficult choices.

The phone rang again and, again, Lisa refused to pick it up. The answering machine kicked in and Mum spoke to it, using her nice voice this time, saying 'Please, Darling, please phone as soon as you get home. I'm so worried about you.'

That made three calls today – the first whingey, trying to make Lisa feel guilty, and the second angry and aggressive. And now all nicey-nicey, pleasey-weasely. And what right did she have to be any of the above? None, that's what. She'd given up those rights when she'd opened her heart to God. Closed her legs to Dad and her eyes and ears to the sobs of the little girl who didn't have that choice. So she had bugger all rights. Fuck all.

There hadn't been a mention in the morning papers. Not that Lisa had expected anything – she'd just hoped, that was all. Then there had been nothing on the telly or the radio either. Or the *Evening Times*, not a line. And that just confirmed it. The body had been found by now. Of course it had. What was his name? Boyd, Danny Boyd. She had his credit card, a souvenir, a keepsake. They must have found him by now. A cleaner, chambermaid. Somebody's seen him. They've all seen him. And the cops have recognised her work. They know all right. They're just frightened to admit it. They've imposed a news blackout. They can do that, censor the press, silence the media during a war or something. In times of emergency, that was how they put it. So that's how they considered Lisa now – a national emergency. They'd have their best team on it – experts – might even call in MI5 or something. It was quite flattering, really. She'd left them all the clues they needed – everything apart from her address and they still couldn't catch her. Three murders in her home city now and they were no closer. They knew Lisa could do it again, whenever she wanted to, whenever the mood took her. And they were frightened. They were lying awake at night. They were wondering when it was going to happen. Maybe saying their prayers. Well good. They could ban all the newspapers they liked but they couldn't pretend it never happened. They couldn't close their eyes and ears to Lisa.

Only one man did that now. The one man she really wanted. Really, really wanted dead. Lisa lifted the phone and called the Royal Infirmary again. It rang for a long time and she said a little prayer.

Please, Simon, Darling, pick up. We're waiting for you. Your lover and your daughter. Please, Darling, come and see us. And we'll be together for ever and ever. Amen.

Just one death, the lowest of lowlifes, and the fifth-floor of the Hilton Hotel was alive with coppers. Danny Boyd's mutilated body had been found by one of the assistant managers. The chambermaid had reported the Do Not Disturb sign still on the door handle after check-out time. No answer when she knocked on the door so she had followed the rules and reported it to reception. No answer when the assistant manager phoned the room so he had gone up there, knocked on the door again, then used his pass key to gain entry. And been greeted by the glassy-eyed, bloody corpse.

Thank God it had happened in the Hilton, Chief Constable Tobias Fastnett said. It was an establishment with a reputation to protect. It had a procedure for sudden death, a rehearsed, dignified response to minimise fuss and avoid raising the fear and alarm of the paying lieges. The first two coppers had been on the scene within five minutes. The others had arrived soon after. No flashing lights, no sirens. It was in their interests to keep it low-key, too.

Digger Burns had been driven there along with Fastnett and James Smith. Digger had suggested that they leave the crime scene untouched until Hunter arrived. No one had disagreed with him. But each had peeped inside the room. Observed the pecking order, Fastnett first, Smith next, then Digger. Each had taken only a couple of careful steps, surveyed the gruesome scene, then back-pedalled. They were in the room across the hall now, whispering because the door was open, awaiting Hunter's verdict.

Nobody could read a crime scene like The Hunter. He had been at it for so long, had done it so often. It was as if he was in touch with the animal instincts that civilisation had wiped out of other mortals generations ago.

No need for his expertise here, though – a blind man could see it. Danny Boyd, in his birthday suit, dead as a dodo. Cause of death – knife blow to the heart. Strangelove's trademark. One wound, delivered by an expert hand. She had signed her work again. A long incision, from Adam's apple to chin. Bloody banknotes, must be thousands of pounds, stuffed into the aperture. And the knotted end of a condom peeped out of his mouth. Her signature, increasingly elaborate, more and more damning, all over the room. Fingerprints on the champagne glass and bottle; hairs in the shower. She had even left a lipstick kiss on the mirror. No doubt about the killer or that she was now wildly insane. More clues than an Agatha Christie book. All of them valid, each one damning and none worth a tinker's curse. Hunter had only one thing to do now. He went over to Boyd's body, looked into those cold eyes and said his silent words. Three words, this time.

'God forgive you.'

Then he called in the photographer, told him to snap away and not to be too fussy. SOCO would be in next and the guys would go through their tasks with a fastidious diligence, but they might as well save themselves the trouble. No error would be seized on by a clever lawyer. Nor was there any fresh evidence here – nothing that would lead to Strangelove's door.

Digger entered the room and said, 'Just about finished.'

Hunter noted that it was a statement, not a question. Just a few days and Digger had outgrown him. He'd lost a Sergeant.

Digger said, 'Three doors down, on the left. The video's set up, Sir.'

Might not be lost after all.

She was just a blur, a black shadow, as she entered the hotel. She'd been here before, knew the position of the camera, kept her head down, went straight to the lift and didn't turn around. Didn't press the lift button, though, just waited patiently for Danny Boyd to do the biz. Danny took the starring role. Swaggered up to the reception desk, pure dead gallus.

Hunter hit the freeze-frame. Familiar face turning round there. Leaving a conspiratorial smile with the receptionist.

Boyson! And the journo had been trying to get a hold of him.

Hunter put a match to his pipe, sucked in the smoke. Couldn't see an ashtray so he put the match back into the box, then pressed the play button.

Danny was flashing the plastic, signing the register and taking the key in his left hand. Big smile as he walks to the lift, puts his right arm around Strangelove's waist, gives her bum a cheeky wee pat.

Hunter pressed the eject button, took the cassette out of the VCR and replaced the yellow Post-It sticker on which Digger had printed 'ONE'. He removed a similar sticker from cassette two, put it in the VCR and pressed play. Danny and Strangelove getting out of the lift on the fifth floor. Danny's head up, up for it, and her face snuggled into his shoulder. She has to walk awkwardly, kind of knock-kneed, to keep her face in there, hidden, but she does, all the way along the corridor. Danny's right arm around her waist, probably still touching up her arse, and his left hand zips the plastic key thingy in the magic slot and they disappear. The time, recorded on the top right of the video, was 9.13 p.m.

Hunter stopped the video and checked Digger's sticker. It said 'FAST FORWARD TO 10.27 p.m.' He stopped the tape three times, settled for 10.23 p.m. and watched four minutes of empty corridor.

What did Boyson know? Had he recognised Danny? He should, fundamental part of his job, surely, being able to identify the biggest crooks in his city. When Boyson had phoned, he'd told Digger it was about the Partick Hilton. Hunter couldn't work it out. He decided to put it on the back burner.

The clock on the video ticks on to 10.27 p.m., and Strangelove comes out of the room. Head down, dammit, she turns away, back to the camera, and nonchalantly strolls towards the lift. Then she stops.

Why are you stopping?

And she turns. All the way around. Full face! Can't make out any detail at this distance but the techie guys'll love it.

What do you want to tell me?

She's swaying. Kind of dancing. Dirty dancing. Like the hoors in the dirty clubs. Her right hand is up to her right breast. Fondling it. Then up a bit. A bit higher, to the silver brooch.

What are you doing? What are you telling me?

She's stretching the brooch. It is silver elastic.

An alarm went off. An ear-shattering, high-pitched fire alarm, activated by the smoke sensor just above Hunter's chair. He ejected the video, lifted its partner and made a run for it. Got to the door just as the sprinklers went off.

Calder lies so still, so pale against the white linen sheets. An alabaster profile which might have been fashioned by the loving hands of Leonardo. A sensitive, intelligent face from the pictures of his student days, living on Heinz soups and moral debates, too innocent to be burdened by his great potential.

The Ramblers have gone, back to the big houses and fast cars bought with the money from covert operations in the intensive care suite. They were happy to go, never to return. End of chapter.

Hubner and Clive are in the old house. The former listening to music, Beethoven's 9th Symphony, the latter in his room with the whisky bottle.

Only Matthew Whittle remains in Calder's clinic. The nice crook and the nasty lawyer have been discharged.

Only Zara in the intensive care suite. Only Zara and her husband. She is at the machines. Taking the plugs out of the sockets on the wall. It's a moral decision. Removing their entrails from Calder's body. Amoral decision. Pulling the shunt from his vein. He is untroubled, at peace now, with that face which age shall not wither. Let nature take its course. Let Mother Nature decide. She might, in her bounteous mercy, even choose to give him his life back.

And, even then, Zara has choices.

Hunter had stuck his neck out. So what's new? He'd built his career on it. Could write a book. Call it *Giraffes and Gaffes*. He'd made two decisions. Both needed approval, permission. Sensible thing to do. First rule when you were caught with your pants down – cover your arse. The Jug was there, James Smith too – along the hall in the room across from the body – so play it smart, go to them, share your thoughts, weigh up the pros and cons and then simply obey orders. That's where it fell down. Smith was okay, a good guy, an old hand who would be persuaded. But Fastnett? Even with his trousers up he was an arse. So Hunter had just gone ahead.

He phoned Jamesie. Told him Danny Boyd was dead. Said nobody, not even the two coppers standing over the body, knows it's Danny. Told Jamesie to take his time, to think hard. Said keep the heid. Then he said goodbye.

The press were beginning to swarm around the Hilton, excited by the scent of blood in the wind, swooping like vultures to pick at the flesh while it was still warm. Hunter had identified five of the hacks – from the dailies and TV – and sent Murdo and Aine to tap each on the shoulder, tell them to make their way quietly to the back door. He met them there himself, a finger over his lips commanding silence. He cut a comical figure, his hair (what there was of it) dry but the crumpled blue shirt and grubby chinos still wet. When all five hacks had arrived, he led them to the small cocktail lounge. He knew what each one drank and he had set up a round, paid for out of his own pocket.

He downed his own whisky in two gulps, motioned for another, then he started.

'This is not a press conference. There will be no questions. There will be no quotes. You don't repeat a word to anyone. That includes your newsdesks and editors. Okay?'

They agreed. They had no option. They knew that they would be turfed out if they didn't and the loss of favoured status would hurt them in the future.

Hunter relaxed a little. He said, 'Okay. Thanks, guys. It's a big story. Pretty fucking huge, really.'

They were almost afraid to breathe, in case it irked him.

'Another man murdered. By Strangelove again.'

There was a collective intake of breath. Strangelove. Good name. Great headline.

'There's sex. Mutilated body. And a positive ID.'

Hunter's phone started to play that bloody tune again. It was Boyson. He said, 'How come I'm out of favour? It's about the Hilton . . .'

Hunter interrupted, 'Sorry, but I've been a wee bit busy. Give me your number.'

He wrote it on the back of his hand, told Boyson he would phone back and hung up. Then he said, 'Okay, where were we?'

The woman TV journalist said, 'Sex, mutilation and you were about to tell us the name of the victim.'

Hunter smiled. 'You wish. I'll give you it this evening, maybe sooner, promise. Tell you this, though, I know him and you know him. Telly gets a head start. Plenty of time for the main broadcast.'

Then he turned to the three journos from the daily newspapers.

'Twenty-minute start for the telly, right? Then, you three, an hour before the statement goes out on the Presswire. There will be no legal restrictions. You can go to town. If . . .'

The goods were great. The price must be, too.

'If there's not a word broadcast, not a word written till I give you the nod.'

253

The bloke from the Beeb said, 'You mean nothing . . . from anyone? Not just us?'

Hunter said, 'That's the deal. I can't stop them. Can you?'

Hello, Strangelove. Full face, full screen, on the computer. The wonders of electronic science. The little face of a killer, alabaster white above the Gestapo coat at the end of a corridor in the Hilton, washed down to dots and pixels, wrung out in the techies' electronic mangles and brought to life within the hour on Hunter's desk.

So you're, Strangelove. Hello. You spoke to me earlier, remember? At the end of the corridor at the mortuary in the Royal Infirmary.

You said, 'Catch me.'

I can, now. I will, soon. You're not far away. I know that. And I know you. I've seen you. But where was it? Your face is being printed in the lab just now. They've tried various papers, different quality, trying for the best reproduction, to minimise the distortions from the magnification. The wanted posters will be all over town tonight, maybe sooner. You'll be on the telly. The front pages of the newspapers. You don't want that. Not really. You're not one of the sickos who needs fifteen minutes of fame. You're more complex, more subtle. So help me. Where have I seen you? You're too clever for me. Help me again.

Hunter reduced the size of the picture on his computer screen. The techies had shown him how to do that. This button zooms to full screen, that one reduces it. He took it down to three-quarters, half-size, quarter. Then he rose and backed away from her. Sidled off, trying to catch her sideways. The eyes never left him. Like Mona Lisa, the eyes followed him around the room. Sad eyes. Pretty face. But sad, empty eyes.

Hunter stopped suddenly. Afraid to move lest it snapped the gossamer thread of a memory. Rangers sprang to mind. He tried to discard it but it would not go. Let it run, then. Rangers. Ibrox. Heilan hardmen. Porno!

Lisa is taking off her white shell suit, the one Louise gave her a couple of Christmases ago. Some bleach splashed on to the trousers as she was cleaning the toilet. The material, a shiny nylon or something like that, had withered. Turned a dirty yellow and wrinkled. She had cleaned her flat thoroughly, bows to stern, that's what Mum says. Dad used to work in the shipyards. Maybe he still does. A welder. Always burn marks on his hands. Fresh burns, red, angry and weeping. Crusty scabs and bluey-white scars. Those hands. The welder's, not the hands of a father. Those angry, scabby hands that had left her weeping and angry.

Lisa stretches to turn on the shower and gasps as the pain stabs at her belly. Abdul's legacy. She is bleeding again, of course. She takes out the tampon and puts it in a little polythene snap-shut bag. Take it down to the bins later, with the other rubbish.

Her body shows the result of Abdul's brutality. Normally, she wouldn't bother. Wouldn't even look. Just an occupational hazard. Grin and bear it. But today she surveys the damage in the mirror. Most of it superficial. Nothing a week would not cure. Just have to keep it until it goes away, that's what Mum would say.

That's what Mum had said that time at bath night. Lisa's turn to get in first, while the bubbles were still white and fluffy and you could put your head in them and they'd tickle your nose. But she'd dallied, let Louise go first. It was the night before Dad went away and there were bruises at the top of Lisa's legs, at her front bottom. Mum had seen them and asked what they were.

Ha! Ha-ha!

As if she didn't know. As if she didn't know who put them there and how he did it.

Lisa hadn't said anything. Just bent forwards, put her head in the water, although there were no bubbles left. No tickles. And Mum had carried on as normal, hummed a little hymn and allowed Lisa to dry herself. Mum always dried her, always finished it off anyway, rubbed her hair briskly, then made a fuss of helping her on with her vest. Said it was stuck on her ears again. Have to do something about these ears, she'd say. Might get Dad to weld them to your head. But Lisa put on the vest herself that night. And Mum didn't say the joke about her ears. Didn't say it ever again.

The bruises are all over Lisa's body today, the blacks and blues not so painful, not so deep. Like the fingerprints on her bottom. But the big, pinkish-red mark at her liver is sore. Abdul had punched her. Afterwards, when the cameras had stopped rolling, when no one was looking, when she was slipping on her top. He'd punched her. A boxer's jab, short and sharp, and she had doubled up in pain. Didn't fall though, didn't cry. Wouldn't give him the satisfaction. What could he do to hurt her?

Lisa stepped into the shower and scoured her body. Put on the scratchy gloves that looked like coconuts and scrubbed everywhere, even the deep bruises. She would be clean. Squeaky clean.

Simon's not coming. He hasn't phoned and he never will. Just like Dad. Lisa can't remember what Dad looks like. There are no photographs and no one to ask. But it doesn't matter. Dad's not coming back, either.

255

Lisa puts his scabby hands on Simon's head and body and likes the image. What'll I call you. Sidad? Damon? Demon.

Ha! Ha-ha!

Well, Demon, if you won't come to me, I'll come to you. I'll make you sorry. You'll live to regret this. Oh, yes, you will.

The staff nurse closed the door of her little office, kicked off her white, slip-on shoes and sat down with a weary sigh. She rubbed the soles of her feet. They were hot and her ankles were swollen. Never mind, only another five hours to go. She flicked the lever at the side of the chair to allow the lumber support to yield, then leant back and swung her feet up on to the desk. Ah, yes. It doesn't take a lot to please a working girl. A little more, perhaps, just six inches of empty desk, and it would be blissfully comfortable. She could have lowered her legs, shifted the bundle of papers – absence monitoring, staff development reports that were only a fortnight late – but she preferred to perform an inelegant little shuffle, wriggling her toes to nudge the papers aside. She cursed softly as her black tights snagged on the stapler and a little pink fleshy slug appeared at her ankle. She froze, eyeing a bottle of clear nail varnish at the far end of the desk, tantalisingly out of reach. As she stretched out for it, the slug changed into a worm and began to snake up the ladder. It had reached her calf by the time she clasped the bottle, unscrewed the cork and dabbed on the only fatal invertebrate potion known to woman. Dammit! They were the emergency tights, too. Need to buy another pair tonight and still a week till payday. Bye-bye gin and tonic, hello half-pint of lager shandy.

She wondered if she could cope with another agency shift. Catch a few zzzs first, squeeze in a midnight till eight shift in one of the private hospitals, catch a fast black hack, then pretend to have slept in. That would be, what, the third shift this month. Oh, well, you're only young once. Sex and drugs and rock'n'roll. Without the sex or drugs or rock'n'roll. There was always agency work going. But it took a month for the money to come through. No, all things considered, she decided just to have a quiet night in. Watch the box. Sleep in her own bed – if her empty tummy didn't rumble too loud. Skint again already. When was the last time? Oh, yes, she remembered, forever.

The pink worm winked at her. She was tempted to get the black Magic Marker and obliterate it. Wouldn't be the first time. Done it for the best part of a week, when she was a pupil nurse, when she was really, really skint. It would be cheaper just to paint her legs, get Dad to do them when he was putting creosote on the shed. It would probably kill off the hair follicles, save money on razors. But not really. She pinched the odd disposable from the men's ward. Perks of the job.

The office door opened and she snapped her legs shut like a vice. Need not have bothered, though, because Simon never gave her a second glance. He slipped off his white coat and tossed it at the hook on the wall, missing by a couple of feet.

He said, 'Who shifted that hook?'

She said, 'Nobody. I moved the wall back a yard this morning. Bored, you know? Just for something to do.'

He gave her his mischievous little smile. She had good boobs, well goodish. Bit saggy, probably. She was a bit on the hefty side, heavy legs, must be the flat shoes and hard floors. Happened to them all, sooner or later. Then their bums swelled. Too maximus about the glutaeus. Either that or they went scrawny, like old hens.

He lifted the white coat off the floor and put it on the hook.

He said, 'I'm just nipping out for half an hour. Forty minutes, tops.'

'Missing you already,' she muttered, as he closed the door. So Shagger Simon was back in business. Nipping out for a quickie. She was keen, too, the poor soul. Been on the phone four times this morning. Oh, well, she'd learn the hard way. What was it they said? Better to have loved and lost than never to have loved at all . . .

You can never find a policeman when you want one. That's what they say, isn't it? Hunter was discovering just how true that was. He was in the copshop, at the centre of his web, and he wanted one specific copper. One of forty-eight. The heilan hardman with the porno tape that had been on the VCR, at Rangers' stadium, at the party to celebrate the detention of Danny Boyd's thugs. The video of Strangelove at work. Talking dirty, a smile on her face, but her eyes sad and empty.

Murdo had been dispatched to Ibrox. Told that the speed limit was 30 mph and never to drop below it. He had called within twenty minutes. The video was not there. The staff had been interviewed, a couple phoned at home, asked about the tape of 'adult entertainment'. Each one swore blind that they had never seen it. The management emphasised that the suite was used by families and no such video would be allowed on the premises. It must have been brought in by the coppers.

Digger Burns was juggling two calls. Left hand had the railway police, who were telling him where they reckoned the Inverness train was now. Right hand talking on the radio to the Strathclyde Police helicopter pilot, getting his position, trying to figure out where he could intercept the train.

Sixteen coppers had come down from the capital of the Highlands and Digger prayed that all of them were on that train on their way home. The right hand knew what the left hand was doing and it was agreed that the helicopter would reach Aviemore in ten minutes, about three minutes before the train was scheduled to arrive there.

The cops would be questioned. Someone would know something about the video.

'Frisk the buggers, if need be.' Hunter had said. 'Just get me that tape.'

Aine was on a pub-crawl, coordinating the movements of twelve uniformed Glasgow coppers who were doing the rounds of the boozers within a stagger of Queen Street Railway Station. The other thirty-two heilan hardmen – nineteen from the Grampian force and thirteen from Tayside, were due to board the Aberdeen train there in forty minutes. They were certain to have a pint or two before boarding. Weren't they?

One of the young Women Police Constables in CR3 put a phone down, thrust her fist in the air and shouted, 'Yes!'

The room went absolutely silent and all eyes turned to her. Had she traced it? Where was the tape?

She flushed, lifted her hands to her pleated blonde hair and mumbled an apology. The cops returned to their tasks. No one chided her and no one teased her. She was guilty of over-exuberance but she had still done some good work.

Hunter watched her closely. She ignored the Inspector and went to the Sergeant. Straight to the one she considered her gaffer. Interesting.

She gave Digger a sheet of paper. She explained that she had called police HQ in Inverness and had got the mobile phone numbers of six of the cops on the train. Digger congratulated her on her initiative, lifted the phone and called the number at the top of the list. The mobile was not switched on. He started to punch out the second number and, with his pencil, motioned to the WPC to do likewise, working from the bottom of the list up. Again, Digger drew a blank. Perhaps the train was in a tunnel or a hollow. Or maybe the phones were outwith their reception area. But the young cop got a result. She handed the phone to Digger.

He was Mr Cool. A swan swimming, Hunter thought. Gliding along on the surface but working like hell underneath.

Digger introduced himself, said he was calling on behalf of Inspector Hunter. Could he please speak to the ranking officer? He offered the phone to Hunter, who shook his head.

A Sergeant came on the line and Digger explained the situation. Twelve cops were on the train. One guy, who was due leave, had remained in

Glasgow to visit a mate. Eleven coppers were in the carriage. None had the video. The other cop was in the toilet. Two minutes passed, then came bad news and good news. He didn't have the tape but he knew who had.

He said, 'Andy's got it. Guy from Grampian. Well, he brought it, anyway.'

Digger asked if he saw the tape, the box, or the title?

No joy.

He couldn't remember Andy's surname, either. But he knew that he was a Constable.

Digger told him to hold for a sec, then repeated the information. He asked the WPC to phone Grampian, to get a surname for Andy and any mobile numbers. Told another copper to phone Aine. Tell her about Andy. A third officer had to phone the railway police at Queen Street, tell them to delay the departure of the Aberdeen train. It was not to leave Glasgow until he gave permission.

The cops on the Inverness train had been talking about Andy.

The Sergeant was back on the phone. He said, 'Hunter'll remember him. He called Andy a poof cos he only dislocated one of the druggie's arms.'

Digger thanked him, told him to keep the lads together and to phone with any other info on the tape or Andy. And to phone every fifteen minutes anyway.

Hunter put a match to his pipe. Digger tapped him on the arm, then pointed to the smoke sensors. The coppers were watching. Hunter took two deep puffs, then put the pipe back in his pocket.

He said, 'Just testing. I'm told these thingies,' he pointed to the sensors, 'are very sensitive. Never seen it myself, though.'

They laughed. Digger wondered if Hunter had set up the charade to break the tension.

The taxi journey had taken all of three minutes. The first lights had been green and the driver had just put his foot down approaching the next set, at the busy junction of High Street and George Street, and shot through on more red than orange. He'd nipped down a couple of back streets and slammed on the brakes at the flat, stopping with a jolt. Simon gave him a fiver, waited till the change was grudgingly counted out, then took it all and slipped it in his pocket. The surly sod could whistle for his tip. Simon surveyed the building, typical new-build, a big brick box with little windows. Still, she'd done okay for herself. Coming from where she came from, it must seem like a palace. He looked at the list of occupants beside their doorbells. O'Donnell, top left. He pressed the bell and waited. Then the intercom crackled and Lisa said, 'Yes?'

'Simon,' he said.

There was a pause, then she said, 'Ooh, good. Perfect.'

There was a click as the door lock was disengaged. He let himself in, climbed the stairs – four flights – and was puffing a bit as he reached the top. He expected her door to be open but it wasn't, so he rapped three times and waited impatiently, his black mood darkening. It took a full minute before Lisa opened the door but, when she did, his demeanour changed instantly. She was wearing a tiny nurse's outfit, open at the top so her breasts swelled out and so short that the suspenders that held up the sheer black stockings were visible.

He had decided to give Lisa a piece of his mind and he would – later. But first, he would give her another piece of his anatomy.

Ten long minutes have passed and they are reluctant to move in CR3. Afraid to draw attention to themselves. Hunter has never experienced anything quite like it. Close now, so near to the end of the hunt he can scent it. Almost taste it. And nothing to do but wait.

Hunter and Digger share the centre of the web. Murdo has returned from Ibrox. The head of the vice squad is in the room, sitting alone, to the side. He is not one of them. He has not paid his dues. But his experience and contacts might be needed. The cops on the Inverness train phoned in three minutes ago. They had no fresh information. No one in the world had fresh information.

Then the phone rang.

Digger didn't move, giving Hunter his rank. Hunter didn't move, giving Digger his due.

Digger lifted the phone. It was Aine.

She said, 'Well, I've found Andy. Didn't find him, really, he just kind of turned up at the railway station.'

Digger tried to keep his voice steady. He said, 'Yes, Aine.'

The air in the room was electric.

Aine said, 'You'll never guess where he was.'

Digger realised he was meant to respond.

'No,' he said, 'I'll never guess.'

But Aine didn't tell him right away. She said, 'He wants The Hunter to know that he's not a poof.'

Digger said, 'I'll pass on that message.'

'Even though he was in GOMA – the Gallery of Modern Art, just a hundred yards away.'

She was teasing. She wouldn't do that if she didn't have the goods. Would she?

'By the way,' she said, 'he's got the video. It's in a plain white cover, not a word on the outside.'

On the outside?

'Oh, and on the inside it says it is presented by Horny Porny and stars Moaner Lisa – that's . . . she spelled it out, 'M O A N E R L I S A. And it should be with you soon.'

They could hear the motorcycle cop's siren already. He entered CR3 ninety seconds later and no one gave him a second glance. They were all working the phones.

It was wonderful. Absolutely perfect. All of them together at last – all three at home – a family. There was so much to do but wasn't that what mums were for? Lisa wasn't complaining. How could she? It was what she wanted. It was fate. It was their destiny.

Simon was so heavy. He'd gone to seed without her steadying influence. Eating the wrong things and too much beer by the look of the spare tyre around his tummy. But that was okay. Just a minor imperfection.

It had been difficult undressing him. His trousers and pants had come off easily enough. But didn't they always! But the jacket and shirt had been a problem. She'd kind of rolled him on to his side but she couldn't get the arms out. They just wouldn't bend the right way. So she'd turned him on to his face then yanked everything up, jacket and shirt in a oner, up over his head and then kept on pulling. Put all her weight into it and fell on her bum when they broke free of the dead-weight.

His armpits were smelly so she had sponged them, dabbed them dry, then sprayed on deodorant. Then she'd pulled him through to the bedroom. She thought that she would never get him up on to the bed but she managed somehow.

Ha! Ha-ha!

His eyes had nearly popped out of his head when he'd seen the nurse's uniform. She'd led him to the living room, sat him on the couch and allowed him to pluck out a breast. He'd taken it in his mouth, sucking hard, biting the nipple. He wanted her now. Wanted her again. She knew that he would. His arms around her, hands at her bottom, a gasp of excitement when he found that she wasn't wearing knickers. He'd tried to force a finger inside her but she wriggled free. Said no, not yet. She'd planned this for so long. It had to be special. Told him to close his eyes. She had a surprise. She skipped off to the bathroom. Everything she needed was there. Then she hurried back, giggling, asking if his eyes were closed, promise, still closed . . .

She straddled him, pinning his arms with her thighs. He was peeking but it didn't matter now. It was too late. There was a flicker of recognition in his eyes. Then that flash of fear. He had put up a struggle, powerful at first, rising from the couch, twisting his head, fighting to free his arms. But she locked her ankles around his back and gradually his exertions weakened, his legs buckled and he gave in to the inevitable.

Lisa could hardly contain herself. Joy, elation, vindication. She checked the newspaper to make sure that she had the name right. Then she made the phone call. They said he wasn't available. But they promised to pass on the message.

Horny Porny was a new one on the vice squad copper. Not a UK firm, that was for sure. Nor the US. Dutch or German? Possible, but he doubted it. They used their own girls. Italian was more likely, typical Catholic country, communion by day and porn on terrestrial TV at night. But his dosh was on Hungary. Porn was big business there – lots of girls from the former Soviet Union countries who worked for buttons.

They were in a little room down the corridor – Hunter, Digger and the vice cop – and Moaner Lisa was still on screen. It was clear how she got her name. They'd had to turn the sound way down.

Two sharp knocks on the door and Aine entered with Andy. Hunter had the remote control. He wondered if he should cut the power or whether that might be considered patronising. He let it run.

Andy was a bit sheepish. Understandable, he'd been caught with his pants down. But he redeemed himself with one word.

'Amsterdam.'

His mate in Customs at Dyce Airport had found the video during a routine search of a guy coming off the rigs. The oilman said he'd got it from one of the Dutch roustabouts who said he'd got it in Amsterdam.

It took only two phone calls. The vice copper phoned his oppo in the Dutch capital and, ten minutes later, got a call back. They hadn't found Moaner Lisa but they got the next best thing. Her agent. And from him they got her name.

Lisa O'Donnell.

She did live in Glasgow. And she had a phone. Did he have a pen?

Hunter watched the first three numbers – 552, the Merchant City – and hit the stairs running. Digger and Aine hot on his heels.

They were in the car, belting towards George Square, by the time the address was traced on the phone-number-to-address CD ROM. Digger took the call and he gasped. It could be no more than a hundred and fifty yards from where Mr Macintosh had been killed. If he'd pursued his original plan – using the voters roll, checking up on single women, just increased the radius a little – he would have knocked on Strangelove's door.

Murdo was driving. There were no short-cuts through the city centre but he was jumping red lights, giving it welly. A couple of hundred yards from her house, Hunter told him to slow it right down. Then told him to stop a hundred yards on. Her flat was round the corner.

He said, 'Here's how we do this. Nice and slow, right? Don't want to frighten her. Me and Digger in the front entrance, up the stairs to her flat. You two are at the back. If she comes out, do not, repeat do not, confront her. And watch her hands. Watch for a knife. Understood?'

They understood.

Hunter said, 'Now I get out the car first. Digger, follow me in ten seconds. You two, ten seconds after that. Holding hands, you're in love, right? Just in case she sees you.'

The front door to the flats had a security entrance, push-button code, and it was shut tight. Hunter gave it a minute, then phoned Murdo's mobile. Was the back door open?

No, dammit.

An elderly woman looked out of a window in the bottom left flat. Hunter smiled at her, then showed his warrant card and pointed to the door. Ten seconds later a buzzer sounded and he was able to open the door. The old dear came out to meet them. Hunter told Digger to go inside with her. Digger shook his head.

Hunter snarled, 'Inside. That's an order, Sergeant.'

Digger obeyed it.

Hunter took the stairs silently. Thought, glad I'm wearing the Hush Puppies. Rubber soles. No squeaks or creaks. Up two flights. Lisa's top left. Pause here, catch my breath.

Walk up again. One stair, listen, silent. One stair, listen, silent.

Five stairs to go and her door is visible. Getting too old for this. Out of puff again. Or is it fear? Whatever. Onward, ever onward. Top of the stairs now, heart pounding. It is fear. That's good. I'm feart, therefore I am. Something about the door. Something not right. It's not shut tight. Gentle push and it's opening. Squeaks a little. Pause, listen, silence. Into the little hall. Nice, white, bright. Glass door at the end of the hall, light coming through it. No shadows, no figures. Doorway to the left. The toilet, can smell it, nice and clean. It's empty. Door to the right will be the bedroom, just the one. Nice wee flat, though. Bedroom door is closed. Pause, listen, silent. On to the glass door, the living room, kitchen must be off it. Door opens easily and the room is empty. Half-turns, half-expecting her to burst out of the bedroom. But it's silent. Quiet as the grave. On to the kitchen. No one. Turning back, back to the bedroom, holding his breath, listening. Beads of sweat on his forehead. Mouth dry with fear. Part of him hoping she's not there and part of him praying that she is so he can put an end to it. One finger on the door, easing it open. Stopping, waiting for a reaction. It's bright in there. That's always something. No hidden dangers in the darkness. The door is half-open now and Hunter can see the bottom half of a figure in the bed. He freezes but it is still. No movement. No danger. Yet. The door opening more and he can see that it is a man. Then he hears a gasp of pain.

Lisa said, 'Come in, Inspector Hunter.'

He stepped inside. Strange what the mind does to you sometimes. He remembered thinking that it was a nice room. Very feminine. Bright, lace and frills. Nice white bedspread.

Lisa is looking at him. Face very pale. She is on her back but it looks as if she has pulled her knees up. There is a lump in the bed. And the white bedspread is turning red. Hunter can smell it, almost taste it.

Blood. Her arm flops over the edge of the bed. There is a big knife in her hand, blood dropping from the blade.

Hunter went to her and pulled back the bedspread. She has cut herself, ripped her flesh open. One red wound from pubis to sternum. Another across her stomach, like a Caesarian. And the wee mite from the mortuary slab is nestled inside her.

She said, 'What kept you?'

Then she closed her sad eyes for the last time.

Hunter felt the bile rise in his stomach. But he forced himself to stay, to say the silent words.

'God bless you. And God bless your baby.'

They wanted to see her. Digger because he said he should – it was his duty – and Aine and Murdo because they were young. But Hunter wouldn't let them. Just said no and didn't explain it. He despatched Murdo to stand unobtrusively inside the main entrance. Less fuss the better. The others kicked their heels outside the door to her flat. Digger phoned the copshop, called off the troops. Hunter called Arthur, the old photographer, the guy who thought he'd seen it all.

There was a smell off Hunter's breath. Stale whisky and fresh vomit. Aine pointed to the ceiling, said look, no sprinklers. He took out his pipe and kindled it up. Kept forgetting to puff, though, and was forced to light it twice more before he gave up and put it back in his pocket.

The Jug turned up with James Smith. Fastnett wanted to see her and Hunter stood aside, allowed him into the flat, pointed the way to the bedroom. Hunter put a hand on Smith's chest, shook his head and the Assistant Chief Constable stopped in his tracks.

Fastnett had been in the room for all of five seconds before he let out a scream. A shriek of terror. And he came out at a rate of knots, running backwards, pointing and rambling like a lunatic.

It sounded like, 'Moving. His body's alive.'

Hunter and Smith went into the bedroom. The man, indeed, was still in the land of the living. He struggled to his feet – risen from the dead. Hunter and Smith took an arm each, supporting him under his oxters, and half-dragged him to the living-room. Smith stayed with him and Hunter left, closing the door behind him.

Fastnett was ghostly white, a nervous tic at his right eye. He would have risen in Hunter's estimation if he had broken down – fainted or wept. Done something human. Or just buggered off. Just got the hell out of there. Left the mess to the folk who could handle it. But he was too pompous for that. Too arrogant. Too full of his own importance.

He paced the top landing until he got his military stride back, then said, 'Very good. Carry on now.'

Hunter wondered what that meant. Did he want them to pull faces, crack jokes, do something, anything, for a laugh.

Hunter knew what he would find amusing. Giving the plonker a good hard kick in the balls.

9

Hunter looked at his watch again. He put it to his ear, to check that it was still ticking, then remembered it was powered by one of those wee batteries. Bella must have paid cash. No tick. He stuck his head out of his office door, looked at the big clock on the wall at the end of the corridor. Just after 5 p.m. Only twenty-four hours since he'd walked into Lisa's bedroom. That's how he thought of her now. Lisa O'Donnell. Strangelove was dead. And he felt guilty. A bad case of the 'if onlys'.

If only I'd thought of that.

If only I'd done this.

If only I'd got there before . . .

A dose of the 'poor mes'. But he was hairy arsed enough to know that it would pass. Another case would come along, exercise the old grey matter and he'd get back in the groove. Until then, well, there was routine, a mountain of paperwork. He'd ordered Digger to take the day off. The others in the team, too. The least they deserved. They'd hung on last night, filling in the forms, giving the dates and the times, who did what and when, so the basics could be concluded to allow the procurator fiscal to start the ball rolling. He would insert the 'heretofores' and 'hereinafters', then pass it up the legal hierarchy. Pretty soon they'd call in Hunter, ask him to explain it in plain English. And he'd elaborate on the bits that had to be made public, so justice could be seen to be done, and they'd talk about the rest, the bits that no one needed to know, the events that would only rub salt in the relatives' wounds. The sleeping beauty would hardly get a mention. They'd seen to that – Fastnett and the high heid yins – protected the man who could call himself doctor. Smuggled him out of Lisa's flat in a trench coat as if he were a copper.

Simon was a victim, The Jug had said, who would have to live with that hellish experience for the rest of his life. The least the doctor deserved was anonymity. And the establishment figures, ensuring due process of the law, were unlikely to implicate one of their own. So it would be agreed that she killed Knox and she killed Macintosh and she killed Boyd and she killed herself while the state of her mind was disturbed. Sign the papers. End of story.

That was another of Hunter's problems. He could not get what they called in the business world 'closure'. She had been too clever for that. She'd left a trail of clues, led him by the nose, then denied him the satisfaction of talking to her. She had spoken to him and he hadn't fully understood it at the time. Thought it was a reproach for not catching her weeks earlier, after Knox's death, when she might have been saved. It was only when he got back to the copshop, when the Duty Sergeant, pink with embarrassment, passed on the message. She had phoned. Asked for Inspector Hunter. Said he'd been trying to catch her. And left her name and address.

'What kept you?' she'd asked.

Her belly ripped open, her baby safely inside her.

There was no recrimination in her words. At least he didn't hear it. Or maybe that's just what he wanted to think. Whatever, he would learn nothing from her. No secrets, nothing that would make him a better copper. And, Lord knows, it was difficult enough just to be a good one nowadays.

It had been better in the old days when you could play God. The old coppers used to talk about it – the time when there was hanging, when you had their lives in your hands and you could tell them, 'You'll swing for this.' Now Hunter could only sit like Buddha, a toothless one, too. What could you do to them now? Maybe warn, 'Your next incarnation might not be very pleasant.'

But he had adapted, changed with the times. It was a battle of wills now, psychological warfare. He had built up the myth of The Hunter. It was his biggest weapon. The turnkeys in the cells would swagger about The Hunter. Make sure they heard in the cells. Exaggerate the stories, build him into the bogeyman. Digger would put a hand up to his mouth, reverential, when the first interview was well under way, whisper to the young copper to check if The Hunter was free. And he would come into the bare room, take a seat in the corner and sit, silent, while Digger did all the spade work, just waiting for the signs. He watched their hands, the fingers, tapping and tightening, giving away their little secrets. Sometimes he only had to wait ten or fifteen minutes. Other times, it took hours. The timing had to be just right. The timid ones had to be approached with caution, not pushed or threatened. Had to give them some dignity, let them think they were doing a brave thing when they confessed. The cocky ones had to be sweated, kept under pressure and approached only when they struggled –

267

when they were going under for the third time. That was when Buddha rose from his chair, scratching the legs on the lino, ambled over, towered above them, blocking out the light, and whispered in their ears. All the coppers wanted to know what he said – what made them give up, sing like canaries, sign the piece of paper. Hunter never told them.

Lisa never gave him that satisfaction. Never let him take charge. She tugged his chain and he only followed obediently in her wake. In one way, he was glad of that. Because it wouldn't have worked on her. If he'd leant over her and whispered, 'I know.', she'd have whispered back, 'Of course you do, I told you.'

He had found the chloroform bottle in the bathroom. The sanitary towel, still reeking of the anaesthetic, was there, too. And a syringe. What bitter irony. Dr Simon left helpless as a baby by the tools of his trade.

The lads from the City Mortuary had taken Lisa away in a big coffin. Hunter had told them that. Bring a big coffin. The neighbours could not know that it contained Lisa and the baby.

Murdo had insisted on taking the baby (he called her Laura) from the mortuary back to the Royal Infirmary. Aine insisted on going with him. They travelled in a hearse, with Laura's body in a little white coffin in the back. They were met at the infirmary by Charles, Head of Security, and formerly a Chief Inspector of police. They told him that the baby would not be mentioned in any formal proceedings and he said he thought that was the wisest course. The mother was considered to be out of danger and had been asking about the child. Wise to let her say hello and then goodbye. Let her grieve, then pick up the pieces. Life goes on.

Fastnett had addressed the troops in CR3 around 7 p.m. last night. Done it well too, Hunter conceded reluctantly. Struck a dignified balance between the 'sad, tragic outcome to this inquiry and the professionalism and diligence of the police officers in this room'. Would have done well to have left it there, though, and not reminded them that trauma counselling was always available. Then he had called on Sergeant Burns to instruct them on their next duties.

Digger was lost. Tried to hoof it, thanking them, then thanking them again. Hunter caught his eye and he was glad to yield the floor.

He knew how the troops felt. Disappointed, cheated. All the work, all the extra effort and only her body to show for it. So he brought it right back to business. Told them to fill in the forms and told them to do it right. Make sure their mobiles were switched on and the batteries charged – just in case there were any queries. Then he said that Sergeant Burns had recommended that they take tomorrow off. If that was okay with the Chief Constable . . . ?

The Jug thought it was a good idea. Hadn't much choice, really.

The troops started on the forms and Hunter eased Digger towards Fastnett. Said that the relatives of the murder victims had to be informed before it broke on the TV and radio. Murdo and Aine would call on Mrs Macintosh. Lisa's mother lived in Easterhouse. Digger and Hunter himself would take care of her.

Perhaps, Hunter had said, since the Chief Constable has had contact with Mrs Knox, he would want to break the news to her himself . . .

Her sister, obviously pregnant, had been there and that had made it even more difficult.

'It's Lisa, isn't it?' the mother had said at the door of her neat little flat in Easterhouse. 'An accident. I know it. Oh, dear God . . .'

Hunter had ushered them inside, asked them to sit down, then told them that Lisa was dead.

The mother had wailed and the sister had been dreadfully silent.

Mrs O'Donnell knew that it was suicide. 'She killed herself, didn't she?'

Hunter said yes and the mother sank to her knees in prayer. Fingered her rosary and asked God to forgive her daughter this mortal sin.

Louise wanted to know how she did it.

Hunter slung it a deaf one. He'd given them enough bad news and was obliged to give them more. The mother wanted to make them tea but they declined. Better just to get on with it. To get it over and done with.

Hunter told them there was no easy way to say it. Lisa had taken her own life because the police were about to arrest her.

For murder.

Louise cried aloud, 'No. No. Nonono!'

The mother hugged her.

Asked Hunter again how she did it. He knew what she meant but he said, 'She killed three men. Stabbed them.'

Legal obligation fulfilled. Now he could stop acting like a policeman and start to feel a shit.

The mother and daughter hugged and wept. He sent Digger to make tea. The flat was immaculate. Photographs of the girls on the sideboard. In school uniforms, at their first communions, Louise in her bride's dress and proudly holding her first child. No pictures, he noted, of Lisa's father.

As Digger returned with mugs of tea, Louise asked again, clearly, 'How did she kill herself.'

Hunter said, 'I think she took pills.'

The mother asked, 'Was she . . . I mean, did she suffer?'

Hunter said no, he didn't think so. She just went to sleep.

The story had been the second item on the national news on the BBC, after the suspected terrorist bombing in the United States. ITV had led on it, starting with the murder of Danny Boyd. They had still pictures of him and live footage of the outside of his big fortress house. No privacy, no hiding place for Danny Boy's family. Occupational hazard. The Beeb described him as a drugs godfather and gangster known to have killed at least one man. They said that police had later found the body of a young woman and believed that she had killed Boyd and two other men in Glasgow. Simon did not get a mention. The identity of the murderer had not been released. They gave brief details of Knox and Macintosh, then went back to Boyd and speculated that the city faced a bloody battle among rival drug gangs for control of his territory.

The dailies had a field day. Every one splashed on it and the *Daily Record* had it on pages one through to nine. Boyson got a good show in *The Herald* and a picture byline on his page three piece on the painstaking police effort which had zeroed in on the psychotic killer. He also had exclusive pictures and details of Boyd's last hours in the Hilton Hotel.

Committee Room One had been bursting at the seams for the 10 a.m. press conference. Tobias Fastnett conducted the meeting. Smith and the Press Officer were at the top table. Hunter entered quietly after the start and stood at the back. He noticed immediately that the crime correspondents and chief reporters were not in attendance. They would be chasing their own story lines. The hacks in CR3 tape-recorded the entire meeting but still jotted down every syllable. The one piece of information which they wanted, but were not given, was the identity of the killer.

Why was it not being divulged?

Smith answered, 'We have still to inform her relatives.'

Surely the public had a right to know.

'Yes, we recognise that and the information will be released as soon as the relatives have been informed.'

'When would that be?'

'Difficult to say. But the killer's identity will be put out over the Presswire as soon as possible.'

'Was she a Glasgow woman?'

'Yes.'

'Why are you protecting the relatives of a serial killer?'

'Who says she is a serial killer?'

'Who are you protecting them from?'

'You.'

'And she definitely killed all three men?'

'We have never said that.'

The old hands would have let it go at that. It was all over their own bliddy papers and no one had complained. A nod's as good as a wink . . . But the second division got side-tracked here, thought they spotted a weakness where none existed.

Then one guy, a stranger in town, London accent, asked if the police thought they had learned anything from the inquiry.

Smith was sharp. On to him like a flash. He said, 'I didn't catch your name.'

He was *Daily Mail*, sent up from the Smoke to stir up trouble. Bungled inquiry, why did three men have to die? – that kind of thing.

Smith said the police were always learning and went on quickly to pass on condolences to the families of the bereaved. Said he appreciated that the journos had a job to do but could they be mindful of those families? Pointed out that there were children involved. Hoped that their privacy would be respected. Said that perhaps he should point out, to those not fully conversant with the law in Scotland, that the welfare and anonymity of children under the age of sixteen were paramount. Then he had called a halt to the meeting.

Good man, Smith. Wise old bird. Must have been really hacked off to see Fastnett come up as his boss. Might not be too old yet to move up. If The Jug moved on.

Hunter caught Smith's attention in the corridor.

He asked, 'Have you heard any more about the death at the Pet Crem?'

Smith said, 'Yes, definitely murder. Do you have an interest in it?'

Hunter said no, not really, but he believed that they had shared mutual friends.

Almost 7 p.m. and Hunter had just about finished shuffling the paperwork. He walked to the window and opened it up. Lit his pipe, the new briar. It wasn't smoking well. Too wet, too much black, nicotiney gunge. Served him right, though, hadn't treated the pipe with respect. Should have burned it in properly, smoked it once then left it for a day. But it had been going non-stop, like the lum at the rubbish tip, since Tuesday. It would never be right now. Better just to toss it but he wouldn't. It would kick about the desk and the car and he'd keep going back to it, hoping it was better, and he'd met with disappointment every time.

He'd noticed it had gone off last night when Digger was helping to go through the files on Lisa, double-checking that they had covered all the angles. He'd lit up the briar and sucked in an acrid mouthful of the revolting stuff. Bitter, numbing his cheeks and turning his stomach. Had to spit it out into a paper tissue, much to Digger's disgust.

Bliddy born-again non-smoker. Hadn't said anything, though. Didn't need to. Look on his face said it all. He'd asked Digger how he was doing, personally like, how was he living? Been surprised with the answers, too. Married again and a baby on the way. So Hunter hadn't pursued the line about the divorce – how much it cost and that. Just said good, pleased for you. And sent him home to his new wife.

Couldn't bring himself to go home, though. Couldn't really be arsed to do anything. But he did shed the glad rags. The haircut could stay but the oldest-swinger-in-town look would have to go. That was it, that was the jingle on the phone.

You rub on Vick where you used to splash Brut,
You're the oldest swinger in town.

The heilanman had set him up. Said he'd take 'The Billy Boys' off the phone. Did more than that. Took the piss, too.

Hunter had rescued his old clobber from the boutique bags – the twill trousers and checked shirt – and put them on. Transferred his wedge from one front right pocket to the other and wandered into town. Took a fancy for a pint. Thought about the TSB but discarded the notion immediately. The other decent boozers were out for the same reason – crawling with journos. Wondered about giving Boyson a ring – meeting him on neutral territory, just for the company – but he kicked that one into touch, too. Considered catching a black hack, going out to the bools, getting single-fished among some familiar faces. But there were bound to be questions. So he drifted in to a trendy pub in the centre of town – flashing lights and warm beer – and drifted out again after one pint. Stopped at an off-licence and bought a half-bottle of Bells. Putting the wedge back into his pocket, giving it a quick audit. Jesus H, less than £100. Approaching George Square, sees a familiar face. Blondie, the dame from the yacht at Loch Lomond Marina. Big bazookas and a cooked breakfast. Looking the biz, too. And he thinks about it, seriously, and decides, wisely, against it.

272

Takes you all night to do what you used to do all night –
You're the oldest swinger in town.

A young guy in a big car draws in to the pavement and she gets in. Gives him a smacker, on the lips. He's not her son. Good luck to you, Blondie. Hope you don't get a good night's sleep.

Crossing the square, heading for the wee hotel again. Do a Quasimodo, sleep with the Bells.

He had awakened in a cold sweat. Some of it the whisky and most of it fear.

He'd got up and gone to the bathroom. Didn't really need a piddle but needed to put some distance between himself and the nightmare. It was blood and blades and bodies and babies. He'd gone back to bed and been unable to sleep. Lisa wouldn't leave him alone. What had that lassie been through? She wasn't born a vicious killer – though he'd encountered a few who had been – so what had happened to her along the way? Only to her, too, because the sister was okay. But somewhere along the line there had been an event – more likely events – that had cut so deeply that they had severed the perfectly normal pattern of Lisa's life. Simon was high up on the list of offenders. The father of her baby – the one she aborted – Hunter had no doubts about it. That was why she had set up the last scene like a Shake-spearean tragedy.

Bella had lost a baby, almost twenty-one years ago. A miscarriage, after ten weeks. Hunter had taken a week's leave but Granny Pearson had been alive then and Bella had clung to her mum like a bairn. He'd felt useless, surplus to requirements, but he'd hung around anyway. Then tried to keep busy, went for the messages, washed the car, took Alex for walks, to the zoo and the pictures. And when they came home Bella and Granny Pearson would separate, like captured lovers, then drift together again, talking in whispers. He'd gone back to work on the Thursday, said sorry, there's been a murder, you'll be okay, won't you? And he had been glad to return to the kind of unnatural, premature death that he understood. But he still thought about his baby, usually downstairs, with a dram in his hand, and he'd have a wee weep to himself. While Bella was safely tucked up in bed, cosy in her half of the electric blanket.

Why did she leave Simon alive? It wasn't by accident. Wasn't a mistake. Her baby was dead, she was killing herself, why let him live? Uninjured, too. Untouched, really. Was it to show that he wasn't really part of the family? That they didn't need him? Or was it deeper, darker than that?

273

Some kind of strange love . . . It was one for the shrinks to mull over. They'd explain it in polysyllables, maybe even write books about it. Simon was the only one who could shed some light on it but Fastnett had ruled that a no-go zone.

Hunter turned on to his side and watched the rain run down the hotel's mucky window like teardrops. The dirty orange light of the street lamp magnified the image on the opposite wall. He thought he could see movement in the teardrops. Little trapped creatures, struggling to get out. Like a mayfly on the loch. Like Matthew Whittle's pond-skaters. The mononucleic acid, the raw intelligence, of the boy who can remember his dreams.

10

Hunter forced himself to have breakfast. Wasn't hungry, didn't fancy it, but he couldn't remember the last time he'd eaten and it was going to be another difficult day. He ordered the full monty, fried everything, and, once he made a start, it had been just fine and dandy. Stomach must've thought his throat had been cut. Mopped up the egg yolk and tomato with extra toast and drank two pots of tea.

He'd remembered where he'd left the Vectra or thought he did – at Joe's Café – so he tried to hail a cab to take him out to Vicky Road. It was a nice day, chilly, a nip in the air that made you realise, if not appreciate, that you were alive. Nose to tail traffic around George Square. Same out to the South Side, too, so he walked on to Central Station, took the train to Queens Park. No car, though, not where he thought he'd left it. Nicked in to see Joe, asked if he'd seen the Vectra.

Joe said, 'Why, does it do tricks?'

Asked what Hunter wanted to eat. Surprised when he declined, asked if he was taking the negative equity elsewhere. Then, guiding Hunter away from the paying customers, shared a confidence.

'You've no' got a best friend, right? So I'll tell you. You're mingin, Mate. You know, stinky.'

Hunter stuck his nose in an oxter and confirmed the information. The shirt hadn't taken kindly to being stuck in the polly bag for two days then put back into service. Must've reactivated the old sweat, stirred up the stinkies. A no-no – a bit like reheating pork.

It was a bit of a bugger not having the car. On a schedule now, not a lot of time to waste. He had told Mrs O'Donnell that he'd take her to see her daughter. Said he'd pick her up in Easterhouse at 11 a.m. Hadn't mentioned that they'd be going to the mortuary and she would be obliged formally to identify her daughter.

It was 9.30 a.m. Could still take a cab home, tell the driver to wait for him, put on some clean clothes, then take the taxi to the copshop. But he couldn't just body-swerve Bella. Say, hiya, how're you doing, as he was dropping his strides, and cheerio, then, see you sometime, as he buttoned up his shirt and shut the back door.

The suit was in the window of the charity shop. Navy blue with a light pinstripe. Dignified. His size, too – the wee lass in the boutique had measured him – forty-four inch jacket and thirty-six inch strides. Can't be bad at £20. He'd bought a white shirt and a nice woollen tie, fiver the pair. Crossed the road, pair of Ys and a pair of socks out of Henry Hoey's and Robert is your father's brother. A new man. Caught the train back to Central and changed in the lavvies in St Vincent Street. Realised, too late, that it was a favoured meeting place for the shirtlifters, and there he is, in trap two, bare-arsed, and the phone goes off. Oldest effin swinger in town. So he swears at it, in his deepest, gruffest voice, and feels for it in the pockets of the smelly strides. Careful not to call it a bugger, just in case any chaps of a different sexual inclination might be listening. Don't want to offend them. It takes all sorts, after all . . .

It was Aine, calling from the copshop, phoning just to say that she had met with James Smith and he'd said that her move to CID was permanent. So she was just calling Hunter to thank him. Asked where he was. Said he sounded as if he was in the belly of a whale.

He knew, told her to get a car, a big one, dark-coloured, four doors. Told her to pick him up at the tobacconists in St Vincent Street. She didn't know it but said she would get him at the lavatories. Told him to be careful, to watch his back if he was still wearing the chinos and blue shirt.

He finished dressing, buffed up the Hush Puppies with the erse of the old trousers and left the strides and the stinky shirt behind the pan.

The mother was in shock. Dressed in a dignified black outfit, she sat in the back of the big Rover, didn't speak, barely moved. The sister there, in a voluminous red coat, and she hardly shut up. She'd seen the *Daily Record*, so she knew about the murders and she wanted to know why – WHY! – Lisa had done it.

Aine was driving. Hunter did the talking. He said, honestly, that he didn't know. And again, honestly, that he didn't need to know. It wasn't his job. Tried to handle it that way, to keep it impersonal. Spoke about the job and the role of the police and what he was and was not allowed to tell her.

Louise asked if Lisa had sex with the men. He said yes, there was a sexual element to the encounters. She said she knew it, had known it all along. All the big talk about being a model, the fancy foreign trips and everything, and she was nothing but a common prostitute.

The mother had whimpered then.

There was never going to be a right time to tell them but this was as good as any. So Hunter said that they had reason to believe that Lisa had worked in the sex industry. They had to know sooner or later. The papers would be all over it like a rash.

'And you,' Louise said to Hunter, 'did you have her? I bet you did. I bet you got a freebie.'

Aine stuck up for him, said, 'That's not fai . . .'

Hunter cut her off and said, 'She wasn't into that. She did films, that kind of thing.'

'Filthy pornos,' Louise said. 'She was nothing but a wee hoor.'

Her face was red with rage. As red as her coat. But she had vented her anger – for now – and the remainder of the journey continued in silence.

They saw the pale face in the mortuary, through a glass darkly, and the mother confirmed 'That's my Lisa.' Hunter repeated the official wording and she confirmed that the body was that of her daughter, Lisa O'Donnell. Business over.

They declined a cup of tea and, on the way home, it was the daughter who sat brooding and the mother who did the talking. She wanted to know what would happen next.

Hunter told her that there would be legal proceedings to determine how Lisa and the three men died. It was the law, a formality, and there was no need for her to attend. Lisa's body would remain in the mortuary, for about a week. Tests had to be carried out. Again, it was the law. After that, the body would be released. They could make arrangements for a funeral themselves or it could be done for them. There was no need to make a decision at the moment but there was something else that he had to talk to them about. Lisa's name would have to be released soon and it was inevitable that the press would trace them. It would be intrusive and unpleasant. His advice was that they should go away for a few days. Were there relations or friends they could go to? Maybe someone in England?

Louise wasn't having any of it. She had done nothing wrong and, if they came to her door, she would tell them that. And tell them what she thought of the dirty wee hoor.

The mum wanted to get away. But she had nowhere to go. Hunter told her it wasn't a problem. Just to pack some things, enough for a week, and he would see to the arrangements. There was a Bereaved Family Contingency Plan for such situations.

When the mother and daughter were in the bedroom, Aine whispered that she had never heard about the plan.

He said, 'No, you won't have. I just made it up.'

Back in the office and Hunter reckons he might live to regret a moment of weakness. Bruno has just been and gone. Bruno the boxer, who lost his cushy job at the *Record* for being too free with his hands. He'd found out where his shoe gripped him and was really having to work for a living now with the Press Association. But he wasn't a bad lad and Hunter decided to give him an even break.

Bruno had phoned – just mugs for luck, he'd said. The town was crawling with big name journos, sent up from London, so none of his copy would be used. He was wondering if there was any chance of an interview for a personal piece.

'You know the kind of thing – the good guy who got the bad guy.'

Hunter said he'd give him ten minutes and allowed it to stretch to twenty because he had played by the rules. Even said he liked the suit. Hunter made him promise to give Digger a good show and Aine and Murdo too, the bright young things of Strathclyde Polis. That had been a wee bit embarrassing because he didn't know Murdo's surname or how to spell Aine's. Had to call on her to bail him out. She had just put Lisa's mum on the train (Hunter had got a rail warrant, got the cops in Brighton to book a wee hotel, said they'd sort out the cash side later.) Made use of Aine's services when she was there. Gave her the moby, told her to change its tune. Make it ring or buzz or play 'The Laughing Policeman'. Any bliddy thing. Told Bruno technology baffled him – anything after the propelling pencil. Aine left, then returned to tell him that she liked the suit. Was it Italian? Very classy. The tie was naff, though.

Digger had stuck his head round the door and that had been Bruno's interview over. Digger was on a downer. Blaming himself for not pursuing the single women who lived in the area where Toshie's body had been found. Hunter had chewed him out. Told him it wouldn't have made any difference. Lisa was too smart for that. Told him the man that never made a mistake never made a decision. Told him to live with it and not allow the troops to see him with his face tripping him. Said not to worry about it – it was the strangest case. Hadn't seen one like it and didn't want to again.

Digger had something else to say but was having a problem with it. Eventually he got it out.

'We were talking last night, Lorna and me, wondered if you and the missus would like to come for dinner some night.'

Hunter said great, yeah, sounded good.

He'd meant it too. Decided he'd ask Bella – if he ever saw her again. He hadn't been giving her a fair crack of the whip. If Digger could start again (with another woman, admittedly) so could he. New suit, new man, new marriage.

Right on cue, Bella phoned. No, he said, he wasn't busy, all but over now. Yeah, he was alone. And she started to tell him he was a lovely man.

'It's just arrived. What a lovely, lovely man!'

And he's wondering if it's a wrong number. But no, he recognised other members of the cast. She has phoned the Coffee Girls.

'Okay, it's not my turn, it's Celine's day, but I've just got to have them round. They've just got to see it. Even though it's just a huge flat-pack just now, just off the lorry.'

It was a bit embarrassing to have aroused all this passion and not know what buttons he had pressed. Strange creatures, women. An entirely different species. Then, God is good, it came back to him. Yesterday (good Lord, was it only yesterday), on the way out to see how the Pet Crem guy had been incinerated, he'd noticed the sign at the side of the road – 'People in Class Houses', it said. So he'd popped in. Met the wee Irish fella who owned the place. Said one of his pals, The Drouth, was happy with his conservatory and other friends, the Carmichaels, were most unchuffed. He'd flashed the warrant card here, asked if everything was in order, tax, VAT, that kind of thing. Then mentioned that he'd been thinking – but only if the price was right – of a conservatory himself. And the guy had fallen over himself to take the address and assured him that there was a special offer. Once in a lifetime.

Bella had slowed down a bit, to take in some air.

'Sandy Hunter, you are a deep one and a big gem. Just when I was thinking that you'd forgotten our silver wedding anniversary. Well, I can tell you you've put my idea in the shade. Remember Hawaii? Well, I was thinking of a kind of second honeymoon.'

Jesus H, twenty-five years already.

'Was it expensive, the conservatory? No, don't tell me. I know you and I know you'll have struck a hard bargain. But tell me later. Tell me now, how are you?'

Left just enough space for him to say okay.

'It must be a hard time for you. I know that. That dreadful woman, killing those men. I'm glad you got her. I'm proud of you – I don't tell you that often enough but I am really proud of you. I hope you can manage home tonight. Phone if you can. I'll wait up. Have a drink together then we might even practise for the second honeymoon, eh?

Hunter wanders along the corridors to CR3. No coppers there, only the techies, dismantling the equipment, handling the computers with loving care, preparing to transplant them to a new body. There is nothing in the room – no spirit. Even the ghost of Strangelove has gone.

One computer left flickering with life. He asks one of the guys if it can trace a stolen car. It can but he can't. Didn't have access. But if Hunter could log on . . . The guy turned his back while he keyed in his password.

BELLA. She left five black bullet holes on the screen.

Took five seconds for the techie to plunk some keys, tell him, no, the car had not been reported stolen.

Of course it hadn't. A copper and he'd forgotten to report it. Have to do it, though, to claim the insurance. It'd take bliddy months to get settled. They'd offer a grand and he'd tell them to stick it sideways. And they'd show him figures in books, say that's all it's worth. And he'd say that'll be shining bright, you make up those figures, there's no way I can buy a similar car for that kind of dosh. And they'd hum and haw for a fortnight and he'd maybe get it up to £1,200 or £1,300. Then a nasty thought creeps into his mind. Jesus H, hope the insurance is up to date. Who pays the insurance? Has to be Bella, surely that's her domain. If not, he's up shit creek without a paddle.

He wanders on, passing the traffic department, sees a familiar face, an old Sergeant. Pops in, tells the guy, look, it's a bit embarrassing, but he reckons his car's been half-inched. And the Sergeant presses some of his buttons then says, yeah, it's here, bad news. Reported yesterday by a binman, lying outside Polmadie rubbish incinerator. All it's windows put in. And he better shift it soon, before it gets lifted and taken away to the pound and he has to pay two hundred quid to get it back out. The guy has a parting shot, too. Says two hundred quid would be nothing to a bloke with a suit like that. Had he won the lottery?

Heading back to his office, sees The Jug in the distance and gives him a swift body-swerve. It would appear that Fastnett is a happy camper. A wee bird tells Hunter he's had a call from the Met and he's humming 'I Love London Town'. God help them. And God help The Jug, too. They'll eat him alive in the Smoke.

*　*　*　*　*

There's a noise inside his office. A phone.

Dadadada da da
Deedle eedle eedle eedle
Deedle eedle eedle de

It's his phone. Good Lord, Aine, what have you done to me?

It's Jamesie, putting on what he thinks is the voice of authority. Wants Hunter to know that he's taking care of business. Actually said that, taking care of business. He met up with the guy at the other side of town, not paper or scissors, know what I mean.

Stone, yeah, very fucking clever.

Jamesie says they've signed a truce. No more killings. It's back to normal.

Hunter said, 'That's right. It's me against you again. And don't you forget, Jamesie, I've got you by the balls.'

It's dark o'clock. Standing at his wee window, smoking the Falcon, and the aluminium stem is unpleasantly hot in his hand. Better than the gungy briar, though. Life's full of compromises. The wind's turned to the north, a bit too bitter for snow but it's brass monkey weather out there. Have to go out in it soon. Have to go home. Should be okay. Brownie points for the conservatory. Must've scared the shit out of the wee Irish guy. Didn't talk turkey with him, no mention of money, so could beat him down to the bone. Get it for Asda price. The wee guy must know that, know that possession is nine-tenths of the law and ten-tenths of the bargaining power.

The mobile plays its new tune. It's Boyson.

He said, 'I hear you've been busy but we need to talk. Fancy buying me a pint? I'm just down the road – at the Hilton.'

Hunter asked if he had wheels. Boyson said yeah.

Hunter told him that he shouldn't drink and drive.

'Pick me up at the copshop in five minutes. I've got a wee job to do. What? Oh, it'll only take five minutes. Just got to get rid of some old rubbish.'

He spotted the Vectra from the crest of the bridge over the railway. It was sitting terribly alone, on a cushion of diamonds, like a wealthy orphan. Hunter told Boyson to take a right, no, not the one at the fire station, the next one. Then asked him to stop after twenty yards. He got out and told Boyson to stay there. This was something he had to do alone.

281

As he turned the corner, the cold night air caught the back of his throat and he took a fit of coughing. The Vectra had been abandoned at waste ground outside the huge Polmadie refuse incinerator. A statement, perhaps lacking a little in subtlety. The street lighting sparkled off the shattered glass, so much of it on the road that the windows must have been smashed from the inside. The rear, nearside light assembly was broken and there was a long, nasty gash along the bodywork where it had taken second prize in an argument with a wall. The door mirror flapped like a limp dick – a victim of the same altercation. One window remained intact, the one on the driver's door. It was jammed, about three inches down, presumably how the thief had gained entry. The radio had gone, of course. All in all, not a pretty sight but nothing that could not be repaired. It was only glass and metal.

The cough came back. A ticklish annoyance which grew to a painful heaving of the chest. It was the Falcon. Smoked too hot, it wasn't healthy. Hunter opened the driver's door, to check if there was a spare pipe in the pocket.

He smelled it first; saw it soon after. An elephant-size shit on the driver's seat.

He removed his tie. Felt in the pockets of his new suit jacket. Pipe, house keys, car keys and finally the lighter. He unlocked the petrol cap and stuck the tie into the hole. Found a stick and used it to stuff the tie right down in there. Aine thought it was naff anyway. Then he got out his lighter . . . and stopped. It would have been so easy but it wasn't right. He pulled the tie out of the tank and tossed it into the spare ground. It wasn't his colour anyway, petrol blue.

Elbows on the bar in The Mire, the working man's pub round the corner. A boozer, about a mile away, was called the Queens Park Cafe and, farther into town, was The Office. A lot of guys were detained of an evening in the Cafe or the Office. But tonight Hunter was in The Mire.

Boyson was nursing the last inch of a half-pint of Guinness. Hunter had broken his last £20 for another large malt whisky (the first had gone down without touching the sides). Boyson had done all the talking, Hunter all the thinking. He had distilled the journo's information and been left with a few questions.

Why had Paborsky left Patrik, his lover, alone in the Hilton after the concert?

Why had Patrik left the hotel in tears two days later?

Why had Calder Carmichael paid the bill?

Who was the man with them?

And who had gone where from the airport?

Hunter drained his whisky and thought about another. But he knew it wouldn't be one more drink, it would be yet another heavy bevvy session. Anyway, Boyson wasn't up for it. So they left, went back to the old, black car. Through a gap in the buildings Hunter could make out the shape of the Vectra. Then, as if by magic, it burst into flames.

Boyson said, 'You know, I didn't see your lips move.'

Two lads sprinted away, laughing. Hunter thought he could hear the rattle of Swan Vestas. He said a silent prayer. Now he wouldn't have to go to the bad fire.

Then, since he appeared to be without transport, Boyson drove him home.

Hunter stood outside his house and listened as the old, black car farted its way down the street, leaving the oily stink of diesel in his wake. He remembered where he had heard the clunk of Jed's Pet Crematorium van. And knew where he would go tomorrow.

11

A cooked breakfast, the second day in a row, and Bella's was even better than the hotel's. She'd really made an effort. Sausage, black pud, tomato and the bacon singed around the edges. But the special touch was the wee bits of parsley on the poached eggs.

Bella had nibbled on a piece of toast and made a fuss of topping up his tea.

Hunter had the suit on again. She'd said last night that she really liked it – and where did he get it? It was a classic no-win situation so he'd told half of the truth. She'd laughed when he explained about the oldest-swinger-in-town gear (though he had not said why he needed a disguise), then she gave him a row when he told her about the charity shop. He didn't say that it was the one in Vicky Road, cos he knew that would really drive her bonkers, have her worried in case one of the Coffee Girls had seen him.

She'd asked last night if he wanted a whisky and looked a bit surprised when he said no, he'd had a couple earlier. She'd said that was good. She had mistaken Boyson's jalopy for a black hack and said she was pleased that he'd taken a taxi home. She didn't like it when he drove . . . at night. He knew exactly what she meant but let it go. He thought of telling her about the burned-out Vectra but decided to leave well alone.

They'd gone to bed and she said she liked his Barlinnie haircut, stroked his head, and he told her she'd get skelfs. They'd had a cuddle, cos it was cold and she'd forgotten to put the electric blanket on, then he'd gone out like a light. Slept for almost ten hours and really felt the better for it.

She was pleased, really chuffed about the conservatory. The Coffee Girls had been so impressed. He'd had her fooled, she confessed. She thought he'd forgotten all about their anniversary. Then she had asked the hard questions. Like how would they pay for it? Would planning permission be needed? How long would it take to be built? When would they come to put it up?

He'd ducked and dived, said he'd put it up himself on Sunday and she let it rest there. Then he'd changed the subject, told her one of Boyson's stories from last night. About Zara to be put in charge of the UK refugees' project. Boyson had called her Tsarina Zara.

Hunter polished off his breakfast, said it was great, then said that he'd have to make tracks. Bella started to ask if he'd be home tonight but stopped halfway through, in case she broke the spell. He sipped at his tea, not wanting to leave on a sour note. She remembered something, went to the letter rack and gave him the envelope that had arrived yesterday – Bank of Scotland stamped on the back. He opened it – nothing to hide – and was a bit puzzled by its contents. The bean counters in the bank said that they had taken the liberty of moving his current account into another one which offered the same facilities and paid interest into the bargain. Aye, very good. Interest on what? Bella read his expression accurately, asked if he needed some money, for a taxi or something, but he said no, he was fine.

She had walked him to the door and planted a wee cheeper on his cheek. Love's middle-aged dream.

Missed the bliddy train, half an hour till the next one and not enough dosh for a taxi. So he wanders into the bank, shows the letter to the boy behind the glass screen and asks what it means. Cheeky wee shite asks if he's got any ID. So he produces his warrant card, asks if it'll do or would the laddie like to come down to the copshop and ask his questions there. The boy goes crimson, selects a leaflet from a stand-up shelf thing and slides it through the gap under the glass. Hunter gives it a quick shuftie, then says, 'Just out of interest, how much is in this account.'

The boy plunks a few buttons on snazzy wee computer, writes down some figures and passes the slip under the partition. Hunter reckons he's made a mistake. Forgotten to put the point in that'll show whether its 6p or 86p. Asks if he's sure that's right. The boy swivels the screen around as far as its wire allows. Hunter has to stretch to see it, so his cheek is pressed up against the glass, and the boy is right enough. It says £4,686.00. Hunter asks if he can take some out and the boy asks how much. So he takes £686. Tucks it into his right trouser pocket. Tidy wedge. Practises counting it with one hand as he waits for a taxi. Half of his mind is wondering how the bank made such a big mistake. But that's the wee half. The big half is saying that possession is nine-tenths of the law.

The *Daily Record*'s front-page story is 'Sex Shame of My Slut Sister'. A big picture of Lisa with her arm around her wee sister. One not yet at school and the other still unsteady on her pins. Ankle socks, ribbons in their hair and sisters' loving hugs. Hunter compiled a mental letter to God.

Dear God,
I know you're busy running the universe and all that but this'll only take a minute. You see, I was wondering when you decided that these wee lassies' lives would turn out like this. Oh, I know about free will, that kind of thing, but you must've thought, at some stage, hey, I'll pop in a porn star loony murderer option here. So if you could answer that, that'd be good. You know where I'll be,
Sandy

So Louise had decided to cash in. What'll she get for it? Maybe a grand – and the rest of her life to feel guilty about it. Still, it would get the other hacks off her back. And her mother's too, hopefully.

Aine knocks twice on Hunter's office door and he tells her to come in. Nice tie, she says, asks if it's real polyester, and he wonders if she's taking the piss. He says he's not sure about her fancy wee number, maybe she'd look better back in uniform, with her long, black hair piled up on top of her noggin and stuffed under a WPC's hat. And she says keys, boss, J for joke and just how high would you like me to jump?

She'd been doing some digging for him into Lisa's financial affairs. No real reason, just turning over stones to see what was there. A lot, really. She hadn't traced everything but she reckoned it would run into six figures – and that was without any decimal points.

He asked, 'Who gets the dosh?'

She said, 'I haven't been able to find a will, so it'll be the mum and' – she tapped the picture in the paper – 'the loving sister.'

Hunter said, 'What about a father.'

Aine said, 'Oh, he's still on the go. Around somewhere but he bogged off when they were about that age.' She nodded at picture.

Hunter told her that, legally, he was entitled – maybe even to the lion's share.

She didn't like that, said it was unfair. He agreed, said it didn't have to be fair, it was the law. She twisted her long hair round a finger, popped the ends in her mouth.

'What if we don't tell him?' she asked.

He said, 'We have nothing to do with it. Our bit's done.'

She didn't like that either. Started to argue. But he told her that there was a time to let go and this was it.

He thought of something to divert her, threw her the slip of paper the boy in the bank had given him. Hunter had written the account number on the top and asked if she could use her electric skills to wheedle some secrets out of the computer.

She said, 'Easy-peasey. What do you want to know?'

He asked for details of when the money was paid in, when it was taken out and where it came from.

She asked, 'Are you logged on?'

He said he was. She said, 'Right, let the dog see the rabbit!' and she made a dismissive gesture with the back of her hand, to get rid of the novice and make way for the expert.

He got up obediently and they swopped seats. She pretended to type away at the keyboard. Said oh yeah, tricky, this might help, yeah, good, okay. Then she made a phone call, spoke in whispers and jotted down some figures. Then she hung up and triumphantly waved the slip of paper.

He said, 'That's not fair.'

She said, 'No, but it's using the power of the law.'

He smiled. Sharp kid. Got her own values. She wouldn't be stopped by rules and regulations.

She said, 'So, what we have is thirty-five pay-in transactions, first of the month, every month.'

Pay day.

'One withdrawal, today, want to guess how much?'

He shook his head.

'But, and I'm only guessing here, you would like to know where the money came from, am I right?'

He told her she was right and reminded her of the WPC uniform.

She rhymed off the number of another Bank of Scotland account and it sounded familiar to him.

He went round the desk, took a photocopy of an expenses sheet from the top drawer and asked her if she knew how much had been deposited last month.

She had to phone again and she said the figure out loud this time. 'Yeah, got it. £46.80. Ta. See you tonight. Your turn to make dinner, by the way.'

It all came back to him. It had been agreed at an early board meeting of Sandy Hunter Finances (very) Ltd. The Chief Financial Officer had pointed out that his expenses were paid through salary and, since they were bona fide expenses, they should not be part of the general financial pot. So she proposed, and he seconded, the motion that the separate account be set up.

Aine was smiling. She knew that he had shared an intimate secret.

Hunter said, 'And you can wipe that bliddy smirk off your face. I could have done that myself. Who was it, incidentally? Boyfriend?'

She thought carefully before answering. Finally said, 'Girlfriend. My girlfriend. Any probs with that?'

He said no, not at all.

'In fact,' he said, 'it resolves a problem.'

She looked puzzled.

He said, 'Explains why you haven't tried to get inside my pinstriped pants.'

Aine was in the boss's chair, using his superior security clearance, switching from e-mail to internet, from phone to hacker. She'd asked Hunter to give over with humming 'Mhairi's Wedding'. Her exact words, which he said had shocked him, were 'It was getting on my tits.'

He said that he was humming in admiration and appreciation of her network of contacts. If her girlfriend didn't know how to break into (Aine said access) a financial institution's computer network, she knew someone who did.

They had obtained nothing of any interest on Zara Carmichael. Her fertility clinic had shown a profit of £45,000 in the last financial year. Not bad for a second income. She had two credit cards (one, a Visa, run through the Bank of Scotland, the other American Express) and both were run in a manner which would have pleased Bella herself. The transactions were perfectly ordinary household expenditure, with the occasional purchase of clothes. The amounts due on both accounts were cleared each month, by cheque.

Aine explained the tricks and shortcuts as she tiptoed through the electronic tripwires and he quietly hummed.

Step we gaily on we go . . .

Calder's finances were more interesting. He juggled four plastic cards and was near to the borrowing limit on them all. The payments over the past four months had been to cover only the minimum amount necessary. Aine called up a calculator on-screen (Where the hell had she found that?) and worked out that he had more than £30,000 of plastic debt. But this paled into insignificance compared to the mortgages. Three of them – one for the big house, the others for the extensions – for a total of more than £290,000. And there was another interesting figure, a negative one. Calder's clinic had shown a loss of £5,000 in the financial year. And, if that was what he was admitting, what was the real figure?

But, according to his business account, the tide was turning for Calder. A cheque paid in last week for £50,000. Aine said she didn't recognise the sort code (whatever the hell that was). She reckoned it was foreign and, she said, that would be a whole different bag of nuts to crack. The cheque for £20,000, paid in last Friday, was a dawdle. Royal Bank of Scotland, account holder, Sir Ranulf Jedbugh.

Aine stretched back in the chair and let out a sigh of satisfaction.

Then she said, 'My mammy has an expression for the likes of the Carmichaels – fur coat and no knickers.'

Hunter held up a hand for quiet. He was going back over his week. Back to last Thursday, to the marina on Loch Lomond and Sir Ranulf signing a cheque in the cabin at the blunt end. His liver buggered, no longer able to cope with the booze.

Now why would a dying man hand over £20K to a medical clinic?

Then he understood. He phoned Murdo, told him to take a jaunt up to the Royal, have a chat with his new pal Charles, check out if Sir Ranulf was waiting for a transplant.

And then he told Aine to phone her girlfriend, tell her to get a fish supper on the way home, tell her that her new boss was a bastard and there's no way she'd be home before midnight.

Then they really started work.

A great thing, the internet. A library at your fingertips, no need to wade through all the heavy books and none of those itchy wee paper mites. Hunter left Aine to do the donkey work and listened as she got all excited about sites and keywords and search engines. But he directed the traffic.

It was transplants and livers.
Transplants and hearts.
Transplants and blood types.
Transplants and Hubner.

His name had come up when they checked out Calder's plastic card from Sunday. He had paid the bill with it at the Hilton, then another guy had helped the weeping Patrik out to the silver Merc. And, what do you know? The same card had bought two flights to Paris. A single for Patrik and a return for Hubner. The internet had provided nothing useful. A million mentions for some Tally footballer but nothing on a doctor. They had been stumped for a while, then Aine decided to try a different search engine. The Reuters database.

She said, 'It logs newspaper entries from all over the world.'

She keyed in Hubner and pressed the magic button. The Italian footballer had more hits than the Mafia.

Then she refined the search. Hubner and transplants. Half a dozen entries. Worked as a transplant surgeon in the former Soviet Union. Trained in Moscow, moved on to East Berlin, Riga, Tirana, on to Milan. Bingo! Retired from practice two years ago and took the post as personal physician with the world's leading violinist Josef Paborsky.

Hunter said, 'Call up Paborsky on that thing. See what his health's like.'

She boobed, just used Paborsky as a keyword and got more than nine hundred entries.

'Oops,' she said, 'we'll just refine that search a little.'

She entered Paborsky and health. Only one hundred and thirty-seven this time.

She said, 'I suppose when you get to that age health's a constant problem.'

She was trying to wind Hunter up but he didn't bite. Just asked, 'What age is he? Or was he?'

Aine looked stunned. She said, 'Do you think he's dead.'

He said, 'I'm sure of it.'

She said, 'At Busby. He died there?'

'Died, killed, murdered. But one thing at a time. His age.'

She scanned several of the entries and his age was put at anything between fifty-six and seventy-five.

He said, 'Try heart. Paborsky and heart. Type it in.'

Two hundred and forty-eight entries. It appeared, from scanning half a dozen of the most recent newspaper stories, that the maestro's music came straight from the heart.

Hunter said, 'Why are we farting about. Go for heart attack.'

Only eighteen entries – seven of them mentioning a suspected heart attack in Switzerland in 1991 and four reporting a heart attack in New York seven years later.

Hunter had taken a thinking break, shoved his window open and kindled up his pipe. Aine had joined him, perched on the window ledge and lit up a Silk Cut. He'd asked her if the Frankenstein theory fitted, held true with her feelings about Mr and Mrs Weird. She'd nodded her head but added a rider. Said that she wanted them to be guilty so her judgment wouldn't be tainted.

They sat in silence for a few minutes, then she threw her cigarette out of the window, watched it arc down towards the bins. She went back to the computer, back to the internet.

After a minute or so, she said, 'Do you want to know how it's done. I mean, the actual operations. There's a technical piece here.'

Hunter continued to look out of the window. Then asked if there was an idiot's guide.

She said, 'Hardly. We're talking about the ultimate in surgery – the cutting edge, literally.'

He put his pipe on the window ledge. Then said, 'Well, I'm not likely to understand it. Anyway, I know what I need to know.'

'Oh really,' she said, a note of sarcasm in her voice. 'Well, explain it – to an idiot.'

He said, 'It's just a kind of hokey-cokey. You take your old bit out, you put your new bit in – that's what it's all about. It's like a car mechanic but with scalpels instead of spanners. Okay, so Ford and Vauxhall don't do hearts and livers but the theory is the same. You have a listen to the engine, maybe take it for a wee drive, decide what bit's knackered, then take it out and put a new bit in. Attach all the tubes, tighten up the nuts and bolts and add the lubrication. And, just as you can't fit a Mondeo starter motor to a Vectra, you have to be a bit choosy with your organ transplants.'

She said something about him missing his true vocation. She was on the net, keying in Inspector Sandy Hunter, just for fun. Well what do you know? An entry today, on the Strangelove murders, and the man who had solved them.

'Sacré bleu,' she said. 'But the man's big in Paris.'

Hunter was only half-listening. He was thinking back to a TV programme, one of the big drug companies ripping off the National Health Service for treatment for transplant patients. What was it? Something to stop the body's defences attacking the new organ, to fool the immune system. Immunosuppressants, that was it.

Aine said, 'Listen to this, it's from today's edition of *Le Monde*. Tell me when you recognise someone.'

She put on a voice like a newsreader, 'He's a loose cannon, a throwback to the time when policemen were above the law. He's more at home with the thugs he arrests than the authorities who lock them up. His dress sense makes Colombo look like a fashion model. But an animal cunning separates . . .

'Come on,' she said, 'you're supposed to guess.'

He said, 'I don't know any Froggie coppers.'

'Guess. And he's not French.'

He said, 'Poirot.'

'Wrong,' she said. 'Try Hunter. Inspector, Sandy.'

291

She turned the screen round so he could read it.

He said, 'Bruno, you bastard. You stitched me up.'

She said, 'It's not bad, actually. The bit about Colombo's out of date, though. He can't have seen the executive suit. Where did you say you got it?'

He said, 'I didn't. Now, playtime's over. Back to work. Tell me things I don't know.'

She thought for a bit, then asked, earnestly, 'Do you honestly think they could do it in Busby? Do transplants? How would they get the equipment, for one thing?'

He answered with one word.

'Money.'

Then added, 'If you've got enough, it'll buy anything. It'll buy a kidney and it'll buy a man.'

Or four or five men. He thought of the four who had confronted Boyson at the Carmichaels' empire on Tuesday. The same four who had breathed life back into Calder when Boyson thought he was a deader.

He spoke his thoughts out loud, 'And that place has taken in seventy grand in the past week.'

The more he found out the more he was convinced that was what was going on behind the posh metal name plates at Chateau Carmichael. It all fitted.

Murdo phoned from the Royal Infirmary. Surprise, surprise, Sir Ranulf's liver was on its last legs, so to speak. He had his own dialysis machine and full-time nurse at home.

Murdo said, 'He's on the transplant list all right – has been for eighteen months – but the problem is that he has a rare blood group, so finding a match is extremely unlikely.'

Hunter gave Murdo and his new pal another task. Hush-hush – asking questions only of computers so as not to alert any human beings. He wanted to know about immunosuppressants – whether any had gone missing, if any surgical unit had been ordering a lot recently.

He hung up and answered before Aine could ask.

He said, 'I remembered from a TV documentary. Drug companies running a cartel, setting their own prices. There was a wee girl, just about five, down in England who got a heart transplant. The operation went well, but she couldn't cope with the immunosuppressants. Seems that the body treats a transplanted organ like an invader. Starts to attack it. And the immunosuppressants kind of switch off the body's natural defence mechanisms. But the wee soul couldn't cope with the tug of war inside her and she died anyway.'

Aine thought about it. Working it through. But something was worrying her. Something didn't quite fit in.

She said, 'Okay, it's all possible. Far-fetched but possible. So – stop me if I'm way off beam – but we're building up all this circumstantial evidence.'

Hunter nodded in agreement.

She continued, 'But we don't have anything concrete. That's the wrong word, I know, but do you think we could get a search warrant?'

Hunter said no but told her to continue thinking out loud.

She said, 'Okay, we want a witness but we're not going to get one. Right? Because any witnesses must be involved in it and so open to charges themselves. What would the charge be, incidentally?'

He said, 'Murder.'

'Can you believe this? There are people in poor countries who sell their organs. Can you imagine that?'

Aine was on the Reuters website, reading about transplants and third world countries. 'Your family's starving and you've got two kidneys so you sell one.'

Hunter said, 'But you've only got one heart. One liver.'

She admitted that there was a flaw in her theory. Then he told her how it was done. How Zara's refugees' charities were lauded because of the extensive health checks they carried out.

She caught on quickly. 'So they know the blood types, tissue matches. It's like Marks and Spencer – that easy? Just take the waist size and leg length off the shelf. But Rupert or Rudolf or whatever his posh name is can't get one to fit.'

Then the full implications hit her.

'So they . . . kill people.'

Hunter nodded his head.

She said, 'Are you sure? Are they capable of that – how can you know that?'

He strolled over to the window. Took his time lighting his pipe. Then he told her. Just said it, by the way.

'They tried to kill me. A bit of a drastic measure, so it shows I was getting too close to . . .'

She said, 'Hold it right there. You did say they tried to kill you?'

He said, 'Yes and no. The charge would be complicity to commit murder.'

She said, 'Would be? You mean the bloody charge is . . .'

He told her to shoosh. Told her just to listen.

He said, 'I wasn't aware of it, of course, but I was getting too close to their secrets. And they panicked. Or one of them did. Anyway, they got a third party to approach a certain well-known figure in the criminal fraternity – let's call him Danny Boyle – and asked him to arrange the early departure from this world of yours truly.'

She interrupted again. Couldn't stop herself.

'When was this?'

He said, 'Monday, I think.'

'You think! What did the Chief Constable . . .'

He hushed her again. Told her there was no danger now.

She said, 'So we go for the guy they used – the go-between – to set up the contract on you. Do a deal with him if we have to. And that gets us the warrant to get into their transplant unit.'

He said, 'No can do. Remember the fire at the wee place outside East Kilbride. Guy fried in highly suss circumstances?'

She said, 'It was him?'

He said, 'The very man. Do you remember what he did for a living.'

Her eyes opened wide. 'Pet crematorium. He burned the bodies. They took hearts and livers out of living bodies and he burned the evidence. Then they burned him. Oh, my God! Then there's nothing we can do.'

He chided her for such negative thinking. Said that, where there's life, there's hope. Told her to go for lunch, take her girlfriend out, put it on her eccies. Then he headed for the door.

She asked, as a child would, 'Can't I come?'

He told her no. This was something he had to do alone.

Still without wheels, Hunter headed for the garage to take a car out of the pool. The zippy wee Peugeot wouldn't go with the image and the dark blue Rover had unhappy memories of Lisa's mum's tears. Then he saw just the job. Keys still in the ignition, too. It started up like an old tractor, drove like one too. And, he thought, in a strange way, it matched the new suit.

It had been a mistake. He could see that, was perfectly willing to admit it. But, Jesus H, he thought the police helicopter was over the top.

Hunter had driven to Busby and been pleased to see the matching silver Mercs in the forecourt of Chateau Carmichael. So he'd driven in there, burled the van around and picked a nice spot. Parked at an angle, so they could see the signwriting on the side of the van but not his face. He kept the diesel engine running, then leant on the horn.

Only Zara came out of the big house. He watched in the mirror. Front door opened at a rate of knots, she stamps out with her Mrs Angry face on, then stops as if she'd hit a glass wall.

Old black van, sooty from its master's fire, 'PET CREMATORIUM' writ large in gold letters.

It was Stephen King meets Hitchcock.

Then a little smile appeared on Zara's face. Of course, Hunter could never prove it. And it would be laughed out of court.

So, Mr Hunter, you were looking in a wing mirror, through smoky, dark-tinted glass, over a distance of ten metres, and you say you detected a smile. Might that have been a look of shock. Horror and disgust, even?

But it had been a sleekit, wee smirk. It had only lived for a second or so, because Zara had turned around then and run screaming into the big house. He had taken his hand off the horn and lit up his pipe. Quite apt, he had thought, to have a stream of smoke escape through the open inch of driver's door window. Decent smoke it had been, too. The meerschaum, filled, after he had liberated Jed's van from the evidence compound, and just burned in on the drive out.

The helicopter was first to arrive. Buzzing like an angry wasp, it circled a couple of times, a bit wary. It took a sweep across the park and approached with caution. Giving wee jinks, swerves left and right, like a boxer feinting a jab, trying to draw an opponent's lead. Then it settled about thirty feet above the hawthorn hedges, guarding the entrance (or was it the exit?) at the Carmichael empire, with a pointy-down nose like a playful Labrador puppy.

Hunter had been surprised to see it, then angry, then felt okay about things. It had to have been Aine. She wouldn't have volunteered the information – wouldn't have clyped. But someone must have squeezed her. The Jug, maybe even James Smith. Asked where he was, what he was doing. Then, if she had remained faithful (and he had every reason to believe that she had), ordered her to tell.

The first police car was on the scene within four minutes. It screeched to a halt across the drive. The driver opened his door and tumbled out like a stunt man. Then he did a creepy-crawly away into the hawthorn bushes. The chopper lifted a little in the air then but still kept its snout down on the scent of its prey.

Hunter thought it looked daft from this angle. Overkill, like a bad movie where the director has demanded a lot of action. And there was more to come.

Six other police cars arrived before the ambulance. And then The Jug turned up, James Smith in the back seat too and Digger driving. It was at this point that Hunter saw the armed response team. Protective armour and rifles. And he thought, 'Fuck this for a game of soldiers.'

He switched off the old diesel engine, opened the door and made to get out. Some numpty was barking orders though a loudhailer. It was one of those slow-motion moments, like when a car crash is inevitable and there's sod-all you can do about it and God, in mischievous mode, presses the slo-mo button to give you time to put your head between your knees and kiss your arse goodbye.

'Put your hands on your head.'

That's what the copper was saying.

'Put your hands on your head.'

Getting a bit ratty too. Hunter hopes that the guy puts his hands on his head because this copper is struggling to keep the panic out of his voice.

Then somebody's calling his name.

'Sandy. Sa-andy.'

As if he's shouting on a puppy.

'Saan-daay.'

It's Digger and he's walking over. The Jug's telling him to come back.

'Now. That's an order, Sergeant.'

Digger's ignoring him. Only three or four yards away now. There's a metallic, slidey sound. Like a rifle being primed. Then Digger says, sorry, sorry about this. And, next thing you know, your arm's halfway up your back and your face is up against the driver's door window and you can taste the smoke and soot from it.

Then all hell breaks loose.

Zara had heard the car horn and immediately thought there had been a crash. She might even have said it out loud – she couldn't remember. It's funny how a notion just jumps into your mind and the image is so strong that it becomes reality. But, before she left the room, she was sure she could see the car upside down, at the bend at the foot of the hill, its front wheels still spinning, a tongue of flame starting to lick at the engine.

Clive is in Calder's bedroom, too, telling her to ignore the noise. Saying they had more important things to do. Pointing to Calder's body, still in the wheelbarrow they had used to bring it from the high-dependency unit. Clive saying they shouldn't attract attention – couldn't run the risk of anyone coming into the big house. Not now. Not when she was so close to starting another life.

But she'd said that she could not ignore it. She had a position now. It would look bad in the press if she ignored it. She was, after all, a leader, appointed by the Prime Minister himself. But Clive couldn't see it. Couldn't see the big picture. A great brain but such narrow vision.

Zara had gone out alone and been confronted by Jed's Pet Crem van. Quite a shock it had been, too. But she'd held it together. Kept her nerve. Junkie Jed had been no match for her in flesh and blood and his ghost certainly was not about to scare her off.

Then she had smelled him. The infernal policeman, Hunter. Smelled the smoke from his stinking pipe, saw through his stupid little ploy. Did he really think he could fool her with such an obvious trick?

Then she saw the way to get him out of her life for ever. She had gone back into the house, locked the door and dialled 999. Clive tried to stop her but she held his hand to reassure him.

'Leave it to me. Leave it to Zara. Zara knows exactly what she's doing.'

The 999 woman saying, 'Emergency, which service, please?'

Zara saying, 'He's killed him, he's finally done it. He's killed Calder.'

The 999 woman telling her to calm down. Quiet, authoritative voice. Asking for her name and address.

Zara telling her. Then saying, 'Sorry, I'll have to go. But, please, please, send an ambulance.'

Then hanging up.

Still holding Clive's hand. Leading him by the hand back to Calder's bedroom. Talking quietly, reassuring him, soothing him. Clive tugging, now, reluctant. Telling him that it's all right. It's fine. It'll all be fine.

'Just trust me. Trust Zara. Please, Clive, I need you. I need you again. Help me do this. I always relied on you, Clive. Just this one more thing then we're free.'

And he lifts Calder under the arms and she takes his feet and they stumble slowly and awkwardly because neither of them is strong but they keep on, Clive walking backwards and Zara kind of steering, left leg down a bit, towards the front of the house.

The phone's ringing but she ignores it.

Into the front room over towards the window. The curtains still drawn. And she says now, Clive, let him go now, but Clive is reluctant.

And she says, 'Please, Clive, trust me in this, we can't hurt him now, can we?'

And Clive lets go and Calder falls head first on to the pitch-pine floorboards.

Zara tells Clive to get the wheelbarrow, take it out the back, then remove all trace of it from the house. Shake up the rugs. Remove the wheel marks. Clive is crying but he does as he is told. Then Zara runs to the phone, practises her sobbing before she picks up to talk to the 999 woman. Then she lifts the handset and gives the performance of her life. The distraught wife, the new widow, showing a restrained dignity, but unable to stifle the odd sob. But thanking the 999 woman, asking when the ambulance will come and throwing in a few oh Calders and oh my darlings.

Just for the tape.

They took Hunter to one of his own cells. Read him his effin rights, then took away his belt and his shoelaces and banged him up. Told the boys not to talk to him. Left him for more than two hours till the police federation lawyer, a sharp cookie called Angela, turned up. Then they charged him with taking and driving away a vehicle, interfering with evidence and obstructing police officers in the course of their duties. Told him that further, more serious charges would be put to him at a later date. These were likely to include the police harassment of Ms Zara Carmichael and the culpable homicide of Mr Calder Carmichael.

Angela told him to say no comment to anything. He simply collected his possessions from the Duty Sergeant, then turned to face Chief Constable Tobias Fastnett and Assistant Chief Constable James Smith. They took him straight back to the interview room to tell him that he was suspended from duty with immediate effect. They told him to have no contact with any serving police officer and to take no part in any active police investigation. Then they took the keys to his desk and office, and his warrant card.

The Jug then took a delight in telling him he was free to go.

12

Hunter had rummaged among the rubbish and retrieved Friday's *Herald*, the one with the job adverts. Bella said she would get it, she knew where it was – in a Safeway's bag at the back of the wheelie-bin – and it would be easier, but he said, no, it's okay, I'm doing nothing else anyway. Tacked on a wee smile to let her see it was a joke. They'd been doing that, walking on eggshells, overly polite, careful not to create friction.

A job on the front page of the appointments section caught his eye right away. Fraud manager in the council's housing and property services department, salary £24.5–26.8K. About £500 a week, can't be bad. He realised that he didn't know how much he earned at the moment. Bella could tell him, of course, but best not to ask her. Eggshells and that.

The job was to run a benefits fraud squad.

Good, he thought, I can do that. Could probably teach them a few dodges.

And something called the verification framework team.

Fine, tell me what it is and I can do that too.

A proactive approach was required to fraud prevention and detection.

No sweat – just suss out the crooks and lean on them. Proactive is my middle name. Retaliate first.

PINS accreditation was required.

I can finesse that. Just say pins, sure, got two of them, left and right, but isn't it a bit monopedist? Got to be careful not to upset the politically-correct police but I won't tell if you don't tell.

They kept the hard ones till the end, though. The successful applicant will be computer literate on mainframe and PC systems.

Literate? Don't even know what they are.

Next ad.

Part-timers needed who want to earn over £20 an hour. Self-motivated.

No question about it.

Ambitious.

Could bullshit that.

Four days a week.

What, every week? Only joking, that'll be no problem.

Working between 6 p.m. and 8 p.m.

Hang on, that's eight hours, £160 a week. They want ambition for that? Jesus H, look who it is. The *Evening Times*, wanting folk to join its highly successful home delivery door-to-door canvassing operation. Knock, knock. Who's there? *Evening Times*. *Evening Times* who? *Evening Times* they are a-changin.

Next ad.

But there wasn't a next. Everybody wanted qualifications and nobody was crying out for a middle-aged copper who had blotted his copybook.

Bloody newspapers. Nothing in them. Settle for that today, though. Not a line in the Sundays about his suspension. He'd been prepared for the top cop shock in the tabloids. The broadsheets, a little more subdued, better informed, going along the lines of senior policeman suspected of killing tsarina's husband. He'd told Bella to expect it. But there wasn't a dicky-bird. The dailies would be on to it tomorrow. Had to be. Probably working on it just now, getting the gen, digging the dirt, drawing straws to see who would call him later for a comment. He'd wondered about phoning one of them, maybe the nice lass on Radio Clyde, giving her the inside track, trying to spike the guns of the big boys. It was the sensible thing to do. He'd have done it for Digger. But it was different when it was yourself.

Bella had been great about it. Said if it happens, it happens. He'd given her the worst case scenario, too, though he didn't believe it for a moment. But he'd warned her, all the same, that he could get the jail, the pension would be down the swannee and it would do no good at all to his chances of getting an OBE in the New Year's Honours list.

She had smiled at that and told him not to worry. Hadn't that new Chief Constable been out to get him for a couple of years now? And, even if he managed it this time, well, they hadn't starved a winter yet, had they?

He'd said that it could make things difficult with the Coffee Girls and she'd looked a bit surprised at that. Then said that they would understand, they'd stand by her. And anyone who didn't was, well, . . . she would be better off without them anyway.

He'd told her about the Vectra, too. Why not? Might as well get all the bad news over and done with. She'd told him not to worry about it, that was what insurance was for, then, God bless her wee cotton socks, she'd disappeared, saying she had something to do.

The phone rang and he ignored it again. Hadn't even listened to the messages. And he'd switched his mobile off. It wasn't the phone, though, it was the doorbell. And the caller was most insistent. It was one of the guys from the mortuary, civil fella with a crap job. Hosed down all the blood and guts when the doctors in death had done their worst. The guy said he wouldn't come in, bit of a hurry and that, just wanted to tip him the wink. The post mortem on Calder Carmichael had thrown up something funny. He'd eariewigged while they were bumping their gums. Seemed that the guy had been dead for longer than his missus had said. And the death docs were very interested in marks on the body's thighs and upper back. Said it was as if it had been carted about in a wheelbarrow.

'Hope that's good news for you,' the fella said.

Hunter said, 'Yeah, yeah, I think so, anyway.'

Asked the guy if he wouldn't take a drink, just one for the road. But he refused.

Hunter said, 'But tell me this and tell me no more. How did you know I was in the shit.'

The guy explained that the top brass, the English plonker, had gone on about it.

'Said that he never thought he'd see the day when one of his officers faced a murder charge. Well, my lugs cocked up at that. They never see me, just ignore me, so you can hear all kinds of good gossip. Anyway, the English guy said that it probably wouldn't be murder, more likely culp hom or something, then he mentioned your name.'

The guy looked a bit embarrassed. Didn't want to repeat exactly what had been said but Hunter said he'd probably heard worse, just to spit it out.

The guy continued, 'Well, he said that, if any policeman had to face the disgrace, he couldn't think of anyone more suitable than Sandy Hunter.'

Hunter thanked him. Said the gen was helpful. It had taken a weight off his mind.

The guy looked pleased. He said, 'I'm for the off then. One good turn deserves another.'

That had puzzled Hunter. Till the guy explained that his nephew shared his trade.

'Shooey,' he said, 'the sister's boy. You sorted him out, Mr Hunter. He's never looked back since he got the job at the mortuary at the Royal.'

The phone in the hall rang so Hunter thanked the guy and said goodbye. He answered the phone this time and was relieved to hear Celine's voice. She said she would phone Bella later. He pressed 1571 and listened to his messages. Digger, wanting to know if there was anything he could do. Aine, telling him to phone her and to switch on his mobile. Murdo, saying this episode would make a great chapter in Hunter's autobiography and would he please remember the nice teuchter when he was Chief Constable. Aine again, telling him to bloodywell phone her. Digger again, saying he'd try to get him tonight, just before 6 p.m. Finally Aine, saying, if he didn't phone her, she would bring all her lesbian friends round to his lawn for a barbecue and love-in.

'And,' she said, 'we'll bring our own sausages.'

The doorbell rang again. It was James Smith, in his Sunday best – a big Shetland sweater and a pair of denims. He stood in the hall, said that he couldn't stay. Just wanted him to know on the q. t. that Carmichael had been dead for some time before the 'incident' with the Pet Crem van.

Hunter was tempted to say yeah, I know, but didn't. The Assistant Chief Constable was breaking the rules by telling him, facing the wrath of The Jug himself.

Smith said that there were other suspicious circumstances surrounding the death. But he didn't elaborate and Hunter didn't ask. Smith said that he had persuaded the Chief Constable that Hunter was due time off and was, therefore, to be considered to be on holiday.

He said, 'Of course, Sandy, you're still suspended from duty. There's still to be an internal inquiry. So, take it easy. Take a rest. It'll work itself out. Just give it a chance.'

He was out the back, looking at the flatpack conservatory. Seemed just the biz. Double glazing, white, plasticky frames. It would even match the house windows. He must have put the fear of God into the wee Irish guy. And that was just as well. Could be that he would get paid out of the lump sum from the pension of former Inspector Sandy Hunter. The frames were already bored with holes to take nuts and bolts to hold it together.

A glint of sunlight on the glass caught his eye. What could that be? Surely not? It bliddywell was. A crack in the glass, just a hair's breadth, but a definite crack. Aye, well, if he thinks he can palm shoddy goods off on The Hunter, he had another thing coming.

'Can you see it, eh?

It was Bella. She said, 'Can you just picture it up here, catching the afternoon sun? It'll be lovely, just you wait and see.'

Then she said, 'Why don't you make the most of your time off. Go to the golf or the bools.'

She let him think on it for a moment or two. Then she threw him a set of car keys.

* * * * *

Hunter's got the clubs in the boot of the new Vectra and he's driving out of Newton Mearns heading for the golf club. Nice car, less than 3,000 miles on the clock and more gadgets than you could shake a stick at. Bella had taken care of the car insurance, of course. Gone for top of the range, everything covered except your bald spot and a car thrown in until your own wheels were repaired or the claim was settled. No need to accept the first offer, then. Or second or third for that matter.

At the turn-off for the golf club now and Hunter drives past it. His heart wasn't in it. Not even for a pint and a listen to the chat. He was a different person at the golf, a quiet man, quite content to remain on the fringes and let others direct the traffic. But today he didn't feel that he deserved it. He had done nothing to earn the leisure time.

He took a left, over the moor, and just followed the bonnet of the car. Hands doing the driving and his brain in neutral. Fifteen minutes later was surprised to find himself on the road to Jed's Pet Crematorium. He was a good boy, though, drove straight past it and soon saw the hand-painted sign at the road-end – 'People in Class Houses'. He drove up the rutted road. Decided to take a crack at the wee Irish guy. There were no cars at the top of the road. The display units had gone. And the Portacabin which the wee shite had used as an office had been emptied.

Yer man had done a moonlight flit. So it looked like a free conservatory for Bella – with one pain in the glass.

Back at the bottom of the road, Hunter waited for one car to pass. A familiar car, a Fiesta, with Digger driving. Hunter nipped out sharpish, flashing his lights and giving the occasional, restrained wee toot on the horn. Digger recognised him, stopped the car and got out. His hand went to his jacket pocket and brought out an evidence bag.

He said, 'What do you think?'

Hunter said, 'I think you shouldn't be here. It's the kind of thing that got me in the shit, remember?'

Digger said that he'd been at a loose end. Just out for a drive . . .

Hunter took the clear, polythene bag and had a shuftie. Then said, 'It's the tooth but not the whole tooth.'

Digger said, 'Exactly. So what's missing?'

Hunter said, 'Apart from my job?'

Digger said, 'Seriously. What's missing?'

Hunter looked at the bag more carefully. It contained a molar, blackened as if it had been in a fire and he knew then where Digger had got it. But he couldn't see the significance. Digger had to point it out.

'You see here, the inside, see the hole? It's not rotted, not caused by decay. It's been drilled. The filling's missing. And how many dogs do you know with fillings?'

Hunter said, 'Well, there's The Jug's wife . . .'

Hunter in the coffee shop of a garden centre on the outskirts of East Kilbride, eating a treacle scone, sipping a cappuccino and thinking about fillings. Good man, Digger. Hunter had told him yesterday that he thought Jed had been burning more than bunny rabbits in his incinerator. Hadn't gone into any details, just said it was a hunch, that was all. And Digger had shelved all his own work to follow it up. Gone out to the Pet Crem, tied his hanky round his nose and mouth and poked about the ashes with a stick. Found a number of teeth and took one, left the others in situ. No bliddy good in a court of law, though. No coppers at the crime scene. Pollock or Pillock or Bollocks had waited till Jed's body was removed, all black and crispy, then shut up shop. Not a bliddy cop in sight. So Digger's work was all for nothing. Unless they could work a wee fiddle . . . He knew the very girl to do it, too. His mobile played its annoying wee tune. He knew it was Aine before he heard her voice. But he couldn't, in a month of Sundays, have guessed what she had to tell him. Another dead man, a macabre sexual death and the body found at the exact same spot where Toshie had breathed his last.

He strolled around the garden centre – just another guy passing the time, swithering over a box of winter pansies, wondering if the ornamental cabbages were worth the dosh. Could be at that. Might keep the slugs off the path. Bella had gone her length last December, arse over tip, after skiting on a slug that the frost had welded to the slabs. There was no serious damage, neither to path nor Bella because, over the years, she had acquired a considerable amount of padding to reduce the impact of such an eventuality. But she'd gone her dinger nonetheless.

It was his fault, of course, the other men had scraped their paths clear and put down salt or grit. He'd said sorry, he'd do it right away and offered to kiss her bum better. She had declined, which was just as well because it would have been a big job and he was in a bit of a hurry.

He picked up six of the pinky-purple cabbages, then put one back, remembering the TV programme where they said that you should always plant odd numbers. It must have been *Groundforce* (it was the only one he watched) because it had the big ginger-haired bint who didn't wear a bra. They never missed the opportunity of filming her in the rain, to show where she kept her dibbers. Could've dangled a couple of hanging baskets on them.

He was at the fruit trees, trying to negotiate safe passage between two grannies with toddlers in buggies, when it all fell into place. The death was connected to Lisa, of course. But it wasn't a murder. Not a twisted copycat killer. It was a sacrifice or a penance. The man had cut off his penis and he had bled to death. And, for once in his life, the bastard had done the decent thing.

Hunter phoned Aine, asked who was there from SOCO and got a good result. An old pro, a good guy, so he had a quiet word with him. It was an unusual request but he agreed to fingerprint the body in situ. Then Hunter told Aine to run the prints through the computer. And he told her which name to check first.

Onions frying and death. Hamburgers and hot dogs, at Paddy's Market, and cold bodies in the mortuary.

Hunter skulked in the shadows at the rear of the morgue, like a defrocked priest pressing his ear to the confessional. He could not do the job himself but he had to be close. Then, if it all went wrong, he could claim responsibility. Say the police officers were acting on his instructions. What more could they do to him?

The fingerprints had been a gamble but it had paid off. Two convictions, many moons ago. The first was run-of-the-mill – a £25 fine for fighting in a posh Aberdeen hotel after he'd come off the rigs where he was working as a welder. The other was more interesting. He had taken a hammer to the statue of the Virgin and Child at the church in Easterhouse. Such deviant desecration earned him twenty-eight days in the Bar-L. Aine matched the dabs. Peter O'Donnell, once of this parish.

Hunter saw the car arrive. Digger getting out, walking round to the passenger's side, considerately opening the door. The young woman getting out, her face deep in the collar of her coat. A bright red coat.

All the better to hide you with.

They paused for a few seconds, just to draw breath, to steel themselves for what they had to do. Then, head bowed, they disappeared through the cold doorway to do their duty.

Only one guy working in the mortuary, waiting for them. Digger had phoned earlier. Told him what to expect.

'The young woman's had a hellish time. Identified the body of her sister on Friday and back today to see her father.'

And what a death he had chosen. Hacked off his dick with a bread knife. The guy hoped that the dad had been mad. Better that than to think about the sins that compelled him to end his life in such a way.

He showed them to the viewing room, then went to get the body. He wheeled it to the widow, removed the sheet from the face, pulled open the curtains, then stepped aside. The lassie hardly lifted her head. He heard the copper say the legal words, for the record, and the lassie confirming that it was the body of her father.

The guy closed the curtains, waited a minute or so, hoping that they would leave. Then slid the body back on to its icy shelf. When he returned to the room, they had gone. The copper and Little Red Riding Hood.

They had agreed to meet up in The Mire. Aine had shed the big red coat. Digger said that his wife wouldn't even know that he'd borrowed it.

Hunter was waiting for them, with what looked suspiciously like a pint of lager shandy.

Aine said, 'On the wagon?'

He tried to smile but failed. He ordered drinks – a pint of beer for Digger and a Bacardi Breezer for Aine. They sat at a table in a quiet corner by the door, then he asked them how it had gone.

Digger said that he had been right about Louise O'Donnell. She wasn't answering her phone and the handful of journalists camped outside her Gorbals flat had said that there had been no sign of life all day. They reckoned the *Record* had spirited her away. Put her up in a hotel so none of the hacks could outbid them for the next instalment of her story. One of them had asked about the death in the Merchant City. Anything in it?

Aine said, 'You'd have been proud of him. He said it was just a lowlife. How'd you put it?'

She turned to Digger, then continued, 'Oh yeah, you said it might be the hundredth junkie of the year and that took the lead out of their pencils.'

Hunter said, 'And the mortuary? No probs?'

Digger said, 'No. Just as you said. The bloke didn't give her a second glance.'

Aine flicked her long black hair à la filmstar.

It was Digger who mentioned Mrs O'Donnell. Said she'd have to be told. Hunter told him not to worry about it. He'd take care of that. Peter O'Donnell would be buried in a pauper's grave. He would be neither missed nor mourned.

They sat for a bit, sipping their drinks. Then Aine said, 'Well, I've got news. And you'll want to hear it.'

Hunter shooshed her, said he had orders and said she wouldn't want to hear them.

The plan was straightforward. She was to find Josef Paborsky's dentist. He might be anywhere on the planet but how hard could that be with her electronic skills and the World Wide Web? What was really needed was the pictures, x-rays or something, so they could match them up with the debris from Jed's incinerator.

That was where Murdo came in. He had to get a hold of Pollock's SOCO officer, the good guy, the one who wore white gloves at the scene of a fire. They would empty out Jed's furnace. Bagging everything, ashes and all. The SOCO guy would know what to do. He was a pro.

Digger would coordinate the operation. Give Smith a bell at home. Get permission.

Aine said, 'My turn now?'

Hunter nodded.

She started with a confession. 'I've been reading your e-mail.'

Hunter said fine, he didn't know how to drive it anyway.

She said, 'Listen. You'll want to hear this. Do you know where to put your hands on your passport?'

Hunter had made up his mind that he would go back in the springtime, take Bella and she would love it. He had spent little more than an hour in Paris and had not set foot outside the airport. Just time to meet up with his man, buy Bella some perfume, have a beer (though it tasted more like lager) and get back on the plane again.

The fasten seatbelt sign was on. They would be touching down in Glasgow in five minutes or so. Hunter and poor Patrik, the broken-hearted partner of Josef Paborsky. The little man who would humble the mighty.

He had told Hunter his story in Charles de Gaulle airport. He was afraid but he had his passport with him. He was ready to return to Glasgow and he was willing to tell the truth.

He had begged Josef not to go through with the transplant operation. Josef had said that it was his last chance. They had a heart, a perfect match, and Hubner would supplement Calder Carmichael's team. But Josef had refused to say how they got the heart. They had argued. Patrik had told him it was wrong, immoral. His last words to the lover he adored were, 'It's nothing short of murder.'

Patrik had seen Bruno's story in *Le Monde*. Said he had liked the bit about Colombo, the man who did not fit in, a man who was not afraid to face up to the authorities. He had also seen the story about Zara Carmichael, the Prime Minister's new ambassador for asylum seekers – the refugees' tsarina. And he had gone to an internet café and e-mailed The Hunter.

307

They had jumped in a taxi at the airport and Hunter had told the driver to take them to the copshop. But he'd changed his mind halfway there and asked the guy to take them home.

Bella's heart had gone out to Patrik. A maternal thing (though he was at least ten years older than her) and pretty soon she was giving him a wee cuddle and a large whisky.

She had told Hunter that the phone had been red hot. Digger, Aine and Murdo. He decided not to call them tonight. He wanted to see their faces when he told them he had cracked it.

A D-notice, a legal gag, had been taken out by the Lord Advocate himself. It had been served upon all members of the media, instructing them that nothing could be published or broadcast about Ms Zara Carmichael, her late husband, Calder, or any matter associated with their medical practices at their premises in Busby, near Glasgow.

Tobias Fastnett had been called to Edinburgh to meet lawyers representing the Lord Advocate. He had been left in no doubt that any inquiries into the Carmichaels and their empire had to be terminated forthwith. It was a matter of state security, they said, and would be protected as such. Meanwhile, Special Branch officers had descended on police headquarters in Glasgow and removed all records, including computers and disks, which might have been used in inquiries into the Carmichaels. Furthermore, all police personnel who had had any dealings with any matter concerning the Carmichaels had to sign the Official Secrets Act immediately and be made fully aware of its legal constraints and the dire consequences of contravening it.

Just when Hunter thought he had the upper hand, Zara had played her ace. All he had to do now was work out how to trump the Prime Minister.

The story had first run in Iraq, Libya and China. Countries which had no love for the United Kingdom. It had been picked up in Russia, Afghanistan, Italy and France. Sky News had broadcast it in Europe. And TV stations in the US had taken it from there. Several of the Prime Minister's back bench MPs made it known that they intended to raise questions in the House of Commons, where absolute privilege enables the UK media to report the proceedings.

A sleek, black limousine had drawn up at Sandy Hunter's door and the Lord Advocate had got out. He wanted the answers to three questions:

Did Inspector Hunter have sufficient evidence to bring a case against

Zara Carmichael and others for what he called 'the goings on' at the premises in Busby?

He did.

Was Inspector Hunter in a position to press charges?

He was.

And, finally, did Inspector Hunter know how the reports had appeared on the internet?

'How could I know?' Hunter said. 'Ask anyone, I'm a Luddite – a right bliddy dinosaur.'

EPILOGUE

The seven surviving members of the Busby transplant team had been taken into custody that night. Three were arrested at the Carmichaels' big house – Zara, Clive and Hubner. Police in England swooped at the same time and apprehended the three so-called Ramblers – Ramsay, Black and Erskine. Sørensen, the anaesthetist, was taken into custody from his home in Bearsden, in the north side of the city.

They had appeared in court the following day on a number of charges, the most serious of which was murder, and had been remanded in custody.

Only Clive had offered information. He had given detailed statements which would convict each and every one of them. He had gone back to Busby with Hunter, removed the loose floorboard in his bedroom and handed over the Polaroid picture Zara had taken during the heart transplant operation on Josef Paborsky. Clive had then shown police where to dig beneath the willows at the bottom of the garden in Busby and the body of The Skunk had been recovered.

Sørensen's half-brother, whose kidney transplant was the first and only successful operation, had been traced to the south of Spain. Extradition proceedings were under way and he was due to arrive in Scotland in time for the trial date which had been arranged early in the new year.

Clive had given full details of how he cut up the bodies of the people the Carmichaels called donors – NM_2, neither missed nor mourned – and how Jed had taken away the black bin liners and burned their contents at his Pet Crematorium. Five human teeth had been removed from the incinerator but they had been badly burned and none could be linked to Josef Paborsky.

Patrik's statement was not as detailed as Clive's but, in the case of Paborsky's murder, it was equally damning.

Patrik had returned to Paris, to live with his sister.

Hunter had gone to see Sir Ranulf Jedburgh in his home overlooking the Firth of Clyde. He had given Sir Ranulf a bottle of malt whisky and told him to do the decent thing. The next morning, Sir Ranulf was found dead in his bed. The cause of death was liver failure.

The Prime Minister had washed his hands of his new champion for asylum seekers. The *Sun*'s front-page headline read, 'Tsarina Zara Loses her Tiara'.

Clive had also spoken freely about the illegal activities at Zara's little enterprise. He knew that babies had been bought from refugees in this country and also smuggled in from abroad. But he could provide no proof – nor could any be found at Zara's clinic. No charges had been brought but the file remained open.

The one remaining patient in Calder Carmichael's clinic had been liberated on that first night. Matthew Whittle, the boy who could remember his dreams, had been taken by ambulance to a hospital on the outskirts of Edinburgh. He had undergone extensive medical examinations which showed a high level of illegal drugs in his bloodstream. It was also established that he had the same blood and tissue as Calder Carmichael and would have been a suitable donor for a heart transplant. Matthew's physical health had improved but his mental health was a major cause of concern. He would remain in care for the foreseeable future.

Calder Carmichael's body was cremated six days after it was found in the front room in Busby. The procurator fiscal had noted irregularities in the circumstances leading to its discovery, but the cause of death had been established as coronary thrombosis.

Zara and Clive, under separate police escorts, were allowed to attend the service. Hunter was there too. As the curtains closed on the coffin, he said three silent words.

'God damn you.'

The body of Lisa O'Donnell was buried seven days after she killed herself. There were only five mourners. Her mother, Hunter, Digger, Aine and Murdo. Hunter had already asked God's forgiveness for Lisa but he did so again. In her will, Lisa left £10,000 to her mother and £10,000 to her sister. The remainder of her estate, which would amount to more than £180,000 after the sale of her flat and investments, she left to the anti-abortion charity, The Innocents.

Three days after he took his own life, Peter O'Donnell's body was put in a pauper's grave as darkness was falling. No words were said over him. No marker was erected.

Simon is on sick leave from the Royal Infirmary. He cannot sleep. When he closes his eyes he smells chloroform and remembers Lisa overpowering him. When he opens his eyes he sees the syringe but he can never remember what she did with it. He thinks that he knows. He found the puncture mark and little bruise on his left buttock. He had gone to the phone a hundred times but never made the call. He was entitled to ask and they would have done it for him. Taken a sample of Lisa's blood and tested it for AIDs.

There are two phials of morphine in his fridge. He has taken them out a hundred times. One day, when his anguish becomes too much to bear, he will not put them back.

Tobias Fastnett is still Chief Constable of Strathclyde Police. He was not appointed Commissioner of the Metropolitan Police. He was not even interviewed for the post.

The Hunters have a new car. Not brand new but a new second-hand car. It is a small Peugeot with a soft-top. Bella is not fond of it but did not want to make a fuss, even though the roof leaks a bit. Sandy had, after all, paid for the conservatory out of his own pocket money and then the company had gone out of business.

They employed a local firm to construct the conservatory. The project was not straightforward. The first problem arose when it was discovered that the holes drilled in the frames to take bolts to attach one to another did not match up. As new holes were drilled, some panes of glass were broken and replacements were not cheap. It appears, too, that the surfeit of holes is contributing to the dampness problem. However, the building firm is diligent, responding swiftly to Bella's pleas when puddles appear. The costs, of course, come out of the general household funds, although she leaves Sandy to hand over the cash. He has a special arrangement with the firm.